Lions

The Invader

The driver half-turned. "Car kaput," he said. He pulled over to the side of the road, braked and turned off the ignition. "Bad men here," he went on, pulling up the bonnet catch and getting out of the car. I got out too and stood by the car.

Suddenly, I heard movement, and glimpsed the outlines of a man scrambling on to the road. There was another man behind him.

Sometimes, when the adrenalin flows, you think so fast that the thoughts are just a blur. Before I knew what I was doing, I dodged round the car and dived into the darkness. My bag came with me, more by accident than by design.

And as I dived, the gun went off...

Also available in Lions and Lions Tracks

THE INVADER

ANDREW TAYLOR

Lions
An Imprint of **HarperCollins***Publishers*

First published in Great Britain in Lions 1994

3 5 7 9 10 8 6 4 2

Lions.. is an imprint of
HarperCollins Children's Books,
part of HarperCollins Publishers Ltd,
77-85 Fulham Palace Road, Hammersmith,
London W6 8JB

ISBN 0 00 674656-X

Printed and bound in Great Britain by
HarperCollins Manufacturing, Glasgow

THE INVADER

ONE

For an instant I didn't believe my eyes. An instant? It lasted maybe half a second and felt like half eternity. Then I swung the wheel hard over and the car careered on to the wrong side of the road.

To my horror the other car did the same. It was still coming straight for mine. The driver was aiming to ram me. I didn't know why. I didn't have time to ask questions, let alone answer them.

The approaching headlights were on full beam. Everything was unnaturally clear: the leaves on the hedge on my left and the railings on my right, the glistening tarmac and the rain rushing out of the west from the Welsh hills. The wipers slapped to and fro. The rivulets of water on the windscreen were like streams of diamonds.

Two cars, each travelling at, say, 50 mph, would collide with an impact of 100 mph. And I was driving Carson's mobile rust heap, which would give me roughly the same wrap-around protection as a paper bag. I braked automatically but too abruptly – the rust heap tried to go into a skid. The rain had made the road slippery. The tyres were barely above the legal minimum. Another of Carson's economies.

Still braking, I tried to haul the car back to the left-hand side of the road. The lights of the other car wavered. For a moment I thought its driver was going to copy me once again. Instead, the oncoming car went into a long skid, its tail swinging on to my side of the road. The headlights sliced across the narrow grass verge and shone full on the line of railings. Worst of all, the car was still moving.

Beyond the railings there was nothing but the rain against a backdrop of darkness. Above the noise of the two engines I heard the crunch of the impact and the grating sound of metal under strain. The railings bowed out into the darkness as the car struck them. But they didn't break.

I must have registered all this because I remembered it afterwards, detail by detail. But at the time my mind was concentrating on survival. The other car was blocking most of the road. I didn't know if there was enough room for my car to get between it and the hedge. There was a jolt as my nearside wheels left the road. The suspension threw a fit.

The car slowed, but not enough. I couldn't stop in time. The gap wasn't wide enough to let me through. I steered into the hedge and shut my eyes.

Branches scraped like claws along the windows and the paintwork. The car slowed a little more. All the while it jerked like a wild thing. Suddenly it stopped, throwing me hard against the seat belt. The engine stalled.

I opened my eyes. I was trembling. The wipers still slapped to and fro as though nothing had happened. The other car was so close I could have leaned out of the window and touched it. There was less than a metre between us.

I'll be late – Carson will be furious. This wasn't the time to worry about that. I switched on the hazard-warning lights and scrambled out of the car. The rain and wind hit me like a wet towel. The two cars made a metal barricade across the road. In the short term that didn't worry me too much because our lights should give plenty of warning in either direction.

I ran across to the driver's side of the other car. It was a silver Honda Civic, the previous year's model. The engine was still running. The front of the car was nudging the railings. The lights were on and the wipers were beating time on the windscreen. I heard something slithering and grinding away on the ground. I smelt burning rubber. Suddenly I realized that the wheels were turning. The slippery grass on the verge didn't give them much purchase, which was just as well.

I yanked open the door. The courtesy light glinted on short fair hair. I felt a surge of panic like an electric shock. A woman was slumped over the wheel. Dead? I tried to speak but nothing came out. No one else was in the car. She was wearing jeans and a blue sweatshirt. There was an Ordnance Survey map folded open on the passenger seat beside her.

"Are you OK?" I said at last.

To my relief she stirred and mumbled something. The keys were in the ignition. I reached into the car and switched off the engine. Relief gave way to anger.

"What the hell were you doing?" I yelled.

She turned her face up to mine. I saw slanting

eyes, high cheekbones like an American Indian's, and a wide mouth with full lips. She shook her head as if I'd brought her back to life by throwing a bucket of cold water over her.

"Me? Are you crazy?" The voice was American and just as angry as mine. "Or stoned or something?"

"You were on the wrong side of the road," I snapped. "You can't argue with that."

Her face was very white. "Because you were all over the place," she said. "What were you trying to do? Kill someone?"

"I was leaving that to you."

As I spoke, the woman blinked. It was as if she was having difficulty focusing on my face. I remembered she'd been sitting with the engine running and with the car on the edge of a drop. She must be in a state of shock. Maybe she had briefly lost consciousness.

"Come on – get out," I said. "I've got to move your car."

"*You* have?"

The voice stopped me like a slap. She made it sound as if I were planning to steal her car.

"Why don't you move yours?" she went on. "Then maybe I'll be able to move mine."

I shrugged and walked back to Carson's car. What made me really angry was the fact that she was right: unless I reversed out of her way, she'd need a helicopter to move the Honda. I felt she'd made a fool of me, which wasn't fair to her – I'd managed that by myself without any help. The rain had soaked my tee shirt and jeans, and water ran continuously down my face and neck. I thought of her sitting as dry as a bone in her smart little car.

The VW started first try. There was a good engine under all that rust. I reversed slowly down the hill, the hedge scraping off some more paint and rust from the near side of the car. As I turned off my engine, the Honda's came to life. I heard the woman revving the engine like a lunatic. Sprays of mud shot up from under her front wheels and streamed through the railings into the darkness. The Honda didn't move.

I got out of the car and walked back to her through the rain. Her window slid down. She didn't say anything. She just looked at me and her shoulders twitched.

"You could try again," I suggested. "And I'll push."

There was only one sensible place to put my shoulder, and that was against the door pillar. So I opened the door. She recoiled. I explained what I was going to do. She didn't look too happy. Presumably the thought of having me a few inches away from her didn't appeal. But she realized she didn't have much choice. She put the engine into reverse.

The effect was much as before except that it made me considerably wetter and muddier, and a little rain drifted into the car. We tried a few times more. Then she turned off the engine and looked up at me.

"You got a tow rope?" she asked.

"No."

We had in the Range Rover but not in the Polo.

"There's a hotel about half a mile down the road," I said.

"Ardross Hall?"

"You know it?"

"I'm meant to be staying there."

"I'll give you a lift down there if you want."

"Why don't you go?" she said quickly. "Ask them to send someone."

The implication was that she didn't trust me enough to accept a lift from me. I shrugged. What did it matter? In any case it was probably better that someone should stay with the car. I turned away.

"Do you hear that?" she said. "Is that someone coming?"

I listened. A few seconds later I heard the sound of an engine. A car came round the bend below us – just a pair of headlights coming up the road from the direction of the hotel. We waited – she stayed in the car, and I was standing in the rain. I could hardly get any wetter.

The oncoming driver must have seen our lights. The car slowed as it came up the hill. It stopped beside the Polo. A blue light began to flash from side to side on its roof. I heard the woman let out her breath in what was probably a sigh of relief.

A couple of uniformed policemen sauntered over. They were carrying torches which they shone in my face. The beams swung back to Carson's rust heap and then across to the neat little Honda. One of the cops was a sergeant, a burly man with a black beard. He didn't bother to introduce himself. The other was tall and thin with black-rimmed glasses.

First they got their shoulders behind the Honda's

door pillars and pushed it back on to the road, where they tucked it in front of my car. Then they started asking questions. They were slow and very methodical. Standing in the rain didn't seem to bother them.

The woman said she was called Elvira Bladon. She showed her passport, her international driving licence and the papers from the car hire firm. They liked that. They liked it even more when she said she was staying at the Ardross Hall Hotel. She pitched it very well. She wasn't arrogant, just quietly confident and obviously pleased to see them. I figured she was younger than I'd thought, maybe around my age.

"And how did all this happen, Miss Bladon?" the sergeant said. "Could have been very nasty."

"This guy just came at me, officer. He was driving like a maniac."

"Listen," I said, "you've got—"

"You'll get your turn later," the sergeant said. "Don't interrupt."

There wasn't any point in arguing. It was true I'd been driving fast – I knew the road well and I'd been in a hurry to get back because Carson wanted to brief me before he went to Turkey. But I'd been within the speed limit and on the right side of the road.

"I braked hard – too hard, maybe, I don't know this car; I only got it this morning. And I went into a skid."

"Lucky you weren't going faster, Miss. You might have gone right over."

He knew and I knew what lay there in the

darkness: a steep-sided valley with a stream at the bottom perhaps twenty metres below. Before you got to the stream there was a stone wall running parallel to the road.

"The tyres wouldn't grip," Elvira Bladon was saying to the nice sympathetic policeman. "I couldn't reverse back on to the road."

"Front-wheel drive," the sergeant said, shaking his head. Then he jerked a thumb at me. "And what was he doing?"

She hesitated. "He tried to push the car back on the road. Then he offered me a lift down to the hotel."

"I see."

The sergeant made it sound as if what he saw wasn't very edifying. It was her hesitation that did it, that and her tone of voice. No one actually accused me of being a talent-spotter for the white slave industry but I had the feeling that the thought was present in everyone's mind. The torch beams converged on my face.

"Your name?"

"Adam Davy."

"I think I'll see your driving licence," the sergeant said.

"Sorry. I haven't got it on me."

I'd been in such a hurry when I left I'd only taken some money. Carson was convinced I would be late.

"You do surprise me," the cop said. "Nor the log book, I suppose?"

"No." By now I wasn't feeling very helpful.

"Insurance?"

14

"No."

"But surely you know the number of your car?"

"No," I said. "You see, it's not my car."

"At last. Now we're getting somewhere. Whose is it, then?"

"Mr Carson's. Up at Hill Farm."

"Does he know you've got it? Are you insured to drive it?"

I nodded.

"OK, son, how old are you?"

"Eighteen."

His eyes narrowed, perhaps because I looked older than I was. "And where do you live?"

"At Hill Farm."

"At the Sanctuary?" By now the hostility in his voice was unmistakable. "Well, well. D'you work there too?"

I nodded again. I tried to tell myself not to take this personally. Carson wasn't popular with the local constabulary, and nor was the Sanctuary. It had nothing to do with me. Not yet.

"And what's your explanation of all this?" The sergeant waved his torch from the Polo to the Honda.

I said, "She was on the wrong side of the road. Maybe she's not used to driving on the left. Visibility was bad, and she doesn't know the road." I wondered whether her driving had been affected by jet-lag, but I didn't mention that. "Anyway, we both had to brake. She went into a skid."

"And?"

"And what?" I said, a little more loudly than I'd

15

intended. "I tried to help her, of course. And unblock the road. What did you think?"

"None of that, lad."

The sergeant came closer. He didn't touch me but I could feel the menace oozing out of him. He was longing for me to do something stupid like throw a punch or start running. Suddenly he bent forward. For an instant I thought he was going to head-butt me. Instead he sniffed.

"Been drinking, have we?"

"No."

They breathalysed me anyway, just for the hell of it. First, however, they sent Ms Bladon off to the comforts of Ardross Hall. There was no question of breathalysing her, of course, or of searching her car. I felt lonely when she went, and very much at the mercy of the Beard and his silent sidekick. They wanted me to be guilty of something. After all, it was Saturday night, the traditional time of the week for trouble, which meant the traditional time of the week for improving arrest quotas.

Once the appliance of science had persuaded them that I wasn't drunk, they took a look inside the VW. They examined the ashtray and made sure I didn't have a consignment of crack in the boot. They found several kilos of frozen day-old chicks instead. Then they checked my pockets. After they'd discovered my cheque book and credit cards, they grudgingly accepted that I hadn't given them a false name; but they didn't start calling me "Mr Davy".

I waited, arms folded, and getting wetter and

wetter, which amazed me because I had thought I had got as wet as I could some time before. Their investigations seemed to take hours. I thought about the woman being welcomed by the flunkies at Ardross Hall. By now she was probably having a long hot bath. I wondered what she would look like in a good light.

The Beard gave me plenty of time for thinking. Carson had been even more neurotic than usual today, partly because of the Turkish trip and partly because of the latest letter from his bank manager, which had arrived this morning. My little problem with the cops would enrage him even more. He'd be angry with the police but he'd probably take it out on nearer targets, like me. I could cope with that because I knew the reason he got angry so often was that he was always worried.

The rain went on falling. I was starving. I decided that Elvira Bladon was out of the bath by now. She was probably ordering a little something from room service. *Yes, Madam, of course, Madam.*

That's when I started to wonder what she'd been doing on the road in the first place. Ardross Hall Hotel was only just off the main road, and it was very well signposted. But she'd made a completely unnecessary diversion up in the hills. I didn't think she'd got lost: she had a good map, and there'd be no reason for her to come up here.

So what had she been doing? Our little road made a big northerly loop round the village of Quanton St John. Each end of the loop joined the main road. Apart from the Sanctuary, the loop also served a couple of farms and a hamlet higher up in the hills. We get people coming up to the Sanctuary, of course, and sometimes walkers and other tourists. But there's not a great deal to see or do after nightfall during a rainstorm, even on Saturday night.

At last the Beard decided to call it a day. He didn't apologize. I had the sense not to show my annoyance at the delay. It was one of our busier times at the Sanctuary, and with Carson away I'd have even more to do than usual. I climbed into the Polo and started the engine. The sergeant came over. I rolled down the window.

"I got my eye on you, boy," he said. "So watch it."

I smiled at him and closed the window. I drove slowly up the hill. I glanced in my rear mirror and saw the police car reversing into a turning point. I guessed they were going back to the station for a well-earned cup of tea and a good gossip about the weirdos up at Hill Farm.

I drove on, keeping my speed down. The road levelled out and widened. It ran along a ridge. On the left-hand side a mass of shadow marked the beginning of the eight acres of land belonging to the Sanctuary. It was still raining – typical English summer weather – and the wipers slapped a rhythm on the windcreen. I was shivering.

The thudding began as the VW reached the trees. The steering wheel tugged at my hands: the car wanted to turn left. I swore. The last thing I needed right now was a puncture.

There was a lay-by just beyond the trees. I let the

car stagger into it, and switched off the engine. I was damned if I was going to change the wheel – it could wait till morning. I decided to leave the car and walk back to the Sanctuary.

I was just about to turn off the lights when I saw the glint of metal a few metres away. I peered through the windscreen. The glint came from the chain-mesh fence that marked the boundary of the Sanctuary's land. Part of the mesh looked out of line with the rest.

Leaving the headlights on, I got out of the car and went over to the fence. Someone had made a hole in it with a pair of wire cutters.

TWO

I crept through the darkness. I stumbled over tree roots and branches slapped my face. My eyes were still dazzled by the glare of the headlights.

The trees dropped away and the squall of rain hit me. The sky was the colour of faded black ink. I was in the field we used as a flying ground. I jogged across the grass until I heard the crunch of gravel beneath my feet, at which point I hopped back on to the grass and ran parallel to the path. The five-bar gate loomed up. We usually shut it at night after the dogs had had their last run. But now it was propped open.

Beyond the gate the path forked. If I went right, I'd reach the house. If I went left I'd come to the barns where much of the real work of the place was done. I turned right. The first thing to do was find Carson.

I ran past the owls' pen and up the hawk walk towards the house. It was a plain, redbrick building which dated from the time when Hill Farm had been a working farm. There was a light in Carson's study, and another in the bedroom Kenneth used. I tried the side door. As usual it was unlocked. The dogs were waiting in the hall, desperate to get out. They nudged my legs with their noses and streamed past me. I heard them barking.

Why hadn't Carson let them out?

I went along the hall to the study. The big desk was covered with papers. But Carson wasn't there. I stood at the bottom of the stairs and shouted for Kenneth.

At last he appeared on the landing. He was a big man with grey, wiry hair and a crumpled face that looked permanently on the verge of tears. He was already in his pyjamas – they had lurid purple and green stripes; very unlike the dull colours he wore in the day.

"Where's Carson?" I said.

"I – er – I think he went out...a few moments ago."

"Why?"

"The alarm went for one of the incubators."

This wasn't a burglar alarm: it was wired to the temperature gauges in each of the incubators. Carson had planned to install a security system but he'd run out of money.

"He didn't take the dogs?"

"No... Ah – too wet. They've already had their run."

"Someone's cut a hole in the fence on the other side of the flying ground," I said. "We've got a visitor."

The shock of the news spread over his face. He opened his mouth but didn't say anything.

"I'm going down to the barns," I went on. "You'd better get dressed. If I'm not back in five minutes maybe you should phone the police."

He frowned at me as he tried to register all this information. Kenneth was perhaps twenty years older than me, but it seemed natural to be giving him orders.

"OK?"

"I – um...yes. I think so."

The dogs were barking in the distance. I left Kenneth quivering with indecision on the landing and went back down the hall. Carson had a 12-bore for shooting clay pigeons, and for a moment I was tempted to take it with me. But if this were a false alarm, I'd be wildly overreacting; and if it were not, a shotgun would almost certainly make the problem escalate. And I could imagine what the police would think.

I switched on the outside lights in the hope that they would frighten our visitors away. Then I took Carson's walking stick from the rack by the door and went back outside. The barking was louder.

I ran back the way I'd come. The dogs were definitely down by the barns, which were still in darkness because their outside lights were on a separate circuit from the house's. As I was passing the pens, I heard many of the birds moving restlessly. My eyes had been dazzled once again, this time by the lights inside and outside the house, so my night vision was back to zero.

The barns were arranged round three sides of a square yard. They were a little younger than the house and built of redbrick walls with roofs of corrugated iron. As I came into the yard I heard the sound of breaking glass. It sounded as if someone had smashed a window.

The noise was coming from the barn we used for breeding, the one on the left-hand side of the yard. Carson had converted it, with no expense spared, into a range of rooms and pens. What with the renovation and conversion of the barn, plus all the specialized equipment for the incubator room, not to mention the office, the brooder room, the emergency generator and the separate kitchen, the cost had been astronomical. Carson said it was vital capital investment, because captive breeding offered the only chance of making the Sanctuary a going concern.

Now one of the dogs was snarling. There was a sound like a smack, and the other dog began to howl – a savage and hopeless noise. There was something unearthly about it. Imagine the noise a dying wolf might make.

"Stop that!"

It was Carson's voice, muffled but obviously shouting; he was probably inside what we called the breeding barn.

"I've phoned the police and—"

He stopped shouting. For an instant everything went quiet. The whole place seemed to be holding its breath.

I ran across the yard, careless of the noise I was making. A light shone in the doorway of the breeding barn. Someone had flicked on a torch. The beam swung up to my face. Then the light vanished. The door slammed shut. I was alone in the yard with a howling dog. I'd seen the dog picked out by the light of the torch. Just for a second, and that was quite long enough to burn the sight on my memory. It was Sammy, Carson's setter. He was lying on his side, writhing, just in front of the entrance to the breeding barn.

I rattled the handle. The door wouldn't budge. I tried to force the lock, but that didn't work. I hammered on the door with the walking stick. There was one hell of a racket inside the barn – clatters, thuds and crashes. And all the while Sammy howled and writhed.

There were few windows on this side of the building, and they were either barred or high above my head. I left Sammy and ran out of the yard and round the end of the barn. I was just too late.

The door at the back was open. Light poured through the doorway. Carson lay across the threshold, his legs inside and his head and shoulders outside. On this side of the barn there was an overgrown shrubbery, and it sounded as if a small army was retreating through it. The other dog, an English pointer called Leila, was somewhere inside the building, still barking.

I dropped the walking stick and knelt down by Carson. The rain was coming down harder than ever. He looked almost as wet as I did. The grey hair was plastered against his bony skull. You could see the little bald patch at the crown of his head. Usually he combed his hair to conceal it, which always struck me as odd because he wasn't a vain man in other ways. He was breathing shallowly. His eyes were closed and his face was a bad colour.

I heard an engine starting up somewhere near the house. The starter motor had a high-pitched whine that carried over the sound of the rain and Leila's barking. Then the car – or whatever it was – moved off, the engine backfiring once. I couldn't tell which way the car was going.

The escape vehicle? Maybe, but I thought the timing was cutting it fine. Whoever had run out of the barn must have had an Olympic turn of speed to reach the road at the front of the house in the time available.

I knew enough not to risk moving Carson. But I couldn't let him get colder and wetter. I went inside and opened the door to the kitchen. Leila shot out, crazed with rage and fear and perhaps guilt. I grabbed her collar and tried to soothe her. Nothing worked; so I let her do what she wanted, which was go to Carson.

The little kitchen was immaculately clean and tidy – unlike its counterpart in the house, which was a complete tip. Only the very best would do for Carson's birds. I opened a cupboard under one of the work surfaces and took out the sleeping bag inside. Carson had been known to spend the night down here. I went back outside and draped the sleeping bag over him. Leila looked reproachfully at me and whined softly. Sammy wasn't howling any more.

Where the hell was Kenneth? Frightened to come out of the house? I stepped over Carson's body and poked my head inside the incubator room. Everything movable had been thrown on the floor, including the five hugely expensive incubators themselves. The floor was a sticky sea of glass and eggshells. The damage in this room alone must run into four figures.

If we were lucky, Carson was fully insured. But he was too short of money to make that any more than a possibility. Besides, all the money in the world couldn't replace what was lying wrecked on the floor:

hundreds, maybe thousands of birds that would never get a chance to fly; a season's breeding programme.

The silence alerted me. Leila had stopped whining.

I went back to the doorway. Carson hadn't moved, but his eyes were open. Leila nuzzled his hand, trying to make him stroke her. I crouched beside him. His eyes moved: he'd seen me.

His lips twitched.

"It's all right," I said. "Just lie still."

A flash of irritation crossed his face. For an instant he looked almost normal. "Adam," he said in a voice not much more than a whisper. "You'll have to do it now."

"Do what?"

But his eyes had closed again. Leila whimpered. In the distance I heard the siren of a police car.

THREE

"Over here," I called.

The torches swung towards me. Heavy footsteps crunched on the gravel, and then trod more quietly on the strip of grass between the shrubbery and the barn. Leila tried to burrow more deeply into Carson's side. She wouldn't stop whining.

I noticed that the gutter on this side of the barn was blocked. Water was cascading down the wall. Carson would want that cleared. I made a mental note to get Kenneth to do it in the morning. While I was doing that, I was watching the water splashing on to the grass. The ground sloped, and the water had turned into a little stream running down to Carson's head. The light from the doorway made the water look golden. The water that got past the head was stained a pinkish red.

"Oh my God..." Kenneth said, his voice rising. "Is he...Oh dear – I mean – ah—"

"He's alive," I said. "Get a doctor."

Kenneth reached the area of light spilling from the doorway. He'd covered his pyjamas with a waxed jacket, corduroys and Wellington boots. He was even wearing a scarf to keep out the draughts and a flat cap to keep his hair dry. Behind him were two taller figures, the bearded sergeant and his skinny colleague in black-rimmed glasses.

The sergeant pushed me aside and knelt beside Carson. He glanced at his colleague. "Doctor."

The younger man ran off. Kenneth stared at Carson and said nothing. But his hands crept out of his sleeves and clung to each other. They looked like pale little animals in search of reassurance.

"There's blood under his head," the sergeant said. "Have you got a towel or something?"

I fetched a clean towel from the kitchen. He arranged it around Carson's head. Leila tried to bite him, so I grabbed her by the collar. The sergeant looked at me.

"What happened?"

I told him everything from the puncture onwards. I was surprised how calm my voice sounded. I think so much had happened in the last hour that I'd temporarily mislaid the ability to feel surprised. Besides, I was too tired to feel surprised. I didn't have the energy.

"How many of them were there?" he asked.

"Probably two. But I didn't actually see anyone." Then I remembered that Sammy was lying in the yard on the other side of the barn. "We need a vet as well as a doctor. They did something to one of the dogs."

"Later."

"Now," I said. "Let Kenneth go and phone. It's the Breams' practice in Quanton St John."

The sergeant thought about it, then nodded.

"OK, Kenneth?" I said. "The number's by the phone. You'd better take Leila up to the house. Shut her in the study."

Kenneth clicked his fingers at Leila, but she wouldn't go with him.

"Oh dear," he said, his eyes darting between me and the policeman. "Usually she's so – so biddable."

Kenneth took off his scarf and looped it through Leila's collar. He dragged her away. I noticed the sergeant looking oddly at me, presumably because I was giving the orders although noticeably much younger. Then the constable came back. While we waited for the ambulance, we tried to rig up a shelter made of blankets to keep the rain from Carson. The sergeant asked me all the obvious questions, such as who had done what and why, and I gave him answers that satisfied neither of us

The doctor and the ambulance arrived in convoy. Bag in hand, the doctor ran down the path and knelt down beside Carson. He exchanged a few words with the sergeant while his fingertips probed the wound on Carson's head. After a moment, the sergeant left him to it and sauntered into the barn.

"Where are you taking him?" I asked the doctor.

He looked up. He was a heavy, middle-aged man with a rubbery face and ginger hair. "The Royal Hospital. You'd better phone in the morning."

I wanted to say *Will he be all right?* But there's no point in asking questions that can't be answered. The doctor stood up and gestured to the waiting ambulance men. He stared at my face. He looked angry. I wondered whether this was because he hated violence or because he was annoyed at being dragged away from his television.

"Can't take chances," he said brusquely. "You understand?"

"Yes."

He grunted. The sergeant reappeared, and the doctor murmured something to him. The ambulance men moved Carson on to the stretcher with incredible gentleness. The doctor followed the stretcher down the path without bothering to say goodbye.

"Lot of mess in there," the sergeant said to me.

"Yes," I said. I bent down and picked up the towel, which was sodden with rain and Carson's blood.

"Doesn't look like robbery to me. Looks more like revenge."

I said nothing. So far I wasn't very impressed by his forensic skills. But it was early days yet. I dropped the towel inside the doorway. There was a glint of metal between the mat and wall. I looked more closely. Carson's keys. They must have fallen out of his pocket when he fell, and his body had hidden them.

"Do you know if Mr Carson's got any enemies?" the sergeant asked.

"It depends what you mean by enemies. A lot of people round here don't like him."

Including the local police, the farmers and even the press. By his voice the sergeant was a local man. He'd know that Carson had threatened to disembowel a local reporter who had publicized the site of an easily accessible nest of goshawks in the wild. It was the first mating pair they'd had in this area for over a decade, apart from those in captivity in the Sanctuary. People who've lived in the country all their lives don't get sentimental about animals; and they don't appreciate newcomers like Carson telling them what they can and cannot do. Carson had many good qualities, but tact wasn't one of them.

The sergeant was moving back to the path. "Yes," he agreed over his shoulder. "Anyway, we'd better have a look round."

I scooped up the keys and put them in my pocket. I followed him round the gable end of the barn to the yard on the other side. Sammy had stopped writhing. He was still alive but I didn't dare touch him. He lay very still, his eyes half closed, with the air rasping in and out of his lungs in short, shallow breaths. He didn't look like a dog any more. He looked like a soaking wet hearthrug. I fetched a blanket and draped it over him.

"Don't give much for his chances," the sergeant said.

We walked back to the house. Kenneth was filling a kettle in the kitchen. Leila was with him, not in the study. He had quietened her down, which in the circumstances was quite an achievement.

"Did you hear anything?" the sergeant asked. "See anything?"

Kenneth went bright red and looked even closer to the verge of tears than usual. "No, nothing. Honestly. I – ah..." He ran his fingers through the wiry hair. "Carson shouted upstairs about the alarm on the incubator, said he was going to fix it. I – er – I heard nothing after that. Well – not until I heard Adam calling me. I was in bed, you see."

It didn't surprise me. Kenneth was usually in bed by ten o'clock. The sergeant stared hard at him, and Kenneth quivered. Then the sergeant went back outside with me in tow.

"Is he always like that?" he asked.

"Kenneth? Only with people."

We patrolled the rest of the Sanctuary. At present the name Carson had chosen for Hill Farm seemed ironic: sanctuaries are meant to keep intruders out. The sergeant and I checked everywhere, at least superficially. As far as I could see there was no other damage. Some of our birds are very valuable – we had two golden eagles, for example, and a gyr falcon in pens near the house – but they were untouched.

"Difficult to sell something like that, of course," the sergeant said. "Lot of regulations these days."

"You'd be surprised what you can do on the black market," I said. "Some maniacs just want to kill them and stuff them. Then they hide them behind the telly and bring them out occasionally to have a good gloat. Or they try and fly them in the wrong sort of country, and get the bird killed. Or they keep birds like that in their garden shed and show them off to the neighbours until they die of maltreatment."

He looked sharply at me but said nothing. We walked across the flying ground and out into the lay-by where I had left my car. He wanted to have a look at the hole in the fence.

"You heard them driving off, didn't you?" the

sergeant said. "So we know they had a car."

"The engine I heard couldn't have been theirs. They ran off this way. The engine was up at the other end, near the farmhouse."

"Easy to be mistaken about the direction of a sound at night. Especially at a time like this."

I said nothing. I hadn't been mistaken.

The cop sniffed. "Of course it was their car. Not exactly the weather for an overnight hike, is it?"

"They might have hidden their car somewhere near the lay-by – and then coasted downhill without starting the engine."

"The road's level here," said the sergeant triumphantly.

"But it soon starts sloping."

I stared into the darkness. The hill I'd driven up earlier this evening began about fifty metres away. There were several places you could leave a car without its being noticed. If I'd been planning the break-in, I might have arranged it like that: it would throw any investigation on to the wrong track right away.

The sergeant and I walked up the road to the farmhouse. Hill Farm used to be a tenanted farm with a couple of hundred acres, one of several on a big estate. When the owners sold up fifteen years ago, Carson had bought the house and as much land as he could afford.

The police car was sitting by itself in the Sanctuary's car park. The constable was munching crisps and listening to the chatter of the radio.

"Not a lot more we can do till morning." the sergeant said to me. "Someone'll be up first thing. Have a good look round when it's light." He got into the car. He rolled down the window and added awkwardly: "You'll be all right?"

"Fine," I said, standing shivering in the rain.

The policemen drove off. I glanced towards the house. There was a light in the kitchen. I guessed that Kenneth would have made a pot of tea. He was always making pots of tea, which on balance was a point in his favour. But before I could head towards it, I heard the sound of another engine. The driver was slowing down. I saw the orange flicker of an indicator.

I thought briefly of Elvira Bladon with her cool American voice. Meeting her was something that seemed to have happened months ago. To all intents and purposes she was now on another planet. I didn't know whether to feel relieved or sorry.

Headlights cut a bright swathe across the car park. The Breams' Land Rover came to a halt with a spray of gravel. To my relief it was Jack who got out. His father was said to be a very good vet but I knew him much less well than Jack, who was only a few years older than me. He'd qualified last year.

"So what's all this?" he said. He reached inside the Land Rover for his bag and his torch. "One of the dogs hurt? I couldn't get much sense out of Kenneth."

I explained quickly as we walked towards the yard.

"Nasty," he said. "And you look half-drowned. Are you OK?"

"Yeah. But Sammy isn't."

34

Ignoring the rain, Jack knelt beside the setter, removed the blanket and began to examine him. He was a tall, stooping man with dark hair and a thin and misleadingly melancholy face. Animals liked him, as they did Kenneth, for reasons I could never quite understand.

The yard lights were bright, and when necessary I held the torch for him. Jack was very thorough. Sammy's back and his left ear seemed to interest him in particular. At the end he stood up and rubbed his eyes. The dog's eyelids flickered. He whined softly.

"Well?"

Jack shrugged. "It's bad. I think someone may have shot him in the ear. They also gave him a hell of a battering with something heavy. His back's broken."

"Will he live?"

"He might last a day or two."

He bent down and stroked Sammy's head. He did it automatically. I watched him.

"Will he be in pain?" I asked.

Jack glanced up. "What do you think?"

"What about pain-killers?"

"Trouble is, they can only cope with pain up to a certain level. It's the same with humans. There comes a point when if you increase the dose you kill the patient."

"Either way it wouldn't be much fun for Sammy?" I said.

Jack shook his head and carried on stroking the dog. He was waiting to hear what I wanted him to do. He'd given me the facts and his opinion, but he couldn't make the actual decision.

We both knew that there was a special bond between Carson and Sammy. I wondered if the attackers had known that too. My hand closed round the bunch of keys in my pocket. I squeezed the cold metal until it hurt my fingers. I thought about the options. I could have Sammy put down without consulting Carson. I could hope that Sammy stayed in his coma until he quietly died, thereby letting me off the hook. Or, if he came out of the coma, I could let him live in pain until Carson was well enough to have the responsibility of deciding what to do.

I hated these stupid phrases people used to disguise the ugly fact of death. *We had to have him put down. He's passed away. We lost him in the summer. It was a kind way to go, really. He had a good life.*

Sammy whimpered softly.

His hand on the dog's head, Jack looked up at me. "Well?"

"Kill him," I said.

FOUR

When I woke up the first thing I saw was Carson's keys.

Before I'd gone to sleep I'd hooked the key ring on to the belt round the waist of my jeans. The jeans were draped over the back of a chair. The keys glittered in the morning sun.

The people who worked at the Sanctuary had a running joke about Carson's keys. There were seven or eight of them on the ring, all different shapes and sizes. He was terrified of losing them and incapable of organizing a complete spare set. On average he mislaid them about twice a day, and life became unbearable for anyone he met until they were found.

"I can't understand it," he'd say, time and time again. "I had them in my hand a moment ago."

The sight of those keys triggered a rush of memories. Carson lying in the doorway and muttering, "You'll have to do it now." Do what, for God's sake? Sammy writhing in the yard. Jack Bream with his hypodermic needle bringing a gentle end to a savage way of dying. The endless rain. And the American girl saying, "What were you trying to do? Kill someone?"

I groped for my watch. It was still early. I'd slept for about four hours. It surprised me that I'd got any sleep at all. I climbed out of bed and went to the window. The sky was a cloudless blue, and the world had that fresh, unblemished look it has after a night of rain.

I took a shower, first with hot water and then with cold. Clean and shivering, I pulled on my clothes and went downstairs. The house felt empty. Usually Carson would be whistling while he shaved, and the dogs would come trotting along the hall in search of company and breakfast.

There was hot tea in the pot, which meant that Kenneth was up. His normal regime was early to bed and early to rise; it seemed to keep him healthy if nothing else. I poured myself a mug, took a few sips of tea and went to phone the hospital.

In the end I got through to a woman with a harassed voice. Yes, Mr Carson was on their ward, and yes, he was awake. In fact he had made rather a disturbance because he wanted to go home. But when he got out of bed he'd fallen over. The doctor was seeing him now. I explained who I was and asked if I could come and see him.

"Please do," she said. "Maybe you can reassure him that life's going on perfectly well without him. He seems to find this hard to grasp."

I chuckled, partly because this sounded like the authentic Carson and partly because I'd been privately terrified he'd end up like Sammy. Jack Bream had taken the setter's body away last night – all bagged up and ready for an autopsy.

I asked when I could come to see Carson.

"This is an open-access ward," the nurse said. "Any reasonable time's all right. How about in an hour? He'll have had breakfast then."

"Fine." It would give me time to sort myself out at the Sanctuary.

"I'll tell him you're coming."

I hung up the phone and went outside to look for Kenneth. He was always the first up. He liked to do a round of all the pens and make sure his beloved birds had survived the night. I think this was his favourite time of day – there were no humans about to make things complicated. Once or twice, when he thought he was alone, I'd heard him talking to the birds in a wordless mixture of clucks and coos.

He was down in the yard. He and Leila were in the barn in the middle, which was open-sided at the front. Usually we didn't let visitors come too close to it. Carson had converted it into several pens which he used for the later stages of his captive-breeding programme – aviaries for chicks that were just fledged, and ready to leave their parents. The birds were too young to be able to cope with members of the public. The pens were large enough for them to be able to fly around and gain a degree of independence before we took them outside to be trained.

Kenneth was examining the side of one of the pens. Leila came over and sniffed my hand. She was much less bouncy than she usually was at this time of day. I guessed she was missing Carson and Sammy. Kenneth looked over his shoulder. The creases deepened in his lined face.

"Ah – Adam?"

"Yes, it's me," I said in case he was as unsure of my identity as he sounded.

"It's – um – a bit of a worry..."

He drew back as I came closer, and his hands fluttered towards the wire mesh as the side of the pen. There were some hybrid chicks inside – crosses between a peregrine and a gyr falcon. Carson had great hopes of them. If you get it right, and it's a big if, hybrid vigour allows you to get the best of each parent species. These ones should be large, hard-feathered and very fast – well over 100 mph in the right conditions – but not as big and temperamental as the pure gyr. Carson called them his GTi longwings and thought if all went well they should go down very well with his richer American and Middle Eastern customers, many of whom were very competitive; they would buy a fast bird for much the same reasons they'd buy a fast car – status, and the sheer excitement of speed. You needed to have miles of open countryside at your disposal if you wanted to fly birds like that. To get the best out of them in Britain, you'd have to have the use of a grouse moor in the Highlands.

"What's wrong?" I said.

The chicks were fluttering around. The prospect of breakfast always made them excited.

"Two of them are missing."

"Sure?" I'd have had to check the records to find out.

"Quite sure," Kenneth said, without any trace of his usual hesitation. "And look at this."

The hands fluttered over the mesh again. The light wasn't so good here. I bent down. Someone had cut a neat little opening. And when they'd got what they wanted, they'd fixed the wire roughly back in place – well enough for the robbery not to be obvious to the police and me when we looked around last night. Luckily the makeshift repair had kept the other chicks inside.

"I'd better phone the police," I said. "Can you check the records in the office? They may want documentary evidence that we had the chicks in the first place."

I told Kenneth that Carson was conscious and demanding to be let out of hospital.

"He'll – um – be all right, won't he?" Kenneth waved his arm with sudden violence in a gesture that embraced the Sanctuary as a whole. "I mean, if he – ah – went, all this would go too."

"It didn't sound as if he's in immediate danger."

I explained that I was going to see Carson, and told Kenneth how I thought Carson would want him to spend the day. It's not easy giving someone orders when you haven't any authority to do so. But if I didn't, no one else would.

Maybe that's what Carson had meant: "You'll have to do it now."

To my surprise, Kenneth took it as a matter of course that I should give him his instructions. I went back to the house to make some phone calls, have some breakfast and plan the day's work. My mind was already running over the problems ahead, most of which related not to birds of prey but to people. I had a horrible suspicion that one way or another I would have to shoulder many of Carson's responsibilities over the next few days – not out of choice, but by default; there was no one else who could. The prospect terrified me.

The biggest potential problem was our administrator, a woman called Phyllis who lived in a bungalow in the village. I had never worked with her, because she reported directly to Carson, but she had a reputation for being difficult and eccentric. If she took against me, or decided I was too young to cope with the extra responsibility, I wasn't sure what we would do.

At this time of year the Sanctuary employed ten or twelve people, some of them part-time. We often had one or two students in search of practical experience. Carson was the director in fact as well as name; he owned the place, and he wasn't much good at power-sharing. I was one of the younger ones, but experience and aptitude counted much more than age. In theory I had one big advantage: unlike most of the others, I lived at Hill Farm, which meant I was available for twenty-four hours a day, seven days a week. But would Phyllis see it like that?

I'd been working there for about six months – ever since that terrible Christmas at the place I used to think of as home. My father and I had quarrelled; we'd both said things that should have been said before and things that should not have been said at all; and I'd walked out. At present, the Sanctuary was the nearest thing I had to a home.

Much of the routine care of the birds devolved on Kenneth. He just needed someone else to tell him what to do; and he seemed happy enough for that someone to be me until Carson came back. Carson concentrated on the breeding programme, which was the Sanctuary's main source of revenue, and did a lot of the demonstrations and the PR side. I often helped him, and I could probably deputize for him for a week or two. In any case, it didn't look as though we'd be doing much breeding for a while.

When I got up to the house I went into Carson's study and phoned the police. I learned that the sergeant with a beard was called Todd. I left a message for him about the stolen chicks. Then I dialled Phyllis's number. She answered on the second ring.

"Yes?" she barked.

"I know it's Sunday, but do you think you could come in today?"

I explained what had happened last night. While I was talking I heard the scrape of a match as she lit a cigarette. Phyllis saw to the Sanctuary's accounts, she managed the shop and the café, and she was in the throes of computerizing our records; she was said to be brilliant at what she did, but like Kenneth she had little interest in what went on outside her area. She used to be a civil servant until she took early retirement. Now she earned less money for more work than ever before.

When I finished she had a coughing fit. Then she said, "I'll be right up. Can you handle it, do you think?"

"Handle what?"

"Pretending to be Carson. It'll have to be you. I can cope with my job but I can't do his."

"I'll do my best," I said, feeling simultaneously relieved, because Phyllis was a useful ally, and apprehensive, because I'd suddenly realized just how much responsibility I was taking on. "I imagine he'll want to do as much as he can by remote control."

"Stupid man. He should concentrate on getting well. Can you ask him what he wants done about the Turkish trip? I'll have to get in touch with them this morning."

"OK."

"And tell him I'll get the insurance claim started. The sooner the better. I'd like to see him fried in oil."

"Carson?"

"No. Whoever did that to Sammy."

She started to cough again. I put the phone down and went in search of some food. Kenneth came into the kitchen while I was ploughing my way through an enormous bowl of muesli.

"Ah – er – did you get the DOC?"

"I put them in the big freezer last night."

DOC are day-old cockerels, which formed the bulk of our birds' diet. Carson and Kenneth were meticulous about keeping the freezers stocked with several months' supply, because the cockerels could be hard to get hold of. The reason I'd driven down the hill the night before was to collect a consignment of blast-frozen DOC; Carson had decided to make a emergency purchase because he felt our stocks were getting dangerously low. Fortunately I'd remembered to fetch them from the boot of the Polo before going to bed.

Kenneth calmed down and started to fix himself some food. But his question reminded me that I hadn't changed the wheel on the Polo. I went off to do it after breakfast.

The harsh morning sunlight made the car look semi-derelict. I quickly changed the wheel, then cobbled up a repair to the fence with the pliers from the car's toolkit.

The hole in the chain mesh was rectangular – perhaps a metre high, and wide enough for a man to scramble through. Whoever had done it had made a cut up the left-hand side and cuts along the top and bottom, though not necessarily in that order. He – or she – hadn't bothered to cut the right-hand side: he'd simply bent the cut-out rectangle outwards as if it were a door on a hinge.

As I was mending the fence, it suddenly occurred to me that if I'd been making a hole like that, my vertical cut would have been on the right-hand side, not the left.

I took a closer look at the severed wires on the horizontal cuts. It was hard to be sure but I reckoned that the wire cutters had been moving from left to right.

Time was getting on. I drove back to the Sanctuary, where I packed a bag for Carson and said goodbye to Kenneth.

"Er – what if – ah – the police come while you're gone?"

It seemed to me that Kenneth was even more jittery than usual. I put it down to what had happened last night.

"Phyllis will soon be here," I said. "Don't worry."

I drove down the hill, passing Phyllis in her MGB going like the clappers in the opposite direction. She had a cigarette clamped in the corner of her mouth. We exchanged waves, and she gave me a flurry of toots on her horn.

Near the bottom of the hill were the wrought-iron gates of the Ardross Hall Hotel. I glanced up the drive. I couldn't even see the house, let alone a silver Honda Civic.

On the main road I pushed the car up to 70 mph and kept it there. Luckily the traffic was light because it was Sunday. There was so much to do, and I was aware of time slipping away. I tried to rein in my impatience.

When I reached the town I followed the ring road round to the hospital. I knew where it was, though I'd never been there before. It turned out to be a scruffy complex of buildings put up at odd moments during the last hundred years. I was looking for Ward 15, which turned out to be in the largest of the newer blocks.

I parked as near to the entrance as I could and went to buy a ticket from a slot machine. It took me a moment to find the right change. People were scurrying around – medical staff, patients and visitors. I don't know what made me look up as I was feeding the coins into the machine. I glanced towards the entrance.

Patients in dressing gowns were standing in a line just outside and puffing cigarettes. The big glass doors slid open. A guy in a white coat waved his hand to concede right of way, allowing someone to come out before he went in.

Not just someone: a slim woman with short blonde hair, slanting eyes and high cheekbones.

She ran down the steps and got into the Honda, which was parked on a double yellow line just beyond the doors. I started to move towards her, but I was too late. She climbed into her car.

"Hey," I shouted, and broke into a run.

Apparently she neither heard nor saw me, though plenty of others did. The Honda's engine roared into life. The car moved swiftly towards the exit, leaving a streak of rubber on the tarmac. It pulled out on to the ring road, forcing an articulated lorry to brake. A horn blared like an angry trumpet.

Several passers-by stared at me. I resented the looks, knowing Elvira Bladon had made me feel foolish again. The girl seemed to have a genius for wrong-footing me. I stuck the ticket on my windscreen and wondered if she'd recognized me or not.

But what I really wanted to know was what she had been doing at the hospital.

FIVE

"We've had a bit of a setback," said the ward sister. "We were trying to walk before we can run. Very silly of us."

She was a heavyweight woman with dyed black hair and a roman nose. If she'd had the hair permed a little higher it could have passed for a guardsman's busby on a foggy night. She was sitting at her desk protected by a barricade of files.

"Can I see him?" I asked.

"No visitors." Her lips were very thin, and she'd drawn attention to the fact with bright red lipstick. "Perhaps tomorrow."

"What happened?" I asked.

She frowned, giving me the impression that she was the only one entitled to ask questions round here. A nurse was passing. The sister beckoned her over. They had an urgent conversation, mainly in whispers. As far as I could tell they began with the menus for cook-chill meals, moved on to the lateness of someone called Margaret and finished with a plot summary of a film the sister had recently seen; but maybe I was doing them an injustice. Finally she noticed I was still standing there.

"Yes?" she said, as though she had never seen me before.

"What happened to Mr Carson?"

"Are you family?"

"I work for him."

"In that case I'm afraid I don't intend to discuss his medical history with you."

I put on my best smile. "When I phoned, I was told there were no restrictions on visiting."

Her eyes bulged behind her glasses. "That may have been so when you phoned. It is not the case now. Not with this patient."

"Did some one else ask to see him? A few minutes ago? An American woman? Short blonde hair?"

"I really don't know." She opened one of her files. "Now if you'll excuse me..."

In the corridor behind her desk a door opened. An Asian in a white coat came out.

"Sister? If someone called Adam Davy—"

"That's me," I said quickly. "For Mr Carson."

He waved me down the corridor. The sister sat in frozen silence. I dared not look at her face as I passed her desk. The Asian gave me a tired smile. His name tag identified him as a doctor.

"Mr Carson tried to get up and discharge himself," he murmured. "For the second time. I'm afraid he collapsed. I've given him something to help him to rest but he's not going to let himself relax until he's talked to you. Something about the Sanctuary?"

"The Sanctuary is a centre for birds of prey. He's the director."

"I'll give you five minutes. All right?"

He let me into the room and went away. There

was a high bed with a cupboard beside it, a blank television, a chair and a window with a view of a brick wall. It was very warm. I put down Carson's bag on the chair and went to stand by the bed.

It's always a shock when you see strong people looking helpless. Carson was a tall man, and normally he was always moving; he had too much energy to be still. Now he was lying like a statue under the blankets. He seemed to have shrunk. There was a dressing on his head. His eyes were closed, and his complexion was a shade of dirty white. I'd seen faces like his in other hospitals. I hated these places where people come when they are ill. They reminded me of my mother.

He opened his eyes. I saw them slowly focusing on me. A trolley rattled down the corridor outside.

"How are you feeling?" I asked.

"Bloody quack," he said, slurring the words a little. "Wouldn't let me get up."

"So you went ahead and did it anyway. Now look at you."

He tried to grin. "There's a note on the cupboard. See?"

I picked up the sheet of paper, which had been folded in two. Phyllis's name was written on it.

"Nurse wrote it for me. But I signed it. You and Phyllis run the place till I get out. Right?"

"Don't worry," I said. "It's all under control. I've already talked to Phyllis."

"And you go to Turkey instead of me. Vital. We need the money. Got a passport here?"

"Yes."

"Blue folder in my desk. Find it. Second drawer down. Phyllis can fax Izmidlian."

"Who?"

"Damn," he said.

"What is it?"

"Drawer's locked."

I held up his bunch of keys.

"Keys of the kingdom," he muttered. "Don't lose them." His eyes had gone out of focus. The lids closed. He frowned, looking puzzled. "I had the keys in my hand a moment ago."

"Did you see who broke in?" I asked.

There was a long pause. I thought he'd drifted into unconsciousness. Then he licked his lips. "No. Just heard. Saw damage. Shouted. Went out the back door, did I? Don't remember."

"Doesn't matter."

But he'd remembered something else: "Sammy?"

"I'm sorry," I said. "He's dead. But the birds are OK."

No point in mentioning the stolen chicks; that could wait, and so could the details of Sammy's death. I watched Carson's lips tightening. As I stood there, my mind shot off in an unexpected direction.

If the American woman had come to see Carson, how had she known that he was in hospital?

Carson sighed. "Sammy..."

The doctor stuck his head in the room. "Come on. That's enough."

I said goodbye. I don't think Carson heard me. In

the corridor the ward sister was dealing with some more would-be visitors – a slight, grey-haired man in a dark grey suit, and a much younger woman.

"We aren't very well," I heard the sister say. "We need all the peace and quiet we can get."

"We'll have to keep him in for another day or two at least," the doctor said to me as we moved down the corridor. "See how things go. Phone the hospital late afternoon."

The sister swivelled in her chair. "Doctor, could you deal with this lady and gentleman?" she said menacingly. "The police for Mr Carson. Do you want to disturb him again?"

The grey man looked up. "I'm Detective Inspector Anthorn, sir. This is Detective Constable Vince. Is there any chance of a word with Mr Carson?"

"He's asleep. In a few hours' time, perhaps. But I really can't guarantee it."

Anthorn looked at me. "And can I ask who you are?"

I told him.

"In that case I'd like a word with you, too."

He had a few words with the doctor and then he escorted me unharmed past the ward sister. We took the lift to the ground floor.

"Let's go outside," Anthorn said. "I can't stand these places."

Between the car park and the road there was a strip of scrubby grass. He led us briskly to one of the wooden benches that stood there. We sat in a row, with me in the middle. It was still early but it was already warm. The DC took out a notebook.

"Going to be a hot day," Anthorn said, stretching out his legs. On the end of his legs were little black shoes, very highly polished. He looked like an assistant bank manager or perhaps an old-fashioned teacher. He glanced at me and smiled, a professional smile without much warmth. "I just missed you at the Sanctuary. They told me you'd be here."

"Any news?" I asked.

"It's early days. I wanted to find out if Mr Carson saw who attacked him."

"I asked him. He said not."

"Pity." Anthorn shrugged. "Could have made our lives a lot easier. Now I've read Sergeant Todd's report, and I've talked to him. And I understand you found a couple of birds were missing this morning. Hybrid chicks, was it? Can you tell me what they are, and why you have them at the Sanctuary? Assume I know nothing about the subject and we can't go far wrong."

He listened without interrupting while I explained. I told him that the Sanctuary had some thirty or forty types of birds of prey from all over the world – from eagles and vultures to hawks and owls, many of which belonged to threatened species. Conservation was our main job, and captive breeding was essential to restore species populations to safe levels. Captive breeding was also a vital source of revenue for us. Interesting hybrids were not just of scientific interest – they could command high prices from the many people round the world who owned and flew birds of prey.

And so on. Most of what I said came from one of

53

the standard spiels we gave to visitors. My voice droned on, and I was only half aware of what I was saying. The DC took notes. Around us people came and went and pigeons hopped as close to our feet as they dared, hoping for charity.

When I'd finished Anthorn said, "Last night it looked as if the intruders just wanted to do as much damage as they could. That was how Sergeant Todd read the situation. He thought it could be a couple of lads with too much lager inside them. Or possibly something more calculated than that. Some sort of revenge. They'd started with the yard because it was furthest from the house. Do you think it's likely that Mr Carson surprised them before they'd really begun?"

"That's what I thought last night. That they just had time to hit the barn we use for breeding." I hesitated. "But now it looks as if they went for the chicks before they did anything else."

"Would the chicks have much cash value?"

I shrugged. "You couldn't sell them legitimately. They're ringed before we put them in the aviary. And anyway you'd need a sale licence. The whole business is very strictly controlled."

"What about on the black market?"

"In theory, yes. But it wouldn't be easy. These are chicks, you see. Hardly fledged. They're completely untrained. Very vulnerable. They need expert handling."

"So who do you think would go for them?"

"Either a fool who didn't realize what he was taking on, or a falconer with quite a lot of experience and confidence. If they survive, these will be very unusual birds. The odds are that whoever wants them is an amateur."

"Why?"

"Because there aren't that many professionals around," I said. "It's a very small world. Everyone would know if one of them was in the market for stolen birds."

"Sergeant Todd thought Mr Carson might have upset a local farmer. Someone like that."

"Yes, but they wouldn't want to steal a couple of chicks. Carson thinks that one or two of them shoot birds of prey. That's partly why there's bad feeling. But it could well be someone who knows the area. Whoever did it knew their way around."

Anthoni gave an almost imperceptible nod. "I'd like a list of local enthusiasts. Especially those who've quarrelled with Mr Carson."

"Kenneth and Phyllis would be the best people for that," I said. "They've been here much longer than I have."

He looked curiously at me. I thought I was going to have to fend off another set of questions about myself.

I said quickly, "And there's something else. Something I noticed this morning." I told him about the hole in the fence.

He saw the implication at once. I could see it in his eyes. But he said, "And what does that suggest?"

"A left-hander. Assuming the hole was cut from the outside. And there'd be no point in cutting it from the inside, would there?"

"Know of anyone who'd fit the bill?"

I hesitated. "Not for certain."

"We're not going to overreact," Anthorn said. "Just tell me what you know and let me handle it."

"There's a man called Jason," I said reluctantly. "I don't know his other name. He's a year or two older than me. I think he lives somewhere up in the hills. He tried to buy a hawk from us, but Carson wouldn't let him. But he started to write out a cheque and he used his left hand."

The bird had been a goshawk, a kind which is both temperamental and expensive. Carson began to ask Jason the standard questions, which are designed to investigate whether the prospective purchaser is a suitable owner for a bird of prey. Jason assumed that this was a roundabout way of haggling, so he pulled out his cheque book; he was the sort of man who thinks you can solve anything with a cheque book.

"OK, OK," he said, writing Carson's name on the cheque. "Just tell me how much, will you?"

I'd noticed that he was one of those left-handers who hunch their whole body round so they can pull the pen from left to right. In the end, it was all a waste of time because Carson wouldn't let him buy. They'd had a blazing argument about it in front of a coachload of schoolkids from the Midlands.

"What was the snag?" Anthorn asked. "Thought the cheque would bounce, did he?"

"This guy Jason drives a Lotus Elan," I said.

"Then what was the problem?"

"Carson felt he wasn't the right sort of person to own a budgerigar, let alone a goshawk."

Anthorn, like many people, hadn't realized that the money-raising aspect of the Sanctuary wasn't run like a normal commercial operation. It was true that most of our profits derived from the sale of birds. But we had a policy of vetting our new customers very carefully. We wanted to know why they wanted a bird of prey, what experience they had, what sort of quarry they intended to fly the bird at, and over what sort of countryside. Carson also insisted on seeing a photograph of the quarters they intended to use for the bird. We weren't unique in this – all reputable British breeders of birds of prey had a similar vetting process, partly because of legal requirements and partly because they cared about the birds they sold – but ours was more stringent than most.

I explained all this. I thought Anthorn found it hard to believe. I also suspected that he wanted to be elsewhere. He cut me short in mid-sentence and nodded to the DC. She shut her notebook. They both stood up.

"Thanks for your help," Anthorn said. "I expect I'll be coming over to the Sanctuary later today."

They walked off, leaving me on the bench. I stared after them. Off to find Sergeant Todd, I guessed: he was the sort of man who could give them chapter and verse on Jason. I thought of calling them back: "There's a couple of other things..."

But was there any more worth saying? I wasn't sure, any more than I was sure that the police wanted to listen to me. Besides, Sergeant Todd should have mentioned both points in his report.

There were two irritatingly inconclusive items, which might mean something or nothing. They led to two questions. Why had Elvira Bladon been coming down the hill from the direction of the Sanctuary to the Ardross Hall Hotel? And what about the car I'd heard just after I found Carson last night – the car with the whining starter motor and the engine that backfired?

The American girl's behaviour was the point that really bugged me. I wasn't entirely sure of my motives. Maybe I wanted an excuse to think about her.

But it wasn't just that – because now she'd given me a third question. What had she been doing at the hospital? You could take your choice about the answer. Either her visit was pure coincidence, just like her appearance last night – or it had something to do with Carson.

SIX

Jack Bream flagged me down as I was driving through the village on my way back from the hospital. I pulled on to the forecourt in front of the veterinary surgery and rolled down my window. My conversations with Carson, the ward sister and Anthorn had left me feeling worried and angry, an uncomfortable combination. I was glad to see a friendly face.

"Thought you'd like to know," Jack said. "The police have asked my father to do an autopsy on Sammy."

"Will it help anyone?"

He shrugged. "They like to be sure of the precise cause of death. Especially in a case like this."

I got out of the car. I was glad of an excuse to delay going back to the Sanctuary. Jack stared at the passing traffic. His mind worked quickly but he spoke slowly. I guessed he had something else to say.

"My father reckons he should be able to find the bullet. There wasn't an exit wound. He's not sure, but he thinks it's something pretty small, like a two-two."

I remembered the sound I'd heard last night, just before I rushed into the yard to find Sammy writhing on the ground: a sound like a smack. A bullet would be solid evidence, the sort that helps to get a conviction. I knew that if the police could trace the gun, they might well be able to match the scratches on the bullet with the peculiarities of the rifling.

"Have you been to see Carson?" Jack asked.

I gave him the news. Then, on impulse, I said, "Do you know a bloke called Jason? Drives a Lotus?"

"Jason Ford." He paused; I waited. "Lives up Quarry Hill," he went on. "Place called Well Farm. Why?"

"He had a row with Carson."

"So did a lot of people." A ghost of a smile flitted across Jack's face. "Do the police think it was Jason last night?"

I told him about the hole in the fence and how my attempt to reason like Sherlock Holmes had made me think a left-hander might be responsible. "I had to tell Anthorn, but now I feel bad about it. Jason's probably no more guilty than I am."

I'd always hated the thought of people being accused of something they hadn't done. Since Christmas I'd had a personal reason to feel even more strongly about the subject.

"I wouldn't waste too much sympathy on Jason Ford," Jack said.

"You don't like him?"

"He's one of these townies who like to play at living in the country. Someone said his dad's got a chain of betting shops in Birmingham. No shortage of money – doesn't seem to need to work."

"So what does he do with himself?"

"Plays with his toys, when he's here. He's got a couple of horses, a dog." He glanced at me. "And

60

occasionally a hawk."

"Occasionally?"

"They tend to die on him. Or lose themselves."

"Is that why you don't like him?"

"We sometimes see the animals that survive," Jack said. "That's the main reason."

He shut his mouth tightly, as if there was nothing more that needed to be said on the subject. I knew him well enough to fill in the gaps. He and his father saw a lot of animals which were neither well treated nor sufficiently ill treated to justify legal proceedings. Jack had told me that was the most frustrating part of his job.

"Anyone else live there?" I asked.

"There's a girlfriend."

"Local?"

Jack shook his head. "Sounds like another Brummie. She's no pushover, either."

I had my hand on the car door. I was just about to get in and drive away. Things would have been very different if I had.

Out of the blue Jack said: "Do you want to come up there?"

"What – now?"

He nodded. "I haven't done my calls yet. There's always a few on Sunday. I was just leaving."

"You're going to Well Farm?"

"I wasn't intending to, but I could. I treated one of their horses for a sore on its leg. I said I'd look in sometime and check how it was healing. Today's as good as any."

"How long would it take?"

"We could be there and back in half an hour."

I said yes, which was utterly stupid of me. I had a hundred and one things to do at the Sanctuary, including sorting out this Turkish trip. But I wanted to see Jason for myself, because lurking in my mind was the possibility that I'd landed him in a lot of trouble. Either he deserved it or he didn't. I wanted to make up my own mind on the subject.

We left the Polo in the surgery car park. Jack drove the Land Rover. We took a left-hand turn into a lane just beyond the Ardross Hall Hotel. I knew that the family who used to live there had once owned Hill Farm; Jack said that Well Farm had been part of the same estate.

At first the lane ran along the boundary wall of the hotel grounds. Then it zigzagged between high hedges in need of cutting back. I hadn't been up this way before. The countryside round here is full of hidden pockets: it lends itself to secrecy. Eventually we reached a crossroads and plunged into another lane, this one not much more than a metalled track with a line of grass sprouting in the middle.

"Is he likely to recognize you?" Jack said.

"I don't know. The only time I saw him at the Sanctuary, he was concentrating on Carson."

"We'd better play it by ear. I can always say you're a student."

"Of what?"

"Human nature?"

Jack braked. The lane ahead had shrunk into a

track suitable only for horses and mountain bikes, but there was a white-painted five-bar gate on the left-hand side. It was obviously new, with WELL FARM painted on the top bar in fancy lettering. Beyond it was a gravelled drive.

"Used to be a mud track," Jack said sourly. "I can remember when this was a working farm."

The drive ended in the sort of farmyard that belongs in a glossy magazine: exposed stonework, fresh paint, flowers in pots, and a total absence of rusting tractors, rotting tyres and mucky, noisy animals. The house backed on to the yard: it was older and larger than the one at Hill Farm, and looked far better maintained.

I jumped down to open and close the gate. As I was unfastening it, I heard a car starting up out of sight in the distance – perhaps behind the curving ridge that lay almost a mile away on the far side of the farm. I knew that up here soundwaves could travel a very long way, and sometimes by unexpected routes, bouncing off hillsides and round obstacles; it was often impossible to pinpoint where they came from. But one thing was certain: the starter motor had a whine to it. Then the engine fired and I heard the car moving off. The engine didn't backfire. It was possible that it was the same one I heard last night at the Sanctuary. I had no way of knowing.

I followed Jack's Land Rover up the drive. One of the barns was used as a garage. I glanced through the open doors and saw the Lotus, a brand-new Land Rover Discovery and a mud-splashed Toyota pick-up.

A dog was barking somewhere out of sight. I glimpsed a woman with streaked blonde hair at an open window on the first floor of the house. She vanished. I heard her shout for Jason.

Jack parked in the yard. As he got out, the back door opened. The woman filled the doorway. She was wearing tight jeans and a tee-shirt. She folded muscular arms across her chest.

"Yes? You're the vet, aren't you?"

Jack nodded. "How's Milly?"

"Seems OK. Leg's healed."

"Mind if we take a look?"

"Help yourself. She's in the paddock."

She went back inside the house. Jack led the way round the back of one of the barns. There was a range of stabling here, and beyond it the paddock.

Jack jabbed a thumb in the direction of the ridge. "See that track up Newton Hill? He owns the first two fields on either side as well. He must have about ten acres altogether. And all he does with them is drive round them in his new Land Rover."

Two horses, a grey mare and a black gelding, were nibbling grass. They came over to investigate us. Jack climbed over the gate and began to examine the mare.

He clicked his tongue. "See that?" He stroked the mare's flank: the hair was dull and matted. "Still, at least the sore's gone."

The gelding nudged him, demanding attention. I left him patting both horses and wandered back to the stable block. Someone had been doing some heavy-duty pruning. There was a small mountain of cuttings on a patch of wasteland at the side. I looked more closely: not just cuttings – cardboard boxes, newspapers, scraps of plywood, even a few feathers.

Feathers?

I bent down and picked up a couple. They were small, fluffy feathers from a very young bird. One of the tips was flecked with blood. Jack came up behind me.

"What do you think?" I said.

Jack took the feathers from me. He put them in the palm of his hand and stirred them with the tip of his forefinger. "Hard to be sure."

"Sure of what?" said a voice behind him.

We turned. Jack slipped the feathers smoothly into his trouser pocket. The first thing I saw was a hooded Great Horned Owl. It was in good condition but it didn't look pleased with life.

"Difficult to be sure you won't get similar sores developing," Jack said. "We've just been to see Milly."

"You've done a good job there," said Jason Ford.

He was a good-looking man, about my height, with thick, golden hair and grey eyes. He had an easy charm – the sort that comes so easily that you wonder whether it really means anything. He raised his right arm so we could admire the great bird on his gloved wrist; left-handers use their right arm for the bird's perch.

"Like my new baby?" he asked.

I opened my mouth, then shut it. That bird was not a baby and it was not enjoying life. The Great Horned Owl is a big, aggressive American bird, a little lighter than the European Eagle Owl and definitely not a bird for a beginner. It must have cost a small fortune.

"I've decided to call her Victrix," Jason said.

Jack chatted about Milly and about Jason's new acquisition. Jason didn't ask who I was and Jack didn't tell him. He managed to bring the conversation round to captive breeding.

"Yes, I tried it," Jason was saying. "But I just don't have the time to do it properly." He waved towards the feathers. "That was the last chick I had. Tragic, it was." The face was grave, but I swear there was laughter in the eyes. "The cat got in." He stroked the owl. "Easier to buy them as adults, ready-trained."

He offered us coffee, but Jack said we had to be going. We left in a flurry of pleasantries about vets and their bills. On our way out I opened and closed the gate. As I was climbing back into Jack's Land Rover I glanced over the gate and up the drive.

Jason was standing in the yard with that great bird on his wrist. He gave me a wave and turned round to have a word with the woman, who was coming out of the house with an overweight alsatian beside her.

"Well?" Jack said as we bounced down the lane. "What did you think?"

"I don't know. I'd like you to keep those feathers."

"If he really has been trying to breed, you'd find it hard to prove those feathers belonged to your hybrids."

"But not impossible. That's why I want you to have them. Just in case it comes to court. You're an unbiased witness."

"Look, the only way you could prove a match

beyond reasonable doubt would be genetic fingerprinting. You'd need samples of genetic material from the chicks you still have, and then you'd have to have them compared with what you've got there."

"I know," I said.

"It's a highly specialized job. And it doesn't come cheap."

"Just keep the feathers for me, OK? And if necessary be ready to say where and when we found them. Eventually I may ask you to take blood samples from the chicks we've still got."

Out of the corner of my eye I saw him glancing at me. He said nothing, and for that I was glad. I probably knew as much or more about genetic fingerprinting as Jack did. But he wasn't to know what my mother had done for a living and I didn't want to talk about it, because all that belonged to my old life, the one I had left behind.

Suddenly Jack braked and edged the Land Rover off the lane and on to a patch of ground in front of the gateway to a field. A Renault was coming in the opposite direction. The driver waved his thanks as he passed. I shrank back in my seat, hoping I hadn't been seen. The driver of the Renault was Detective Inspector Anthorn.

We drove on to the village as quickly as possible. Jack was late for his appointments. He dropped me off at the surgery. I promised I'd buy him a drink when I got back from Turkey.

"Now look," he said, leaning out of the window of the Land Rover. "Don't do anything stupid, will you?"

I shook my head. "Jack?"

"What?"

"Thanks. Thanks for everything."

He grinned, let out the clutch and drove away.

Feeling unexpectedly cheerful, I got into the Polo and drove on to the Sanctuary. My mind was in a whirl. There were too many half-glimpsed possibilities, and too few facts. I didn't know what to think about Jason Ford. I didn't like him, but that didn't mean he was guilty of anything. I was sure that if he had all that money he could have found a breeder less scrupulous than Carson to sell him a captive-bred goshawk, just as he'd found someone prepared to sell him the Great Horned Owl. Would he risk everything he had for revenge, and the chance to steal a couple of unusual hybrid chicks?

It didn't seem rational. But people aren't rational, particularly when they're angry. And it's also true that many people find it hard to be rational about birds of prey. They arouse strong feelings, for and against. Third, if Jason Ford had been spoilt rotten all his life, he might be just the sort of person to throw a tantrum when thwarted.

I turned into the Sanctuary car park, and other worries took over. How the hell was I going to cope with the Turkish trip? I just didn't have the experience to deal with wealthy foreign clients.

With another part of my mind I automatically recorded the welcome fact that there was already a healthy sprinkling of cars. I slotted the Polo into a vacant space next to Phyllis's elderly MGB. The entrance to the Sanctuary's combined ticket office and shop was only a few metres away. As I cut the engine, I glanced at the car on the other side.

It was a silver Honda Civic. It was the same make, model and colour as Elvira Bladon's car.

SEVEN

"Took your time, didn't you?" Phyllis bellowed across the shop.

Several of the customers looked instantly shifty, as if fearing that their browsing habit might be under threat. Phyllis was manning the till, catching up on her correspondence and negotiating with the woman who made the cakes we sold in the shop. She had a genius for what she called simultaneous multi-tasking. As I moved towards her, she brought the negotiations to a swift and favourable conclusion.

I gave her the note from Carson and told her briefly what had happened at the hospital.

She looked relieved to hear Carson was no worse. "By the way, there was a phone call for you—"

"Has an American girl come in?" I cut in. "About my age. Tallish. Short blonde hair."

"Wearing jeans? She went through about twenty minutes ago." Phyllis frowned, sniffing an unhealthy romantic attachment in the offing. "Why?"

I relaxed a little. If the Bladon girl wanted to leave the Sanctuary, she'd have to come through the shop. I took a moment to set Phyllis's mind at rest. "Nothing personal. She drove past the Sanctuary last night. In fact she nearly ran into me as I was coming up the hill. Claimed it was all my fault, which it wasn't."

"Tourist?"

"I don't know. She said she was going to stay at Ardross Hall."

"In that case I don't think much of her map-reading," Phyllis said. "This is miles out of her way."

"There's another thing. She was leaving the hospital when I arrived there this morning. And she wasn't coming out of the casualty department or anything like that. She was coming out of the block where Carson is, which has got nothing to do with outpatients."

"Coincidence?" Phyllis said doubtfully.

"And now there's another coincidence: she's here."

A woman came up with three postcards in her hand. Phyllis automatically browbeat her into buying Carson's video about the Sanctuary as well.

"All right then," Phyllis said, a moment later. "How did she know Carson was in hospital? It doesn't add up."

I shrugged.

She had a fit of coughing, which seemed to bring her inspiration. "I wonder... Was it Geoff Todd who came up last night? A sergeant with a beard?"

"Yes. And he was also there when that woman nearly drove into me. Took her side, as a matter of fact."

"Do you know Mrs Todd?" Phyllis said, reaching for her cigarettes. "No? She's Geoff's wife – bit of a gossip. She works part-time at Ardross Hall. Mornings only, I believe."

Our eyes met. In a place like this, the raid on t'

Sanctuary and the attack on Carson added up to a major news item. If Mrs Todd worked at the hotel, probably everyone, staff and guests, had known about it down to the last gory detail by breakfast time at the latest. Elvira Bladon would have been among her potential audience.

"I'm going to find her."

"I'll stop her if she comes through here," Phyllis said, her eyes gleaming. She lit up with a flourish. "I'll head her off at the pass. We've got her trapped, partner."

She squinted at me through the smoke. I think she was trying to look like Clint Eastwood. Phyllis was a film buff, and in times of excitement she had an embarrassing tendency to talk like the script of a B movie.

I went outside. We already had a healthy sprinkling of visitors – in the summer, Sundays were often very busy – but there was no sign of Elvira Bladon. I walked quickly down the hawk walk. It was only a matter of time.

Some kids were watching one of our part-timers feeding a family of chicks; they were asking the usual questions about the diet and saying "Yuk!" when they heard the answers. Kenneth was at the end of the path with Leila at his heels. The pair of them came towards me.

"Um – Adam? I was – you know – wondering..."

"I'm looking for somone." I described the elusive ⁺s Bladon. "Have you seen her?"

"Er, no. That is... I don't think so. I wanted a

word about something... ah, the padding on the sparrowhawks' bow perches—" He broke off, his eyes drifting away from my face. "Is that – um – the girl you're looking for?"

I swung round. Shock jolted through me: for an instant I thought I saw Carson, miraculously restored to health and brought back to Hill Farm. Then my mind caught up with what I was seeing. Ms Bladon was standing where she had no business to be, in Carson's study staring out of the window. The sheet of glass between us made her look insubstantial, like a ghost; it blurred her outlines and drained much of the colour from her, so her fair hair could have been as grey as Carson's.

The house was out of bounds to visitors. Usually we locked the doors, but it was easy to forget – especially on a day like this when all our routines were upset. When we forgot, it was amazing how many visitors would ignore the notices and just wander in. Last year Carson found a total stranger making herself a cup of tea in the kitchen.

I walked quickly towards the house. The girl vanished. I swore, and broke into a run. Looking back, I realize I acted stupidly – I ran straight for the side door of the house: I should have pretended I hadn't seen her; I should have got Phyllis to cut off her line of retreat before I went after her. I twisted the handle of the door and pushed: it opened. I went into the house and down the hall to the study.

The room was empty. Nothing seemed to have been disturbed since earlier that morning. I thought I smelt a hint of perfume, but I might have imagined that.

In the distance a heavy door closed with a bang that shook the house.

I knew it was the front door, which gave on to a strip of garden that bordered the road. But there was still a chance of preventing her escape. I started to run – down the hall and out of the side door. I cannoned into Kenneth. Leila started to bark. I ran round to the shop with the dog at my heels.

The shop was more crowded than it had been. There was a queue at the till and a crowd of children were picking through the cheaper souvenirs. Phyllis looked up, startled. Leila's barking confused everyone. I dodged between visitors and display stands, bumped into the counter and lurched through the doorway.

I was half a minute too late. I reached the car park just in time to see the Honda Civic turning into the road. I quietened Leila and went back to Phyllis. I told her what had happened.

"Police?" she said.

"Do you think they'd be interested? I don't, not if nothing's been taken, that is. People wander into the house all the time. She could just say she panicked when she saw me coming."

"But with all the other things?"

I shook my head. "They don't add up to anything that would impress the cops. If she's still here when I get back from Istanbul, I'll go and talk to her."

"Do you want me to go?"

"Don't bother. You've got enough to do."

This was only partly true. My other reason for wanting to talk to Elvira Bladon myself was more personal: she'd made a fool of me last night and a fool of me this morning at the hospital. There was unfinished business between us.

I got the part-timer to take over the till. I made a pot of coffee and took it to Carson's study, where Phyllis and I spent the next hour. The first thing we needed to discuss was the Turkish trip, for which I had to find the blue folder Carson had mentioned. While I was looking in the desk for it, I checked the other drawers. All of them were locked, and so were the filing cabinets; they showed no sign that someone had tampered with them.

We flicked through the contents of the folder and added what we saw to the information we'd gleaned separately from Carson in the last few weeks. Carson had been retained by a wealthy Turkish businessman to advise on a proposal for a large private mews project. The idea was that we would submit plans for it, including detailed costings. According to a friend of Carson's in the City, the client was well on the way to becoming a dollar billionaire, so money shouldn't be a problem if he decided to go ahead with the project. If the plans were agreed, we would be employed to oversee the construction. The client would also buy both birds and specialized equipment from us, and it was possible that we would train a falconer for him. Carson hoped that we'd be retained indefinitely consultants, and also that such a substant commission would lead to others of a similar nature

"What's Izmidlian's angle?" Phyllis asked. "Sport? Conservation?"

"Both. Or that's what he'll say. He'll never admit it's really a mixture of tax avoidance and prestige."

For many of our Middle Eastern clients, hawking had a glamorous, upmarket image, rather like hunting and shooting used to have in Britain. And investing in it could make financial sense too: often they could pick up grants or tax credits for protecting threatened species and helping their country's ecology.

Phyllis produced a folder of her own: she'd faxed Izmidlian's Istanbul office that I'd be coming, and received an acknowledgement from his personal assistant. She'd also managed to transfer the tickets to my name. As it was such a short trip, Carson hadn't intended to take traveller's cheques. Instead, Phyllis had ordered him some Turkish liras and US dollars for emergencies. She'd typed up the flight details and the arrangements at the other end.

"You've got a credit card, haven't you? You'll be able to use that, I'm sure."

I nodded.

"I've given you a note of the address and phone number of our consulate in Istanbul, and also the embassy in Ankara. Just in case. You never know, do you?"

"No," I said, "you don't." The spectacle of Phyllis acting like a mother hen was beginning to unnerve me.

"And your passport's in order, isn't it?"

"Don't worry."

"You know how to get to Heathrow airport, don't

you? It can be a little confusing with four terminals. I'd allow—"

"Phyllis," I said. "Please don't fuss."

She looked sheepish. I never thought I'd see the day when Phyllis showed a trace of embarrassment. She coughed, and then cleared her throat. We moved on to the next hundred-and-one items on the agenda. We had a couple of school coach parties booked for later in the day, and another tomorrow. We had to arrange for someone to do the demonstrations in my place; fortunately one of the students had a knack for it, and I thought she would be all right if she used some of our calmer birds.

Phyllis and I discussed how we were going to clear up the mess left by last night's visitors. Though it was Sunday, she had already been in touch with Carson's insurance broker, a local man whom she'd run to earth in the golf club; after a little persuasion, he'd promised to bring her the claim forms during the afternoon.

"I'm surprised Carson managed to pay the premiums," I said.

Phyllis cackled. "I practically had to put a gun to his head to make him write the cheque."

I glanced at my watch. I was a long way behind schedule. "One other thing. Do you think you could move up to the Sanctuary while I'm away?"

"Why?"

"I'd be happier if you were here. Kenneth can't cope by himself. He needs someone to tell him what to do, especially if we get another emergency."

"Surely that's not very likely?"

"As far as Kenneth's concerned, a visit from the police counts as an emergency," I said. "Haven't you noticed?"

She looked thoughtful. "Now you come to mention it, yes."

"And we might get journalists too. As soon as Carson's conscious he'll be trying to get maximum media coverage out of this. Can you imagine Kenneth dealing with a TV interviewer?"

"Damn Carson. Why'd he have to get himself knocked on the head? If he's not careful he'll get Mrs Fettercairn down here."

"Mrs who?"

"His big sister. She lives in Scotland somewhere."

"I've never heard of her."

"They don't get on," Phyllis said. "Apparently they fight like cat and dog. Usually on the lines of why doesn't he do something sensible with his life. I've talked to her on the phone a few times. If she hears he's in hospital she'll be down right away. Like a ton of bricks."

The coffee pot was empty, and we both had work to do. As we were walking down the hall, Phyllis stopped abruptly and smacked her forehead.

"I must be going senile. You had a phone call."

"Oh yes?"

"A girl." She looked up at me. "Another girl. This one was English. You're a dark horse, aren't you?"

"Who was it?" But I'd already guessed.

She cackled again. "Playing the field, eh? Becky the name. Wants you to call her."

Why did my old life have to muscle its way into my new life today of all days?

"Said it was urgent," Phyllis went on, "and that you'd know the number. In my experience it always is urgent."

She grinned at me and went out of the side door. I waited for a moment, trying to calm down. If Becky phoned me here, it could only be bad news. The question was, how bad?

I went back into Carson's study and shut the door. I sat down at the desk and reached for the phone. I dialled the number for the private line. Becky answered on the second ring.

"It's me," I said.

"Adam, I'm sorry..."

Her voice sounded as though someone were beginning to strangle her.

"It's all right," I said. "Don't worry."

At the other end of the line I heard my sister beginning to cry.

EIGHT

British Airways flight 680 drifted down to Atatürk Airport, a few miles west of Istanbul. You felt, rather than heard, the roar of the engines. The airbus touched down like a rubber ball in slow motion. I felt the impact and waited for a bounce that didn't come. We taxied along the runway. It was nearly ten o'clock in the evening, local time.

I was flying economy; Mr Izmidlian's generosity had stopped short of providing Carson with a club class ticket. As it was a scheduled flight, most of the other passengers were either business executives or well-heeled tourists.

I spent much of the time worrying about Becky – which in a sense was a blessing in disguise because it meant I had less time to worry about what I would have to do in Turkey. On the other hand, it wasn't really a blessing at all because thinking of my sister made me feel so helpless. She was stuck in that big, formal Lodge with only my father and the ghosts for company. No wonder she needed to hear a friendly voice. I also felt guilty for not phoning her more often.

I was one of the first to get through immigration ~~nd~~ customs because I didn't have to wait for my ~~~gage.~~ I had all I needed in the bag I'd had with me ~~~he~~ cabin. It was an old leather shoulder bag of

Carson's, scarred and scratched with use and festooned with old labels. There was room enough for a change of clothes and the papers I needed, which included a folder of plans and photographs.

We filed into the arrivals hall. I saw the man immediately. He was standing near the barrier and carrying a rectangle of cardboard with a crudely lettered sign on it: KARSON. SANCTARY.

I paused by him. His eyes flickered over me, then away. He had carrot-coloured hair, a freckled skin and disconcertingly green eyes. There are a lot of Western European genes floating around in the Turkish population. He was wearing an artificially distressed black leather jacket, very tight designer jeans and Nike trainers. It didn't take much imagination to realize that he thought he was really something.

"Are you from Mr Izmidlian?" I said.

The eyes swung back. He looked puzzled. "Mr Carson? You?"

"I'm representing him, yes. I'm—"

"Carson," he said. He was looking at an old flight label on the bag. It had Carson's name on it, and the Hill Farm address. "OK. We go."

"You've had the fax we sent?"

The question didn't get through. "OK," he said. "No more baggage?"

"No more baggage."

"Mr Izmidlian says urgent, top priority. You come with me."

He set off at a walking pace that was the next best thing to a run. I followed him out to a car park.

warmth hit me, and the alien smells and sounds: as always the first exposure to a strange place sent a surge of excitement through me. I caught up with my guide.

"Are we going to Mr Izmidlian's house tonight?" I asked. "Or to a hotel? Or where?"

He looked blankly at me. "Soon," he said. "Soon, OK?"

"OK," I said wearily. It had been a long day. "Whatever you say."

He shepherded me into the back of a white Mercedes 230E, though I would have preferred to sit in the front. I stared at the boil on the back of his neck while he slotted a disc into the CD player. Perhaps he wanted to discourage conversation he wasn't equipped to handle. Tom Petty filled the car at concert-hall volume. While the driver was negotiating his way through the car park he pulled out a Marlboro and lit it one-handed, a process which nearly brought us into a head-on collision with a taxi.

By now it was nearly night. We took the motorway eastwards, towards Istanbul. At first we could have been driving towards almost any modern city in the West. On the outskirts, however, we pulled off the motorway and headed north through the suburbs. Maybe my driver planned to skirt the city and bring us to the villas that line the Bosphorus. Alternatively we might be heading towards Istanbul's high-tech enterprise zone; I remembered Carson telling me that Izmidlian's business had something to do with computers.

I was getting increasingly thirsty. Flying dehydrates

you, because the cabin of an aircraft in flight is drier than the driest desert. I considered asking my driver to stop so I could buy a Coke or something. But I doubted if he'd think this was a good idea, even if I could make him understand what I wanted.

Outside my tinted window, houses, flats and offices gave way to slums and factories. The road surface became rougher and the street lighting worse. Suddenly it was obvious we were on the edge of Asia, on the fringes of a different culture from the West's. We passed mosques, beggars, shanties made of what looked like cardboard and corrugated iron, men drinking tea and playing backgammon in pavement cafés lit by paraffin lamps; and everywhere thin children and thinner cats swarmed, like flies on carrion.

The first prickles of foreboding ran up my spine. This was ridiculous, I told myself: I had no reason to distrust this man. And, like a fool, I listened to the voice of reason.

Gradually we left the city behind. I knew we must still be in the European part of Turkey because we hadn't crossed the Bosphorus.

"Are we nearly there?" I said loudly.

The driver half-turned and shrugged, miming his lack of understanding.

I tried the same question in French. He didn't bother to turn or even shrug. He simply ignored me. So I tried German, which is a second language for many Turks, and got the same result.

Meanwhile the road surface grew worse and w

The man was driving fast. Occasionally we overtook other vehicles, but no one overtook us. By now I had completely lost my sense of direction. Scattered lights in the distance only emphasized the immense loneliness of the night.

Suddenly the engine stopped.

But the car glided on. Tom Petty thumped out of all four speakers. Lights glowed and flickered on the dashboard. The road was rising slightly and running along the side of a valley. We were losing speed.

The driver half turned for the second time. "Car kaput," he said. He pulled over to the side of the road, braked and turned off the ignition. "Bad men here," he went on. His face looked genuinely anxious, though it can be hard to judge expressions on a face you don't know well.

He leant across and pulled up the bonnet catch. He got out of the car. I did the same, bringing my bag with me. I stood by the car. It was good to be outside after the sterile, air-conditioned atmosphere inside the car.

It was almost completely dark. The courtesy light inside the car was on, because our doors were open; but this made little difference. On the left the ground sloped steeply upwards. On the right there was a drop.

The driver lifted the bonnet and peered at the engine, which ticked softly as it cooled.

"Kaput," he said again. "No good."

I wondered how he could be so confident. He n't even have a torch. Then I heard movement nd him. I glimpsed the outlines of a second man scrambling on to the road from the drop to the right of the Mercedes. There was a third man behind him.

Bad men here.

The driver screamed something in Turkish.

One of the men had something in his right hand – a torch or spanner perhaps? He lifted his hand, as if holding it out to me.

Sometimes, when the adrenalin flows, you think so fast that the thoughts are just a blur. In a flash I must have linked the loneliness of the road with the object in the man's hand, and the darkness of the night with the prickles dancing up my spine. And before I knew what I was doing, I dodged round the car and dived into the darkness. The bag came with me, more by accident than by design.

As I dived, the gun went off.

I saw the muzzle flash as I hit what felt like a pile of rocks. An instant later I heard the crack of the shot. Simultaneously I yelled with pain and I rolled sideways, trying to get to my feet. There was another shot.

I was up and running – away from the road. As well as sloping upwards, the terrain was rocky – bad enough for running in daylight; almost suicidal at night. There were strange, vivid scents. My left cheek and my left hand were on fire. My breathing sounded like the noise you make when you tear strips of paper. I felt a flash of intense pain in my right ankle. I think I screamed.

There was a third shot, and running footsteps behind me.

I ran on. Fear filled my mind and pumped energy through my muscles. Several times I stumbled and almost fell. Someone was shouting. The man fired another shot. I glanced back, and saw below me the light inside the car glowing faintly in the distance. I had covered a surprising amount of ground. A moment later I tripped and fell full length with a jolt that squeezed the air from my lungs.

I lay on the ground and felt exhaustion creeping over me. Despair followed. I wasn't sure I was capable of running any further. I waited for the pursuing footsteps. I waited for the final bullet.

The men scurried about. Occasionally they called to one another in Turkish. They dislodged stones and small rocks, some of which skidded down the hillside and caused several false alarms.

One of them came within a couple of metres of me. A match flared. I held my breath and slipped into suspended animation. He lit a cigarette, tossed the match on the ground and moved away. I saw the match end glowing for a few seconds in the darkness.

I lost all sense of time. It's possible that at least an hour slipped past without my noticing. I found I was registering unimportant details with an intensity that was almost hallucinatory: the cool night air flowing over my bruised cheek; the stars wheeling overhead, seemingly so much nearer than in England; the smells that reminded me of cooking – thyme, was it, or rosemary? Perhaps people condemned to die experience their last sensations more vividly than normal. I thought perhaps there were footsteps in the distance. It didn't seem to matter very much.

The Mercedes's engine started up, which brought me out of my trance. I waited. The car moved off. I waited a few more seconds. I sat up cautiously. Far below, I saw the car's lights moving along the road. The tail lights vanished round a bend. I was alone.

I realized that largely by accident I had done the best thing I could: I had run off into the darkness and lain low, so the men could neither see me nor hear me. If any of them had had the sense to bring a torch they would almost certainly have found me.

I started to shiver – partly with cold, made worse by the cooling sweat on my body, and partly because the departure of the immediate threat gave me time to realize how close I had come to being killed.

People do get killed, of course. Many of them die violently not by accident but because someone actively wants them dead. You see it in every newspaper, in every television news. You get used to it.

But it's different when you're the intended victim. Believe me, it's different.

After a while I stopped feeling sorry for myself and started pulling myself together. I foraged in the bag and put a layer of clothing over what I was already wearing. I forced myself not to hurry. Every few seconds I stopped to listen. One of the men might have stayed behind, waiting for me to move.

I found a bar of chocolate and made myself eat it for the energy. The trouble was, as I realized too late, it made me thirstier than I had been before. Sweating had dehydrated me even further.

The first thing I needed to find out was how badly I was hurt. Very slowly and cautiously, I stood up. I tried my weight on my right ankle to see how seriously I'd sprained it. Pain stabbed up the leg but I reckoned I could walk on it if I was careful. I'd cut my face and my left hand, which were still throbbing; but the blood was drying, and making the skin underneath itch like crazy.

I listened. I heard nothing except the noises of the night: tiny scratches, ticks and scrapes, perhaps caused by small animals moving or by the cooling of the hillside; an engine revving in the distance; a jet plane even further away; a barking dog, with another answering it. There was also a continuous rustling. It seemed to come from further up the hill. It might even be a stream.

It was getting colder. I looked at my watch – a digital one with a light: it was already after midnight. If I tried to spend the night here, I was going to get very chilly indeed. But I didn't want to go down to the road in case those guys with the gun decided to patrol it in search of me. My safest option was a cross-country walk in search of human beings or somewhere more sheltered to spend the night.

I glanced up the hill. The possibility of that stream haunted me. If there was water, I knew it would almost certainly not be fit to drink. Not worth taking a chance on it. Finding the stream would just refine the torture by increasing my thirst. But people live near water.

I calculated that I was at least twenty miles from

Istanbul, possibly further. I knew there must be nearby villages and perhaps towns, but we hadn't driven through any of them for some time. I guessed my driver had taken us by the back roads.

It shows how the shock had affected me. All this time had gone by since the man had tried to shoot me, and I hadn't asked the obvious question, Why?

The obvious answer was that they'd wanted my money. Maybe the guy with the gun wouldn't have tried to shoot me if I hadn't run away. Had there been two criminals or three? In other words, had the driver set me up, or had he been as much a victim as I was? It was possible that the breakdown had been perfectly genuine. I hadn't liked what I had seen of the driver, but that didn't mean he was a crook.

If he was innocent, then presumably the motive for the attack had been straightforward robbery. The Mercedes wasn't a poor man's car. But it was surely a barely credible coincidence that the breakdown should have happened in a remote country road with a couple of gun-toting hoodlums standing by. So was the driver in it too? But that didn't make sense either. If anything had happened to me, then Izmidlian and the authorities would naturally want to have a word with the chauffeur.

The chauffeur was working for Izmidlian. Could Izmidlian have stage-managed the whole affair? But why should he want to rob me? Or why should he want me dead? Izmidlian had never even heard of me; he'd never even met Carson, come to that.

I pushed the problem to the back of my mind: I

wasn't equipped to solve it. This was a strange country. Find a stream, I told myself wearily. Follow it. Then find a policeman. Let him deal with the problem. That's his job.

Slowly and painfully I moved up the hill. I kept stopping to rest and listen. In my mind were pictures of Coke cans dripping with moisture and straight from the refrigerator, and tall glasses of mineral water topped with ice cubes and slices of lemon.

Sometimes it seemed to me that the rustling that might be a stream was getting louder and closer. Sometimes I thought the sound was all in my imagination.

The ground began to level out. I bumped into yet another jagged and malevolent chunk of rock. Perhaps this walk wasn't such a good idea. I now had as much night vision as I would ever have, and it wasn't enough to keep me from getting damaged. I could come to a precipice and just stroll over it.

Once again I stopped and looked around me, my ears straining to decode the noises of the night. Was that a yellow glow in the sky? For one mad moment I wondered if dawn was on its way. I looked at my watch again. I didn't think the sun came up at two in the morning, even in Turkey.

Then what was the glow coming from? Not a town, surely, because there would have been noises as well.

I moved on, still climbing, but at a gentler gradient than before. Gradually the glow grew brighter. Then I saw, outlined against the sky, three parallel lines of barbed wire. A few metres later I saw the wall beneath it. I came closer.

Where there's a wall, there must be a house. The idiotic jingle was going round and round my mind. Where there's a house there must be a phone. Where there's a phone—

A sharp pain stabbed the shin of my right leg. I tripped. For the third time that night I belly-flopped painfully on the rocky hillside. I let out a yell. And immediately all hell broke loose.

A tripwire? In the middle of nowhere? A siren started to wail. I heard raised voices on the other side of the fence.

"Help!" I shouted, but in all the din I don't think anyone heard. I stood up and tried again. "Help!"

Feet pattered among the rocks. A dog barked very close to me. I saw a dark wolf-like shape. I smelt its warm fetid breath.

The dog leapt up at me. Automatically I dodged. It missed me by inches. I kicked its flank but did no damage at all: I just enraged it even further. It snapped at my foot, but missed. I took a step backwards. The dog snarled and gathered itself to spring. I was dimly aware of more running footsteps – human ones, this time. The dog leapt at me again. I held out Carson's bag and rammed it between the dog's jaws.

The brute's weight hit me. I staggered and fell, this time on my back. The dog was apparently trying to bite the bag in half.

There were torches like criss-crossing searchlights. The light dazzled my eyes. A man was shouting. He seized the dog's collar and pulled the beast off me.

Another man in some sort of uniform bent over me and waved an automatic pistol in my face. He yelled at me in what I think was Turkish.

There was a third man too. This one had a sub-machine-gun and he was pointing it at me.

"English," I said. "*Ingilizce.*"

The dog dropped the bag and tried for the third time to leap at me. It took two of the men to hold him back.

I tried to explain what had happened in the mixture of French and German. They shut me up by pointing the sub-machine-gun at me. The men had a lively and incomprehensible conversation. Meanwhile the dog snarled quietly and tried to sink its teeth into my leg.

I heard the word *polis* and took a chance.

"*Polis,*" I said. "Yes, please."

This confused them. Then the man with the sub-machine-gun said something, evidently a command. He picked up my bag. One of his colleagues grabbed my arm and twisted it behind my back. The other concentrated on controlling the dog. We set off, following the line of the fence. I staggered along. Every now and then I muttered, "*Polis.* Yes, please."

We came to a road. We followed it for about thirty metres until we reached a pair of gates, which were closed. The rustle of water had grown steadily louder: it looked as if the stream ran under the wall and then through a culvert under the road and onwards down the hill. Behind the gates was a lowered boom flanked by guardhouses. For the first time I saw what the wall was protecting: a complex of floodlit buildings. I couldn't tell whether it was a military or civilian installation.

Two more men in uniform emerged from one of the guardhouses. One of them was muttering into a mobile phone. The gates swung silently open, operated by remote control. A couple of closed-circuit TV cameras panned to and fro above the guardhouses.

The gates swung shut. A plump young man in a loose-fitting, lightweight suit strolled towards us. The guards straightened themselves. You could tell that they were doing their best to look alert and well-disciplined. No one said anything. Suddenly it occurred to me that the guards were scared.

The man paused in front of me, keeping a safe distance away, and looked me up and down. I was surprised to see how young he was – hardly older than me. Then I realized with a far greater shock that it wasn't a man but a woman, and a very attractive one at that.

She said something in Turkish. The guy with the sub-machine-gun answered. He sounded apologetic. He waved his gun at me.

"*Polis?*" I said.

"American?" the woman said.

"English." I decided to keep it simple. "I was attacked by robbers on the road below."

She frowned. "Why are you here?"

"In Turkey? I've come to see someone called Izmidlian."

One of the guards sucked in his breath. I sensed

that there had been a change in the atmosphere, but I didn't know why.

The woman grunted. She had a full, petulant mouth and plump cheeks. There was too much puppy fat under the expensive suit. She looked me up and down, as if contemplating buying me.

"Oh yes?" she said. "My name's Izmidlian."

NINE

What woke me, several hours later, was a dream.

I was chasing Elvira Bladon across a sun-parched Turkish hillside because I had something vital to tell her – vital for her, not me. The sun glinted on her fair hair. Every now and then she would turn her head and glance back, and her slanting eyes were full of mockery. I knew that I would never catch up with her. But I went on running because I had no choice in the matter. And the more I ran the thirstier I became. Then she stooped, picked up a rock and threw it at me. It hit me in the chest, on the right-hand side. The impact shocked me awake.

Her face was still in my mind, though fading fast. How different, I thought, from Marguerite Izmidlian's.

The sunlight poured through the slats of the shutters and made golden stripes on the wall opposite the window. I got out of bed. There was a robe of fine white cotton on the wooden chest between the windows. I put it on, opened one of shutters and stepped on to the balcony beyond.

The balcony was the size of my room at the Sanctuary and bordered on three sides by a stone balustrade. The ground below dropped sharply to a formal garden arranged round a fountain in the shape of a great white shell; beyond the garden the land fell away in a series of terraces. Two gardeners were weeding – I guessed they were doing as much of their work as they could before the day warmed up.

Beyond the terraces was the Bosphorus, the waterway linking the Black Sea with the Sea of Marmara and dividing European Turkey from Asian Turkey. The rising sun had turned it into a sheet of molten gold. Birds were wheeling to and fro in the sky.

I perched on the balustrade. On the left I could see part of the main villa, an enormous neo-baroque building erected in the last years of the Ottoman Empire for one of the Sultan's ministers. I knew all about that because the Izmidlians had thoughtfully left a folder of information in the guesthouse; I'd fallen asleep over it.

The Izmidlians were still an unknown quantity – apart from Marguerite, the young woman I'd met the previous night. Her father, John Izmidlian, was the man I had come to see. Marguerite couldn't have been kinder. This was after she had heard who I was and seen the documentary proof of it in the shape of my passport and a letter from her father to Carson. Suddenly, nothing was too good for me. It made a pleasant change.

It seemed that the installation I had stumbled on was the family's main Turkish assembly plant. There was no coincidence in this, she told me – the driver had been taking me to the villa, and the road along the valley beneath the plant was on the most direct route. When in Turkey the Izmidlians lived mainly at the Bosphorus villa, which was convenient not just for the plant, but also for the Istanbul head office and the airport. But I had been lucky to find her at the plant in the middle of the night. The night-shift manager had been taken ill just after midnight. Marguerite had been summoned to sort out the chaos which had followed. She had been on the verge of leaving when I stumbled into the perimeter tripwire.

First she gave me a drink of iced water, which tasted like liquid heaven, and then whisked me off to the factory's medical officer. He brushed aside my protests that I just had a few bruises and gave me a thorough examination.

Afterwards Marguerite settled me in her black BMW and drove me down to the villa. We talked most of the way. Her English was very fluent; she spoke with an accent which was part American and part French; her mother, it turned out, was Parisian. I started off calling her Ms Izmidlian.

"No, no," she said. "That is ridiculous. You must call me Marguerite. And I shall call you Adam. Yes?"

I agreed, of course, because I didn't have any option. I wasn't sure what was causing all this friendliness.

She hadn't heard about what had happened to Carson. As I was telling her, I saw headlights reflected in the nearside wing mirror. There was a car on our tail. I mentioned this to Marguerite.

"It's just the bodyguards," she said casually. "Wherever we go, we take bodyguards."

She made them sound as unremarkable as toothbrushes. F. Scott Fitzgerald was right: the rich are different from us. But it's not just that they've got more money. They think differently from the rest of the world.

"What about the police?" I asked as we drove through the night with a carload of weaponry behind us.

"What about them?"

"When do I talk to them? I take it you've told them what happened."

"No. Not yet."

"But why not?"

"I have shocked you, yes?" She sounded amused. "The point is, this isn't England. It will be best to discuss the matter with my father before we do anything. He may think it wiser to mount our own investigation."

I didn't like the sound of this. "Is he at the villa?"

Marguerite shook her head. "He was called away this morning. We have another factory near Samsun. I tried to phone him just now, but his plane's out of radio contact. It seems that there's a storm over the mountains."

I described the car and driver which had met me at the airport. "Do they sound familiar?"

"It could possibly be one of our cars. But it doesn't sound like one of our chauffeurs."

I wondered how many chauffeurs they had. "Why not?"

"Most of them are middle-aged, and they speak several languages. Also, they are trained to be polite to our guests."

I shivered. "This guy wasn't exactly polite."

"Don't worry. One way or another we'll find out what happened. Our security people are very good."

After that we talked about other things. It turned out that the falconry project had originally been her father's idea, but Marguerite had supported it with enthusiasm. She was spending a few months in Turkey gaining practical work experience in the family company before going on to business school. But she had been on a falconry course while she was at university in the States.

"As soon as I felt a bird on my wrist, saw it flying – I knew this was for me. You know?"

I knew. I'd been bitten by the same bug.

Her father had made the initial enquiries and then invited Carson over; but otherwise he was leaving the development of the scheme almost entirely to her. She referred to it rather grandly as "The Izmidlian Falconry Centre for the Middle East". She rattled on about the environmental and educational benefits. Neither of us was tactless enough to mention more sordid subjects like strategies for avoiding tax or generating good publicity.

There were more guards at the villa, with more automatic pistols and more sub-machine-guns. It was too dark to get an overall impression of the place, though I estimated that the drive was at least a mile long. Marguerite took me to a guesthouse in the grounds; I gathered it was one of several. A servant was waiting for us.

Marguerite told me I had only to ring the bell, day

or night, and the servant would bring me whatever I wanted.

"If only he could," I had wanted to say. "If only he could."

Now, here on the balcony in the early morning sunshine, I watched the seagulls wheeling overhead and a couple of Romanian cargo boats moving slowly down the Bosphorus. I couldn't hear their engines.

For a few moments as I sat there, all the problems dropped away – the previous night's business, Carson and the Sanctuary, the Bladon girl and the ones to do with Becky and my family. It was good to be alive.

There were footsteps on the gravel below.

"You're awake already?"

I looked down. Marguerite smiled up at me. Her dark hair glistened as if lacquered, and she was dressed in a towelling robe.

"I thought you'd sleep till lunchtime," she said. "If I'd known you were awake, I'd have asked you for a swim."

"I've been admiring the view."

"When you live with it, you hardly notice it. Do you feel up to a working breakfast with my father?"

I agreed – as far as I was concerned, the sooner my business here was finished the better. She left me, saying she'd send a servant to collect me. I took a shower and got dressed. My body had some interesting bruises. The cuts on my face and hand had scabbed over and were healing nicely.

There was a desk with stationery in the room. Among the stationery were coloured postcards of the view from the villa. I sat down at the desk and addressed one of them to my sister. Becky would like the view – she longed to travel, or maybe just to get away from England and home.

This is the view from my balcony, I wrote. *I'll be back soon, and we'll talk properly. Everything will be all right. Most of all, DON'T worry. Love, Adam.*

I didn't want prying eyes to read what I'd written, so I put the postcard in an airmail envelope. As I was addressing it, there was a tap on the door and the servant floated into the room. He saw what I was doing and offered to post my letter while I was having breakfast. That sort of well-oiled obsequiousness may not be beyond price, but it comes extremely expensive.

I was glad to have his services as a guide. The villa turned out to be a maze of marble-floored halls and corridors and anterooms. We passed at least two immense stone staircases decorated with wrought-iron rails and assorted statuary. Everything seemed about two-and-a-half-times normal size. Living there must have been rather like living in the British Museum: one up on the neighbours, but not exactly cosy.

At last we came to a room overlooking the sea. I was the first to arrive. The servant left, giving me a moment to look at my surroundings. The cornices were liberally gilded, and there was a good deal of pink paint on the walls. High in the corners of the room twinkled the red and green lights of the alarm system. There was a gleaming parquet floor; it was partly covered with a huge Turkoman carpet, obviously very old. A Monet hung on one wall with a Pissarro opposite it. In the middle of the carpet was a round table, laid with three places.

The long windows were open. I went outside onto a stone-flagged terrace above the formal garden. I was just in time to see a couple of guards strolling along one of the terraces further down; they were equipped with sub-machine-guns and a Dobermann. I wondered whom Izmidlian was afraid of, and whether he minded living in this luxurious prison.

There was movement behind me. I smelt perfume and turned. Marguerite had changed into a dress. She looked plump and pretty.

"What were you thinking of, Adam?"

"I was wondering how your father felt about all this."

"Proud." She saw the question in my face, and explained: "We're partly Armenian, you see. The Turks massacred a lot of the Armenians seventy years ago. My grandfather lost everything except his life. And now my father has got it all back. And more."

There was a deep chuckle from the doorway. Mr Izmidlian came towards me with his hand outstretched. He was no taller than his daughter but a little plumper. Another manservant, wheeling a trolley, followed him into the room.

"Marguerite is an incurable romantic, Mr Davy," Izmidlian said. "Or may I call you Adam, as she does?"

We shook hands. Izmidlian had a firm grasp and a way of looking you in the eye when he was talking to you. The top of his bald head was only just on a level with my chin, but his actual size was unimportant; he carried himself like a big man. His English was as good as his daughter's, but more florid and old-fashioned, as if he had learned much of it from the Collected Works of Charles Dickens.

"The real reason why we moved here was more prosaic," he went on. "It almost always is, don't you think? The Turkish government wanted to encourage foreign investment. And that meant attracting multinational companies like ours, and they were prepared to offer very considerable inducements in the way of tax concessions and low-interest loans."

"Are you a manufacturing company?" I asked.

"Partly. We put our eggs in several baskets. Electronics is our principal field. Not exactly high-tech - more like low to middling."

He paused for me to show my amusement; the joke had a well-rehearsed air about it. Marguerite had turned away to pour the coffee. She looked sullen, I thought, or perhaps bored.

"We make a few of the simpler parts ourselves and do a lot of assembly work for American and European wholesalers and retailers. Our labour costs are relatively low, you see, but the skills our workforce can offer are increasing with dramatic rapidity. This country has a unique—"

"Papa," Marguerite interrupted. "You sound like a press release. I'm sure you're boring Adam. Come and have breakfast."

Izmidlian grinned at me, one male seeking sympathy from another; and despite myself I grinned back. I liked him for the way he accepted the criticism. The apparent frankness and the easy charm were unexpectedly familiar. He reminded me of people I'd met when my parents were trying to raise funds – my mother for the department and my father for the college. The rich share a family resemblance which has nothing to do with blood.

We sat down. Marguerite fussed over us.

"How do you like your coffee, Adam? Or would you prefer tea?"

The coffee tasted freshly roasted as well as freshly ground, and the bread and the croissants had been baked that morning. Izmidlian swiftly brought the conversation round to Carson.

"I'm so sorry to hear he's in hospital. I understand you're his deputy."

"In a sense," I said.

He glanced shrewdly at me. "This trip must have been very inconvenient for you. You must be even busier than usual at the Sanctuary."

"Mr Carson was very keen I should come," I said diplomatically.

Perhaps I imagined the glint of amusement in Izmidlian's eyes. I wondered if he had guessed how badly the Sanctuary needed an injection of capital, and how important his commission could be for us.

"And I must apologize for the breakdown in communications. The fault was entirely ours."

He explained that the fax which Phyllis had sent to his Istanbul office had been dealt with by his personal assistant. The crisis in Samsun had taken him away from the office, and the message notifying him that I was coming in Carson's place had gone astray. The problem had been compounded by the breakdown in radio communications owing to the storm near Samsun yesterday evening.

"But what about the car, Papa?" Marguerite said. "What happened?"

All the charm vanished from Izmidlian's face. "I have already put in train an investigation," he said bleakly. "Adam, I cannot tell you how distressed I am that this should have happened to you, my guest. Believe me, the perpetrators will be found and severely punished."

"But what *happened*?" Marguerite persisted.

Izmidlian was still looking at me. "I had arranged for the car to pick up Mr Carson at the airport. The chauffeur has been with us for years, a very reliable fellow. My secretary had given him written instructions. Which flight to meet, your name – or rather Mr Carson's name. And so on. We don't know what has happened to him yet. The man who collected you was not one of my employees, I can promise you that."

"I can understand him stealing the car," Marguerite said. "But why go to the airport and collect Adam? It doesn't make sense."

"It doesn't make much sense if their motive was simple robbery, I agree." Izmidlian paused. "But I don't think they were stealing a car. I think they were stealing a Trojan horse."

"A Trojan what?" Marguerite snapped. "Papa, you're—"

"You mean they wanted a way to crack your security and get inside the villa grounds?" I said.

"Precisely." Izmidlian nodded approvingly at me. "Our security is very good here. But imagine what would have happened if the Mercedes had turned up at the gates last night. One of our private Mercedes. At the expected time. Apparently with the guest it was meant to be bringing. It's even possible they were planning to force the chauffeur to cooperate when it came to getting the car through the gates." He glanced at Marguerite. "We must be grateful to Adam, my dear. He may well have saved our lives."

Marguerite smiled at me. She had her own brand of charm, and she turned it on at full force.

"I don't follow," I said.

"I suspect, my dear fellow, that the only thing that stopped them from trying to carry out their plan was the fact that you'd escaped. There was the risk that you'd raise the alarm while the attack was in progress. And there was also the problem that you'd seen their driver's face. Which reminds me, I wonder if you could talk to my head of security after breakfast? He would very much appreciate a full description."

I glanced at Marguerite, wondering if she had told her father about our conversation last night. "What about the police?" I said. "Shouldn't I talk to them as well?"

Izmidlian's manicured fingers were tearing apart a croissant and scattering the pieces of pastry on his plate. It struck me that he had drunk two cups of coffee but eaten nothing. As I spoke, the fingers stopped moving.

"That depends entirely on you," he said, letting the remains of the croissant fall on to the plate. "If you want, of course you shall talk to the police. Say the word, and I'll tell them to bring you a phone. Or you can have a car and driver and go into Istanbul."

I kept my voice as neutral as I could: "But you'd rather I didn't?"

"My dear Adam, my feelings shouldn't come into it." The dark eyes stared into mine. "But I should warn you: if you personally report this to the police, you'll be lucky to get back to England before the end of the month. In this country a formal investigation entails a great deal of red tape. The red tape multiplies if a foreign national is involved. You don't even speak Turkish, do you?"

I shook my head.

"Which means you'd have to do everything through an interpreter. I can give you one of ours, of course – that's no problem. But it would all take time. And the fact you were coming here would make it even worse."

"Why?"

Izmidlian spread out his hands. "Because the investigating officer would know who I am. He'd know his superiors would be double-checking his every move. So he'd have to do everything by the book. And there might even be other considerations."

"Political ones?" I said brightly.

"Indeed. This isn't England, you know, or the United States."

I sipped my coffee. The thoughts rushed through my mind. I had to get back to England as soon as I could. Carson needed me; so did Becky, and Phyllis and Kenneth; and I had all those questions to find answers for. If I insisted on staying to see the Turkish police, things at home would go from bad to worse in my absence. And I suspected that Izmidlian, for all his apparent willingness to do whatever I wanted, might be sufficiently peeved to cancel the projected commission.

"What would you advise?" I asked.

"It's your decision, as I say," Izmidlian said, reaching for the cafetière. As he talked, he refilled my cup and then his own. "Personally I'd be inclined to let our security people take over. They'll notify the police, of course, but by that time you might well be out of the country. It wouldn't just be more convenient for you. It would also mean the investigation would get off to a faster and more efficient start."

"Don't think Papa is criticizing the Turkish police," Marguerite said with a touch of sarcasm. "It's just that he thinks that no one can do a job as well as he can."

"But in this case it's true, my dear. Speed may be of the essence." His eyes came back to me. "If the Trojan horse theory is correct, I don't think it will be difficult to find out who was behind the operation. Proving it, of course, would be quite another matter." He smiled at me again. "But then it always is, don't you find?"

I nodded, and watched his face beginning to relax. "I'm sure you're right," I said. "After all, I'm a stranger here. You know the ropes."

I wondered why he was quite so anxious to avoid my going to the police. But perhaps everything should be taken at its face value. Perhaps too little sleep and too much excitement were making me imagine a Machiavellian scheme where there was nothing but a simple desire to help.

"Have you fixed it all up between you?" Marguerite said impatiently. "Can we please talk about falconry now?"

For the next quarter of an hour, we talked about the project in broad terms. Izmidlian was prepared to set up a foundation to provide an income for the centre; he would provide land, and a capital sum for the buildings and for the purchase of birds. On the other hand, he wanted to be sure that the Sanctuary had sufficient expertise to provide him with what he wanted; he was particularly concerned about our ability to deal with Middle Eastern conditions. I reassured him with the information that Carson had spent a total of almost three years working on contracts in Saudi Arabia and the United Arab Emirates. I had come equipped with a list of Middle Eastern clients who would be happy to provide references.

At first I was a little surprised that Izmidlian knew so little about falconry. I soon realized that he was leaving all the practicalities to Marguerite and whomever they hired to oversee the job; he wasn't interested in the details.

Izmidlian glanced at his watch. "I have to make some phone calls, I'm afraid. You've brought some plans and photographs, I understand?"

I nodded. "Also some costings. Just to give you a very rough idea of what you'd have to pay to stock the place, and for specialist equipment."

Izmidlian gave us his orders in a practised way that made them sound like suggestions. Marguerite and I spent the rest of the morning doing exactly what he said. First she took me down to see the villa's head of security, who had an office filled with television screens in the basement.

He looked like a successful business executive in his lightweight suit and striped Pierre Cardin shirt; he also had a silk paisley tie with a matching handkerchief peeping out of the top pocket of his jacket. The only discordant note came when he leant forward to give Marguerite a glass of iced water. His jacket fell open and I glimpsed the gun in its holster strapped under his left arm.

Fortunately his English was good, and when it wasn't good enough Marguerite helped him out. He set his tape recorder running and spent nearly an hour grilling me. He extracted everything I could remember about the events of last night; if there was anything I'd forgotten he'd have needed deep hypnosis to get it out of me.

Afterwards I said something complimentary to Marguerite about how thorough he'd been.

"He would be, wouldn't he?" she replied curtly. "His job's on the line."

We spent a long time at the guesthouse going through the material in Carson's folder. Marguerite asked a lot of questions that suggested she'd inherited a good deal of her father's business acumen. She was particularly interested in what I could tell her about the economics of commercial breeding.

"Carson's the real expert on that," I said, at last. "And I'm sure our administrator would show you the figures. But if you have a breeding programme, it's vital you get the right person to run it."

"Would you run it for me?"

I thought the question might be a little more complicated than it sounded. I said, "You'd really need someone with more experience than I've got. A specialist. But why are you so interested?"

She looked at me and answered, very seriously, "I want the centre to make money. It's not just a toy, you see."

I did see; and I liked her better for it.

It was nearly midday by the time we'd finished. Marguerite said we had better find her father. We went across to the villa and climbed one of the huge stone staircases. Izmidlian had an office on the second floor. It had a full-sized billiard table at one end and a conference table at the other.

He was on the phone when we went in. "*Mais c'est pas lui*—" he was saying. "But it's not him—" He sounded irritable, and also on the defensive, which was not what I expected him to be.

He smiled, waved us to seats and went on with his call. Now his voice was calmer. Speaking rapidly in French, he said something about being only too glad to help; and that he was sure a solution to the problem would present itself.

There were magazines on the coffee table in front of our chairs. I glanced idly towards them. Suddenly I sat up. One of the magazines was open at a double-page spread. The text was in Arabic, and so were the captions below the photographs at the head of the pages. One picture showed a couple of men shaking hands and looking not at each other but at the camera. The other was of two women. They were standing on the deck of what looked like a yacht and chatting to each other. The one on the left had her head covered and looked Middle Eastern, though she wore Western clothes.

The other was taller. She had short fair hair. There were slanting eyes above high cheekbones. The mouth was wide, with full lips. It was Elvira Bladon.

Izmidlian put down the phone and came quickly towards us. It seemed to me that he was in a hurry. His face was wreathed in smiles. His voice sounded as if it were coming from a very long way away – the aural equivalent of seeing something through the wrong end of the telescope. I knew it was vital not to betray the shock I was feeling. I had to act normally. I dared not look at the magazine.

"And how have you two been getting on?" he asked, radiating benevolence like Santa Claus in his grotto.

"We've covered a lot of ground," I said.

"I think it's very promising, Papa."

"Let's have a look at those plans," he said.

He swept the magazines into a pile and dumped them on the floor. The photograph of Elvira Bladon disappeared. I glanced at Marguerite and her father, who were apparently absorbed in opening out Carson's plans and spreading them across the coffee table.

"The centre itself needn't be that large, Papa," Marguerite was saying. "But we'll need lots of open country for the birds to fly over. And that will raise questions of access."

Izmidlian was kneeling on the floor almost on top of the pile of magazines. I thought about what had happened last night and about all the very sensible reasons Izmidlian had found for my not talking directly to the police. I thought about that phone call.

"*Mais c'est pas lui*—"

The villa and its grounds were Izmidlian's private kingdom, policed by his private army. I thought about the man with the gun who had tried to kill me last night. Then I thought of asking Izmidlian who Elvira Bladon was, and why she was hanging round the Sanctuary, and why her photograph, if only in a magazine, had been lying on his coffee table.

Better not, I thought as I stuffed my hands in my pockets to stop them trembling. The rich are different from the rest of us: they make their own rules.

TEN

I didn't believe that Izmidlian was really going to let me go. I suspected that he was playing with me, a cat-and-mouse game, perhaps, which at the last possible moment would end with a very dead mouse.

Perhaps I was overreacting; perhaps fear, fatigue and uncertainty were making me paranoid. But it didn't feel like paranoia. It felt like common sense – even as time went by and nothing happened to confirm my suspicions. But that's the whole point of a cat-and-mouse game: the cat makes it last as long as possible.

After an early lunch Marguerite drove me to Atatürk Airport in a soft-top Porsche with the carload of bodyguards riding bumper-to-bumper behind. She didn't stop talking about her falconry centre. She bombarded me with questions, and I tried to give her coherent answers.

She was full of plans for us. I was to phone her when Carson was out of hospital, and she'd fly over for a few days; I'd come and meet her at the airport, wouldn't I? Could I recommend a nice hotel near the Sanctuary? Or maybe she could stay with me?

Papa was going to get his lawyers to draw up a contract for the first phase of the project: a five-figure sum in US dollars in return for a detailed blueprint of the centre and its contents, expense no object, plus a commitment to act as consultants to the project for the first year; if all went well, the consultancy would be renewed.

Once or twice Marguerite took her hand off the wheel and patted my leg to emphasize a point. She kept saying "we" in a proprietorial fashion. Her behaviour would have worried the hell out of me if I had been capable of worrying about anything other than getting back to England in an undamaged condition.

The minimum check-in time for the 1450 hours flight to London Heathrow was ninety minutes. We got there thirty-five minutes before take-off. "No problem," Marguerite said; and it wasn't. The minimum check-in time was one of those regulations designed to make life complicated for lesser mortals. People like the Izmidlians rose effortlessly above such petty restrictions. For the purpose of getting on the plane I was a temporary Izmidlian. I didn't object because I was desperate to be gone, but I didn't much like it either.

Even when I was on the plane, I didn't believe I was safe. The minutes before take-off stretched into hours. At last the plane began to move. We left the ground. I stared down at the airport.

A Scottish voice came on the PA system and told me I could unfasten my seat belt. I let out my breath in a long sigh of relief. The German businessman in the next seat looked curiously at me. I felt myself beginning to relax. The knot of tension inside my stomach started to loosen.

By now the plane was cruising above the clouds. The stewardess came round with her trolley. The man beside me was counting up a mountain of small change in assorted currencies. It was all so blessedly normal. And blessedly safe.

I struggled to make sense of what had occurred. The word "perhaps" kept tripping me up. Perhaps it was merely coincidence that in his office Izmidlian had an Arab magazine which happened to be open at a page which happened, by another coincidence, to contain a photograph of Elvira Bladon. Or perhaps there was a perfectly innocent connection between her and the Izmidlians – Coincidence Number Three.

The trouble was, when Carson heard about the deal, he'd be in heaven. He'd immediately see beyond the first phase to a second phase and a third phase. He'd be counting all those lovely US dollars in his mind, just as the German was counting his change.

But I didn't believe the deal was on the level, or not as far as Izmidlian was concerned. I didn't trust him. There had been too many hints that something was wrong. Marguerite was a different matter. Unless she was a brilliant actress, she was genuinely keen on the falconry centre, even though it had been her father's idea. What sort of a man would be willing to con his own daughter? There were many things I disliked about my father, but I knew with an absolute certainty which was bred in the bone that he would never be dishonest with Becky or me.

My immediate problem was Carson. I was afraid

that he would so much want to believe in this deal that he would ignore all the warning signals. He hadn't experienced them at first hand.

Somewhere, somehow there had to be a connection between Elvira Bladon, who was linked to the violence at the Sanctuary, and an Armenian industrialist in Turkey. *C'est pas lui* – it's not him: not Carson? Had the whole purpose of the trip been to lure Carson to Turkey? And, once he was there, for the driver of the Mercedes to stage a breakdown? And then for a man to come out of the darkness with a gun—

It just wouldn't add up. Carson had upset a lot of people. He was a man with strong opinions, a mission in life and tunnel vision; he would have been promising Crusader material in the twelfth century. Of course he had made enemies – but not the sort of enemies who consider putting a bullet in your brain on a lonely Turkish hillside. Or who are capable of suborning an Armenian industrialist. Falconry is not like drug-smuggling or arms-dealing. By and large, it doesn't attract people who like living dangerously or getting rich quickly.

Then again, *perhaps*. I began to wonder if I had misread the situation. Perhaps there was a perfectly innocent explanation staring me in the face. Hadn't they let me go?

I had to get to the hospital and see Carson. All I could do was tell him what I knew and suspected and then let him judge; it was his life.

I'd been away for less than twenty-four hours. It felt like a month. Everything in England seemed remote – not unimportant but distant in both time and place. I tried to work out what to do about the people and problems that were waiting for me. Carson, Phyllis and Inspector Anthorn. Elvira Bladon, Jason Ford, Jack Bream and my sister Becky. The people and the problems spun round like a roundabout at a fairground. I couldn't do anything about them because I wasn't on the roundabout but standing uselessly beside it.

I must have fallen into an uneasy sleep. Once again I was dreaming about Elvira Bladon. In the dream I was annoyed about this because I thought she should at least respect my privacy. I didn't want to dream about her. Not in the slightest.

The next thing I knew was that someone was shaking my arm.

"Will you fasten your seat belt, please?" a stewardess said. "We'll soon be coming into land."

As the plane slid through the clouds, the reassuring Scottish voice informed us over the PA that our flight was on schedule. I looked down on England, on a country that compared to Turkey seemed cramped and crowded. The plane touched down just before five o'clock.

Ninety minutes later I was battling with the rush-hour traffic on the motorway. The sleep had refreshed me. Best of all, I was back in England, in a country where I had a better grasp of how the system worked. The problems were still there but I reckoned I could cope with them. It just shows how wrong you can be.

I pulled into the first service station I came to.

Both the car and I needed refuelling. First I headed for the bank of payphones. I thumbed a phone card into the slot and tried to ring Becky. There was no answer, so I broke the connection and punched in the number for the private line at the Sanctuary.

"Yes?"

"Hello, Phyllis."

There was a burst of coughing.

"It's Adam," I went on. "How are things going?"

"Where are you?"

"Beside the M4."

"You're back in England? But Carson thought—"

"He was wrong," I interrupted. This wasn't the time or place to explain how wrong. "Is he in hospital still?"

"Just about. He's coming out tomorrow."

"Is he well enough?"

"Of course he isn't. The doctors want him to stay for a day or two, but he's not giving them the option."

"Sounds like he's more or less back to normal."

"Well, he's not," Phyllis snarled. "Just like a man. Thinks everything grinds to a halt without him."

"I'll call in and see him on my way back. Is everything OK at the Sanctuary?"

"You mean has Attila the Hun dropped in again? Not so far. But we had a woman from local radio instead, and a couple of journalists. And that policeman, Anthorn, called by to let us know he wasn't getting anywhere. Yak, yak, yak – don't they realize that some of us have got work to do? Oh, and a man from the insurance company phoned. He seemed

119

to think there was no particular hurry about sorting out the claim, so I put him right on that. Otherwise it's been business as usual."

As she was talking I listened to the tiredness in her voice.

"Is Kenneth all right?" I asked.

"Less of a pillar of strength than he might have been. Anthorn and the journalists sent him running for cover. How did you get on?"

"I'm not sure," I said. My phonecard was about to expire. "I'll tell you about it later. Have you seen Elvira Bladon?"

There was an almighty sniff at the other end of the line. "She's not showed her face up here. But she's still at Ardross Hall. Jack Bream saw her car this afternoon."

I said goodbye and put down the phone. Phyllis sounded rattled as well as tired. Maybe the unresolved violence of the attack on Carson was worrying her. Normally she came across as one hundred per cent True British Grit, which made it easy to forget that she was also elderly and perhaps not too strong.

I got myself some food and the car some petrol. Soon I was back on the motorway. It was one of those perfect summer evenings that always seem to happen when you're stuck inside a car. I drove west into the setting sun and wondered how on earth I was going to persuade Carson to treat the Izmidlian offer with the caution it deserved. I wasn't to know that there was no need for me to worry. Or at least not about that.

I turned off the motorway and headed north-west

on the long Roman road. I drove as fast as the roads and the Polo would let me. I wanted to reach the hospital before they turfed out the visitors for the night.

I was only just in time. When I got inside the the building where Carson's ward was, I checked at the reception desk. I had fifteen minutes before the end of visiting time. I took the lift and followed the signs until I reached the swing doors leading to Ward 15.

No one was sitting at the desk where the ward sister had been on my last visit. It was surprisingly noisy. At least two televisions were on, but tuned to different channels. One patient and his group of visitors were having a high-volume conversation with another patient and his group of visitors; the patients had rooms on either side of the corridor, and each patient was in bed. A guy in a wheelchair was groaning to himself; no one else was listening. At the far end of the corridor, a flustered probationary nurse was trying to soothe an irate and obviously deaf old man.

I walked past the desk and down the corridor. In a room on the left two more nurses were chatting over mugs of tea. Neither looked up as I passed. I reached the doorway to the room where I had seen Carson. The door was shut, as were several others on the corridor. There was a square window in it, set at eye level. I peered in.

The first thing I saw was a big man in a white coat. He was standing with his back to me and bending over the bed. I could see Carson, too, or at least his face.

121

He was lying on top of the blankets propped up on a couple of pillows. His hair was uncombed and pushed away from his forehead; it looked like a pair of white wings, ragged and distinctly grubby. The dressing on his head was smaller than the one he'd had yesterday morning.

Carson was staring up at his visitor, and he looked obstinate and cross. I had seen that expression so often in the time I'd known him, and I knew exactly what it meant: Carson was doing battle with some form of authority he had decided to disapprove of.

The doctor or whoever he was moved slightly. He had broad shoulders and dark hair. I saw that he was holding a hypodermic in his right hand. He was waving the other hand as if emphasizing a point.

Carson's lips were moving. I couldn't hear the words but it wasn't hard to guess the gist of what he was saying. *I've had enough of you damn quacks poking needles into me...*

The doctor began to wave the arm with hypodermic as well. It was a thick door, but judging by the muffled sounds coming through it, both men were raising their voices.

Find someone else to use as a pincushion...

The doctor's left hand dug into the pocket of his white coat. At first I amused myself by thinking that he'd stuck it there to prevent himself from hitting Carson with it; Carson had a genius for provoking violent reactions from those he disliked. My amusement lasted for about two seconds. The doctor was looking for something. And then he found it.

He pulled out a kitchen knife – a Sabatier with a black handle; the sort of knife that serious cooks go for. It was in a plastic sheath. He put the bottom of the sheath between his teeth and pulled the knife out.

For an instant it all seemed perfectly reasonable. And in that instant all sorts of absurd thoughts cantered through my mind. Medicine is a profession full of processes that seem mysterious to the uninitiated. Here was another little technical mystery. Maybe Sabatier knives were standard issue for doctors. Maybe they used them for cutting open phials or something. In any case, who was I to interrupt a professional consultation? The guy would have me thrown out of the hospital. Doctors knew best, and it was none of my business.

Then I saw Carson's face. I didn't believe what I saw. The eyes were wide open and staring at the knife. His mouth was open. He was shouting. His body began to thrash about on the bed. The doctor flung his weight on the bed trying to pin Carson down. He lifted the knife.

I twisted the handle. I shouldered the door open and charged.

The man in the white coat glanced at me. His face wasn't much more than a blur. I had the vague impression that it was probably the sort of face sometimes described as "hawklike" by people who don't know very much about hawks. He had his back to the window. The long summer evening was beginning to edge towards dusk, and the setting sun was behind him. The light wasn't on. Besides, I was distracted. Even so, there was an elusive hint of familiarity about the man.

Carson was trying to push his attacker off the bed. The man in the white coat stabbed the knife into Carson's chest. It didn't go in very far. Maybe the tip hit a rib.

Carson grunted and writhed. I'd have thought a person in his situation would have screamed, or at least made more noise and tried to raise the alarm. But in practice Carson had neither the time nor the energy. The need to avoid the knife: there was room for nothing else in his mind.

As I careered towards them I stuck out my hand trying to grab the knife. I was too late. The man stabbed again. This time the blade went in and in, nearly as far as the hilt.

The man in the white coat tugged out the knife. The skin clung to the blade. His movements were fluid, like a dancer's. His right hand, the one with the hypodermic, came up and hit me. The blow didn't hurt much, but it threw me off-balance.

His other hand was moving too. The one with the knife. Something exploded above my right ear. I fell sideways across the bed – across Carson's legs. There should have been pain but I didn't feel it.

My eyes focused on a perfect red flower which was growing a few centimetres to the left of the middle button on Carson's pyjama jacket. The edge of the flower touched the button.

I remember nothing else.

ELEVEN

I heard a woman saying, "We don't look very well, do we?"

Other voices were shouting orders. There were running footsteps. Everyone was in a hurry. I was lying down with a blinding headache. Maybe it was a migraine.

My mother used to have migraines. That was how her illness started. I remembered her lying in her bedroom with the curtains drawn during the day. Becky and I would tiptoe round the house. It seemed like a life was in suspension: it was weird then, just as this was weird now.

I felt slightly nauseous. I had been drifting on the borders of consciousness for some time. I knew that they'd moved me to a room that was almost identical to Carson's except that the furniture was arranged differently. I heard canned laughter from a TV sit com. Nothing seemed very important.

Someone wiped my face with a cool, damp cloth.

"I knew that bird man meant trouble," the woman said. "You can always tell."

I opened my eyes to see who was blaming Carson for someone attacking him. There, uncomfortably close to mine, was the face of the ward sister whom I had met on my last visit to the hospital. She was bending down to look at me and the thin red lips were pursed with disapproval.

If she bends any more, I thought confusedly, the busby will fall on top of me. Then I remembered that it wasn't a busby. It was her black, dyed hair piled high on her head. I opened my mouth. But there was so much to say I ended up saying nothing at all.

A man in a white coat came over. I shied away from him. But it wasn't the man with the knife. "It's all right," he said as he bent to examine me. His fingers touched my head and I cried out.

"Adam Davy," the ward sister said. "That's his name. Look, here's his passport."

"There's nothing wrong with me," I said firmly. "I can tell you my name myself."

"He's just like the other one, doctor," the sister said. "Thinks he knows it all."

During the examination, the doctor questioned me briefly about what had happened.

Afterwards I said, "Is Carson alive?"

"Yes. Don't worry about him now."

"That guy with the knife – have they caught him?"

"I don't know. The police are dealing with it. You can ask them tomorrow. Listen, we'd like to keep you in overnight for observation. Is there anyone we should contact?"

"You can't keep me in," I said. "I need to get back."

"Don't be stupid," the doctor said. "No one's that important."

"There's things I've got to do."

126

"The thing you've got to do most of all is rest."

I'd been lucky, he said. If the blow had fallen in a different place on my skull, or if the guy had used the blade rather than the hilt of the knife, I might have been much more seriously damaged. But the fact that it could have been worse didn't mean I could pretend that it hadn't happened.

I knew he was right. To be honest, I felt so tired it was an effort to put one word after another. So I told them Phyllis's name and the Sanctuary's phone number.

"Tell her I'll be back tomorrow," I said. "OK?"

"We'll see," the doctor said. He was a young man with an old face, lined and grey with fatigue. "Man proposes, God disposes."

They gave me a pair of pyjamas and a couple of tablets. A few minutes later I got into bed. It was wonderful to lie down on cool, white sheets and let someone else do the worrying. Suddenly I couldn't understand what the argument had been about.

I didn't notice the transition between being awake and being asleep. This time I went down into a dark place deep inside me and stayed there for hours. I slept heavily in a black silence. Elvira Bladon didn't come to trouble me. There were no dreams at all.

Then I was awake. It was daylight. I was very thirsty. My head no longer hurt. I wasted a little time trying to solve all the obvious questions like who I was, and where and why. There was only one problem: I couldn't work out whether it was Monday or Tuesday. I examined my head. There was a bruise where

Carson's attacker had hit me with the knife's hilt. It was painful to the touch. But otherwise I felt normal.

There were noises outside: the ward was coming awake. I got out of bed. I took it slowly. I was fine. I rummaged around the little room. I found my clothes in the cupboard. The bag was there too, but someone had removed the passport and money, presumably for safekeeping.

I got dressed and wandered into the corridor. A nurse I hadn't seen before was sitting at the desk. She looked up.

"What do you think you're doing?" she said.

"Looking for a cup of tea," I said. "Then I'm going home. Can you tell me how Mr Carson is? The man who was stabbed last night."

"You'd better have a word with Sister," the nurse said. "I've only just come on duty. Why don't you go back to bed while I fetch her?"

"I'll wait here."

I sat down on the visitor's chair. According to the calendar on the desk, it was Tuesday. The nurse looked at me and sighed. But then she put the kettle on and picked up the internal phone. A few minutes later the sister arrived.

"You should be in bed," she said.

But she turned out to be a little less aggressive than her colleague in the busby. When I asked her about Carson, her face went blank. I knew it was bad news.

"Is he dead?"

"No..."

"So how is he?"

"Are you a relative?" she asked, just as her colleague had done a couple of days ago.

"I work for him. And he's a friend."

"He's in intensive care. They've got him on a life-support system."

"Will he live?"

She looked at me. "They're not sure. I'm sorry."

I think she told me everything she could. She'd heard nothing about an arrest.

The sister wanted me to wait for the doctor but I said no thank you. I had to fill in a form and get my passport back.

Less than an hour later I took the lift down to the foyer. It felt as though I were being let out of prison. I went through the swing doors, past all the men in dressing gowns having their early morning cigarettes and into the car park. I shivered, because it was still cool.

The Polo was where I had left it, with a Renault on one side and a Rover on the other. I had a superstitious fear that there might be a silver Honda Civic in the vicinity. But if there was, it wasn't in sight.

I fished out the keys and unlocked the driver's door of the Polo. Behind me a car door opened. I glanced over my shoulder.

"There you are," said Inspector Anthorn, climbing out of the Renault. "Making an early start?"

He had a faint, meaningless smile on his pale face. He was wearing a different suit from the previous time but the overall effect was the same as befor

129

essentially grey.

"I'm just going to the Sanctuary," I said.

"Mind if we have a little chat first?"

"Sure," I said. "But it's a bit chilly. Your car or mine?"

"Mine, I think."

I got in the back of the Renault with him. The woman in the driver's seat – Detective Constable Vince, was it? – gave me a nod of recognition and got out her notebook.

"Is this a coincidence?" I asked.

Anthorn shook his head. "I'd asked the hospital to let me know if you showed signs of rushing off before I'd had a chat with you."

"I was coming to see you."

"No doubt," he murmured in a colourless voice. "But recently you've been rather elusive, haven't you? I expected to see you yesterday afternoon at the Sanctuary."

"I was in Turkey."

"So I understand." He injected a squirt of sarcasm into his voice. "An unexpected business trip. You get back late yesterday afternoon, and you immediately drive here. Isn't it odd how Mr Carson tends to get attacked when you're around?"

"Yes," I said. "Almost as odd that someone was able to attack him in the middle of a hospital. I hope he's under police protection now."

Anthorn's lips tightened. "As a matter of fact he is. At present."

"You mean you're going to withdraw the protection? Have you caught the man who did it?"

"Not yet. Leaving that aside, I meant that we would naturally withdraw it if Mr Carson dies. I gather it's touch and go. No point in protecting a corpse, is there?"

There was a silence. It wasn't so much the news that Carson was close to death as the callous and calculating way Anthorn had told me about it. It was as if he'd deliberately punched my emotions, given me the psychological equivalent of a body blow; he was trying to do damage. The tactic would have affected me worse if I hadn't worked out that he was only doing it in a crude attempt to soften me up. But he didn't need to play games with me. Didn't he realize that we were meant to be on the same side?

"What do you want to know?" I said.

He wanted every detail I could dredge up about what had happened yesterday evening once I arrived at the hospital. He treated me as if I had a mental age of twelve. I did my best not to show that it irked me. He kept coming back to one point.

"So could you identify the man who attacked Mr Carson?"

"I've told you – just possibly. But I doubt it."

I had explained why, twice. Now I did it once again.

Anthorn sighed. "I'd like you to see if you can put together a Photofit picture for us."

"Is that like Identikit?"

"Similar. It's a more sophisticated technique."

"I can try. But I doubt if it'll help you much."

"We'll be the judge of that. This officer could

drive you to the station now. She'll bring you back here when you've finished. Unless, of course, you have something more pressing to do?"

I said I'd be delighted. I knew that trying to construct a Photofit picture would be a pointless exercise, but it would be even more pointless to alienate the police still further.

"Good." Anthorn felt for the door handle. "In that case I needn't delay you any longer."

"One more thing," I said, hoping I'd get a reward for good behaviour. "Or rather two..."

Anthorn looked wearily at me and raised his eyebrows.

"First – is there any news about who was behind the other attack? The one at the Sanctuary?"

"You mean, have we investigated the suggestion you made? Mr Jason Ford of Well Farm? I'm glad to say that he was very cooperative, and we are now looking elsewhere."

"No other leads?"

"We are investigating several possibilities," Anthorn said primly. "What was your other question?"

"Not a question," I said. "It's a piece of information I think you should have. Someone tried to kill me in Turkey. And I think they meant to get Carson."

There was a silence in the car. The detective constable jerked her head round and stared openmouthed at me.

Anthorn said silkily, "No doubt the Turkish police will be forwarding their report. Perhaps it's already on my desk."

"I didn't go to the police."

"Really. How – ah – how refreshingly unusual. Someone tries to kill you and, unlike almost anyone else in the civilized world apart from criminals, you don't tell the police."

"There were reasons."

He smiled at me with no warmth whatsoever. "I thought perhaps there might be. May we have the condensed version, please? We have a busy morning in front of us."

Anger and embarrassment mixed me a cocktail of unwanted emotions, just as Anthorn had intended. He was trying to get me angry. Why? In the hope of surprising me into a confession for something I hadn't done? To give him an excuse to get heavy with me?

"I'll keep this as short as I can, Inspector," I said. I told him how I had been met at the airport; about the breakdown on the road to the villa; the attempts to shoot me; and my escape.

"Dear me," Anthorn commented; he looked like a bank manager faced with an immense unauthorized overdraft. "How very enterprising of you."

I explained about the Izmidlians, and their arguments against my talking to the Turkish police.

"No doubt they will confirm all this?" Anthorn said.

"I'm not sure."

He raised his eyebrows. "I don't understand."

"It depends on their motives."

"Forgive me," Anthorn said with all the humilit

of a striking viper, "but I'm getting a little confused."

"I think our fax hadn't reached Izmidlian. So that means he was still expecting Carson. I think it wasn't me they were trying to kill. It was Carson."

"And why should they want to do that?"

"I don't know. But we know someone does. Remember what happened last night."

"I hadn't forgotten. It's a pity you didn't mention all this before the latest attack on Mr Carson." Anthorn chewed his lower lip for a few seconds. "Look," he went on, and for an instant I thought there was a note of pleading in his voice, "you haven't given me a shred of corroborative evidence. You tell me all these things happened to you in Turkey. We've only got your word for it, that's all."

"Plus a few bruises and cuts," I said, knowing that as far as Anthorn was concerned I could have acquired them anywhere.

"And what about motive? Why should a Middle Eastern businessman want to have Carson murdered? As far as you know this man Izmidlian is perfectly respectable."

I shrugged. "Don't ask me. I'm prejudiced."

"And as far as you know he's not a fool, either. So why would he lure Carson out to Turkey? Why not have him killed in England? Or anywhere but his own back yard?"

"I know," I said. "I thought of that too. It doesn't make sense. Which if you think about it is a reason for believing me."

"Eh?"

"Why should I make up a story that doesn't make sense?"

"People do," Anthorn said dryly, and I thought I saw an unexpected flicker of amusement on his face. "Especially when they're talking to the police. You'd be surprised."

"There's one other thing I should tell you," I said. "There's an American girl who keeps turning up. She's staying at the Ardross Hall Hotel – just down the hill from the Sanctuary. Her name is Elvira Bladon."

I told him about meeting her and later Sergeant Todd on the road on the night of the first attack, about seeing her at the hospital and later at the Sanctuary, and about her photograph in Izmidlian's magazine.

I might have known. Anthorn was thoroughly unimpressed.

"Let me see if I've got this straight. You see this girl briefly at night time. It's dark. You're both upset, and have an argument. Naturally she's in your mind the next morning. Maybe she was at the hospital, maybe she wasn't."

"She definitely was."

He shrugged. "I imagine that quite a lot of women with blonde hair drive Honda Civics. Let's see – then she sees you at the Sanctuary and runs away. Nothing odd about that, if it was the same girl. Hard to be sure through a sheet of glass. Let's say it was her, for the sake of argument. She probably didn't know you worked there. After that quarrel you're the last person she'd want to talk to. So she runs away. Not very dignified, but there's nothing odd in that."

"But she was in the house, searching Carson's study."

"Searching it? You found no evidence of that, did you? And you said visitors often stray into the house. They go anywhere if there's not a locked door in the way. Perhaps she suspected she might be trespassing. All the more reason for her to run away."

"And the photo in the magazine?"

"We know the girl was already on your mind. You saw the photo for a couple of seconds, perhaps, and not close up. By your own admission you haven't seen her in a decent light for any length of time. It's more than possible that you saw someone who looked similar to her."

"I didn't. I'm sure it was her."

"There's no way we can check. You don't even know what the magazine was. And in Arabic too."

I said nothing.

"You don't make it easy for us, do you?" Anthorn sighed and looked ostentatiously at his watch. "Do you want my detective constable to drive you to the station for the Photofit session?"

"I'll drive myself."

"Is that wise?"

"I'm not planning to run away, if that's what you mean."

"I was thinking about your head injury, actually," Anthorn said.

"I'm fine."

"I'm delighted to hear it."

I got out of his car and said goodbye. I drove to the

136

police station. As far as I could see my only possible way forward was through Elvira Bladon. The problem was: how could I persuade her to to talk to me? On past form, she would either demand police protection if she saw me, or run away.

The desk sergeant was expecting me. He told me their Photofit expert would be along in ten minutes and offered me a cup of tea while I was waiting. I asked if I could make a phone call first.

I rang the private line at the Sanctuary. Phyllis answered. She sounded out of breath.

"Thank God," she said.

"Why?"

"I just rang the hospital, and they told me you'd left. But you hadn't arrived here so I was beginning to think that something must have happened."

"I got waylaid by Anthorn. Any news about Carson?"

There wasn't. He was still in a coma. I explained about having to spend an unknown period of time with the Photofit expert.

"By the way," Phyllis said. "There was a phone call for you yesterday evening. Your friend Elvira Bladon wants you to get in touch with her at Ardross Hall."

TWELVE

When I got back to the Sanctuary it was already halfway through the morning. Phyllis met me with the news that Elvira Bladon had phoned again: she'd left a message inviting me for a drink at the Ardross Hall Hotel at eight-thirty that evening.

"No need to call her back unless you can't make it." Phyllis's eyes gleamed with curiosity. "Is this the beginning of a beautiful friendship?"

"Leave it out."

"It's just a line from Casablanca," she said innocently. "Will you go?"

"I'll see how I feel."

"Playing hard to get, are we?"

"Just tired."

We plunged into the business of the Sanctuary. It was a hell of a day. Quite apart from the extra work and the constant worry about Carson, the attacks on him had brought the tourists out in droves. They were good for turnover, if nothing else, which would have pleased Carson. One kid asked me to show him where the bloodstains were.

"Wretched ghouls," Phyllis said on one occasion when at least twenty of our visitors were in earshot. "Quite morbid, in my opinion. No better than grave-robbing."

We phoned the hospital a couple of times during the day. Carson's condition remained stable. He was like a man lying on the edge of a precipice. He was still in just as much danger as before, but at least he hadn't actually fallen off.

In the afternoon, we had to cope with an assessor from the insurance company, a man with a long, lugubrious face which masked a warped sense of humour.

"Had a client who lost a couple of budgies once," he said as he was standing in the doorway of the wrecked incubator room. "But I must say it was nothing like this."

In the meantime I supervised the routine of giving displays and talks, and looking after the birds. Kenneth dogged my footsteps with a succession of queries. By six o'clock, when we shooed the last visitor off the premises, I was dropping with exhaustion. But I wasn't complaining.

We had been so busy that I'd had to give the other problems a rest. The problems like who was trying to kill Carson and what I was going to do about Elvira Bladon. I didn't know what I felt about her, besides confused. She was a complication I could do without. On one level she needed investigation in case she was tied up with the attacks on Carson: I had to check her out because the police had no intention of doing so. On another level I didn't much care for her haughty manners: the way she'd acted at the accident, for example, and the way she'd summoned me to Ardross Hall.

Phyllis and I went into the shop. I tidied up the displays while she emptied the till. I made some remark to the effect that at least the day's takings would help to keep the Sanctuary solvent.

"Take more than a few visitors to keep us going," she said with sudden violence. "This place is losing money hand over fist. I don't know how Carson manages. I really don't."

"I knew it was bad," I said. "But that bad?"

"Worse," she snapped, and she shut her mouth like a trap. "You haven't heard the half of it."

I was about to ask her more when I heard a car drawing up outside. I went to the door. It was the Breams' Land Rover, its sides streaked with mud.

Jack got out – very carefully, as though his long thin body were made of glass. He looked exhausted. I went outside to meet him.

"What's up with you?" I asked.

"I spent the night with a cow in labour. Then I had a long day – had to cover for my father, you see. He was doing the autopsy on Carson's dog this morning."

In all the excitement I'd forgotten about Sammy. I wondered if Carson had taken in the fact that he was dead.

"Any news?"

"Nothing." Jack lowered his voice. "Nothing official, that is. Everything has to go through the correct channels."

"I'm sure Inspector Anthorn will pass on anything he feels we need to know. Next month, maybe."

Jack grinned. "I wouldn't bank on it."

"Did you know the police have ruled out Jason Ford?"

He nodded. "He had alibis coming out of his ears. And they say his old man plays golf with the Chief Constable."

"Who gave him alibis?"

"I don't know. Look, I – ah – I happened to hear my father phoning in his preliminary report on the autopsy. It looks like someone fired a point-two-two airgun slug into Sammy's ear. At close range."

I swore softly.

"Yeah," Jack said. "My feelings exactly."

"Will it help? Can they identify the gun from the slug?"

"Afraid not. Smooth-bore barrel, of course; and anyway the slug was flattened when it hit bone." He stopped and stared into the middle distance, but I knew him well enough not to say anything. After what seemed like half an hour he went on: "I saw Jason Ford trying to shoot rabbits once. With a two-two air pistol."

"A lot of them around. Can you spare a few minutes?"

"Why?"

"Blood samples, remember?"

He sighed. "You don't give up, do you?"

He fetched his bag from the Land Rover. We walked down to the barns together. You need at least two for this job: one to take the sample, the other to hold the bird.

Kenneth emerged from nowhere with Leila at his heels and watched with hot, suspicious eyes as I fetched a couple of the gyr-peregrine hybrids from their aviary.

"He gives me the creeps, that man," Jack said later, when we were back at the Land Rover.

"Kenneth? He's just being protective. He loves those birds."

"Do you know anything about his background?"

I shook my head. "Carson may."

Jack climbed into the Land Rover but didn't close the door. "What do you want me to do with those samples?"

"Keep them for me. Just for a day or two. I want to see if someone will analyse them for me."

"If the genetic profile matches the feathers we found at Well Farm, Jason Ford's got a lot of explaining to do."

He waited, and this time he wanted me to say something: to do a little explaining of my own. But I didn't.

"Ah well," Jack said slowly. "Got any other plans you'd like to share with me?"

He stared down at me like a judge looking down on a criminal waiting to be sentenced. I thought he felt he had earned a little more frankness from me. I also thought he had a point. So I told him what had happened in Turkey, how Anthorn had reacted, and even a little about Elvira Bladon.

"She sounds a right little madam," he said.

After Jack left, I just had time to do my evening

jobs, gobble a stale cheese-and-tomato sandwich from the café and take a shower. I had hardly any clothes with me at the Sanctuary, and none of them was suitable for Ardross Hall. I chose the cleanest on offer and combed my hair with extra care.

I stuck my head in the office to say goodbye to Phyllis. She was frowning at a spreadsheet. She had a cigarette in the corner of her mouth, Humphrey Bogart-style.

"Give her hell, boy," she said. "I can't stand these damn colonial upstarts."

"Colonial? The United States?"

"Time means nothing to me." She squinted at me through the smoke. "How's your head?"

"As good as new," I said.

It was true that I felt much better. The attack on me last night seemed to have left no serious ill effects, and I was less tired than I had been at six o'clock.

I collected the car keys and went outside. It was a beautiful summer evening. Someone had been cutting the grass, and the cuttings made the air smell fresh and sweet. I drove out of the car park. I glanced at the clock on the dash. Unless I drove slowly, I was going to be early, which would never do. There was no other traffic on the road. I rolled down the window and dawdled at barely more than walking pace.

I idled along the roadside frontage of the Sanctuary. At the end of the fence was the lay-by. There were a couple of cars there. I glimpsed a dirty white Metro of uncertain age beside a red Volvo attached to a caravan. I thought nothing of it. The lay-by was public property. There was a campsite a couple of miles further on, and people sometimes stopped in the lay-by to admire the view over the valley.

The road began to descend. I took my foot off the accelerator and let the car roll down the hill. There was very little noise. The fresh air flowed through the window.

For a moment it felt good to be alive. For a moment everything was possible: Carson would get well, the Sanctuary would flourish and my sister Becky would be all right. And as for me—

Somewhere behind me, a starter motor whirred. My moment of optimism nosedived to an abrupt and unsatisfactory conclusion. Not much of a moment – more like twenty seconds.

The whirr of the starter had a curious whine to it, a sound I had heard twice before: once on the night of the rainstorm, when Carson was attacked at the Sanctuary, and once when Jack Bream and I went to see Jason Ford at Well Farm.

I waited. The distant engine came to life. The driver revved it. As on the night of the storm, it backfired.

I was tempted to put my foot down and drive like a maniac. But in that case I wouldn't see who if anyone was following me. I could have pulled over to the side of the road, of course, and waited to see what would happen. There were two snags with that idea. First, whoever was tailing me would know that I had seen him. Second, I wasn't sure that I wanted to run the risk of yet another violent confrontation.

The road wound down the hill in a series of loops to the valley below. I kept my speed down. Sheep were grazing peacefully in one of the fields beside the road. Sounds drifted upwards from the floor of the valley: the traffic on the main road; the snarl of a chainsaw; and the rock-and-roll rhythm of someone having a party in their garden.

As I drove I kept glancing in the rear-view mirror. As far as I could see, the road behind me was empty. But I thought I could hear the hum of an engine, and once I heard a solitary backfire. The fact that the driver didn't have to keep me in sight suggested he knew that sooner or later I would hit the T-junction and have to stop.

A quarter of a mile before Ardross Hall I came to a decision. I rammed the accelerator into the floor. The Polo leapt forwards. In a few seconds we had gone from twenty-five miles an hour to seventy. I braked sharply at the mouth of Quarry Hill and swung the car into the shelter of the lane.

Leaving the engine running, I turned and stared out of the rear window. I didn't have long to wait. The white Metro came hurtling down the road. As it passed the entrance of the lane, I glimpsed the driver's face in profile. He was driving so fast that all I registered was a blur which might have included a dark beard and glasses.

I heard him change down for the next bend. I waited twenty seconds then reversed out of the lane and turned into the drive of the Ardross Hall Hotel.

The drive was bordered by double rows of lime trees. Gravel whispered under the tyres of the Polo. There wasn't a weed in sight. The Ardross Hall Hotel was one of those corners of England designed to reassure tourists from abroad that some things never change. It belonged in the same category as malt whisky, Oxford marmalade and the Changing of the Guard. There were rolling acres of parkland populated by browsing deer and lowing cattle. There was also a helipad, but that was discreetly sited behind a screen of conifers near the west lodge.

I had been there a couple of times with Carson to give displays for the guests. Afterwards, one or two of the braver visitors had played at being Robin Hood falconers. They stood smirking with our tamer birds on their wrists while their friends recorded this glorious achievement for posterity on their video cameras.

The main house came in sight. It was a big, stonefaced block with a pediment and urns on top. At right angles on either side were low wings which enclosed a forecourt. The forecourt was empty apart from a row of expensive cars and a fountain containing a stone goddess.

I slid the Polo between a Porsche and a Bentley. The place seemed deserted but it was so big that you could have had an army here without it being obvious to casual callers. There was no sign of Elvira Bladon's Honda. But that meant nothing. There were other places to leave your car.

I went up the flight of steps leading to the front door. At the top I turned. The drive behind me was empty.

Without warning the double doors opened. A butler stood before me. He had a high wing collar and a black tailcoat. I thought butlers like that only existed in the sort of movies Phyllis watched.

He raised his eyebrows at me. He didn't say anything, just stood there looking at me. I got the impression that unless I did some fast talking he intended to send me round to the tradesmen's entrance.

"I'm Adam Davy. I've come to see Miss Bladon."

The butler looked down his very long nose. "Is she expecting you?"

"I hope so. She invited me."

He took a couple of steps back and waved me into the hall. It was an enormous room, at least two storeys high. It had a chequered, marble floor, enough pillars for a small Roman temple and a life-sized portrait of a bearded gentleman sitting on a horse and wearing a feathered hat.

"If you would wait here," the butler murmured, and added very faintly and as an afterthought, "sir."

He went away down a corridor, his heels clacking on the marble floor. I looked around me. I admired all the portraits and smiled up at the closed circuit cameras. A few moments later the butler returned.

"This way, please."

I followed him down the corridor. The marble gave way to oak floorboards covered with oriental runners. No one else was around. Eventually we came to a pair of glazed doors.

It looked as if there was a small Amazonian

rainforest inside. The butler ushered me in to a large Victorian conservatory. The plants were so big and beefy that someone must have been feeding them steroids. Along one wall ran a glass-topped bar counter, behind which a man in a white jacket was polishing a glass. There were several clearings in the jungle and these were filled with basketwork furniture. Half a dozen people were sitting around having a drink. None of them looked up as we came in. I followed the butler round a clump of palm trees. There at a table by a window was Elvira Bladon.

She was sitting with her head bowed over a Compaq laptop with a colour screen. The butler cleared his throat as he approached. She shut the laptop and looked up.

"Mr Davy, Miss."

"Right, thanks."

The butler slipped silently away. Elvira Bladon stood up, holding out her hand.

"It's good of you to come."

Her hand was so cold it was almost icy. Involuntarily I glanced down at the glass beside the laptop. She had been drinking something long and packed with ice. She followed my eyes and put the wrong construction on what I was thinking.

"You want a drink?"

"Not particularly," I said, more aggressively than I intended.

Her face sort of closed up. She waved me to a seat. I sat down in another chair, the one furthest away from hers. I wasn't in the mood for being polite.

"Why do you want to talk to me?"

"I owe you an explanation, I guess."

"That would be nice," I agreed.

"And maybe you might be able to help me too."

I said nothing. She glanced at me.

"But I guess I should start with an apology."

For the first time I looked directly at her rather than at my hands or at the laptop or at the view of the parkland through the window beside the table. Up until now I had only ever seen her in jeans. Now she was wearing a dress and she had done something to her hair. She looked right for this setting, which made me feel even more out of place.

"That night on the road. I – I – wasn't too friendly. You were trying to help."

"It doesn't matter." I waited to see if there were any more apologies in the pipeline, or even explanations: for example, it would have been nice to know what she had been doing at the Sanctuary. But it seemed that the apology I had had was the only one on offer. I glanced at my watch and said, "What do you want me to do?"

The wide mouth tightened. She flicked a strand of hair from her forehead. "Well, for a start you could stop looking so... so disapproving."

First I was shocked because in this country you don't expect people to be so direct, or not in circumstances like those. Then this awful hotel and the look of outrage on Elvira Bladon's face suddenly struck me as having a comic side. I couldn't help smiling. Less than twenty-four hours earlier someone had been trying to kill me; maybe the experience had done something to my sense of humour.

"You find this funny?" she said.

I stopped smiling. "It's nothing personal."

There was a silence which seemed to go on for a long time.

"Look," she said, leaning forward, "can we start over?"

"That's up to you."

"All I wanted to do is ask how Cousin Roger is."

"Who?"

"Roger Carson."

At this moment the guy in the white jacket materialized by our table to ask if sir and madam would like a drink. Madam said no, but sir was so surprised he asked for a lager. I waited until we were alone again.

"How exactly are you related to him?" I asked.

It turned out that the relationship was more than a little hypothetical. Elvira said that she was in England researching the British part of her family tree; and that she was fifty to sixty per cent certain that Carson was a cousin of hers. That was why she wanted to meet him.

My lager arrived. Elvira made an excuse and left the table. I guessed that she was going to the lavatory. She was away for about five minutes.

When she came back she gave me more of the family history. It was all incredibly vague. She didn't produce any photographs or family trees – none of the stuff that amateur genealogists carry around with them in briefcases shackled to their wrists. At one point she said her family had settled in San Francisco: another time it was Seattle.

When there was an opening, I said, "I don't understand why you didn't just write to Carson."

"I like to do this sort of thing face to face."

"Like now?"

"Like now," she agreed. She went on to ask whether there was any way she could find out if Carson really was her cousin before he came out of hospital. She said there wasn't much point in her waiting round here if he wasn't. She made it sound quite reasonable. What she really wanted was access to any family papers or photographs Carson might have up at the Sanctuary.

"I'm sorry," I said. "That's just not possible." Then I remembered something Phyllis had told me. "But there's one person you can try."

She looked up sharply. "Who?"

"Carson's sister," I said. "Mrs Fettercairn. You must have heard of her. If you're related to Carson you'll be related to her as well."

"Ah – yes."

"If you want to write to her care of the Sanctuary, we could forward your letter."

"Great," she said without obvious enthusiasm. Her eyes flicked away from mine. "Where does she live?"

"I'm not sure."

"So she's not a neighbour or something?"

"Oh no."

I thought I saw relief on her face. We sat and talked for a while longer. It wasn't an easy conversation. I could tell that she was annoyed with me because I wouldn't do what she wanted.

A little after nine o'clock I said I had to be going. She didn't make much attempt to keep me. I took a couple of steps towards the door and then turned back.

"Ever been to Turkey?"

"Sure. Once or twice."

"I wondered if you knew a man called Izmidlian. I thought I saw your photograph in his house."

"No." Her face was as welcoming as a slammed door. "Never heard of him."

The butler appeared out of nowhere like the family ghost and conducted me back to the hall and out through the front door. I said good evening to him as I went down the steps. He didn't reply. Maybe I wasn't wearing the right aftershave.

I walked slowly across the gravel to the Polo. You know how it is when you've just had a meeting like that. Your mind keeps replaying every twist and turn of the conversation. I kept wondering what Elvira Bladon had been holding back. And I also wondered whether I had seemed like a complete fool to her.

The Polo was still standing beside the Bentley but the Porsche had gone. In its place was a Land Rover. My head was full of that girl inside, the girl with the shut-in face. Still brooding on Elvira Bladon, I stuck my key in the Polo's door.

The nearside door of the Land Rover swung open to its widest extent. Its edge almost touched the wing of the Polo. I glanced up and saw Jason Ford's bottle-blonde girlfriend sitting behind the wheel. On her lap was an air pistol. It was pointing at me.

THIRTEEN

Jason Ford laughed. Not a belly laugh – just a quiet little snigger.

I heard his footsteps on the gravel. I turned. He slipped round the rear of the Land Rover. He smiled at me.

"You've been sticking your nose where it's not wanted," he said softly. "Something tells me you need to be taught a lesson."

"Something?" I said. "Or someone?"

"Get in. You're coming for a ride."

He was holding a Stanley knife in his left hand. My heart was thudding in a most uncomfortable way. It didn't seem possible that they would allow this sort of thing to happen at the Ardross Hall Hotel. Maybe cameras were covering the forecourt, and in a few seconds the butler would appear out of the front door at the head of a riot squad. Then it struck me that the pair of them had boxed me in very neatly between the two vehicles, and no one in the house could have the slightest idea what was happening.

But just suppose somebody was standing at the top of the flight of steps by the front door?

"Over here," I bellowed, waving my arm.

It was a silly trick which only succeeded because Jason didn't have time to think about it. He turned and glanced towards the front door. It must have taken him not much more than a second to see that there was no one there and to swing back to me.

But that second was enough. I dropped like Newton's apple on to the gravel. I half-rolled, half-wriggled underneath the door of the Land Rover. There was a crack – a rush of compressed air. A slug smacked into the driver's door of the Polo. Jason stared down at me, his eyes wide and his mouth making a wide O of astonishment.

"Hey," he said. "Come back."

I scrambled up and started running. Not towards the house – it might take too long for the butler to open the door. I skirted the fountain. I looked back over my shoulder. Jason hadn't moved. I ran on. I hurdled over some railings and sprinted down a long strip of grass that ran parallel to the drive.

The Land Rover's engine fired and I veered away from the drive. I took a five-bar gate at speed and found myself in a meadow populated with surprised-looking sheep. I slowed down. It was a pleasant evening for jogging. I told myself that everything was going to be all right, at least in the short term. I couldn't see Jason leaping out of the Land Rover and coming after me across the fields: his talents lay in other directions.

I sat on another gate and waited. I didn't think that Jason would dare try again. A place like this must have its own security. Last time I had been careless and they had been lucky. They wouldn't get a second chance.

A moment later, the Land Rover rolled down the drive. I walked slowly back to the forecourt in front of the hotel. How very well-timed it had all been. Jason and the girl had turned up shortly before I left. They couldn't have been there long or else someone would have wanted to know what they were doing.

Look at it in sequence, I told myself. Out of the blue Elvira Bladon asks you for a drink. When you get there she leaves you for a few minutes. Time enough for a phone call? She comes up with the missing-cousin business, a story that wouldn't convince a three-year-old. Then you leave. And you find you've walked into an ambush.

Put like that, the events this evening could have only one interpretation. Elvira had set me up. It was a warm evening but I felt chilly with anger. Without giving myself time for more thought, I marched across the gravel forecourt and went up the steps to the front door. I put my thumb on the bell and left it there rather longer than was strictly necessary.

At last the butler appeared. He had a pained expression on his face as he opened the front door.

"Yes?"

"I want to see Ms Bladon."

"I'm afraid Miss Bladon is not at home."

"Does that mean she's gone out or she doesn't want to see me?"

"I'm afraid I'm not at liberty to say."

With a sense of anticlimax, I asked the butler to tell her I had called. He nodded distantly and shut the door on me. I went slowly down the steps. As far as I could see there wasn't anything else I could do but go back to the Sanctuary.

I felt in my pocket for the car key. It wasn't there. Then I remembered: I'd just stuck it in the door of the car when Jason and his girlfriend had decided to make their presence known. I walked round the end of the car. The key had gone.

The next quarter of an hour was one I'd prefer to forget. Nothing totally awful happened. But a series of petty humiliations can have a cumulative effect.

First I had to see the butler again and ask if I could use the phone. Then I suffered Phyllis's ribald comments when I told her what had happened. She said she would drive down with the spare key. The butler didn't want me to wait inside the house, so I kicked my heels on the gravel instead. I added all the humiliations into a sub-total which I transferred to Elvira Bladon's account.

At last the MGB roared up the drive and braked so sharply that a spray of gravel patterered against the radiator of the Bentley.

"Phyllis," I said as she rolled down her window, "you know something? You're a teenager at heart."

"I wish I could say the same about the rest of me."

She passed me the spare key. The butler opened the door and stood watching us from the top of the steps. His expression made it quite clear that he didn't feel we lent tone to the establishment, or not the right sort of tone.

"Have you called the police?" Phyllis said.

"No."

"Why ever not?"

"Who do you think they'd believe?"

Phyllis sniffed. "It's outrageous."

"Yes. But that's the way it is."

We drove back to the Sanctuary in convoy, with Phyllis in the lead. We met no one on the road. By now the light was fading fast. The valley below was full of lighted windows, and I wished I was behind one of them. This whole business was getting on top of me. I couldn't see any end to it. I couldn't even see any reason for it.

The road began to level out as we hit the top of the ridge. Suddenly the MGB's brake lights glowed.

I braked hard myself. Then I let the Polo roll forward until it was just behind the MGB. I saw why Phyllis had stopped.

From this point we could see the lay-by, which was now empty, the Sanctuary's boundary fence and the farmhouse at the end. One of the sash windows on the ground floor was open. Orange flames were licking along the gap between the window and the sill.

It's amazing how quickly a fire can get going. Phyllis went to see if the phones were working while I investigated the blaze. As far as I could tell only two rooms were affected: Carson's study at the back of the house and the room directly opposite on the other side of the hall, which looked on to the road. There wasn't much I could do besides trying to contain the fire by shutting both doors. I checked the rest of the house. It was empty. Kenneth was doing his evening rounds.

Coping with the fire wasn't dangerous or even

dramatic. It was just hard, filthy work, and at the back of my mind was a sick feeling that some joker was out to get us.

Kenneth came back, with Leila at his heels. He had seen the smoke and his face was grey with shock. Phyllis got through to the fire brigade. While we waited for them to turn out the three of us did our best to empty the more valuable and more accessible possessions out of the house.

"Typical," Phyllis said. "Anything Carson cares about is in his study."

I looked at her and found that she was already looking at me. Then the fire brigade arrived and took over. In the lull I phoned the police. I got hold of my favourite policeman, Sergeant Todd, down in the village.

"We've got a fire up at the Sanctuary," I said.

"Oh aye."

"I don't think it started accidentally."

"Why's that then?"

"Because there's not one fire but two," I said. "And they appear to have broken out spontaneously in two separate rooms."

Sergeant Todd said that someone would be along. I suggested he might like to let Inspector Anthorn know. He advised me to do my own job and let him do his.

The firemen got the two blazes under control. The guy in charge asked if I'd by any chance phoned the police.

I nodded. "As soon as we saw there were two fires."

158

"It's not just that. Come and have a look."

He took me along the hall to the doorway of the smoke-filled study. He pointed at the desk. The drawers were either hanging out or strewn on the floor. Good seasoned English oak takes a long while to burn. You could see the splintering around the locks.

"Crowbar job, I reckon," he said. "We found some glass in both rooms."

"From the windows? Because of the heat?"

"No, not like that. More like bottles."

"What are you saying? Molotov cocktails?"

"I'm not saying anything more," the fireman said grimly, "except to a policeman."

What with one thing and another I didn't get to bed until half-past three in the morning. My room smelt of smoke. Three hours later my alarm came on, and I got up to help Kennneth with the early-morning rounds. He was even more nervy than usual.

"Ah – there wasn't much – um – damage, was there?" he asked, staring at his hands and flexing the fingers. "I mean – Carson's had so much to cope with lately."

"Carson may never know."

Kenneth looked at me with the eyes of a frightened rabbit. "What will happen if he – er, er...?"

"If he dies?" I shrugged. "I suppose it would depend on who the place belonged to. And whether they wanted to carry on."

"The – er – sister. Mrs...?"

"Your guess is as good as mine."

When I got back to the house I phoned the

hospital again. Carson's condition was unchanged. Next I tried the Ardross Hall Hotel. Elvira Bladon still didn't want to talk to me. Either that or she wasn't there. Then I phoned my sister.

"Adam, when are you coming home?" Becky said.

"I'll try and get over this afternoon."

"How long can you stay?"

"A couple of hours, maybe." I heard her sigh at the other end of the line. "I'll have to get back here."

I made a couple of other calls. The first was to Jack Bream: I arranged to pick up the blood samples and the feathers which we'd found at Well Farm after lunch today.

"And can you make sure they're in sealed bags?" I said. "I don't want to be accused of tampering with the evidence."

The second call was one I wished I could have avoided. It was to a man called Simon who used to be one of my mother's research assistants.

"Adam, how are you? Are you OK?"

"I'm fine."

"When are we going to see you?"

"Could you make time this afternoon?" I asked. "Around half-past three?"

"Sure. There's a seminar but I can cancel it."

"I've got a favour to ask."

He listened to what I had to say. I didn't like asking favours but I had no option. Simon said it would be a pleasure. My mother had been more than his head of department: she'd helped him through his PhD, and I don't think he would have got his fellowship without her backing. The subject of her last major piece of research had been variations in genetic profiling across species and genera, and he had been part of her team. The previous summer, I had helped them correlate the results.

I fixed a rough-and-ready breakfast for the three of us. While we ate we sorted out the day ahead. As casually as I could, I mentioned that I wouldn't be around in the afternoon. Kenneth took this without a blink – he probably assumed I was going to see a supplier or a client. But Phyllis raised her eyebrows. I smiled blandly at her.

"Let's just hope the police don't object," she said.

When I unlocked the door to the car park a handful of people was waiting outside. I stood back to let them through. Phyllis was already at the till.

An enormous Jaguar rolled majestically into the car park. Even the dents and rust patches couldn't disguise the elegance of its lines. It was painted dark blue and probably guzzled about a gallon of petrol for every five miles it travelled. Thirty years ago it must have been someone's fantasy car. Now it was almost a museum piece.

The Jaguar stopped in the middle of the car park – managing, despite all the space available, to trap two other cars. The engine stalled, and the car jerked an inch forward. The windows were smoked glass so I couldn't see inside.

There was a pause which dragged on and on. Slowly the driver's door opened. A stick appeared, then a leg, then another leg. I heard puffing and panting. A woman emerged. She was as eye-catching as her car, and for similar reasons.

She must have been nearly six feet tall. She was dressed in a huge fur coat that hung below the knees. Usually fur coats turn my stomach. But this one was different. Although an awful lot of animals had contributed to it, they had done so a very long time ago.

Leaning on her stick, the woman limped towards me. She had a broad face, full of sharply defined lines and acute angles. Her eyes were large, blue and watery; they sat on her face like a pair of ragged puddles on crumpled pink tissue paper. She looked all skin and bones and once, I think, she had been beautiful.

"You there!" she called out to me, though there were only a few yards between us. "I want to talk to whoever is temporarily in charge."

"There are two of us really." I moved aside and waved towards the doorway into the shop. "How can we help you?"

"My name," she said, "is Fettercairn. I have come to take charge while Mr Carson is in hospital."

FOURTEEN

It was not until the police arrived that we had an inkling that Mrs Fettercairn might be more of an asset than a drawback.

"Officer," she said to Sergeant Todd, "I'd be obliged if you'd waste as little time as possible. Mr Carson's employees have work to do."

This was not the way to endear herself to the local constabulary. She irritated the hell out of Sergeant Todd and later out of Inspector Anthorn. But in her own way she did it for the right reasons. She was trying to do her best for the Sanctuary and for us, because we belonged to her brother.

It was another busy morning. I noticed that Phyllis kept looking at Mrs Fettercairn. When we were by ourselves in the office for a moment, Phyllis murmured, "I've seen that woman before, I'm sure of it."

"Maybe Carson's got some photographs of her," I said.

"Carson? You must be joking. He's not the sort who keeps photographs of people."

When she wasn't infuriating the police, the insurance assessors or the fire brigade, Mrs Fettercairn was stumping round the Sanctuary getting in everyone's way. Now the day had warmed up, she'd taken off her moulting fur coat. Underneath were pearls, a tweed skirt and a jersey covered in cat hairs.

At twelve forty-five she appeared in the doorway of the incubator room. The police and the insurance assessors had finished examining the evidence, and I was trying to clear up the mess. She looked round without saying anything. I had just picked up a damp towel. It was stained with rain water and her brother's blood. Her bony nose quivered.

"Good God. It's barbaric."

"That's being polite," I said. I opened a cupboard at random and threw the towel inside.

"You know what it reminds me of? The Blitz. I once saw the effect of a bomb on a chemist's shop. I'd forgotten all about it." She frowned – not at me, I think, but at chaos past and present. "It was early on – 1940. I can't have been more than ten or eleven." She shrugged the memory away. "What do you usually do about lunch?"

"We have a sandwich in the café or soup up at the house. But I'd imagine you'd be more comfortable at the hotel."

Phyllis had booked Mrs Fettercairn into the Ardross Hall Hotel.

"You won't get rid of me as easily as that, young man."

I couldn't tell if she was joking, or if she was really offended. I gave her a smile that meant nothing and went back to work. I felt her eyes on me.

"I shall have a sandwich in the café," she said. "I'd like you to join me."

"Now?"

"If you wouldn't mind."

She waited outside while I washed my hands and ran my fingers through my hair. I took her round to the café. There is something unnerving in being in the company of someone who belongs to another age. It wasn't just a matter of calendar years. Phyllis couldn't have been more than ten years younger than Mrs Fettercairn, but she belonged to a completely different period of history. It was as if Mrs Fettercairn had strayed into this world from a place where men were still gentlemen and changed for dinner.

The café was self-service. But the part-timer behind the till took one glance at Mrs Fettercairn and decided that here was a customer who required a waitress. She gave our order priority. The odd thing was that no one in the queue waiting at the counter seemed to mind.

Our lunch arrived. Mrs Fettercairn ate daintily, cutting up her sandwich into bite-sized squares. She took a sip of her coffee, winced and sipped no more.

"It appears to me," she said when she'd had enough of her sandwich, "that the police aren't doing very much to find out what is behind these attacks."

"I'm sure they're doing their best."

"That may be so, but their best isn't good enough."

I tried to explain, as tactfully as I could, that Carson had managed to alienate the authorities in this part of the world, including the police. That didn't mean they weren't doing their job. It just meant that it was easy to get their backs up.

She thought about that for a moment. She said, "Mr Carson and I rarely see eye to eye about things. But I really cannot condone people trying to kill him."

I nodded. The way she was speaking made me feel like an audience, not a person. I glanced at her face. Her eyes were enclosed in folds of wrinkled skin, like a lizard's. They stared back at mine. For a moment, neither of us spoke.

"Yes," she said, as though I'd answered some question to her satisfaction. "I imagine you and the rest of the staff may have your own ideas about what's going on."

"It's easy to have ideas."

"I made much the same point to that woman – Phyllis, is it? And she referred me to you."

I took my time. For the life of me, I couldn't see what I would lose by telling her what I knew, and what I suspected. I felt that all of us were trapped in a labyrinth of coincidences, unexplained violence, confusion and fear. They say that a trouble shared is a trouble halved, and on that principle the more people I told the smaller our troubles would be.

I told her about Jason at Well Farm, and what I thought he and his girlfriend had done to Carson, and what I knew they'd done to me; about the white Metro with the whimper in its starting motor; about my trip to Turkey in Carson's place, and how I was attacked; and about Elvira Bladon.

"A cousin?" Mrs Fettercairn said sharply. "That's most unlikely. We haven't any American connections at all."

"Then why should—"

"How should I know?"

Mrs Fettercairn shifted angrily in her seat. The table wobbled. Coffee slopped from the cup she had hardly touched. I got up to fetch a cloth from the counter. I was glad of the excuse to get away from those reptilian eyes. Part of me had hoped that Elvira Bladon had told me the truth last night. Maybe not all of the truth, but at least some of it. Now I knew that she had fed me a pack of lies.

The old woman watched me as I swabbed up the coffee.

"Well, Adam?" she said with a snap in her voice. "What do you propose to do about all this?"

I took the cloth back to the counter. And when I came back I told her.

Once upon a time there was a harmless medieval market town. Then a bunch of monks decided that they really couldn't get along any longer without a centre of learning. So they founded a university there. Five or six hundred years trickled by. The university and its colleges attracted money like flypaper attracts flies. They had to spend it somehow. They spent some of it on putting up fancy buildings in picturesque surroundings. With hindsight, perhaps this was a mistake. They weren't to know that tourism would be the growth industry of the late twentieth century.

There were other factors too. During the same period the population of the town grew and grew. New industries moved in, bringing their work forces. All these people needed somewhere to live and somewhere to shop. At Cambridge, they stirred all these factors together in the cauldron of history. They turned into a tasty little traffic problem.

I had forgotten how bad the place could be. It was near the end of the summer term, so the town had the worst of both worlds – masses of students and masses of tourists. As a result, I was fifteen minutes late for my appointment with Simon.

I reversed the Polo into the professor's slot in the departmental car park. The insulated freezer bag was wrapped in newspapers in the boot. I slung the bag over my shoulder and strolled up to Simon's lair on the fifth floor. The blinds were down in his tiny office. He was hunched over his glowing computer screen, and grunting softly and with obvious satisfaction, like a wild animal enjoying a mid-afternoon snack.

"Adam," he said, without turning his head. "Won't be a moment."

His fingers fluttered over the keys. I looked round the room. It was strange being back in the department. The place seemed shabbier and more cramped; and the air smelt staler. I had spent a lot of time here when my mother was alive, but now I'd grown used to being outside. I wasn't sure if this was a good thing.

I sat down. Simon turned on his desk lamp and swung round in his revolving chair. He was a small, dark man, and everything about him was wiry: his body, his black hair and the frames of his glasses. He took the glasses off and rubbed the mark on the bridge of his nose.

"Where have you been hiding yourself?"

"If I told you," I said, "it wouldn't be a hiding place."

He laughed. "You haven't changed, have you?"

"Any news?"

"About what? Your father? Your sister?"

I nodded.

"I haven't seen your father since—" He stopped. I guessed he'd been about to say *since the funeral*. He recovered himself quickly. "For quite a while. But I ran into Becky at the market – the weekend before last, I think it was. We didn't talk much – she was in a hurry."

"How did she look?"

"Bit pale, maybe. She said she'd been studying hard. She's got exams coming up this year, hasn't she? They take them seriously at her age." He smiled: a man with a PhD under his belt can afford to take a relaxed attitude towards other people's exams. "I think she misses you, though. But that's only natural."

He wanted to know, like everyone else, why I'd left home so soon after my mother's death, at a time when the survivors of a family usually cling together; at a time when Becky needed me so badly.

I said, "I brought the samples."

I pushed the freezer bag across the carpet towards him. He unzipped it and inspected the two small polythene bags that nestled between the ice packs inside. He got up to put the bags inside the refrigerator beside his desk.

"What's all this in aid of?"

"I want to find out if the two samples came from birds with the same parents," I said. "There's no problem, is there?"

"None at all. Falcons have hypervariable regions in their DNA, just as humans do. The principle's exactly the same." He sat down and looked suspiciously at me. "But you know all that. Am I right in thinking this isn't just something you're curious about?"

"It's a legal matter," I said. "They might be used in evidence. Depends what you find."

"In that case I'll keep back some of each sample. A lawyer may require the tests to be done again by Cellmark."

"Cellmark?"

"A subsidiary of ICI."

"Could I go to them directly?"

"You could. But it would cost you. I don't think you'd get much change from a couple of hundred pounds. And the test generally takes about three weeks."

"I think I'll see what you come up with first."

"I've got a PhD student who's working in this area. She'll give me a hand. But I don't know exactly how long we'll be."

"The sooner the better," I said. "People are getting hurt, and I think it's got something to do with this."

"Are you ever going to tell me what all this is about?"

"One day," I said. "It's a promise."

Jerusalem College wasn't much more than four

hundred years old, which by Cambridge standards rates as middle-aged. It was far enough from the river not to attract too many tourists, which was a great relief to everyone who lived and worked there.

I still had my set of keys for the Master's Lodge, so I could use the private entrance and avoid going through the college itself. I had timed my arrival very carefully. By now it was a little after five o'clock. My father was a man of routine. On Wednesday afternoons during termtime, he chaired a meeting of the Finance Committee which never broke up until six o'clock at the earliest.

I shut the wicket gate behind me and went up the short drive. Becky was standing at the dining-room window. She waved, charged outside and hugged me.

We had a lot of talking to do. You can only pass on so much information over the phone. You can't tell how a person is looking. Sometimes you can't tell how a person is feeling either.

After a while, I said, "How do you feel about these exams?"

"Fine," she said, and her face tightened. "Dad says I should do very well."

"What do you think?"

She shrugged. "Sometimes I wish he didn't expect us to get straight As in everything."

"You don't have to do that."

"But you did."

"I don't any more." I watched her face: it didn't take much imagination to see the worries dancing like shadows behind her eyes. "Is there anything to eat in this place? I'm starving."

We went through to the kitchen, and Becky raided the fridge. My father had entertained an ambassador and her entourage last night. There was a good haul of leftovers. I ate smoked salmon canapés and black Provençal olives, and washed them down with a glass of slightly flat champagne. And while I ate, Becky talked.

She talked about everything and nothing. Even now, she said, she'd hear creaks upstairs and think someone was walking around up there. Or she'd catch a movement in the corner of her eye and look up, expecting to see Mother coming into the room. We talked about things like that, because we both needed to. And we talked about other things too: school, her exams, this boy in the sixth form she fancied, some friends of mine she'd met at a party last weekend.

She asked about life at the Sanctuary. I told her more than I'd meant to. It was a relief to talk to someone who was outside it. I toned down the violence because I figured she had enought to worry about already.

"But how can Simon help?" she asked. "Some sort of blood test?"

"Not exactly. Every living thing from a man to a worm has its own individual genetic pattern. Each one isn't quite unique but very nearly. They're like genetic signatures. If you get them under the right kind of microscope, they look like supermarket bar codes – except prettier."

Becky frowned. "I don't see how that can help you

prove that the feathers you found came from a stolen chick. I mean, the chicks you've still got at the Sanctuary are different birds."

"Yes – but they've got the same parents. And the genes of the child are a sort of mixture of the genes of the two parents. It's as if the bar codes of the parents are blended together to form the bar code of the child. For each child, it's a different bar code – but with the same ingredients."

Watching Becky relaxing was like watching the effect of water on a thirsty plant. She was beginning to look like her old self. My sister was small, dark and pretty: the boys liked her. When she was happy, she sparkled with life. She was very like our mother.

"So once we've got the genetic code, the DNA signature, of the blood on the feathers from Well Farm," I said, "we can relate that to the DNA signatures of the other chicks with the same parents. We can cross-check it with the genetic codes of the parents themselves – a peregrine and a gyr falcon."

"Suppose you can prove that man stole the chicks. What happens then?"

"I don't know. But at least it would be a piece of hard evidence. The police couldn't ignore it. And somehow there has to be a connection with Elvira Bladon."

Becky looked at me across the table. "That girl's really got to you, hasn't she?"

I shrugged. "I don't like being made a fool of."

Becky reached across the table and put her hand on mine. We smiled at each other.

173

"I wish you'd come home," she said.

"You can't turn the clock back."

The happiness drained out of her face. "It's not fair to you. I'm going to tell Dad what really happened."

I shook my head. "There's no point. We've been into all that."

Her fingers tightened round my hand. "But Adam, it's not—"

Both of us heard the side door open, the one that led to the Fellows' Garden and from there to the college itself. Becky looked at me, her eyes startled and full of fear. I glanced at the clock on the wall. It was nearly six-fifteen.

There were quick, firm footsteps on the parquet floor of the hall. I squeezed Becky's hand and gave her what I hoped was a reassuring smile. I pushed back my chair and stood up. My father was standing in the kitchen doorway.

He raised his eyebrows. "Adam. Well, this is a surprise."

The way he spoke made it sound as if the surprise was not a particularly pleasant one. His long bony face was unsmiling. Once I'd read a magazine profile of him in which the writer made a point of commenting on his distinguished appearance. Today he was wearing a dark pinstriped suit, a discreetly striped tie and a white shirt. I thought he looked like a superior undertaker. But I was prejudiced.

"I just happened to be passing," I said. I turned back to Becky. "I'd better be off now. I'll be in touch."

I gave her a hug and picked up my jacket. My

father was still blocking the doorway.

"Are you – ah – managing all right?" he asked.

"Fine, thanks."

For maybe a couple of seconds, we looked at each other. And in those seconds something happened. As we stood there, eye to eye, the balance in the relationship subtly shifted. He was smaller than I remembered. It hardly seemed worth hating him any more, let alone being afraid of him. There were bigger problems in the world.

"I've got to go," I said. "Goodbye."

He stood back to let me pass into the hall. There was a puzzled look on his face that I'd never seen before. His usual expression when I was around was one of disapproval.

I walked down the hall and let myself out of the front door. I didn't look back.

FIFTEEN

Some people never learn, do they?

I was almost looking forward to getting back to the Sanctuary. There were problems there, just as there were problems in Cambridge: but the problems there seemed easier to cope with. I knew there was work to be done. Doing something, whatever it is, gives you the illusion that your life isn't totally out of your control.

This illusion came under fire as soon as I drove the Polo into the Sanctuary's car park. The first thing I saw was a large dark blue van. On its side were painted the words: CUSTODEMUS. And then in smaller letters underneath: PERMANENT PEACE OF MIND.

I parked beside Mrs Fettercairn's Jaguar. Before I had time to turn off the engine, two men came out of the ticket office. Within a couple of seconds one was on each side of the car. The guy on my side had a large alsatian attached to his wrist. It was getting dark by now, and the lack of light made their faces anonymous – white blurs against the darkening blue of the sky.

A torch flashed down on my face. I rolled down my window a couple of inches.

"Good evening, sir," said the one with the designer dog among his accessories.

"Good evening," I said, determined not to be

outdone. "It's a beautiful sky tonight."

The man seemed totally unimpressed by my attempt to make light conversation. He rapped on the window with his torch. On the other side of the car, his colleague had bent down: he was looking at me through the window as if I were a fish in an aquarium.

"Identification, please," the first man said.

"My name's Adam Davy. I work here. In fact I live here too."

"A driver's licence, perhaps. Something of that nature."

I found my wallet, fished out my licence and pushed it through the gap between the window and the door frame. He studied it under the light of the torch. Meanwhile his colleague strolled round to the front of the car and made a note of the registration number. I know that's what he was doing because he walked round the car and showed what he'd written to the guy with the dog. And then the guy with the dog asked me what the Polo's registration number was.

"How should I know?" I said irritably. "It's not my car."

It was all getting uncomfortably reminiscent of my conversation with Sergeant Todd on that stormy night when I first met Elvira Bladon. It seemed like years ago. I couldn't see any point in generating unnecessary hostility, so I explained that most people at the Sanctuary had the use of the car – and probably none of us knew its number by heart. The guards must have believed me. They started to become quite friendly.

"We have to be thorough on a job like this," said

the guy with the dog. He was a Welshman with the ghost of a hymn in the back of his voice. "We've got a classification scheme, see? There's general alert, red alert and black alert. This one's black alert."

I locked up the car and walked with them to the office. I knew the name on the van, of course. Custodemus must have been in the top three security companies in the United Kingdom. You saw their armoured vans outside banks. I had a feeling they patrolled some of the university's buildings at night. The only other thing I knew about them was that their services wouldn't come cheap.

One of the men padded after me into the house. I heard raised voices in the sitting room, which surprised me. Carson rarely used the room and half the furniture was covered in dustsheets. The guard followed me down the hall.

I stopped short in the doorway of the sitting room. There wasn't a dustsheet in sight, and it looked as if someone had done a lot of tidying up. Mrs Fettercairn, Phyllis and Kenneth were sitting round the empty fireplace drinking coffee. They looked like conspirators. Instead of chipped mugs, they had matching cups and saucers. I hadn't known that Carson possessed refinements like that.

As I came into the room, Mrs Fettercairn turned her face towards me.

"Ah, there you are." She glanced past me to the guard who hovered like a badly-trained housemaid in the doorway. "That will be all, thank you."

There was a flurry of activity. Phyllis sent Kenneth

to fetch me a cup and saucer. Mrs Fettercairn patted the seat beside her on the bulging leather sofa. I sat down.

"We seem to have our own private army," I said.

"Yes indeed, and not before time."

Since I'd last seen her, Mrs Fettercairn had changed into a long, fitted dress: it looked as if it was made of velvet and it was the colour of red burgundy. She was draped over the end of the sofa and was smoking a long black cigarette with a gold tip. She wasn't just sitting on the sofa, she was posing on it.

"They're very impressive," I said.

Mrs Fettercairn looked pleased. "Of course, it's rather makeshift, this first night. They tell me that tomorrow they will get themselves properly organized. I imagine that means lots of technology. Radar and so forth."

I glanced at Phyllis and caught her looking at me. It wasn't easy to keep a straight face but I managed. The way I did it was to think about money.

"Who's paying for all this?" I asked.

"I am, naturally."

There was a moment's silence. Mrs Fettercairn put down her coffee cup. She took another puff from the cigarette and ground it out in the ashtray. I looked at her hands. Her fingers were playing restlessly with her rings. Maybe she wasn't as calm as she sounded.

Kenneth stirred. I glanced at him. He was sitting in the low armchair on the other side of the fireplace and staring into his cup. His tongue moistened his lips. The room crackled with suppressed excitement like static electricity.

"How will Carson feel about all this security?" I asked. "Is there any news of him by the way?

Mrs Fettercairn looked up. "No news. I've told them, of course, that expense need be no object – but it seems there's nothing they can do. Nothing any of us can do." Suddenly the eyes seemed bluer and more blurred than before. "Nothing except wait."

"Mrs Fettercairn phoned the Chief Constable this afternoon," Phyllis said. "Unfortunately he wasn't in."

There was an uncharacteristically respectful note in Phyllis's voice. I looked suspiciously at her, but she wasn't taking the mickey.

"And how did you get on?" Mrs Fettercairn asked me.

I told them that I'd found someone who'd test the bloodstained feathers I'd found at Well Farm and compare them with samples from our own hybrid chicks. I didn't go into details, and I mentioned nothing about Becky or my father.

"How long will it take?" Phyllis asked.

"A few days. Perhaps a little over a week. Hard to be sure."

Mrs Fettercairn waved this aside. Diamonds sparkled as her hand moved. "That can wait," she said. "We have some news. The Sanctuary has had an approach from an American company. For some reason, they want to give it lots of money."

She looked confused, as well she might, and also proud, as if the offer of money was due to her hard work.

180

"It's a sponsorship deal, actually." Phyllis leant forward. "You just won't believe this."

I looked from her intent face to Mrs Fettercairn draped across the sofa, and from her to Kenneth, staring at his hands. What did he find so interesting about them?

"Adam!" Phyllis almost shrieked. "They're offering us twenty-five thousand for a twelve-month trial. And if it goes well they'll extend it for another four years."

For a few seconds I was so stunned I couldn't say a thing. Then my mind started working.

"Pounds or dollars?"

"Pounds," Phyllis said.

Mrs Fettercairn beamed at us, as if we were the deserving poor and she were our benefactress. "Isn't it wonderful?"

I said to Phyllis, "Was it a formal approach? It seems strange they've never been here. What's the company's name?"

"Rampro."

"Nothing to do with sheep," Mrs Fettercairn said in a voice that hardly trembled at all. "They're something to do with computers."

"RAM?" I said. "As in Random Access Memory?" Phyllis nodded.

I was doing rapid calculations in my head. Twenty-five thousand pounds a year: one hundred and twenty-five thousand over five years. Not a vast sum to an American computer company perhaps, but to someone like Carson it could be vital.

"Naturally they want to discuss the matter with Mr

Carson," Mrs Fettercairn said. "We've had to tell them that won't be possible just yet. Phyllis says they were very understanding. They won't mind at all if you go instead."

I gawped at her.

"Just for a few informal preliminary discussions," Phyllis said reassuringly. "Nothing to worry about. They want to see someone right away, and really you're the only person who can do it. They'll pay your expenses of course."

"When do they want me to go?"

"Tomorrow. They obviously don't believe in hanging around. You see, if it all goes well, we can set up the deal even before Carson gets better. Mrs Fettercairn can sign on our behalf."

Puzzled, I looked at Mrs Fettercairn. "You've got power of attorney?"

"Oh no. The ownership of the Sanctuary is ultimately tied up with a family trust. I happen to be one of the trustees, so I'm automatically obliged to take decisions when Mr Carson is incapacitated."

I glanced at Phyllis, who nodded. I didn't know what to make of the offer. It seemed too good a chance to miss. On the other hand, this wasn't the right time to leave the Sanctuary. And I couldn't help remembering the Turkish trip. I was fairly sure that John Izmidlian would quietly forget about his planned Middle Eastern falconry centre. I wondered if this would be another of those wild-goose chases. Also, I didn't want to leave the Sanctuary while Elvira Bladon was around.

"I'd like to think about it overnight," I said.

Phyllis and Mrs Fettercairn looked disappointed. They wanted me to share their enthusiasm, and I wouldn't. As for Kenneth, he sat there looking sadder and sadder. He was still staring at his hands.

I went into the kitchen to find something to eat. The smoked salmon canapés and the Provençal olives were just a distant memory. A moment later, Phyllis followed me out. She tiptoed into the room and shut the door behind her. I thought she'd come after me to talk about the Rampro offer, but I was wrong.

"Adam," she whispered, "do you know who she is?"

"Mrs Fettercairn? Carson's sister. Or at least I hope she is."

"Yes, but that's just her married name. She's really Julia Bliss."

I frowned at Phyllis, who obviously expected me to start cheering. "Not Julia Carson?"

"Her stage and screen name was Julia Bliss," Phyllis hissed. My face must have looked as blank as I felt, because she went on, "Oh my God, you don't know who I'm talking about, do you?"

I shook my head and started to cut another slice of bread.

"For about three years in the 1950s, she was everywhere. They said she was going to be the British Garbo. But she gave it up for love." The reverent tone of Phyllis's voice implied that love was spelt with a capital L. "And he wasn't even anyone in particular. A solicitor or something like that, I think." She clicked her tongue at me. "Surely you've seen some of her films? They often come round on television."

It all made sense: not just the rings, the fur and the Jaguar, but the way she moved and the way she held herself.

"Star quality," Phyllis murmured. "You can always tell."

The kitchen door opened. Mrs Fettercairn stood on the threshold. Phyllis jumped about two inches into the air. I nearly cut myself with the bread knife.

"I think I'd better be getting down to the hotel. I wonder if you'd drive me, Adam. One of the people there can bring you back."

She waited in the hall, leaning on her stick, while Phyllis fetched her coat and Kenneth found her bag. The three of us ushered her out to the car. Phyllis settled her into the passenger seat, while I fumbled my way around the unfamiliar controls. Sitting in that car was like sitting in a leather armchair. Driving it turned out to be like driving the QE2, with the Queen on board.

We didn't talk on the way to the hotel. I think Mrs Fettercairn was tired. It struck me that if she'd been a big star in the 1950s, she must be considerably older than her brother.

As the Jaguar purred on to the forecourt in front of Ardross Hall, I took a quick look at the other cars parked there. No sign of a Lotus or a Land Rover Discovery. There weren't any Honda Civics, either.

I parked as near to the front door as I could get. I hardly had time to get out of the car before the front door opened and the butler rushed towards us. I guessed that Phyllis had phoned ahead. Mrs Fettercairn took my arm and we walked slowly up the steps. The butler went before us to hold the door open.

"One of you must take Mr Davy back to the Sanctuary immediately," she announced.

"Very good, madam."

"Perhaps not immediately," I said, seizing the opportunity while I was here under Mrs Fettercairn's patronage. I smiled at the butler. "I'd like to have a word with Ms Bladon if she's in."

"I'm afraid that won't be possible, sir," he said. "Miss Bladon left us early this morning."

SIXTEEN

I heard the phone ringing as I unlocked the side door.

I stepped into the hall in time to see Phyllis darting into the dining room, where there was an extension we had started to use since the fire had turned the phone in the study into a mass of blackened plastic and twisted metal.

I'd had enough of today. Mrs Fettercairn was at Ardross Hall but Elvira Bladon had gone. That girl had made being elusive into an art form, and it irritated the hell out of me. I headed for the stairs.

Phyllis appeared in the doorway of the dining room. She beckoned me over. "It's Rampro," she hissed. "Someone called Mike. He wants to talk to you."

Mike sounded full of energy. It was late afternoon in California, and he was probably looking forward to going home. He said he was the personal assistant to Mr Lange, the chief executive officer at Rampro.

"I have to tell you, Adam," he said, "that I personally am very, very excited about this project."

In fact everyone at Rampro was very excited about it. He explained that Rampro were taking advantage of a European Community grant to open a subsidiary factory on a green-fields site about forty miles south of the Sanctuary. He wanted me, as Carson's representative, to come out to California as soon as possible to discuss the promotional possibilities of the proposed sponsorship deal.

I thought I read a hidden meaning into what he was saying. Someone at Rampro had had a bright idea, but it was still just that – an idea. Perhaps it was Mike himself. Now he or his boss wanted me to sell the idea to their colleagues.

"Now what about the visuals?" he asked. "You know what they say – a good picture's worth a thousand words."

"I can bring photographs and a video cassette."

"VHS?"

"Yes, but do you have a VCR that can decode a British tape?"

"No problem – I'll get on to our technical department." His excitement shot up a gear. "This is going to be really something. Now when can you come see us? Tomorrow?"

I dared not risk giving Mike's enthusiasm time to cool. I agreed to fly out the day after that. He told me there was a mid-morning United Airlines flight from Heathrow direct to San Francisco. He would arrange to have a ticket waiting for me at the airport.

As I put down the phone, the implications rushed into my mind. I had a day to do a week's work. I had to catch up with my jobs at the Sanctuary. More important than that, Phyllis and I had to put together a sales package. I found her alone in the sitting room.

"What's up?" she said. "You look as if there's been a death in the family."

It was an unfortunate choice of words. I explained what Mike wanted.

She lit a cigarette with a devil-may-care flourish. "So? What's the problem?"

"Lack of time, for one thing."

"We'll make an early start. Seven-thirty suit you?"

"But what about feeding the birds?"

"Kenneth will take care of that. Go on – have a bath and go to bed."

I did as she suggested. At seven o'clock the following morning I came downstairs to find she had set up her computer in the dining room. Judging by the fog of smoke, she had been there for a while. When I asked if she'd been to bed, she said that she hadn't felt sleepy. We got down to work.

"Be positive," Phyllis kept saying. "You've got to make them feel this is an opportunity they simply can't miss."

We roughed out a thirty-minute presentation during the day. In the evening we had half a dozen full-length dress rehearsals, and in each of them Phyllis played a different role – from a figure-hungry financial director to a hostile heckler. I was as nervous as a dog in a thunderstorm. I could just about cope with pretending to be a salesman when Phyllis was my only audience, but I couldn't even begin to imagine what it would be like to go through the same spiel in front of a group of unknown Americans in unfamiliar surroundings.

I drove to Heathrow in the early morning. I was relieved to get on the plane: I'd nothing to do but eat,

188

sleep, watch a movie and read the in-flight magazine.

That was the theory of it, anyway. In practice it worked out rather differently. I had all those empty hours to fill with worrying. It wasn't a question of how I'd cope or even whether I'd cope – it was more a matter of how spectacularly I would fail. Maybe, I thought, it would be simpler if I just got on the first flight home.

By local time it was early evening when we touched down at San Francisco International. We filtered slowly through customs and immigration: the process took over an hour. A group of people was waiting to meet incoming passengers. At least half of them were carrying little placards. For an instant I hesitated. The memory of what had happened at Atatürk Airport was uncomfortably vivid. A man banged his suitcase against my leg. I allowed myself to be jostled forward.

I saw Mike almost immediately. He was small, dark and a little overweight. He looked like a swarthy cherub. He was carrying a board with the word RAMPRO in big white capitals on it. I went over. He saw me coming. His face broke into a smile.

"Adam! Great to see you."

He pumped my hand up and down. I found myself responding with a pale imitation of his own high spirits: enthusiasm is catching. He took my bag and led the way to the car park.

"I thought you might appreciate a little local colour. I booked you into the Wharf Lodge Hotel. That's downtown. Within a stone's throw of San

Francisco Bay." He paused, and then added, "I guess you'd have to have a strong right arm."

Mike had one of those rich, slow American voices, though there was a touch of something more exotic in his inflections. Everything about him spoke quietly about money. His hair was well cut and his skin had an even, expensive tan. He was wearing a cream silk shirt, light-blue duck trousers and Italian loafers. His teeth were brilliantly white and regular. He was driving a Japanese car – a top-of-the-range, two-litre Mitsubishi Galant fitted with every conceivable extra.

We drove north on Highway 101. The traffic became steadily heavier. We crawled past the Candlestick Park stadium on our right. A little further on, the view opened up. There was the heart of the city. The buildings crawled up and down the hills. The evening sun glinted on thousands of windows. To the east was the Bay Bridge striding across the water to Oakland.

"We're not going to get to the hotel before seven," Mike said. "It's gotten worse since the earthquake. They had to take down the Embarcadero Freeway. It used to take you right into town."

We came off the highway and drove slowly through city streets. I glanced at Mike. The car was air-conditioned, but he was sweating slightly. He caught me looking at him.

"I was hoping I could show you some of the nightlife here," he said. "But I got a problem – dinner with a client. I can't get out of it."

I told him not to worry, that I could look after

190

myself and anyway what I really wanted to do was to go to bed.

"No, you got to fight that. You got to stay up as long as you can. The longer you last out without going to sleep, the sooner your metabolism will adjust to the time difference. You know what I'd do? Wake yourself up with a long shower. Then go out, have a walk. Find a bar, maybe. Have a beer. Then get some dinner. But keep moving, that's the key. Let's see, what about Coit Tower? That's really something after nightfall. You get these amazing views over the bay. And there's Golden Gate Bridge. It's unique."

"Sounds good," I said. After the week I'd just lived through, the prospect of an evening on my own sounded like heaven. No one to make demands on me. No work to do. No one trying to drive cars at me. No responsibilities.

"Great, great," Mike said vaguely, and something in his face jogged my memory. I tried to chase the resemblance but it was too late.

For the rest of the drive, he talked about the arrangements for the morning. He would send a car for me at nine-thirty, because he himself was tied up with meetings in the first half of the morning. The car would take me out to the Rampro headquarters, where I would give my presentation.

With another flood of apologies for not being able to stay with me, Mike dropped me off at the Wharf Lodge. After I'd checked in, my bags and I were wafted up to a room on the sixth floor with a view of the bay. There was an enormous bed which I dared not lie on in case I fell asleep. The refrigerator contained every drink known to civilized man. The bathroom was like something out of ancient Rome, except I don't think the Romans had jacuzzis and power showers.

By now the jet-lag was getting mixed up with my worries about the next day. I didn't know where the one stopped and the other began. I staggered round the room, trying to unpack. My eyes were playing tricks on me, the way they do when you're running a high fever. The outlines of objects were very clear, the colours very vibrant. Part of me felt I just couldn't cope with an alien city tonight.

Step by step I forced my weary body to follow the programme that Mike had outlined. I stood under the shower for fifteen minutes — ten minutes hot, five minutes cold. After I'd got dressed, I flicked through the notes for the presentation, but I found it hard to concentrate and the type kept wriggling in front of my eyes. I resisted the cowardly temptation to get room service to send me up a sandwich. Tonight, I told myself grimly, you are going to have fun.

There was a folder of information on the bureau. It included a complimentary town map, which I put in my pocket. Apart from a belt holding my money and passport, the only other thing I needed was a jersey.

I took the lift down to the lobby and went outside. It was a grey, windy evening. You could smell the ocean. I walked slowly down to Fisherman's Wharf, fending off requests for small change. Every other person I met seemed to be a tourist.

On Fisherman's Wharf, people were cooking crabs in the open, boiling them alive in enormous vats. Beside the vats were boxes of living crabs waiting to be cooked; they were grey and cream-coloured, and their limbs waved to and fro, as if looking for the way back to the sea. I glanced inside one of the steaming vats and saw that the heat turned the crabs pink. I wondered when death caught up with them. I knew that whatever I had to eat that evening, it wouldn't be seafood.

The wind was coming in off the sea. I walked east along the line of wharves, faster and faster, trying to get away from the cold and my tiredness. Up on my right, the Coit Tower stood like a solitary finger on Telegraph Hill.

The line of wharves swung south east. Ahead of me, according to the map, was the tower of the World Trade Center. The exercise cleared my head but jet-lag was still warping my perceptions. The city seemed to be moving about one-and-a-half times the normal operating speed. I didn't know whether to put that down to San Francisco or my state of mind. Maybe it was both.

I went into a bar advertising something called Anchor Steam Beer, which turned out to be heavy and tasteless, but it was a warm and comfortable bar. The trouble was that was sitting there and twiddling my glass brought all my worries about the following day rushing back. I felt the beginnings of a headache. It was time to go.

For want of anything better to do, I was still

following Mike's instructions. I set out to look for something to eat. I walked back up to Fisherman's Wharf and killed another forty-five minutes in company with a steak and salad.

It was almost dark now. Auras of fog clung to the street lights like parasitic growths. All I wanted was to go to bed and sleep. But obstinacy drove me on. I had decided that I was going to visit Coit Tower this evening and I didn't intend to change my mind. I threaded my way through the grid of streets towards the dark silhouette of Telegraph Hill.

There were two ways up the hill. A road wound like a spiral up to the summit with a line of cars following it up to the car park at the top. But there was a shorter way for pedestrians, a path leading straight up the hill. I looked at it and I didn't like what I saw. It was narrow and badly lit, and in the gathering dusk it looked less like a path than a tunnel.

Part of me wanted to go up the hill by the road. OK, it was longer; but all the people and lights and cars made it seem much safer. Everything I'd heard about the escalating crime rates in American cities came flooding into my mind. I was feeling fragile. I was not in the mood for adventures.

Pride makes you do stupid things. I knew that pride had had a lot to do with my decision to leave home, though I hadn't realized it at the time. Now pride didn't want me to take the easy way out. The wind ruffled my hair. There were dozens of people within a few yards of me and yet I'd never felt so alone. I straightened my shoulders and set off towards the path.

The stone steps were worn and irregular. I walked steadily upwards. For much of the way there were walls on either side. I passed doors in the walls, and I wondered what sort of secret gardens lay behind them. Hidden in the dense, dripping greenery were dozens of houses, turned in on themselves.

The path zigzagged higher and higher. The steps were slimy with moisture. Once I slipped, and only saved myself from falling by grabbing the hand rail. The occasional lights failed to reassure me. They threw shadows and deepened the darkness.

I hadn't gone fifty yards before I was telling myself what a moron I was. I paused to catch my breath. I heard a sound behind me. A footstep, maybe, followed by a scrape as though a foot had kicked a stone and sent it scuttering across a step. I started climbing again. This time I was breathing harder and moving faster. My stomach felt heavy. The beers and the food were weighing me down.

A stitch stabbed my side. I paused and leant against a wall. I needed to get my breath back. I sucked cold damp air deep into my lungs. I also needed to prove to myself that I wasn't totally terrified. The stone wall felt rough and damp behind my head. I listened.

I heard car engines, snatches of music, even footsteps – in the distance. From even further away, out in the bay, came the mournful hooting of a foghorn. But as far as I could tell, nothing or no one was moving on the path below me or above me.

There was nothing to worry about. I congratulated

myself on my calm. If you didn't give in to your fears, I thought smugly, they often proved to be groundless. I carried on up the path, more slowly this time. What was the hurry? I wasn't afraid of anything.

Suddenly something wailed like a tortured baby a few inches away from my ear. In terror I leapt sideways and cannoned into the wall on the opposite side of the path. I saw something furry diving through the vegetation.

Giant rats, I thought. Giant killer rats.

There was another howl. This was followed by a spitting, snarling sound like an angry firework. I broke into a run. I stumbled up the steps, hoping that round the corner I'd find some people or at least a light.

A dark shadow streaked past me. As I rounded the next corner, another firework exploded.

There, dimly illuminated by the lamp overhead, were two cats engaged in a duel to the death. They were huge animals, swollen with rage. Their mutual blood lust blinded them to everything, including my presence. For a couple of seconds, I stood there and watched. Birds of prey aren't exactly peaceable creatures, but I'd never seen such savagery as this.

As suddenly as it had begun, it was over. One of the cats decided that he had better things to do than try to prove his masculinity in open combat. He shot up one of the walls as if it were a level surface and disappeared into the branches of a tree on the other side. The victor followed him. There were more howls and screeches, but the sounds rapidly diminished in volume.

I walked on, still cautious but no longer terrified. A few minutes later I came out on the top of Telegraph Hill. The wind was stronger than it had been on the path, and it was far colder. There were dozens of people, some in cars, some on foot, some standing on the parapet looking out to sea.

I wandered around for a while. Someone tried to sell me a tee-shirt. Someone else tried to sell me a postcard. Far below, headlights made pretty patterns on Golden Gate Bridge. The fog was swirling in from the ocean like an invading army.

I found a statue of Christopher Columbus. He was looking at the ocean, just like me, his hand resting negligently on the hilt of his sword. I squinted up at his face. I thought he looked more than a little puzzled, which was not surprising because he'd somehow ended up on the wrong coast of America.

It was getting colder and colder. I wished I'd brought more than a jersey with me. It was time to get back to the hotel. I thought longingly of the bed that was waiting in my room.

I threaded my way through the cars and people. At the head of the path, I paused and looked back. I'm not sure why. I think some part of me liked this wild and windswept pimple in the middle of a city.

I heard the rasp of a lighter. A flame flared. A second or two earlier I wouldn't have noticed it as I'd been looking the other way. A second or two later, the flame would have vanished.

A man was lighting a cigarette. He was standing in the lee of a car about twenty metres away from me. For an instant, the flame threw light on the face of a small figure beside him. Then the flame died, and the man turned away. Now the smaller man beside the smoker was no more than a silhouette.

I turned and ran down the path. Maybe I was going crazy. Maybe I'd made a mistake. Or maybe I was just jet-lagged and desperate for sleep. Or maybe the guy on Telegraph Hill really was my Rampro contact, Mike. If so, there might be a perfectly innocent explanation.

I didn't want to stay and find out. I'd had enough of being proud. It was safer to be paranoid.

SEVENTEEN

The way I went down that path I nearly ended up with two broken legs. There were running footsteps behind me, or at least I think there were. I thought of pounding on one of the doors I'd passed and screaming for help. But I doubted if the people who lived on Telegraph Hill were the sort who answered cries for help.

The fog had grown worse while I was on the top of the hill. Maybe the wind kept it moving near the tower. There was less of a breeze on the path, and the thick, clammy vapour was trapped between the walls. Moisture dripped from overhanging branches. All sounds were deadened. The lights showed how thick the fog was.

Stumbling and skidding, I went down and down. Footsteps slapped behind me. Or at least I think they did. If they weren't echoes, did they belong to Mike or a mugger? Or was Mike a mugger? Or a killer?

Near one of the lights, I passed another cat. It was crouching, ready to spring, on the top of the wall, and it was staring at me with yellow, baleful eyes.

At last I found myself in a street where people and cars were passing to and fro and illuminated signs glittered on the buildings. A cop cruised by on an enormous motorbike. I was breathing in ragged gasps, desperately trying to drag the air into me. I was shivering. I couldn't even think straight. The fog seemed to have got inside my mind.

Apart from breathe, the only thing I did was watch. But no one came towards me. In fact, people seemed to go out of their way to avoid me. As far as I could tell, no one was following me now. No one was waiting for me to start moving again. As far as I could tell, that is.

After a few minutes, my breathing returned to something like normal. I found the map and worked out in which direction the hotel was. I wasn't far from Fisherman's Wharf. I started walking, keeping a good look out all the time. I stayed near people and bright lights, but I shied away from the kerbside. I didn't want to end under somebody's wheels.

The hotel was as welcoming as a cocoon. The doorman seemed to recognize me. He was a big black man, and I was glad to have him on my side. I walked across the lobby to the desk. The clerk had my room key ready for me; it was that sort of hotel.

"Oh, Mr Davy," he said. "There was a message."

The clerk handed me a sheet of paper, folded once. I opened it. MIKE CALLED. CAR WILL BE LATER THAN SCHEDULED – 10AM.

I looked at the clerk. He wasn't much older than me. He had one of the those freckled, friendly faces.

"Do you happen to know when this came in?"

"Sure. About an hour ago. I wrote it down on the paper."

I glanced back at the note. Sure enough, the time

had been scribbled at the bottom.

"The guy thought you might be asleep already," the clerk said. "Said the message could wait till morning. He really didn't want to disturb you."

I slept like the dead. I woke up feeling like a zombie.

I'd booked an alarm call for eight-thirty as a fail-safe mechanism the night before, and that was just as well. The phone on the bedside table dragged me into the waking world. My first conscious thought was that I couldn't put it off any longer: today was the day I was going to make a fool of myself.

The next item that slid into my mind was equally disturbing, though in a very different way. I remembered what had happened on Telegraph Hill last night: I remembered whom I thought I'd seen. But had I just imagined seeing Mike near the Coit Tower? It had been dark. I had not been exactly clear-headed, for which I had to thank a lethal cocktail of tiredness, jet-lag, worry and, last but perhaps not least, a couple of Anchor Steam Beers.

I rolled out of bed, staggered into the bathroom and had another long shower. After that, I was fully awake. The trouble was, parts of my brain and parts of my stomach still felt as if they belonged to someone else.

I took the lift down and went in search of breakfast. They had a menu as long as my arm, but all I could handle was a glass of orange juice and a cup of coffee.

Back in my room, I tried to give myself a full-length rehearsal. But my mind wouldn't concentrate on it. In the end I went out for a walk.

By daylight the city was busy but unthreatening. I walked up Nob Hill, then down to Chinatown and back on Columbus to the hotel. The more I walked, the less likely it seemed that I'd seen Mike the night before. Now I felt ashamed of the way I'd behaved on Telegraph Hill. I shouldn't have run away. I should have gone right up to the man. Almost certainly I would have found he was a total stranger.

I got back to the hotel at nine forty-five. I collected everything I would need for the presentation, and waited in the lobby. My brain was blank and my mouth was dry.

I'd half-expected that Rampro would send a stretch limo and a uniformed chauffeur. But the company had a different view of my status. The driver who came for me wore jeans, a tee-shirt and a baseball cap.

"Hi," he said glumly, as if being civil was costing him more than he could easily afford. "I'm Jerry. Car's out front."

He was a small man, a Caucasian with rounded shoulders and long arms. A thin black moustache decorated his upper lip. He led me out to a dark brown Datsun which had seen better days. Maybe the Lincoln Continental was being serviced.

I sat in the front beside the driver and tried to make conversation. Tried and failed. After a while, I let him drive through the city in peace. I concentrated on trying to tame the butterflies in my stomach.

Soon we were driving south on Highway 101. The

presentation was due to take place at Rampro's headquarters in Menlo Park. A few miles before the airport, we came off on to a road called Wood Avenue. If there had ever been a wood, there was no trace of it now. The road was lined with office buildings on both sides, most of them new. The only trees in sight were small and neatly clipped.

We drove on for another half-mile, making a right here and a left there. It was nearly eleven o'clock by the time we turned into a car park in front of a three-storey office building. The building was faced with bronze-tinted reflective glass. It looked blank and a little hostile, like a person wearing mirrored sunglasses.

The car park and the offices were set in landscaped grounds. There were well-groomed shrubs, but no flowers. Whoever had designed the gardens had rejected grass, presumably because it was too labour-intensive. Instead, there were wood chips everywhere. It was the sort of garden you'd expect to see in Toytown.

Jerry took me inside. The entrance hall was a sort of atrium going through the whole height of the building. There were fitted sofas, upholstered with leather. In front of them were large coffee tables of light-coloured oak. A grove of glossy palms stood near the reception desk.

The receptionist made up for the surliness of the driver. She knew who I was without me having to tell her. She asked me to take a seat while she called Mike.

I sat on one of the sofas and pretended to read the

Wall Street Journal. On the marble-faced wall in front of me there was a big oil painting of a handsome, fit-looking man in late middle age.

There were footsteps running down the stairs. Mike came towards me, his hand outstretched.

"Adam – how did you sleep? Did they make you comfortable at the Wharf Lodge?"

I smiled and nodded. If I opened my mouth, I had a feeling my teeth would start chattering.

"You took my advice, huh? You liked Coit Tower?"

I managed to say it had been great.

"I was up there myself as it happened," he said casually. "Client wanted to do the tourist bit after dinner."

"I – ah – I wish I'd known."

"Well, we'd better get moving – they're all waiting for you. Except Mr Lange, that is. He called this morning. He's real sore about missing you."

I nodded towards the portrait on the wall. "That's Mr Lange?"

Mike grinned. "Yes and no. That's old Gregory Lange, our founder president. He's retired now, and his son Magnus is our chief executive officer."

Still talking, he led me towards the stairs. As far as I could tell in my state of confusion he kept offering me things. Did I want a cup of coffee, a glass of water, a slide projector, a visit to the bathroom? All I wanted was to be somewhere else.

Mike opened a door. "Come and meet the guys."

He ushered me into a conference room. It seemed to be full of people. All of them were poking hands in my direction. Mike introduced them to me one by one. Names and job titles flooded over me. Including Mike there were five men and one woman. I heard names like Jim, Bozo and Zephir. And titles like Executive Vice President, Director of Communications and Environmental Consultant.

Zephir showed me how to operate the video and I rammed in our Sanctuary tape — the wrong way round. I got it right the next time, and the conversion seemed to have worked OK. I turned round, sweating. Everyone else was sitting down round the big table.

Mike said, "Over to you, Adam."

My fingers were making sweat marks on my notes. I couldn't read my own writing. I put the notes beside the folder of photographs at the head of the table. I licked my lips. I cleared my throat. My brain felt short of oxygen. In my mind I heard Phyllis saying, "Be positive." Easy enough for her to say, I thought. At present I was feeling one hundred per cent negative.

"The Sanctuary is a unique British conservation project," someone was saying. "It is home to over eighty birds of prey from all over the world. Besides conservation, our aim is to educate. Last year alone, nearly fifty thousand people visited the Sanctuary. In that same year, the Sanctuary was featured thirty-nine times on British radio stations and nine times on national television. It is also the subject of a documentary to be shown on German television next month."

How I started, I just do not know. At first I had the weird sensation that someone else was talking: all this had nothing to do with me. Those rehearsals with Phyllis had paid off. I remembered to speak slowly and clearly. After the first sentence, my voice hardly shook at all. The more I spoke, the more confident I became.

I gave them a couple of minutes from the video – a clip from a BBC documentary featuring the Sanctuary. It showed falcons in action, and also Carson on his favourite subject: the international ecological importance of the work he was doing.

I showed them photographs, I showed them plans. I discussed some of the ways we could feature the Rampro logo. It was hard to tell what sort of impression I was making on them. A more experienced salesman might have been able to guess. I had to operate blind.

I came to the end of my prepared material a little sooner than I'd expected. All the people round the table were looking at me. I couldn't read the expressions on their upturned faces: I didn't know the language.

"Well – ah – if you have any questions I'd be glad to try to answer them."

There was a moment's silence. Mike broke the ice by asking for more details about our programme of off-site displays. Then the others started firing questions. The only exception was the environmental consultant, who didn't want to ask questions: he wanted to blind us with science instead. He ran on for a couple of minutes before the Executive Vice President pulled him up.

Most of the questions were easy enough to answer. Essentially they were requests for information. Either I knew the answers, or I had them in my notes.

Then the Director of Communications said, "Mr Carson – he owns the place, right? And he runs it too?"

I nodded.

"But you tell us he's in hospital. What exactly's the problem?"

"Mr Carson was stabbed," I said in a level voice. "The police haven't found the man who did it yet, and we don't know what the motive was. However, we hope that Mr Carson will soon be back at the Sanctuary." I could sense that the man was ready with another question, so I pressed on: "I should stress that the Sanctuary is in fact owned by a family trust set up by Mr Carson. His sister Mrs Fettercairn is at present at the Sanctuary, running that side of things. We also have three resident senior staff, including myself. We're all used to deputizing for Mr Carson."

To my relief, the PR Liaison Officer lobbed me a question on another, less controversial subject. Soon I was deep into an analysis of why former sponsorship deals had failed to do much for us.

"Basically, our two previous sponsors were local firms. They didn't have the resources to do the job properly. But it was more than that. They were also local in the sense that they thought locally. They thought in terms of a fifty-mile radius of their headquarters. But conservation is global business. It has to be. That's why we need a sponsor with international interests."

"I still think we need more information on this

proposal," said the Director of Communications.

"Of course," I said, wishing I could kick the man. "If you'd like to tell me exactly what you need to know, I'll do my best to answer your questions right away. And if you or any of your colleagues would like to come over and see the Sanctuary in operation, we'd be pleased to see you."

The Executive Vice President glanced at his watch. "Well, does anyone have anything else to add...?"

Nobody had. The meeting gradually broke up. People started shaking my hand all over again. All of them seemed very enthusiastic. But nothing concrete was said, like "Who do we make the cheque out to?" I wondered whether the real decisions at Rampro were made elsewhere. Despite their impressive job titles, these people might be no more than makeweights. Perhaps old Mr Lange kept the reins of power firmly in his own hands.

Mike clapped me on the back. "That was great. You've got a natural talent for this."

I didn't believe him, but it was nice of him to say so.

"Let's go get some lunch."

I gathered up my belongings, and we went downstairs. Mike was asking me about what sort of food I'd like. I said I could eat anything but seafood.

"Brings you out in an allergic reaction?"

"Something like that."

In the entrance hall, the receptionist smiled at us both. "Mike," she said, "Mr Lange wants you to call him."

Mike nodded. "I'll be right back," he said to me.

He was gone for five minutes. While I waited, the receptionist told me things I already knew about the major tourist attractions of London. Mike returned and the receptionist told me it had been really great to meet me.

Mike and I walked across the parking lot towards his Mitsubishi. It's odd how the future continually fools you. I'd thought that the worst thing the day could hold would be this presentation. In fact, it hadn't gone too badly, and I'd had the bonus of discovering why Mike had been on Telegraph Hill last night. But there were far worse things to come.

A red Nissan Patrol swung into the access road. It seemed to be coming straight for us. Mike and I ducked back into the shelter of a Porsche. The Nissan surged across the lot and braked sharply. It came to a halt in the bay marked PRESIDENT. The driver's door opened.

Elvira Bladon got out. Her face was white and furious. She glared at me. "What the hell are you doing here?"

EIGHTEEN

Mike grinned at Elvira. "What am I doing here?" he said, choosing to take the question personally. "I'm working, that's what. Which is more than we can say for all of us."

"I don't mean you." She stabbed her finger at me. "It's this guy."

"I'd like to ask you the same question," I said.

Our eyes locked. She was wearing blue jeans, cowboy boots and a faded UCLA sweatshirt. There were streaks of red dust on the boots. The colour surged into her face. Maybe she was hot. Or maybe she was just angry.

The passenger door of the Nissan slammed. Elvira's eyes released mine. All of us looked towards the noise. I heard Mike mutter something I didn't catch. For an instant I seriously wondered whether a combination of San Francisco and jet-lag had permanently warped my mind. I thought I was seeing things. Or rather people.

Another girl was coming towards us. She had her dark hair tied up in a scarf. A dark green dress revealed more of her curves than was entirely flattering. As she drew nearer, her face filled with pleasure at the sight of me. It was Marguerite Izmidlian.

"Adam! Isn't this great?"

If my face showed even ten per cent of what I was feeling, I must have looked like a total idiot. My brain just couldn't cope with the implications. There was so much to figure out. But in that instant all I could think about was the fact that Elvira had lied to me. When we'd met at the Ardross Hall Hotel, I'd asked her straight out whether she knew Izmidlian. She had said no. But if Marguerite was some sort of friend, Elvira must have known about Izmidlian, even if she hadn't met him.

Marguerite laid her hands on my shoulders and kissed me continental-style on both cheeks.

"I see you guys have already met," Elvira said.

Marguerite let me go. "Sure," she said to Elvira. "We met in Turkey a few days ago. Adam's going to build a birds of prey centre for Papa."

"Would someone like to tell me," I asked, "whose idea it was that Rampro should sponsor the Sanctuary?"

Marguerite gave what I can only call a trill of girlish laughter. "It was me, of course. We were having dinner with Elvira's uncle, and I was telling him about you and the Sanctuary, and about what good publicity you were going to give my father, and Mr Lange said it could be just what Rampro was looking for too."

"I've got to go," Elvira interrupted.

She turned and walked quickly towards the Nissan Patrol.

"Hey," I said, starting to walk after her. "There's things we need to talk about."

Elvira opened the driver's door and climbed up into the seat. "I don't think so."

Her eyes flicked from me to Marguerite. She slammed the door, started the engine and reversed out of the parking lot. Thirty seconds later, the Nissan was out of sight.

"Something on her mind, I guess," Marguerite said.

I said nothing. I was too busy being furious that Elvira had run off once again. She didn't answer questions, she ran away from them. Also I didn't like it when a girl's eyes had the same effect on me as a stoat's have on a rabbit. It made me feel vulnerable.

Marguerite sidled closer to me. "I didn't realize you knew Elvira."

"I didn't realize you did, either."

"Where did you meet her?" Mike asked.

"We bumped into each other in England. But I wouldn't say I know her very well."

"I'm starving," Mike said. "Let's go."

The pair of them swept me towards the Mitsubishi. I was too confused to argue. Suddenly it seemed possible that if Carson got better, he might have both the Izmidlian consultancy and the Rampro sponsorship. As far as I could see, everything was on the level. Everything, that is, except Elvira Bladon.

We got into the car. Mike and I were in the front and Marguerite behind. She leant on the backs of our seats and put her head between us.

"So where are we going, Mike?" she said. "How about seafood?" She turned towards me and I felt her warm breath on my cheek. "You tried the crabs yet?"

In the end Mike drove us to a Lebanese restaurant. He used his car phone to book a table en route.

The manager greeted Mike and Marguerite as if they were his favourite customers. The three of them talked in rapid French together. The manager made several references to *monsieur le patron*. Each time he used the phrase, he bobbed his head. Waving aside his own waiters, he ushered us personally to our table. He held Marguerite's chair for her. I got the impression that if she'd asked him to drop a curtsey, he would willingly have obliged. It was at that moment that the penny dropped.

When we were alone with our aperitifs and the menus, I said to Marguerite, "Monsieur le patron - that's your father, isn't it?"

She smiled. "Of course. How did you know?"

"Just an inspired guess," I said. "He owns this place?"

Marguerite nodded. I looked from one dark face to the other. I had another flash of inspiration.

"I don't suppose," I said to Mike, "that monsieur le patron happens to be your father too?"

He smiled at me. "I think you understand French pretty well."

I shrugged. "It wasn't just that. There's a resemblance."

"I wanted it to be a surprise," Marguerite said. "So I made Mike promise he wouldn't tell you."

"It was certainly a surprise."

213

The manager and the wine waiter came to take our orders. They gave me a breathing space – time for a little thinking. On the whole, it was just as well that I hadn't known before that Mike was Izmidlian's son. Until this morning, I'd been inclined to think that the Izmidlians were bad news. I still wasn't certain that they were good news, but I felt that the balance had swung in their favour. Marguerite set my teeth on edge but she was only able to do that because she was so obviously sincere.

While we were eating, Mike told Marguerite about this morning's presentation. "Adam was very impressive," he said.

"I know," Marguerite purred. "I've seen him in action before." She leant across the table and nudged me. "Haven't I?"

I tried to keep things on a businesslike level. "How do you rate our chances of getting the sponsorship?" I asked.

"I'd say we've got an eighty to ninety per cent probability here," Mike said. "But the guys you met today won't be making the decision. That's down to Elvira's uncle."

"He's Mr Lange?" I said. "The president of the company?"

Mike shook his head. "Not that Mr Lange. That's old Gregory – the guy in the portrait. I'm talking about my boss – Magnus Lange, who's Gregory's son. Magnus is the one who really runs the company. And one day soon, he'll own it too."

"You mean he'll own fifty per cent of it,"

214

Marguerite said.

Their eyes met. For an instant, the resemblance between them was much more marked. They looked like a couple of cats sharing a secret, a sly secret. For some reason I felt depressed.

"Let me get this straight," I said. "Magnus Lange is Elvira Bladon's uncle? And Gregory's her grandfather?"

"You got it," Mike said. "Her mother was Magnus's sister."

"Was?"

Mike nodded. "She died last year."

The manager appeared with an aubergine dip which was one of their specialities. Mike showed no signs of wanting to tell me more about Elvira Bladon or her parents, and I didn't want to ask. The fact that both our mothers were dead was a small but unsettling coincidence.

"You're staying a few days, aren't you, Adam?" Marguerite said.

"I really need to get back as soon as I can."

"Tomorrow, maybe?" Mike stared at me across the table. "You know I had to call Magnus just before we left the office? He wanted to hear how your presentation had gone."

I waited.

Mike scooped up some more of the aubergine dip and swallowed it. "He'd like to meet with you."

"Where? At the office?"

"At the ranch. He—"

"But that's miles away," Marguerite interrupted. "I was hoping—"

"That guy who brought you from the hotel is going up to the ranch this afternoon. He'll give you a ride."

"How long would it take?" I asked.

Mike said, "Magnus wants you to stay over. Which makes sense – it's four or five hours' drive."

"There and back," I said. "Plus an overnight stay."

He shook his head. "There's not much in it, timewise. If you came back to San Francisco from the ranch this evening, you'd have to come by road. But if you wait till tomorrow morning, you can get a ride in the company plane. It's at Auburn right now, and Magnus is planning on flying here tomorrow."

"Auburn's near the ranch?"

"Maybe ten or twelve miles west?" Mike picked up his glass and looked at me over the brim. "You know, Magnus would really appreciate it if you went. Me too, in fact: this sponsorship deal's big for me personally. But of course it's up to you."

He made it sound like a request, but I felt the pressure behind it. Magnus Lange wanted to assess me himself. That was good news, I supposed – it showed that he was serious about the sponsorship. But if I didn't go, I guessed that we could kiss the sponsorship goodbye.

"Why don't we all go?" Marguerite asked.

"Because we've got work to do," Mike said. "You've got to fill me in on the situation in Turkey, remember?"

Marguerite started to say something. As she spoke she glanced across the table. Mike was looking at her. She gave up after one mangled syllable, shrugged and closed her mouth.

"Besides," Mike went on, "Adam's not going there for a vacation. You know what Magnus is like. The man who invented the eight-day week."

"Elvira said nothing about Magnus being at the ranch," Marguerite said. "When did he get there?"

Mike shrugged. "How should I know? I guess he flew in after she left." He reached for the wine bottle. "That reminds me – how come Elvira was giving you a lift?"

"She came by the Oakland office on the way. I hitched a ride. I don't know what's wrong with her today. She hardly said a word." Marguerite turned to me and there was a glint in her eye. "Look, why don't you spend a night in San Francisco on your way back? We've got business to talk about – the Birds of Prey Centre."

Mike grinned. "She doesn't give up easy, does she?"

Marguerite looked as if she wanted to bite his head off. There was an argument going on here, an argument without words, and I wasn't sure what it was about.

"They'll need me at the Sanctuary, I'm afraid," I said diplomatically. "And I have to see what the police are doing."

"About that guy who attacked Mr Carson?" Mike said. "Now I'd be careful what you say to Magnus about that. It might give him the wrong idea about the Sanctuary."

Marguerite bit her lip.

"I hope you'll be coming to England soon," I said to her. "Then you can see how things work for yourself. It'll be much more effective."

"But Adam—"

"Hey, you guys," Mike interrupted. "That's enough business. We're here to celebrate, OK?"

The oddest thing about that meal in the Lebanese restaurant was that in the end it really did feel like a celebration. I knew that nothing had been settled. Elvira Bladon was as much of a problem as ever. Despite what had happened today I still wasn't sure whether I could trust the Izmidlians. As far as I knew, Carson was still hovering somewhere between life and death. And Marguerite's attempts to mix pleasure with business were getting harder to cope with.

For all that I was almost happy. I think it was because of the presentation. I hadn't chickened out. I hadn't fainted or stumbled over my words or talked nonsense or otherwise made a fool of myself. Instead I felt I'd done the best I could in the circumstances, and we still had a chance of getting the sponsorship. I told myself that I deserved a little relaxation.

Mike and Marguerite seemed to relax as well. We laughed a lot. We might have been a bunch of friends rather than business associates; there was no reason why the two categories shouldn't overlap. The wine waiter produced another bottle of wine, a Chablis, with the manager's compliments. I remember thinking that maybe, just maybe, this was the beginning of the end of the nightmare which had begun when Elvira Bladon nearly drove into me on the road to the Sanctuary.

Nothing lasts for ever, I told myself. Even nightmares have to end some time.

While we were drinking coffee, I was even tempted to tell them about what had been happening in England. I thought that, if anyone could, Mike and Marguerite might be able to help me solve the riddle that was Elvira Bladon. I was just about to raise the subject when Marguerite lobbed me a question about our conservation programme. The chance slipped away, and soon after that the meal came to an end.

Mike slapped my right shoulder as we left the restaurant. "That was great. Let's do it again soon, huh?"

"Maybe in England," Marguerite suggested, nuzzling against my left arm. "All of us, eh? Adam, you got to find Mike a nice English girl."

I grinned and nodded at two smiling people beside me.

Looking back, I was amazed by my ability to fool myself. It wasn't much later before I saw that lunch in Menlo Park for precisely what it was: the lull before the storm.

I glanced across the restaurant's parking lot. A brown Datsun was waiting beside Mike's Mitsubishi.

NINETEEN

Four hours is a long time to spend alone with a man like Jerry.

Once again I was sitting in the front of the Datsun. Jerry grunted occasionally. I got the feeling that he'd already used up his ration of words for the day.

For most of the journey he kept the radio tuned to a Country and Western station. As we drove north west towards Sacramento on Highway 80, the music began to have a hypnotic effect on me. During the last few days, I had been pushing myself hard. Now the release from tension combined with the effects of the long and relaxing lunch. I dozed off. Or rather, I fell in and out of sleep. The music and the advertisements which punctuated the songs made a soundtrack for my dreams.

In my more wakeful periods, I sometimes watched Jerry out of the corner of my eye. He drove at a steady 55 mph, with a permanent frown on his face. His fingers tapped in time with the music on the steering wheel. Every now and then he relieved the monotony by picking his nose.

By the time I woke up properly, we were on the other side of Sacramento. It was late afternoon. We were still heading north-west on Highway 80. The countryside had changed in character – we were in the foothills of the Sierras. We came to Auburn, which had a clapboarded church with a steeple. My throat was getting parched. I glanced at Jerry.

"I'm thirsty," I said. "Any chance of stopping for a drink?"

"No point. Soon be there."

A few miles beyond Auburn, we turned off the freeway. The Datsun bounced along a rough, single-track road flanked by dry storm drains. On either side were huge enclosures separated from each other and the road by post-and-rail fencing. There wasn't much vegetation, and what there was looked scraggy and as dry as a bone. In front of us the parched hills rose in layers towards the snow-capped mountains.

Glancing back, I saw that the car was sending up a cloud of ochre-coloured dust, just like the dust I'd seen on Elvira Bladon's boots.

"How far is it now?" I said.

This time Jerry didn't answer.

A moment later, the Datsun began to lose speed. The monotony of the fence on the left was broken by an archway made of two upright pieces of wood with a third on top. A wooden sign was suspended by a pair of chains from the crossbar. It read: GOLD VALLEY RANCH.

Jerry swung the Datsun through the arch and over a cattle grid. The Datsun's suspension didn't like it but Jerry didn't care. We drove up a long drive which was even more dusty than the road.

Suddenly we came round the lee of a hill and I saw the house. It was a sprawling, one-level building on the crest of a low knoll. The walls were built, or at least faced, with redwood, which had weathered to a silvery grey colour. At one end there was a tapering chimneystack of undressed stone. At the other end was a flagpole. Beyond the ranch house itself, there was a smaller building – perhaps a bunkhouse or staff quarters. I could also make out a couple of corrals and a big barn.

Nothing moved except the Datsun and the dust. There were no horses or cattle, there were no people or cars.

The Datsun rolled to a halt at the front of the building. Jerry got out. He bent down and looked at me through the open window.

"You wait here," he said. "I'll go find Mr Lange."

He went inside the house, shutting the door behind him. Leaving me in the car struck me as odd, to say the least. But I already knew that Jerry's social skills were not his strong point. In any case, I could decide for myself what he meant by "here".

I got out of the car and walked slowly towards the barn. It was still warm, but the sky was overcast and there was a wind getting up. The house was much less pretentious than I'd expected. The place looked as if it hadn't always been a rich man's toy: once this might have been a working ranch.

I glanced at the windows, but nothing moved behind them. The absence of life surprised me. This was only a holiday house, I reminded myself, and it was probably empty for most of the year: perhaps that explained why it felt so desolate.

"Hey, man!" Jerry shouted behind me. "Where you going?"

I turned round. He waved me towards him. He was carrying a heavy-duty canvas bag, the kind designed for carrying tools. He opened the driver's door and put the bag carefully on the back seat. He straightened up.

"Mr Lange is at the mine," he said. "Let's go."

He got back into the car. I followed.

"What mine?"

Jerry started the engine and glanced at me. "Used to be a gold mine. What else? This is gold country."

He gunned the engine and we roared off down a dirt track that ran along the side of one of the corrals. This took us in a direction roughly parallel to the drive. But I couldn't see the drive itself because a long, low hill blocked it from sight.

"What's he doing down there?" I asked.

"Looking for a dog." He glanced at me again. "Dog named Bluey."

The track sloped downwards and went into a hairpin bend round a spur from the hill. After the bend, Jerry braked sharply. The rear wheels went into a slow skid. The Datsun slid to a halt beside a battered pick-up truck. The dust slowly settled round the car.

The hill enclosed us on three sides, making a small natural amphitheatre. The branches of a gnarled oak tree overhung the entrance to the mine, and a tunnel sloped down into the hill. It was one of those almost horizontal shafts called adits. The opening was supported with rough-hewn timbers.

The remains of a windlass stood in front of the entrance. A rusting, narrow-gauge railway ran into the mouth of the shaft. A small bogie with only two wheels lay across the track. It was a long time since they'd hauled any ore out of this mine.

There was something stagey about the scene. All it needed was an old boot and someone singing *Home on the Range*. It wasn't quite a cliché but it was trying hard.

Jerry put his hand on the door handle. There was a bead of sweat on his trim black moustache.

"Right, boy," he said. "Let's go."

We both got out of the car. Out of force of habit, I looked up into the sky. Two black dots which might have been vultures were circling high above us. I took a step towards the mine shaft.

Jerry slapped his thigh. "We'll maybe need a flashlight."

He ducked back into the car. I was aware of him rummaging in the bag on the back seat. I wandered over to the entrance of the mine. The tunnel sloped gently down into darkness. It was dry and rocky underfoot. The rails were still in place, though some of the sleepers had rotted. The part of the roof which I could see looked solid enough – it was supported at intervals by timber joists.

The Datsun's door slammed. I turned round. The first thing that struck me was that Jerry was smiling. This was weird in itself, because I had grown used to the idea that smiling didn't come naturally to him. It was also weird because it was the sort of smile you give when you've broken wind in front of your girlfriend's parents: the guy was embarrassed.

The smile widened until I thought his face would fall apart. He waved the torch, which was in his left hand, and moved out from the shelter of the car. Then I saw what was in his right hand. It was a gun.

The shock made my brain seize up. I knew I should do something. But there was nowhere to run to. I would be an easy target if I tried to scramble up the steep sides of the amphitheatre. Jerry was between me and the track that led back to the ranch. That only left the mine itself – and what chance did I have in the darkness against a man with a torch and a gun?

"Can't be too careful," Jerry said, moving towards me. "Know what we found down the mine in the fall? An old bear with a wounded leg. Meanest animal I ever saw."

I nodded. I didn't trust myself to say anything. I wondered whether the last few days had made me paranoid, too scared to think straight and prone to overreact. After all, this was America, where guns were as common as walking sticks.

I followed Jerry into the mine. The sweat was streaming down my back. I looked at the gun that dangled from his hand, the muzzle towards the floor. It was a heavy automatic, big enough to knock out a horse.

At first the going was easy enough because we had the light behind us, the shaft was straight and the gradient was gentle. The torch beam swung from side to side.

"Like a maze down here," Jerry said, without turning his head; he was getting more talkative by the minute. "You could wander for miles."

"Why can't the dog find his way out by sense of smell?" I asked, just to keep the conversation going.

"The dog? Right – poor old Bluey ain't got much sense of smell left. Must be twelve or thirteen by now. And if he gets down to the lower levels, there's a couple of big pits filled with water."

The track curved gently to the right. As we walked we dislodged pebbles, which skittered down the tunnel in front of us. While Jerry was speaking, the natural light behind us faded gradually to nothing. Now there was only the torch, its beam leaping from wall to floor, from floor to ceiling, from ceiling to wall.

"Watch the track," Jerry advised. "It can trip you up if you're not careful."

There was enough room in the tunnel for the pair of us to walk abreast with the track running between us. The further down we got the cooler and mustier the air became. I wished I had thought to bring a jersey.

"Shouldn't we give Mr Lange a shout?" I suggested.

"No point till we've got past that," Jerry said.

The torch beam snaked down the tunnel to a pile of rubble twenty yards ahead. The rubble blocked about three-quarters of the tunnel. There was a patch of darkness in the top right-hand corner – I guessed that was the way through.

"A roof fall?" I said.

"It's safe enough. We shored it up."

We reached the rubble. Jerry scrambled up it and wriggled through the hole, still holding the gun and the torch. He waited for me on the other side, holding the torch for me.

I followed him through the gap. Here, apart from the torch, it was completely dark. Jerry flashed the beam around in a circle. Immediately in front of us was a gate made from a lattice work of iron bars, with its hinges sunk into the rock itself and a heavy lock mounted on the other side. Beyond it the tunnel widened out into a junction where four or five tunnels met.

"What's it for?" I asked.

"Security. It's as old as the mine. This was a very rich seam."

Jerry pushed the gate and it opened with squeals from the hinges. I followed him into the little junction.

"Mr Lange," he called.

The echoes of his shout bounced off the rock faces and went whispering off into the distance. I listened. I heard nothing – only Jerry's breathing and the diminishing whisper of the echoes.

"Mr Lange!"

Once again we waited. Once again the echoes became whispers and the whispers diminished into silence. Jerry's torch beam moved restlessly round the crossroads.

Suddenly another torch beam, more powerful than Jerry's, leapt out of the tunnel on my right. The light hit my face like a blow.

"That's him."

It was a man's voice, a voice I'd never heard before. And what I heard, even in those two words, was the note of triumph in it.

"What is this?" I snapped. "Who are you?"

It was not exactly an inspired reaction. Sometimes inspiration requires a little warning. I turned towards Jerry partly to get away from the torch beam. But Jerry was no longer beside me. I was standing alone in the darkness. The two torch beams were dancing back towards the iron gate. Footsteps pattered after them. The hinges squealed. Iron clanged on iron. There was a metallic scrape which I knew must be the lock shooting home.

For a second, one of the torches was on the hand holding the key. The light glinted on a heavy gold ring. The beam slid through the bars and across the floor of the tunnel to me.

"Wouldn't it be better to shoot him?" Jerry said. "Just to make quite sure."

"You could bring the tunnel down," said the first voice. "Besides, I want it to be a natural death."

The other beam shone throught the bars and caught me in the face again.

"He's young," Jerry pointed out. "Looks fit, too."

"It's cold down there."

"He might find the water."

"What the hell?" said the first voice. "If he finds the water, he could live for a month – maybe even two. If he doesn't, I'd give him a week, ten days at the most."

At last I managed to speak. "Why are you doing this? Who are you? What's going on?"

But the torch beams had already slipped away from me. For an instant one of the beams backlit a head in profile: someone who knew nothing about birds of prey could have described the silhouette as hawklike. I heard the two men scrambling up the pile of rubble.

"Whichever way it goes," the first voice was saying, "it's going to be one of those tragic accidents."

They had reached the other side of the pile of rubble. I stared at the dim light from their torches as if wishing hard enough would make the light grow brighter; instead, it grew dimmer. I listened to their footsteps as they walked up the tunnel towards the light. When I could no longer hear the footsteps, I listened to the rustling of small stones dislodged from the rubble. When even the stones had stopped moving, I listened to the silence.

I thought about shouting. But I didn't. Even if they heard me, I knew it would be no use. Nothing I could say was going to make them change their mind. I knew for sure it was me whom they wanted to kill. They had shone the torch on my face. And I thought I knew why, too: they thought I could identify the man who had attacked, perhaps murdered, Carson.

I moved slowly in the direction where I thought the light had been. After what seemed like an age my outstretched fingertips touched bare rock. I'd lost my way in less than ten metres. Total darkness is completely disorientating. I stretched my left arm out as far as I could. I touched rock, nothing but rock that felt like cool, fine-grade sandpaper. I tried in the other direction. More rock. I opened my mouth to let out a howl of anguish.

My fingertips touched iron.

I pushed and pulled the gate – just in case: maybe they had forgotten to lock it. The gate refused to move. I tried to lift it off its hinges. I tried to rattle it open. I tried to knock it open by using my body as a battering ram. I tried to kick it open. And when all that had failed, I tried prayer. That failed, too.

I sat down with my back against the cold iron of the bars, and tried to work out what to do next. Despite the physical exercise, I was cold. I had just had a sentence of death passed on me. Terror lowers the temperature. I made a half-hearted attempt to persuade myself that this was a cruel joke. It went like this: other people knew I was coming to the ranch, and sooner or later they would want to know what had happened to me; therefore locking me up down here must be somebody's idea of a joke.

That idea foundered as soon as I'd thought of it. Only four people had known I was coming to the ranch. Marguerite and Mike Izmidlian, Jerry, and the man with the gold ring and the predatory profile – who I assumed was Magnus Lange. Mike worked for Magnus Lange; and what had happened here and in Turkey would only make sense if the Izmidlian clan were in alliance with Magnus Lange. I was still no nearer finding out why. I knew that Carson was – or perhaps by this time had been – a threat to them: so they tried to kill him. Had they intended to destroy the Sanctuary as well – or would that have been merely a by-product of Carson's death? And where did Elvira Bladon come in?

It is not a pleasant sensation to realize you're just an insignificant piece in someone else's game. I didn't know who all the other pieces were, I didn't know the rules, and I didn't even know the object of the game.

I tried to think about the situation from another angle. What would happen if I didn't get in touch with Phyllis at the Sanctuary in the next day or two? What would happen if I didn't go back to my room at the Wharf Lodge? The answer to both questions was not a lot. Phyllis would start telephoning Rampro, and so perhaps would the hotel. And in both cases, they'd get Mike on the other end of the line. Rampro would pay my bill at the Wharf Lodge, and Mike would collect my belongings. He'd tell Phyllis about the presentation, and he'd say how well it had gone. He'd stick to the truth, as far as he could.

There was absolutely no reason why he shouldn't tell her about our celebratory lunch at the Lebanese restaurant owned by his father. It didn't take too much imagination to realize that the manager would say whatever monsieur le patron required of him. Anything Mike said would be confirmed. Mike would probably tell Phyllis that I told him and Marguerite that I was going to spend the afternoon sightseeing, and that when he left me I had intended to take a bus or a taxi back to San Francisco. Jerry had been waiting for us in the parking lot of the restaurant. I didn't think there had been any witnesses to see me climbing into the Datsun.

No, as far as I could see there would be nothing to connect my disappearance with the Gold Valley Ranch. I remembered that long, cheerful lunch with Mike and Marguerite, and how it had seemed possible to mix business with pleasure. Which business? Whose pleasure?

The bars of the iron gate were digging into my shoulder. I was sitting with my back against one of the rock walls and my arms wrapped round my legs, trying to conserve heat. I was getting cold. And the colder I got, the sooner I would die.

I still had my watch. It had its own light, so I thought I'd find out what the time was: nearly seven o'clock in the evening. Knowing I could measure time made me feel a little better. I had regained a tiny fragment of control. On the other hand the light that illuminated the display made no impact whatsoever on the profound darkness all around. That was depressing.

I tried to distract myself by thinking what Jerry and his boss might do now. They would find my coat and bag and destroy them. They would clean the car thoroughly to remove any trace of my presence.

They'd mentioned that there was water underground. I was desperately thirsty. I knew that water would give me a much better chance of survival, because Magnus Lange had been kind enough to tell me, but could I be sure there was any water to find? Perhaps that remark had merely been designed to set me wandering deeper and deeper into the dark labyrinth of tunnels.

I did what I should have done at the start of my imprisonment: I made an inventory of my possessions. I was still wearing the clothes I had worn for the presentation and lunch, though I'd left the jacket in the Datsun. I had my passport in a shirt pocket. At least they should be able to identify my body, assuming it was ever found. I also had my watch and some money in a trouser pocket. Apart from that, my sole possession was a paper napkin emblazoned with the logo of the Wharf Lodge Hotel. I wondered if they were edible. My wallet was made of leather, and I'd heard of people reduced to chewing leather in sieges.

I stuffed my belongings back in my pocket. I huddled down against the wall again. No sense in wasting energy. Soon, I thought, I would try exploring. Ten metres to the left and back to the gate. Ten metres to the right and back to the gate. If I always followed the wall I couldn't lose myself – could I?

I sat there squeezing my legs and trying to summon up courage to move. Despair had taken away my will to act.

The darkness was inside me as well as outside. I sat there, and time ticked by unnoticed. I felt my life was running out like a stopwatch counting down to zero.

I heard a sound. I hadn't heard anything but my own breathing for what seemed like hours. It was the noise a pebble makes if someone kicks it. I listened. I heard nothing.

"Is anyone there?" I called.

I listened. There was no answer. The silence lapped around me like a black tide.

Then, just as I had given up hope again, I heard footsteps.

TWENTY

"Adam Davy?"

The whispered words stirred echoes that ran deep into the mine. I shivered.

"Here," I yelled. "Help!"

"Hush."

Whispers make voices strangely anonymous, but the urgency in that one word was unmistakable. I stood up. My knees screamed with pain. I'd been crouching in the cold for too long. I heard someone scrambling over the rubble that partly blocked the access shaft. I started to tremble with a mixture of hope and fear. My hands grasped the bars of the gate and squeezed.

A torch beam leapt out of the darkness and locked on to my face. After the hours of darkness, the light had the impact of a slap. I let go of the bars and reeled back, covering my eyes with my hands.

"It's me. Elvira. Don't be scared."

"I'm not scared," I snarled. I remembered to whisper: "Just move the light off my face."

I wasn't scared – just terrified. But that was my affair. The torch beam moved away.

"Don't talk, just listen," she hissed. "We haven't much time."

As she was speaking she tried to push something

between two of the vertical bars. I couldn't see what it was. It was too large to get through. She swore.

"Try at the bottom," I suggested. "There's more room."

She bent down, and so did I. By the light of her torch, I saw what she was pushing underneath the gate: it was another torch, a small one encased in black rubber. As I took it, my hand brushed hers. I almost gasped. For me, the extraordinary thing was the living warmth of her skin. For her it must have been like touching a corpse.

"They're going to dynamite the roof of the tunnel tonight," she murmured. "You've got to get out. It could set off a chain reaction down there. Half the timbers are rotten."

"All I need is the key," I said.

"I haven't got it. You'll have to swim."

"Swim?"

"Hush. Sound travels at night. Listen. You got to turn round so your back's to the gate, then take the first shaft on the left. After that, every time you have a choice, you go right. You go right and you go down. Then you come to water. It's an underground river. Follow it downstream as far as you can. Then dive. Use the torch. There's an underwater channel. It'll bring you out in the open. I'll be waiting."

She pushed something else underneath the gate.

"A bag for your clothes."

As I picked up the bag, our hands touched again. I had a hundred questions I needed to ask. For example: why should I believe her?

But she left me no time for questions. She turned and scrambled up the pile of rubble. I switched on the torch she had given me. I was just in time to see her legs disappearing through the gap. But she turned back. For an instant I saw her face. Neither of us spoke. Then she was gone.

I switched off the torch and listened. She moved very quietly. Occasionally I heard the scrape of a pebble. That was all.

Though I didn't trust her in the least, I was cheered by what had happened. I had a torch, which increased my options. Even if Elvira Bladon had been telling me lies again, she had managed to improve my morale.

I decided that I had nothing to lose by exploring. I folded the bag, which felt as if it were made of heavy-duty polythene, and tucked it into my belt.

As I moved towards the shaft on the left, I thought I heard the faint rumble of an engine. I might well have imagined it. I was probably too far into the mine to hear the sound of a car coming into the amphitheatre. But even the possibility I had heard a car made me anxious to be gone. I had no desire to be buried under a mound of rubble for all eternity.

The shaft on the left was the smallest of the five that met at the junction. It was very narrow, and curved slightly like a bow – perhaps following a fault in the rock. The walls were irregular, and the ceiling was low. Pit props reinforced the roof. There were no rails here. Maybe this had been a subsidiary shaft designed for emergency access or ventilation.

The shaft was so narrow in places that I had to

wriggle sideways to get through. I began to worry about the quality of the air. Once you start to worry about ventilation, it's easy enough to begin thinking that you're feeling faint. I wished that Elvira had given me an idea of how long it would take to reach the underground river.

The shaft forked. I took the right-hand turning, even though it seemed to me to be going down less sharply than the one on the left. After the fork the shaft gradually widened. But it made up for this by being not much more than a metre high.

There was a sudden sharp pain in the crown of my head. I reeled back. I had hit a knob of rock projecting from the ceiling. I touched the place where it hurt, and then I put my hand to my mouth: I tasted blood. Unexpectedly, a laugh forced its way out of me. I wondered how long you could survive by drinking your own blood.

After a second I stopped laughing and started to worry instead – partly because the laughter suggested I was getting delirious; and partly because I might be wasting oxygen. The trouble with being shut up by yourself, I told myself, and especially in a place like this, is that you begin to lose contact with reality.

As I stumbled down and down into the depths of the rock, I found my mind filling with thoughts of hermits and political prisoners and lunatics in solitary confinement. To my horror, I realized that I was panting, and had been for some time. The air was getting worse.

I tripped and fell heavily against the wall of the

tunnel. I grunted with pain. Worst of all, I dropped the torch.

The next few seconds stretched into a century of horror. As the torch was falling, thoughts galloped through my mind in a panic-stricken horde. If the bulb broke, I would be trapped in the darkness. If the torch rolled away, and I couldn't find it, I would be left down here for ever. If the air was getting worse, then the longer I had to spend down here, the worse my chances of survival. It seemed to me that the rock was pressing in on me from all directions – above, below and from the sides. The rock squeezed me like a vice and pushed the breath out of my body.

The torch hit the floor. It bounced and rolled. It came to rest against the wall. The beam streamed down the shaft. I picked up the torch and held it tightly in both hands. Despite the chilly air, the sweat was pouring off me.

Twenty metres on, I reached another junction. On the left and in the middle, broad shafts led downwards; and to the right there was a hole at the level of my chest.

"Every time you have a choice," Elvira had said, "you go right."

I poked the torch into the hole, which was not much wider than my shoulders, and peered into it. The shaft wriggled down through the rock like a corkscrew. But was it really a shaft? How do you define a shaft? When was a shaft a shaft and not an accidental hole? The questions set up a buzzing in my head. I felt faint.

I hoisted myself up to the opening and crawled into it. The hole was as narrow as I had feared, if not worse. I edged forward on my stomach. The air was getting worse and worse. If the hole became much tighter, I wouldn't be able to move. I would be jammed in this forgotten cranny in the earth's crust for all eternity.

I forced my mind to go black and blank. Forward and downward: move an elbow, move a knee; over and over again. Thinking was a luxury I couldn't afford. My only chance was blindly to obey Elvira's instructions.

I had the torch in my right hand as I snaked slowly downwards. My forearm ran up against a sliver of rock like the blade of a carving knife. It sliced into the skin. A few seconds later it cut open the front of my shirt. If I didn't suffocate or starve to death, I thought, then I'd probably bleed to death instead. Oddly enough, I found this idea almost cheering. The odds were so stacked against me that I felt I had nothing left to lose.

The hole wriggled round one of the turns of the corkscrew and suddenly opened up. I found I could stand up to my full height on a level surface. I panned the torch around. This wasn't a shaft: this was a long, cigar-shaped cave, so long that the torch beam wouldn't reach the end. The rock was a browny-reddish colour, but the torch beam caught on a million metallic reflectors, minute but glittering.

A gold mine, Jerry had said; maybe the gold down here wasn't economic to work, or maybe it wasn't really gold. I set out walking towards the end of the cave. My shoes crunched through the fine, soft sand that lay on the floor of the cave.

The torch beam picked out the glinting sheen of water. I'd found the river.

My breathing was ragged by the time I reached the water. I knew why. It wasn't from the exertion, but from the air. My lungs were crying out for oxygen.

The water was moving very, very slowly from left to right. I crouched and stuck a finger in it. It felt ice cold. I swung the torch from one side to the other. I couldn't see where the water came from or where it went. I turned right and began to follow the river downstream.

The cave through which the river ran was narrower than the one I'd just left. There was just enough room for the river and for the shelf of rock along which I was walking. Judging by the markings on the walls, when the river was in spate it was much higher and the path I was on would be submerged.

My head felt as if someone had stuffed it with cotton wool. I concentrated on keeping my breathing as shallow as possible. I had the torch in my left hand and I used my right to steady myself against the wall. At one point the path narrowed, so suddenly that it took me by surprise. I staggered, and my body swung out over the water. The glistening river was ready to receive me into its darkness. I wrenched myself back. Not yet, I thought, not yet.

Without warning the path vanished: it ran like a ramp into the water. I shone the torch downstream. The river flowed on for another ten metres. After that there was a wall of solid rock. Either the river turned a corner or it flowed through an underwater outlet.

I wondered whether I'd misheard Elvira. Maybe she'd said upstream not downstream. In my heart of hearts I knew quite well that she had told me to go downstream. What I really wanted was an excuse for not having to get into that dark water. I was afraid I would never come out of its cold embrace. To my fears of suffocating, starving and bleeding to death were added a fourth: drowning.

A dull boom ran along the river. At first it was so faint I could hardly hear it. The volume increased for an instant and then diminished to silence. It was the first noise I'd heard other than those made by me for what seemed like hours. All that cotton wool must have been making my mind work slowly. It was at least three seconds before I realized what the sound signified. They had dynamited the roof of the access shaft.

Now there were other and nearer sounds. Pattering and cracking and creaking and a rushing of air. The entire mine complex could be on the verge of collapse.

The new fear, of being buried alive, gave me that final impetus I needed. I tugged the plastic bag out of my belt and opened it up. The bag, the torch, the quick, clear directions – Elvira seemed to have thought of everything. Almost everything – if only she could have thought of a way to make me trust her. Her instructions might be designed to save my life. But they could just as well amount to a labour-saving method of persuading a murder victim to dispose of his corpse before he actually died.

That line of thought led to madness. I propped up the torch on the path. I heard the buttons plopping into the water as I ripped off my shirt. Shoes and socks were next. I put the trousers in the bag, fastened the neck and looped the handles through the belt. I strapped on the belt, picked up the torch and walked slowly into the water.

It was so cold I nearly screamed. The water slid up my body like a band of iron. I wished I'd left my socks and shoes on because the rock cut into my bare feet.

The water reached waist level. The chill was agonizing: I heard myself making a continuous keening wail. I shone the torch in the direction the river was flowing. There was a blank wall of rock in front of me, and rock to either side. Somewhere down there, if Elvira was right, there was a way out to the open air. I'd hoped that the current might guide me to the outlet channel. But the river was moving too slowly for that.

A pain lanced through my chest, piercing the duller agony of the freezing water. Air – I needed air more than I'd ever needed anything. I launched myself into the water with a great splash of spray. With the bag bobbing behind me and the torch in my hand, I swum a few clumsy strokes towards the wall of rock.

I tried to dive. The water streamed past my open eyes. My chest was a mass of stabbing, twisting pains that pushed outwards against my ribcage as though trying to tear it apart. The water was almost clear. In the underwater world, shapes and colours took on a strange, fluid life of their own.

The pains grew worse. I had to surface for another

mouthful of bad air. My teeth were chattering. I twisted in the water and dived down again. With the torch in front of me I explored the face of the rock. Somewhere there had to be a channel.

Then I saw it. The channel was no more than a patch of darkness in the bottom right-hand corner of the river bed. I dived down and swam into it. I swam perhaps a couple of metres, my chest bursting, before my free hand jarred against a barrier of rock which blocked the tunnel like an immovable curtain. I flicked the torch beam over it. It was solid. I turned the light on the walls, the floor and the ceiling. I couldn't see the smallest crack. There was no way round the barrier.

A red haze of pain filled my mind and body. I had reached a dead end. Maybe Elvira had betrayed me after all. But surely the water had to go somewhere? Maybe there was another channel. I tried to ignore the possibility that instead there might be a vertical sinkhole dropping down into the bowels of the earth.

I struggled to turn round in the narrow space. My limbs thrashed against the wall. Careless of cutting myself on the rock, I used the torch to lever myself round. At last I was swimming back the way I had come. I rushed up to the surface of the river. My head burst out of the water. I sucked the foul air deep into my lungs.

As I let out my breath in a long, shuddering sigh, the world went completely dark. The torch had given up.

The darkness settled around me. Automatically I

swum towards the bank. My feet scraped on rock. I stood up. The water was up to my waist. The soles of my feet were much less painful than they had been. They were so cold that I could hardly feel them at all.

So this, I thought, is it: the end of the road. Time was running out. Without light, my chances of finding out where the river went to had narrowed to vanishing point.

Instead of despair, I felt angry. I started to swear. I was going to die: that was all I could think of. I no longer cared about how to conserve air and energy. My voice rose to a shout. I used every swear word I knew in three languages. When at last I ran out of steam, I threw the torch as hard as I could into the darkness.

There was a thud as the torch's rubber insulation hit the rock. Suddenly there was a light in front of me. My eyes were dazzled. I blinked.

The torch had fallen on the path running along the river. The jolt had made it work again – there must have been a faulty connection somewhere inside. The beam shone upriver; after a few metres the light lost itself in the immensity of the darkness.

I scrambled back to the path and picked up the torch. I waded back towards the rock face at the end of the tunnel. I carried the torch gingerly. I was terrified that the light would vanish again. On the other hand, my legs felt heavier than lead and I wanted more than anything to lie down and close my eyes. The humiliating truth was that part of me wished that the torch had not come on again.

For the third time I dived down to search for the

water outlet. This time I concentrated on the left-hand side. There was nothing – just shiny, smooth rock.

I resurfaced for some more air. My strength was ebbing fast, and so was my will. I had never realized how much survival depended on the will to survive. I wasn't sure I could manage another dive. "One more time," I told myself, "just one more time." I knew that if I didn't try now I would never try again. Tiredness, cold and lack of oxygen had sapped my energy.

For the last time I dived – clumsily, like a wounded animal. I swam lower and ran the torch along the rock wall. It was a smooth, unbroken surface. The torch beam dipped down to the sand on the floor. Out of the corner of my eye I saw a shadow.

I swam towards it. It wasn't a shadow, but the mouth of a hole. It was just to the right of the cul-de-sac I had already explored. I hadn't noticed it before for two reasons. First, it was not at the end of the tunnel but round the corner to the side. Second, it was set low down in the angle where the rock wall met the rock floor. It was shaped like an eye. The opening was about a metre wide and two-thirds of a metre high.

I swam into it. A narrow channel sloped downwards at a gentle gradient. It was too narrow to swim properly so I kicked my legs and pulled myself along with my hands. Here, unlike in the river itself, the force of the current was perceptible. It drew me onwards and downwards.

The pain in my chest was worse than ever. It felt as if someone had hammered nails into it. The need to breathe anything, even water, was also impossible to resist.

I let the torch go, so I could claw myself a little faster down the channel. The blood drummed in my ears and the beat grew faster and louder. The pain in my chest vibrated with the thudding of the drums.

Sheet lightning streaked across the darkness, pulsing in time with the pain. By the light of the flashes I saw faces: my mother's, Becky's, Elvira's. I saw an intensely blue sky, empty except for a single hawk wheeling and turning, readying itself for the kill.

I heard rushing water. I felt cool air on my shoulders. I tried to breathe. I got a mouthful of air mixed with water. I opened my eyes. I saw the moon.

TWENTY-ONE

I lay in the darkness. I wasn't sleepy. I watched and listened. I smelt woodsmoke and coffee.

The fire crackled. The wind sighed in the branches. In the distance, a woman was singing an Irish folk song, a lament for someone or something, and accompanying herself softly on a guitar.

My teeth had stopped chattering about twenty minutes earlier. I was lying wrapped in two blankets inside a sleeping bag. My body was a mass of dull aches and pains, as though a gang of skinheads had been kicking the hell out of it. I didn't mind much. The aches and pains were petty in comparison with what I'd experienced a few hours before. The main things were that I felt warm and the air smelt clean and fresh.

I didn't like to think how lucky I'd been. Another twenty minutes down the mine would probably have killed me. If the channel had been much longer, I would have drowned. And if Elvira hadn't been waiting to drag me out of the pool below the spring, I wouldn't have had the energy to pull myself out of the water.

My memories of the last few hours were a jumble. I remembered Elvira pounding my chest to make me bring up the water I'd swallowed. But I didn't remember how she'd got me into the back of the

Nissan Patrol, or how long we'd driven through the night. She'd put me across the back seat and covered me with the sleeping bag and a mound of blankets. I must have slipped in and out of a doze, neither awake nor dreaming, but oscillating uncomfortably between the two. The next thing I remember with any clarity was her opening the door of the Nissan and saying I could come out and sit by the fire.

There were big trees all around. The stars were brilliant specks of silver. The air was cool on my face. There was a slight breeze, enough to make a healthy draught for the fire.

Elvira's silhouette reared up between me and the flames. She crouched down beside me.

"You want some coffee now?"

I sat up slowly. She gave me a mug. I clasped my hands round it; my fingertips were still numb and dead.

"How are you feeling?"

"Improving." I took a sip of coffee. It was black, scalding hot and very sweet. "Thank you."

She looked away. "Are you hungry?"

"Not yet. We need to talk."

"Yes."

But for the moment neither of us said anything. We sat there, blowing the steam from our coffee. I watched her. Half her face was in shadow. The other half was lit by the fire, giving skin a golden-red glow. I noticed that she was breathing quickly.

"Where are we?" I asked. "Some sort of campsite in the Sierras?"

"Yes – I figured it was safer to go someplace with

other people around. Though if we'd have gone to a motel, we'd have been easier to trace."

"By your uncle Magnus?"

There was a pause. Then she shrugged. "I guess so."

Another silence settled over us. It was comfortable sitting there and drinking coffee. There was no hurry. We didn't have all the time in the world but at least we had a few hours of it. Elvira threw a branch on the fire. Sparks shot upwards and fizzled into the darkness.

"Where exactly are we?"

"About halfway between Auburn and Lake Tahoe. Give or take a few miles."

"How far from the ranch?"

"Fifty or sixty miles. They won't think of looking here."

I stared at her. "They?"

She was silent. She looked at the fire and I looked at her.

"Magnus Lange, your uncle," I said. "Jerry – the guy with the little moustache." I waited but she gave no sign that she'd heard. "The Izmidlians. Mike and his father for sure. I'm not sure about Marguerite. Then of course there's the British contingent who hang around the Sanctuary. That guy Jason up at Well Farm and his girlfriend. They were the ones who jumped on me outside Ardross Hall. Did you know about that? Then there's the middle-aged man with a beard who drives an old Metro. It adds up to quite an army."

This time the silence wasn't at all comfortable. It grew longer and longer. If I wasn't careful she was going to clam up on me again.

"Have I missed anyone out? Is there anyone else we should be looking out for?"

Elvira shook her head.

"Listen," I said. "We can't turn the clock back. I'm part of this now. When people start trying to kill you, you don't have a chance to stay on the sidelines. It's just not an option."

She was silent for a moment longer. Then she said, "What happened when you got to the ranch?"

"Jerry said Magnus was at the mine looking for a dog named Bluey."

"He was my dog." She sounded irritated. "He died last fall."

"When we got there, Jerry produced a gun. There was another man down the mine."

"Magnus?"

"I didn't see his face."

"Pity."

"They locked me in." I stopped, remembering the despair I'd felt. "Then you came. How did you know I was there?"

"I knew there was something wrong when I saw you in Menlo Park with Mike and Marguerite. First I thought I couldn't trust you, that they'd done a deal with you. Then I thought maybe they were fooling you. So I followed you to the restaurant. But I didn't get a chance to see you on your own. Then Jerry showed up and collected you from the parking lot."

"They said Magnus wanted me to stay the night at the ranch."

"So I tailed you. Had to keep well back, but it was obvious where Jerry was going. I skirted the ranch, went into the hills and watched what happened through the binoculars. I saw Jerry driving you down to the mine. Next thing I knew, he and Magnus came out and started loading dynamite and detonators into the pick-up. They went inside the house and I came to look for you."

She made it sound easy, but suppose Magnus and Jerry had seen her? They couldn't have afforded a witness.

"You saved my life," I said.

She hurried on, as if she hadn't heard. "I knew the stream that feeds the pool came out of the mine. When I was a kid, Bluey got trapped up there one summer when there wasn't much rain. It was easy to crawl up the hole to the cave. The stream just trickled out of the rocks. But today it was more like a flood. I thought you wouldn't be able to get through... I thought maybe I'd killed you."

"It wasn't you who was trying to kill me." I saw that she was trembling. "What is it?"

"I'm frightened," Elvira said.

"Then we'd better go to the police."

"Going to the police is one of the things that frightens me most of all."

"What have you done? I'll help you, whatever it is."

For the first time she looked at me. I saw all of her face in the firelight. It looked like a golden mask.

"You don't understand," she said. "I'm not

frightened for myself."

"Who are you frightened for?"

"An old woman. This could kill her." She hesitated. "It's not just that. It's no good going to the cops if I don't have proof. Rock solid, absolute, incontravertible proof. If I start making unsupported allegations, Magnus's lawyers will sue the hell out of me."

"But he's your uncle." I realized that was a stupid thing to say before the words were out of my mouth. "I'd back you up."

"That won't stop him suing." As she was speaking, her voice, never loud, grew fainter and fainter. "Not if he thinks there's money in it. Something like that would give him just the chance he wants. And even if you backed me up he'd find some way to undermine your testimony. You didn't see his face down there, did you?"

She started staring at the fire again. It was true that it would be difficult to implicate Magnus directly, however strong the circumstantial evidence. He operated through intermediaries for most of the time. Had it been Magnus whom I had seen at the hospital: the hawkfaced man who had stabbed Carson? I didn't know. But if it was, it would explain why Magnus had tried so hard to murder me. He thought I could identify him.

I decided to approach from another angle: "Why were you trying to find out about Carson?"

"I'm trying to stop him getting killed."

"By Magnus?"

Elvira ignored the question. We concentrated on our coffee. I glanced around. There were several other camp fires. The nearest was about twenty metres away. The distant guitarist had crossed the Atlantic and started playing a cowboy song about boots and saddles. At another fire, a guy was laughing – a real belly-laugh that sounded as though it would go on for ever.

The warmth of the mug was making my fingertips tingle. My mouth widened into a smile. The memory of the mine, of that cold and suffocating living death, seemed to belong to someone else. The importance of everything else had diminished, if only for the time being. The only thing that was really important was the fact that I was warm and alive.

On impulse I turned to Elvira. "If you won't talk to the police, you might as well talk to me. It can't make things any worse. And it may just help."

She looked at me over the rim of her mug. "Why should I trust you?"

The rich are always suspicious of other people's motives. They have to be. That's another of the things that makes them different from the rest of us.

I said, "Because I owe you. Because I already know some of it. And because you've got nothing to lose." I waited a moment and then added: "If you don't, I'll have to go to the police myself. Look at it from my point of view. I can't just hang around waiting for Magnus to dream up another way of trying to kill me."

She sighed, and it was as if all the resistance was seeping out of her.

"You're in trouble," I said. "I'm in trouble. The

way I see it, our only hope of working something out is if we work together."

Suddenly she said: "Do you know what Rampro is worth?"

I looked blankly at her. "Of course I don't." I'd never known anyone who had such a knack of taking me by surprise.

"Neither do I. But last year the profit was nearly forty-eight million dollars on a turnover of three hundred and fifty-four million. And that's just the tip of the iceberg. It doesn't take into account everyone who depends on Rampro – the subsidiaries, and the suppliers, and the dealers."

"For example, it doesn't take into account the Izmidlians?"

She nodded. "If Rampro goes down, so will they. And if Rampro goes on growing, they will too. That's assuming Rampro chooses to go on doing business with them. It's as simple as that."

"Are you telling me why the Izmidlians are happy to do what Magnus Lange wants?"

"Yes, but it's more than that. In the end this is all about Rampro. Rampro is a great big money-making machine. You know – like the goose that lays the golden eggs."

"I don't get it. I doubt if Carson's ever heard of Rampro."

Elvira rubbed her eyes. "It's hard to explain to an outsider."

"Try. You have to try."

"There are two things you have to know. The first

is that Rampro isn't a public company. It's privately owned. In theory it's administered by a trust set up by my grandfather, Gregory Lange. When he dies, the company's going to be equally divided among his children. Or at least that was the idea. My mother died last year, but I'm her heir – so her share will come to me."

"Your mother and Magnus – anyone else?"

"That's the problem. I don't know." She got up in one easy, fluid movement and stood over me. "The second thing is something I want you to read."

She went over to the Nissan and pulled out a bag, which she brought back to the fire. First she took out a jersey, which she pulled over her head. Then from a zipped pocket in the lining of the bag, she took out an airmail letter. She rummaged in the bag and dug out a torch, which she gave to me, along with the letter.

"It's from my grandfather to my mother," Elvira said. "She deposited it with her lawyer. When she died, it came to me. I've never shown it to anyone else before."

I weighed the letter in my hand. The envelope felt as if it contained several sheets of paper. There was a handwritten address – to a woman called Mrs Jean Bladon living in San Francisco. The sender's name and address was on the top left-hand corner of the envelope. When Gregory Lange had written the letter, he'd been staying at the Gold Valley Ranch.

"Are you sure you want me to read this?"

"Right now I'm not sure of anything," she said roughly. "Except I know that they were trying to kill you. That must make us more or less on the same side."

She threw some more wood on the fire and crouched down beside me. I took the letter from the envelope and unfolded it carefully. The paper had the dry quality that comes with age. The creases were deep and discoloured. There was a date at the head of the letter. It had been written over ten years earlier. Elvira must have been a child, still in single figures. I couldn't imagine her as a little girl.

Gregory's old-fashioned handwriting marched stiffly across the pages of his letter. He'd used black ink. I guessed that he'd been the sort of man who likes a fountain pen. It occurred to me that I was thinking about him as though he were dead – whereas he seemed to be very much alive. So why couldn't Elvira go to him for help? He was the obvious person.

I smoothed the letter out on my lap and began to read. The light was bad but the black, four-square writing was easy to decipher. And after the first few lines, I was fascinated. Reading that letter was like getting a private view of someone else's life.

Dear Jean,

Sometimes it's easier to give bad news in a letter. And I hope this won't come as too much of a shock to you. Your mother isn't a well woman. If she gets another coronary like that, the doc says it will kill her. I'm going to retire. She needs to live somewhere quiet, somewhere without people always making demands on her. Maybe we'll stay here at the ranch – but more likely we'll go back to Santa

257

Barbara. She would like that, I know.

When someone you love is near to death, it has a way of making you face up to your other responsibilities. And maybe you see them in perspective too. First, I need to discuss the money side of things with you. I want Magnus to take over the day-to-day running of the company as CEO. I'm planning to appoint some trustees as well, to share the responsibilities – both Rampro and the real estate business. They will include you, of course, and John Izmidlian. The handover process isn't going to be easy for anyone, but I had to stop running Rampro some day. It's better to do it like this than come out feet first in a wooden box.

My guess is that in the next decade the company is going to expand and expand. This is a growth industry. Think how mini- computers have taken off in the last five years. How you choose to run the company will be your affair – yours and Magnus's and the other trustees. I'll try not to look over your shoulder.

The next thing I have to tell you is that I've redrafted my will. Yesterday the lawyer brought it up to the ranch for my signature. In the old one, everything eventually came to you and Magnus, apart from a few bequests. This is the hardest part for me to write. In the new will, I have directed that once your mother and I are dead, my estate should be divided between my three children. Not two. If that is a shock to you, imagine what it would be to your mother. It is vital that she never hears of this. The news would kill her.

Perhaps most of us have something in their lives that they're ashamed of. This is mine. All I can say in my

258

defense is that it was wartime, and things were different then. Often it was hard to believe we would ever get back to the States. Responsibilities at home were unreal. They didn't amount to a row of beans beside the fact we might well be killed before we had a chance to live. I'm not trying to excuse what I did, I'm trying to explain it.

I married your mother at the end of '43. The army gave us three days for a honeymoon, and then they shipped me off to England. That was a bad time. I missed your mother. I was scared as hell I'd get killed. And England was a god-awful place. The Brits used to stare at us. You could see the envy in their eyes. What they really felt sore about was that we'd missed having the hell bombed out of us. We'd missed the rationing and the queues and all the dreariness of life in wartime. All the girls wanted to be your friend because of the nylons and cigarettes and chocolate.

Not all the girls – Lorna wasn't like that. That was her name. Lorna Carson. She lived in a town called Lewes, in Sussex, which was near the camp where we were stationed before we went to Normandy. She worked in a jewellers' shop in the hill that goes up towards the castle. I went in there to buy a ring for your mother. There was no one else in the shop. I don't know why but we started talking. Then she said it was her lunchtime and I'd have to go. I said we could finish the conversation over lunch.

That's how it started. We had lunch a few times, saw a couple of movies. It was all very innocent. We never talked about the war. Does that seem strange to you? We didn't talk much about our spouses. I knew her husband was in the army. He was in the engineers, I think, in Italy.

259

They had a daughter too, but I didn't see much of her.

It was a strange time, those months before D-Day. Nothing seemed real. A lot of the guys I was with felt they had to pack in as much life as they could. Once we invaded France, there might not be any life left. I guess I'm trying to make excuses.

We used to go for walks in the country. One afternoon in April, it started raining. It was always raining in England, but this was something different. The water came out of the sky like it was never going to stop. We got caught in it. The nearest shelter was a church in the middle of nowhere. That was when it happened. It was only the once. But that was enough.

Jean, I didn't mean to tell you all this. But once you start remembering, the memories keep coming back. Not much more, I promise. A few weeks later, we were moved to another camp. And soon after that, we were in Normandy. I never saw her again. I never went back to England. I could have done in '45, on my way back to the States, but I didn't want to. I thought some things were better left as they were.

But I had a letter in the summer of '44. She said she was pregnant, that I was the father. I sent her some money, because I didn't know what else to do.

I was too much of a coward to go see her myself. I told myself I'd just be a complication. Besides, I had to think of your mother. But a friend of mine was posted to London early in '45, and I asked him to go to Lewes and give Lorna some money, find out if the husband had come back. But she'd left left town, and she hadn't left a forwarding address. The guy who owned the shop said that Lorna had gone up north to live with her parents. That was a month or two before the baby was due. So I don't know whether it was a boy or a girl. All I know is that it was probably born around January 1945.

The guy said that Lorna's husband had been killed. I thought that would make things easier for her, especially because she had moved away from Lewes. She could make a fresh start, and so could I.

But no one makes a fresh start, Jean. Humans aren't made that way. We carry round our past like so much excess baggage all our lives. I've had the child in the back of my mind for forty-odd years.

I guess you're wondering why I've done nothing about finding it – him or her, alive or dead. The main reason was your mother. The shock of knowing I'd fathered a bastard on someone else, and while we were married too, would kill her. And if that was true ten years ago, it's even more true now – with her heart in the state it's in. There were all the selfish reasons as well. Like I was too busy, too lazy, too scared to open what I thought might be a can of worms. I told myself I had to think of the effect this might have on you and Magnus.

Most of those reasons are still valid. I don't want to see this child of mine, you understand, if it's alive. I just want to pay my dues, to feel easy with myself. But only when your mother and I are dead. I don't want this to hurt you or Magnus, either.

I guess that just about wraps it up. I wanted you to have advance warning. I don't think Magnus will care one way or the other when he hears, except that it means less money for him. So I shan't tell him – he'll find out when

261

I'm gone, when he sees the new will. But I wanted to tell you myself, so we can talk about it, or not, just as you want. Don't think too badly of me.

Your loving Dad.

I folded the letter and returned it to the envelope.

"Well?" Elvira said.

For a moment I said nothing. I wasn't sure I liked the sound of her grandfather. Wasn't it rather late in the day to start having pangs of conscience about the bastard he'd fathered? He seemed too keen to accept his own excuses, too eager to delegate the responsibility, and too fond of playing God. Most of all, I felt sorry for Lorna Carson.

Leaving that aside, I felt a sense of relief. If money is a good motive for murder, then a lot of money is an even better one. At last a pattern was emerging – a pattern that linked the Sanctuary with an Armenian businessman and a West Coast high-tech outfit. If Gregory Lange was Carson's father, and Lorna was his mother, then there was a blindingly simple reason why his paternal relations might want him dead: Carson stood to inherit a third of Rampro, a third of a business with a $354 million annual turnover.

"Your grandparents are both alive."

Elvira nodded.

"Then isn't this a bit premature? I thought he said—"

"I think Magnus could have peeked at the will," Elvira said. "He was at law school with one of the partners at the firm my grandfather used. Very buddy-

buddy. But Magnus didn't know my mother knew. He didn't know she'd had this letter. Though by now he must have figured out she had some way of knowing about Lorna and the child."

"Because he knows you were hanging round the Sanctuary in England?"

"Right."

"So your Uncle Magnus isn't content with a third of the cake? He wants half?"

"No," Elvira said. She shivered and stretched out her hands to the fire. "I think he wants it all."

TWENTY-TWO

"Is that gold?" I asked.

I stared at my hand, which looked as if it had been lightly dusted with golden glitter. I was standing with my trousers rolled up to my knees in a little stream that zigzagged along the floor of a narrow valley, about fifty metres below the camp site. The water was shallow, swift and cool. Wherever it had touched my skin, it had left flecks of gold behind.

"They call it fool's gold," Elvira said in a hard voice.

She was sitting on a fallen log and dangling her feet in the water. As she spoke, a bluejay flew up through the trees. Something had startled it. I saw the bright plumage above, and the drab, greyish-white feathers beneath. When the bluejay went, I stopped enjoying myself.

We had slept in sleeping bags under stars which were almost as bright as those I'd seen in Turkey. The coffee didn't keep me awake – nothing could have done. I woke up first. The sun was already high in the sky. I came down to the stream to wash.

In a while, Elvira had joined me. For a few minutes, I forgot the shadows hanging over us, and I think she did too. I splashed her accidentally. She thought I'd done it on purpose. She flicked water at me. I flicked some back at her. Soon we were dripping wet. We could have been any two people fooling around in the sunshine.

Elvira was laughing so much that she had to sit down. She collapsed on to the log. I glanced at my hands and then down at my feet. That's when I asked her about the gold and the bluejay flew away.

I went and sat beside her. I didn't know what was on her mind, except that I guessed it was something to do with the kind of things that money can't buy.

"I thought of something just now," I said abruptly.

She looked at me the way you look at a TV commercial you've seen too often already.

I pressed on: "It could be important. It's about Magnus. Why's he doing all this?"

"We've been through all this. It's greed. There's a lot of money at stake."

"But I don't think it can be as simple as that. He's not some sort of psychopath, is he?"

She shook her head. "Ambitious, yes. Out for Number One. But he's not crazy."

"Then something doesn't quite add up," I said. "He's a very wealthy man, with a job that gives him every chance of becoming even wealthier. When your grandfather dies, Magnus will own outright a large chunk of what he already controls. Why should it matter to him if he owns a third of Rampro or half of it or even all of it? Why should it matter so badly that he's ready to kill for it?"

Elvira lifted one of her feet from the water and examined the specks of gold on her skin. "Money makes you do strange things."

"It doesn't hang together. He's got too much to lose. You think he's acting rationally. Then why is he taking so many risks? He's set up this huge operation. He's tried to kill Carson and me. He—"

"There's something I didn't tell you last night—" Elvira interrupted. "My parents were killed in a car crash last year. They were coming back from a party one night. There was a lot of rain – visibility was bad. Car went off the road." Her eyelids closed. "And down a hundred-foot drop. No witnesses. Just one of those things, huh?"

"It was an accident?"

"That's what everyone thought at the time. Including me. The shock nearly kiiled my grandmother."

I waited; she said nothing more, which suggested that she had no hard evidence to offer. I would have liked to reassure her, to tell her that her uncle couldn't possibly have killed her mother and father. But the idea tied in all too well with what I already knew and suspected.

"Go on," she said, without opening her eyes. "I'm still listening."

"It's not just that Magnus is taking the risk of killing people. It's the fact that he's doing it all in such a chancy way. When he tried to kill Carson in the hospital, he could have so easily been caught. Anyone could have walked in and seen him. And I *did*. Except I didn't see his face clearly."

"We don't know for sure it *was* Magnus. Maybe

some weirdo just wandered in from the street and—"

"You don't believe that. Nor do I."

Elvira shrugged. "OK. So maybe Magnus didn't plan it. Maybe it was a spur-of-the-moment thing."

"Then why was he carrying a knife? And what about all these people he's got running errands for him? I know he's covering himself by delegating some of the work. But he's also stacking the odds up against him even more. The more people know something, the bigger the risk that sooner or later someone will talk out of turn."

"All right," she said. "But if you put it like that, it sounds like he's running scared. And why would he need to do that?"

"I don't know. But it's as if time is running out for him. He's desperate."

Elvira said wryly: "Time's running out for my grandparents, not for him. Each time I say goodbye to my grandmother, I think it could be the last time. And Grandfather's got Alzheimer's Disease. They figure it's a only matter of weeks now."

"Who are the trustees?" I asked.

She frowned. "Used to be my parents, Magnus, John Izmidlian and the lawyer – that friend of Magnus's I told you about. And after my parents died, they co-opted a couple of other guys." She glanced at me. "I guess Magnus must have had a big say in who was chosen."

"When your grandparents die, everything's going to change, isn't it? The terms of the will are going to come into effect. I suppose they'll wind up the trust

267

and transfer the assets to the legatees. I don't know how it would work in the States, but if there are several legatees, then you'd think that each of them would need a lawyer to watch out for their interests. Someone to make sure that none of the trustees had been dipping their hand in the till. But if there was only one legatee..."

My voice drifted into silence. We sat on the log with our feet in the water, thinking about embezzlement and collecting fool's gold.

"White-collar crime," Elvira said. "Hell of a job to prove it."

"If Magnus is so desperate, it can't be that hard to prove."

"They'd need to see the company records first."

"Could you get someone to do a private audit for you?"

"I could find someone easy enough. The problem would be how to get access to the records without Magnus knowing what was happening."

"And to be sure you were seeing everything?"

She nodded. "And he'd fight it in the courts every inch of the way. It could take years."

"That's one possible line of approach," I said, trying to sound less pessimistic than I felt. "The other is Carson."

"You've lost me."

"You can't even be sure that he really is your uncle. All we know is that Magnus is acting as if he was. But if you had proof, the sort of proof that would stand up in a court of law, both of you'd be in a much stronger position. You could act together. It would make it hard for Magnus to have a second shot at killing Carson without the police asking awkward questions."

As I spoke, I crossed the fingers of my right hand. I wasn't usually superstitious but at present I was happy to do anything I could that might keep Carson alive.

I shut my mind to the possibility that he hadn't come out of his coma: that Carson was already dead.

Breakfast didn't take long. Afterwards we packed up the Nissan and drove south-west through the heat of the day. Elvira had changed her clothes and was looking crisp and cool in a loose white tee-shirt and khaki shorts. My chin was prickly with stubble, and my clothes were torn and filthy after my journey through the mine; despite the sun, they were still damp from our splashing session in the stream.

We travelled on a roundabout route across country, using minor roads whenever possible. The way I saw it, we had two big advantages. First, Magnus and his hirelings thought I was dead. Second, they didn't know where Elvira was. We planned to hold on to those advantages for as long as we could.

At Stockton, we found a glorified scrapyard off Highway 99 that sold second-hand cars. Elvira traded in the Nissan for a battered Ford Mustang that had gone round the clock at least once. The guy who ran the place checked the papers very carefully. He must have thought we'd stolen the Nissan. But everything was in order. He gave us the keys to the Ford and counted out $4500 in hundred dollar bills; he smiled when he handed Elvira the keys, and winced as he parted with the notes.

I had my driver's licence with my passport, so I drove. On the way out of town we passed what I called a charity shop and Elvira called a thrift shop. She made me stop. We spent ten minutes buying me a change of clothes and a bag to put them in.

The next thing we needed was some petrol. We found a self-service station and filled up. The shop sold soft drinks and snacks, so we both went in to stock up. Elvira got out her wallet to pay. As we were standing in line by the till, she eased out a credit card. I touched her arm.

"Does the company pay the bills for that?"

"Yes. It does for all the cards."

"Better use cash. Harder to trace."

We drove south on Highway 99. Being a fugitive was a curious sensation. It was very unlikely that the police would be looking for Elvira, but it was reasonable to assume that Magnus would be doing everything else that a rich and desperate person could do to find her. We might be driving into a trap. But time was running out. We didn't have much option if we wanted to prove who Carson was before it was too late.

It was as if Elvira had read my thoughts. "He can't watch everywhere, can he?"

"No," I said. "But four and a half thousand dollars won't last you for ever. And you can't spend your life going from one motel to the next."

It was a warm day, though as we drove the sky

clouded over, and we had the windows down. For nearly thirty miles neither of us spoke. Elvira had her eyes closed and I thought she was asleep. The next time I glanced at her I saw a tear on her eyelashes.

A few minutes later, she said: "Why are you doing all this, Adam?"

It was the first time she'd called me Adam. "I told you: you saved my life back there."

"It only needed saving because of me and Magnus."

"That wasn't your fault. Anyway, if it makes it easier you can think of me as looking after Carson's interests."

"He's your boss," she said; and what she meant was that you don't give that sort of loyalty to someone who just pays your wages.

"I like what he's doing at the Sanctuary," I said, answering the question she had been too polite to put into words. "I know he's a crank, but sometimes you need cranks to get things done." I grinned at her. "And this particular crank needs as much money as he can lay his hands on."

"He may die first – before my grandfather," Elvira said in a small, hard voice. "He may never come out of the coma. He may not even be my uncle."

"Magnus thinks he is."

"I promise you one thing. Whatever happens, I'll help fund the Sanctuary."

I kept my eyes on the road. "You don't have to do that."

She made no reply. The white lines unrolled for another few miles on the other side of the windscreen.

The next time I looked at her, her eyes were closed again. The wind was pulling through her hair like an invisible brush. In repose her face looked gentle, which was not a word I had previously associated with Elvira Bladon.

I drove on. The next big town was Merced. My ears filled with the roar of the wind, the noise of the engine and the rumble of tyres on tarmac. For the first time, I made myself face the truth: that I wasn't really doing this for Carson or the Sanctuary; or rather, I wasn't doing it for them any longer. Otherwise I'd have been on a plane to London or hiding under a table in the nearest British consulate.

It's one thing to make a fool of yourself: it's quite another to realize it. However this worked out, there wasn't any future for me and Elvira Bladon. Nevertheless, I kept asking myself those stupid, unanswerable questions. Why did she have to be so beautiful? Why did she have to be so rich?

The motel was on the southern outskirts of Fresno. The manager was a balding guy with greasy hair and a beer belly. He couldn't keep his eyes off Elvira. But the rooms were inexpensive, and this wasn't the sort of place where Magnus Lange would start looking for his niece.

We registered as a couple. Our room contained a television, a double bed and not much else. Elvira took a shower. There was a phone beside the bed. I picked it up and dialled the Sanctuary.

In England it was getting on for midnight. I heard the phone ringing at the other end. It occurred to me that it was Saturday night over there – almost a week to the hour since I met Elvira on the hill in the middle of a rainstorm. It seemed much longer.

"Yeh-es?"

Mrs Fettercairn's voice drew out the word until it sounded as if it had two syllables rather than one. I had hoped that Phyllis would answer the phone. By this time of the evening Kenneth would be in bed.

"Ye-hes?" The voice was sharper now. "Who is calling?"

I couldn't afford to tell the truth. Someone from Rampro, probably Mike Izmidlian, must have phoned the Sanctuary to say that I had gone missing yesterday afternoon, that I hadn't been seen since the lunch at the Lebanese restaurant, and that my belongings were still in my room at the Wharf Lodge Hotel. I could have trusted Phyllis to keep her mouth shut – she knew me, and she already knew something about what was going on. Mrs Fettercairn was different.

"Sorry to ring so late," I said breezily in a West Country accent that made me sound as though I were doing a cider advertisement. "This is the *Paulstock Observer*, news desk, just wanted an update on Mr Carson before we put the paper to bed. How's he doing?"

"It's a ridiculously late hour for you to telephone." Mrs Fettercairn's voice sounded so clear that she might have been forty miles away rather than four thousand. "But to answer your question: I regret to say that there's been no change."

"He's still in a coma? Sorry to hear that."

"So are we." She sounded a little less annoyed, so perhaps my sincerity had reached her, despite the cider-swilling accent. "I saw a doctor today, and he said it could be worse. Meaningless drivel! The man treated me as though I had a mental age of five."

I felt relieved that Carson was still alive and sorry for the doctor.

"In my opinion, the medical profession has got far too much technology these days. They've forgotten how to deal with people. Now, if you will excuse me, I'm going to put the phone down. You may not need to go to sleep but I do."

I thanked her and said goodbye. I hadn't realized that I wanted to talk to Phyllis so badly. For a moment I toyed with the idea of calling Jack Bream or Becky but neither of them knew enough of the background, and my sister had enough on her mind already; in any case, my father might answer the phone, and I had nothing to say to him. I stayed on the bed, with the phone on my lap, staring out of the window.

"What are you thinking about?"

I hadn't even heard the bathroom door opening. I looked at Elvira. "My sister."

"Are you going to call her?"

"Not now."

Elvira sat down on the other side of the bed and towelled her hair. She wanted to know about Becky – whether she was older or younger than I was, whether we had any other siblings.

"You sound very protective of her," she said.

"She's had a bad time lately."

"How come?"

"Our mother died just before Christmas."

I'd hoped I wouldn't have to tell Elvira that. She might have thought I was trying to claim common ground between us; worse, she might have thought I was asking for her pity.

But Elvira didn't say how sorry she was, or look embarrassed, or act in any of the other stupid ways that people usually do. She wrapped the towel round her head like a turban. She got up, came round the bed and sat down beside me – close but not touching.

"What happened?" she asked.

"Cancer. We thought she'd beaten it, but we were wrong. It broke out somewhere else and suddenly there wasn't any time left."

Neither of us said anything because there wasn't anything to say. In the room next to ours a man and a woman were having an argument with a news programme in the background. Canned laughter and the chink of glasses came from the room on the other side. Kids were screaming in the play area. But inside our room, there was only the sound of our breathing.

TWENTY-THREE

Elvira had the bed and I had a sleeping bag on the carpet, which smelt of cigarette ash and stale beer. Judging by her comments about the mattress, I had the better part of the deal.

We checked out of the motel early the following morning.

"Have a nice day," the manager said, leaning forward to see if he could peer down Elvira's shirt.

She scooped up her change. "I guess it can't be much worse than the night we had."

We had a long drive in front of us — over two hundred miles. There were faster ways to get to Santa Barbara, but we figured that this was probably the safest. There was no especial reason why Magnus should think Elvira might be heading for her grandparents. But if he did, she thought that this approach was the one he was least likely to expect her to use. Furthermore, if Magnus had hired watchers, they would be looking for one person in a Nissan, not two people in a Ford Mustang.

The car gave us some anxious moments — the engine toiled when we went up the gentlest hills, and the brakes had the grip of a wet sponge. There was a hole in the exhaust system: the engine noise increased as the hole grew larger. South of Bakersfield, one of the hoses in the cooling system sprang a leak. I managed a temporary repair with a roll of Scotch tape a previous owner had left in the glove compartment.

On the outskirts of Santa Barbara we started arguing.

"You can't come in with me," Elvira said. "What happens if Magnus is there? He thinks you're dead. Or even if he isn't there himself, someone would tell him."

"But if he's there, he's not just going to say hello to you, is he?"

Elvira took her hands off the wheel and waved them in the air. "Why not? He knows that I know he's up to something. But he doesn't know that I know that he knows that I know." She laughed and, to my relief, put her hands back on the wheel just before the car sailed into a left-hand bend. "Even if he's there, he couldn't do anything. Too many people around. And don't forget the private army."

"The what?"

"The house is in a place called Summerville Palms. The residents have their own police force. That's the private army."

"I still think it's better if we go together."

She flared up: "It's got nothing to do with you. It's my life, Adam Davy. I'll live it how I choose."

"I just hope you live long enough to enjoy it," I snapped.

I glared at her, and found she was smiling at me. I grinned back, which effectively derailed the argument for the time being. But it didn't stop me worrying.

"All right," she said softly a mile or two down the road. "If you feel so strongly about it, how about this? We'll call the house and see if Magnus is there."

She pulled on to the forecourt of a roadhouse named the Lazy Q. The only living things inside were a bored Mexican woman behind the counter and a couple of flies on a reconnaissance flight over the stove. We bought some coffee. I sat down by the window and Elvira went to use the phone. When she came back to the table she was smiling.

"I talked to the housekeeper. They haven't heard from Magnus for a couple of days."

"So I can come with you?"

She shook her head. "So there's no reason why you should. If my grandmother sees you she'll want to know all about you. And the next time Magnus calls her, she'll tell him all about this nice English guy Elvira brought to see her."

"I needn't meet her."

She stirred her coffee slowly. "Are you always as pigheaded as this? Or is it only on a full moon?"

"I could wait in the car or something. Just in case."

She made a face. "Ah well. If it makes you happy. But you're being totally irrational."

We drank our coffee in silence. I wondered whether she wasn't used to people who argued; she was accustomed to make decisions and give orders without being questioned.

I wasn't sure why I was being so obstinate. I'd like to say it was intuition, or the result of a brilliant exercise of deductive thinking, or even because my psychic antennae had beamed a warning to me from the future. But it was none of those things. The truth of the matter was far more confused, as truth is apt to be. It had something to do with the feeling that there was safety in numbers. But I also didn't want to let Elvira out of my sight for the simple reason that I liked looking at her.

At all events, it turned out to be just as well that I wouldn't take no for an answer. In some cases there is a lot to be said for being irrational.

As we drove the last few miles I got tired of waiting for her to be the first to break the awkward silence between us.

"What's this place like?"

She talked about Summerville Palms in an offhand way that made me realize that for her this was how people normally lived. It was a large development of luxury houses overlooking the Pacific, a few miles outside Santa Barbara. It had its own country club with its own golf course. The private police force helped to keep undesirables out of the place. Elvira said that there were only two entrances by road. A discreetly sited fence lined the landward boundary of the enclave. The barrier was reinforced with every kind of electronic gadgetry known to man.

It struck me that what keeps people out also keeps people in: Summerville Palms was a gilded prison.

We turned off the highway and drove slowly up the winding access road to the estate. At the top there was a boom operated by an electronic keypad. Elvira stopped beside it and wound down her window.

A beefy man wearing a khaki uniform and mirrored shades strode out of a single-storey building beside the road. His right hand rested negligently on the holster.

"Yes?" he growled.

"Hi, Jake," Elvira said.

He straightened his spine. "Ms Bladon – uh, sorry – didn't recognize the car."

I guessed that Summerville Palms was accustomed to a better class of automobile. The boom went up. Elvira gunned the engine and drove through. The guard sketched a salute as we passed.

"Do you usually have that effect on people?" I asked.

"Rampro owns the freehold."

"That explains it."

We drove down quiet, tree-lined roads. All the houses were set back in their own grounds. Everything was very clean. Even the mailboxes sparkled in the sunlight; maybe they were given a wax job every morning. There was little traffic.

We turned into a cul-de-sac. Right at the end there was a pair of tall, cast-iron gates which looked if they had strayed from a French chateau.

"If you put your head down below the dash," Elvira said casually, "the camera won't pick you up."

This time I didn't argue. I put my head down and waited. The car slowed and stopped. I guessed there was another electronic lock. A few seconds later we moved on. Then we stopped again.

"You can get out here."

I sat up and looked around. The drive was in the middle of what looked like a tropical plantation.

"As long as you're careful, no one will see you," Elvira said. "There's ten or twelve acres, and the gardeners don't come on Sundays. But keep away from the back of the house. That's where the service quarters are, and the path down to the beach."

"How will I know—?"

"When it's time to meet me here? You'll hear the car. Oh, and keep away from the boundary wall and don't go too near the house. Sometimes they leave the alarm system switched on during the day."

"But what happens if—"

"If I'm going to be long, I'll let you know. OK? But I shouldn't be more than an hour or so." She smiled mockingly at me. "And if I run into trouble, I'll just scream, OK?"

I got out of the Mustang. This was her little revenge for the way I overruled her earlier. She'd made it sound as if all she had to do was rush into the house, stab a needle into her grandfather, suck out a blood sample and rush out again. I didn't think it would be that simple.

Elvira gave me a wave and drove off. Within seconds the car had disappeared round a bend of the drive. I slunk into the undergrowth. It was cool and moist; all the green was restful.

I tried to push Elvira out of my mind. I'd been living in a state of high tension for days. I wanted to relax. There was no risk of my not being able to hear Elvira when she came back down the drive in the Ford

Mustang. In a place as quiet as this, the engine's throaty roar could probably be heard half a mile away.

I worked my way through the trees and shrubs until I came to a winding gravel path. If I turned right, I guessed I'd reach the drive again. I turned left. I walked almost noiselessly on one of the narrow strips of grass that bordered the path. What struck me was the silence, which lay like a heavy blanket over the garden. There were no birds. The mini-jungle petered out. I moved cautiously forward to the shelter of a monkey puzzle tree.

Everything was as still as a photograph. In front of me was an area of lawns, shrubs and flowerbeds laid out with the glossy perfection that only a really good firm of landscape gardeners can provide. On one side was a little ornamental lake shaped like a lopsided hourglass. A balustraded bridge crossed the lake at the waist. The end nearer me was carpeted with water lilies, and there was a Japanese pavilion on a wooden platform which projected over the water. Beyond the lake were a couple of hard tennis courts.

Directly ahead was the house itself – or at least some of it. It was older than I'd expected – a long, split-level place with whitewashed walls and a roof of green pantiles; perhaps the house predated the Summerville Palms development. A verandah with a wrought-iron rail ran the length of the façade. Directly beneath it was a sickle-shaped swimming pool.

Like the garden, the house looked perfect. It was all so perfect that I felt a stab of nostalgia for the shabby comfort of the Sanctuary and the messy informality of the countryside around it.

A door at the end of the verandah slid back. A sturdy woman in a white uniform came outside. I ducked behind the monkey puzzle. I lay on my stomach and wriggled round the trunk of the tree.

The woman pulled a wheelchair out of the house. She began to push it along the verandah. She moved very slowly, as though drugged or dreaming. In the chair there was a hunched, grey-haired figure in a blue-and-white striped dressing gown. They were too far away for me to be able to see the face clearly. When the woman, presumably a nurse, reached the end of the verandah, she made a 180-degree turn and moved slowly back the way she had come. They moved with precision, like figures in a slow-motion dance. Gregory Lange was taking his exercise. I lay there and watched them going from side to side with the regularity of a metronome.

Something unexpected happened. For the first time, it occurred to me that there were different ways of dying, and that some were better than others. After they had discovered that my mother had cancer, it had taken her just over two weeks to die. I had been angry because she had been given so little time; it had seemed an unnecessary cruelty. But she had gone out fighting all the way. Whatever had happened to her body, there had been nothing wrong with her mind or her spirit. That way of dying seemed a lesser evil than the one reserved for Gregory Lange.

Suddenly there was a flurry of activity around the swimming pool. A little procession appeared through the archway at the right-hand end. First came Elvira with a tiny old lady clinging to her arm. Behind them were two women, each carrying a tray. The old woman gestured up to the nurse on the verandah. The procession came to a halt while she conferred with the nurse. The nurse nodded and pushed the wheelchair and its cargo into the house.

Elvira and her grandmother set off across the grass towards the pavilion on the lake. They walked very slowly, with many pauses. Keeping at a respectful distance, the two maids overtook their employer and shot ahead to the pavilion. Mrs Lange had elaborate ideas about what was appropriate for a Summerville Palms tea ceremony.

The rest of the afternoon drifted away. In this garden, time seemed to move more slowly than it did in the outside world. The nurse and the wheelchair did not appear again. After what seemed like half a century, Elvira and her grandmother began to make their way back to the house at a pace that would have given an athletic snail a run for his money.

I hoped that this might mean Elvira was on the verge of leaving. I worked my way through the mini-jungle to the edge of the drive. I settled down to wait behind an enormous clump of bamboo. I was tired, hungry and thirsty. I was not in the best of moods. I wondered if Elvira had thought to fill a bag of leftovers for me. I put the chances at about five to one against.

After a much longer delay than I had expected, the Ford Mustang's engine came to life in the distance. I stood up and stretched. My stomach rumbled. The engine went on roaring. Elvira was revving it too high. The car was coming nearer now, moving very slowly. I almost waited for her in the drive. What stopped me was the faint possibility that she might have someone with her. There was no point in taking unnecessary chances. I peered through the screen of bamboo shoots up the drive.

The car appeared round the bend; it was slowing down – by now it was travelling not much faster than walking pace. Elvira was alone. I stepped on to the drive. And in the same split second, so did someone else.

The man was nearly twenty metres ahead and just in front of the car. He wore a baseball cap with its peak at the back. I recognized the man's rounded shoulders and long arms even from the rear. It was Magnus's driver, Jerry.

The car stopped. Jerry stepped up to the car – to the passenger side. He opened the door with his left hand and climbed inside. He moved quickly and smoothly, as though he'd been practising exactly this manœuvre for months. While this was happening, Elvira sat there with her hands on the wheel, staring ahead through the windscreen. Her lack of movement wasn't surprising. In his right hand, Jerry was carrying a gun.

I slipped back behind the bamboo. I heard the passenger door shut. A moment later, the car started to move – not towards me and the gates, but in reverse up the drive. I ran through the jungle, hoping that the sound of the engine would cover the noise of my pursuit.

Somewhere out of sight, the car stopped. A second

later it started again. In a moment I knew why. Just round the bend, another road, little more than a track, joined the main drive. I guessed that Jerry had told Elvira to back up to the junction and take the smaller road. I sprinted across the drive and followed.

This branch of the drive was not only narrower than the other, it was much less well-maintained. It ran through a belt of tall trees planted along the slope of a ridge. Once, perhaps, this had been a service road. But judging by the weeds pushing up through the tarmac and the overhanging branches of the trees, it was not regularly used at present. As I ran, I glimpsed a boundary wall down on the right.

The car stopped again, and so did I. At first, all I heard was my own laboured breathing. Keeping parallel to the road, I inched forward through the trees. There was movement ahead, and the jingling of keys.

The trees thinned. I hit what had once been a footpath – the layout suggested it might have led down through the trees to the main gates. I followed it up to a thick and unclipped hedge of Leylandii which ran at right angles to the road. Above the hedge were green pantiles like the ones on the main house.

The hedge was so overgrown that I almost missed the gate. Like the main gate and the verandah railings, it was made of wrought iron. I crouched and looked through it.

Until now, I hadn't been thinking about what was happening, or at least not consciously: there hadn't been time. Inside me, anxiety for Elvira gnawed like a physical pain.

In front of me was an L-shaped, single-storey house that had once been whitewashed; from the tiles downwards, it was like the baby brother of the big house. Unlike the big house, however, it was not in good condition. Tiles were missing, one of the windows was broken and the paint was peeling everywhere. The walls were streaked with damp. There was a door in the right angle of the L. It was shut.

I shifted position so I had a better view of the roadside frontage. The arms of the L enclosed an area of hardstanding with room for two or three cars. The Ford Mustang was parked there. Both its doors hung open, giving it an abandoned air. Jerry came out of the house. He moved quickly towards the car, not so much running as shambling.

Slowly I tried the handle of the gate. It wouldn't move. It was either locked or rusted solid.

Jerry dived into the back of the car and came out with an armful of our belongings. He had both our bags, the sleeping bags, Elvira's coat and even my new second-hand jacket. He rushed back to the house.

I forced myself through the undergrowth towards the road. I wasn't sure what I planned to do when I got there – make a citizen's arrest? Make Jerry put down his gun by sheer force of personality? At times like that, you act on autopilot. I was terrified that at any moment I might hear a shot from inside the house.

I had hardly taken a couple of steps before I heard Jerry coming out of the house. I couldn't see him because of the Leylandii. There were running footsteps. A car door slammed, and then another. The engine fired. I was just in time to see the Ford Mustang make a U-turn and go back down towards the main drive.

I ran on to the road, across the hardstanding and up to the door. It was locked. I shook the handle. Nothing happened. The door had lost most of its paint, but the wood was still solid. I stood back. There were four windows in sight, two on either side of the door. All of them were masked with decorative ironwork – decorative, but also functional. I made my way towards the window with the broken pane. When I stood on tiptoe, my mouth was level with the hole in the glass.

"Elvira! Elvira!"

There was no answer. I peered through the hole. On the other side was a kitchen. No one had cooked a meal there for a very long time. The refrigerator and the cooker looked the next best thing to antiques. I shook the bars, but they didn't move.

I didn't waste any more time but ran round the end of the house. There was another decorative grille over the window in the gable wall. I turned another corner. Here, on the long arm of the L, was a flagged terrace. Beneath it, the land dropped steeply away. Once there must have been a view, but the trees had grown too high. Among the higher branches were patches of blue sea.

Halfway along the terrace was a small fountain. The fountain had a dry bowl, in the middle of which was a statue of a boy wearing nothing but a fig leaf.

Facing the fountain was a pair of French windows – the only windows without bars.

The glass was opaque with dirt. With the heel of my hand, I rubbed a circular peephole on the surface, revealing a large, gloomy room. Its furniture and light fittings were shrouded with dustsheets. Armchairs, a sofa, tables, a bureau and a standard lamp: they looked like a company of ghosts.

The sense of urgency was growing. I turned and took a running jump into the bowl of the fountain. The statue was only about eighty centimetres high. The boy's mouth smiled; his eyes were blind. I pushed the statue gently. It rocked away from me. It was resting on a stone base, probably secured by a pin; once, it must have been concreted in, but now it was held in place by gravity.

I flung my arms round the statue, took a deep breath and lifted. There was little resistance, and the stone boy was lighter than I had expected. With a grunt, I hoisted the statue on my shoulder. I stepped out of the bowl of the fountain. I stumbled across the terrace. With a heave that seemed to wrench every muscle in my body, I threw the statue at the left-hand side of the French windows.

There are few sounds quite as shocking as breaking glass. The statue tore a jagged hole in the pane that filled one of the two doors. The noise seemed loud enough to wake the dead. Forcing myself to slow down, I picked out large triangles of glass from the bottom part of the hole until there was a large enough space for me to climb into the room beyond.

The grime on the windows filtered out much of the light from outside; I felt as though I were moving through brown fog. I tripped over something on the floor. Looking down, I saw that it was a head lying face upwards on the carpet among the shards of glass. The lips were still fixed in their serene smile; the blank eyes stared into mine. Sweat broke out on my skin: for the instant between seeing and recognizing the head of the statue, I had thought that the head was real.

I went quickly from room to room, tearing off dustsheets, opening cupboards, looking under beds. I even remembered to check the ceilings; none of them had a hatch to the roofspace.

The search didn't take me long: in the long arm of the L there was the big living room, the kitchen and a tiny bathroom; and in the shorter arm, a large bedroom and a smaller one. The bathroom had been hit by a blizzard of plaster because part of the ceiling had come down. The rooms all smelt the same – of damp and stale air.

I went back into the living room. There was an old black telephone on the bureau. I picked up the handset. The phone was dead. I jiggled the receiver rest but the phone didn't come back to life.

It just didn't make sense. It was true that I hadn't actually seen Jerry taking Elvira into the house but I had seen him carrying our belongings inside. They couldn't have vanished. I stared through the shattered French windows at the bowl of the fountain. Beyond the terrace, the land dropped sharply down to a pile of weeds and stone which might once have been a rock garden. The trees clustered thickly at the bottom.

The land dropped sharply down...

Suddenly I had the answer. The house was built on the side of the hill. There was plenty of room for a cellar. I forced myself to think it out. Assuming there was a basement, its entrance was unlikely to be in the bedrooms because of the lie of the land – they were on the shorter side of the L nearer the road, where the ground was higher. The living room and the little hallway had wall-to-wall carpeting which made either of them an unlikely choice. The bathroom was tiny. That left only the kitchen.

A second later, I was standing in the kitchen doorway. The floor was tiled. I ran my eyes over the tiles. They were as regular and as unbroken as the day they were laid. There was only one possibility – a piece of matting that stood beneath a table that was pushed against one wall. I pushed the table away and pulled the matting aside. And there it was.

The trapdoor was tiled like the floor. In the centre a ring had been let in to it. As my hand touched the cold metal, my excitement died away. If the basement was in the foundations, which were dug partly into the hill, it must be nearly soundproof. It was almost certainly well enough insulated to mask a shot from a handgun.

The trapdoor came up with unexpected ease. I fell backwards, colliding with the refrigerator. I pushed the trapdoor away from me and scrambled to the hole. An iron ladder was bolted to the wall. The murky daylight from the kitchen window seeped downwards and showed me an unplastered brick wall and a bare cement floor. At the bottom of the ladder I could see a sleeping bag and my jacket.

"Elvira," I whispered.

There was no answer. I realized that I had no need to keep the volume down, so I shouted her name instead. An echo threw the last syllable back at me. There was no other answer. By this time I was climbing down the ladder. In the gloom, I saw first her sandal and then her leg. It was much colder down here than it was above, but that wasn't why I shivered. I knelt beside her, saying her name again and again. In the semi-darkness, her body was grey and unmoving.

I touched her feet and ran my hands up to her ankles. They were strapped together with what felt like elastic luggage ties. She was lying on her stomach. I moved my hands up to her waist. Her hands were strapped together too. Still muttering her name over and over again, as though it were a prayer, I let my fingertips trace the line of her arm to her shoulder, and then ran them along the curve of the neck to her face.

Her skin was cold. There was a gag over her mouth. I would have given anything to feel the warmth of her breath on my fingers.

The only sound in that cold, dead place was my own voice saying, "Elvira, Elvira, Elvira."

TWENTY-FOUR

You don't gag a corpse. There's no need to truss it up like a turkey. Just as the realization hit me, Elvira's head stirred on the concrete floor.

The tiny movement galvanized me into action. My fingers were still resting on her cheek. I ran my hand round her head until I found the knot at the back. I tried to pull it apart by brute force. Elvira grunted with pain and I broke a fingernail. I forced myself to slow down and approach the knot more scientifically.

A few seconds later the knot fell apart. Elvira spat out the gag. She retched, but nothing came out. I moved down to her wrists. She moaned softly. Neither of us tried to talk. There wasn't time. Somewhere outside there was a man with a gun.

The luggage ties were cruelly tight. But they were easier to undo than the gag had been because Jerry had just hooked their ends together. When I had undone her hands, Elvira rolled on to her back. I helped her sit up. She rubbed her wrists. I undid the ankles.

"Jerry went off in the Mustang," I said. "He was in a hurry. Now see if you can stand up."

Elvira gripped my arm. I pulled her up. She swayed against the wall, and kept hold of me.

"Can you manage it up the ladder?"

She nodded. She kept trying to moisten her lips. The gag had dried out the inside of her mouth.

I guided her towards the ladder. She looked up at the trapdoor. The sight of daylight gave her a shot of energy. She climbed the ladder slowly, but without any help from me. At the top she sat on the edge of the opening and looked down.

"The bags?" she croaked.

"I'll leave the sleeping bags. Too bulky."

Elvira said nothing, which I took to mean that she agreed. I passed the rest of our belongings up to her and climbed the ladder. There was no point in replacing the trapdoor. Jerry could hardly help noticing that the house had had a visitor while he was gone.

By the time I reached the kitchen, Elvira was standing in the doorway that led to the living room and staring at the shambles.

"No one answered the door," I said.

The attempt at humour did nothing to lighten the atmosphere. Elvira took a step in to the room and tripped over the legs of the statue. Dropping her bag, she stumbled against a tall, dustsheeted piece of furniture. Before I reached her, she managed to regain her balance. The dustsheet slid to the carpet, revealing a dark-stained oak bureau.

"Are you all right?"

She shook my hand away from her arm. "I guess I fainted down there. I'm still muzzy."

The hole in the French window looked like a mouth surrounded by teeth. It seemed a minor miracle that I had managed to get through it without leaving my arms behind. I picked up the dustsheet which Elvira had dislodged and wrapped it round my hands.

"What are you doing?"

"I thought I'd make that hole a bit bigger."

"There should be a key someplace."

She opened one of the bureau drawers and began to rummage through its contents. We didn't have time to waste so I knelt by the window and, using the dustsheet to protect my hands, I picked up the head of the statue from the sea of broken glass. I used it as a hammer to enlarge the hole in the door. Four blows were enough. I glanced over my shoulder. Elvira was still standing beside the bureau, whose drawers were hanging open.

"Come on," I said, irritated that she hadn't spent the time bringing the rest of our belongings from the kitchen to the living room. "If Jerry comes back—"

"Do you recognize him?"

She held up a black-and-white photograph in a blackened silver frame. It was a head-and-shoulders portrait of a dark-haired man with a strong, arrogant face.

"It's not Magnus, is it?"

She shook her head. "It's my grandfather, maybe forty years ago."

"It's not much like the portrait in Menlo Park. Can we get moving?"

She ignored the question. "He was much older then. Lost all his hair. But this must have been taken when he was about the age that Magnus is now. The likeness is amazing. They could be twins."

"OK. But let's go."

"But is this the man who attacked Carson?"

"I don't know." As I spoke, I went in to the kitchen and gathered my bags and our coats.

"But you must know."

There was desperation in her voice. For the thousandth time, I tried to picture clearly the dark, predatory face I had seen hovering over Carson's bedside. But the light had been behind the intruder. Besides, the knife had compelled my attention.

I came back into the living room. "It could be the same face. But I can't be sure." I saw her disappointment in the way her shoulders slumped. "But why don't you bring the photo? Maybe someone at the hospital could use it to identify him. Or is there one of Magnus himself?"

She shook her head. "There won't be a recent one. My grandparents haven't used this place for guests in years."

I held out my bag. She opened it and put the photograph inside. I thought I heard a car outside. I grabbed Elvira's wrist and pulled her to the window. I scrambled through the hole in the glass. The terrace was how I'd left it. The only sound was the wind in the trees. Elvira passed her bag through to me and then followed me on to the terrace. I put out my arm to steady her. She ignored it. I turned away.

"Up to the main house and call the police?"

Elvira shook her head. "It would all come out. There's no way to keep this from my grandmother."

As she was speaking, she started to walk along the terrace. I followed her. At the end a flight of steps led down into the little garden.

"Where are we going?"

"Nothing's changed," she said. "I got the nurse to take a blood sample. So now we'll go to England."

On this side of the garden, there was a fence instead of a hedge. Elvira climbed over and plunged into the trees beyond. I followed. As we went, she threw sentences of explanation to me, like scraps to a dog.

"There's another reason why we don't want to get tangled up in a police investigation here. Magnus is in England too."

"How do you know? I thought you said the housekeeper -"

"He called my grandmother last night. The housekeeper didn't know. He said he had to go away on a trip for a few days."

"To England?"

"I called our travel section at Menlo Park. They booked him on a flight to London yesterday."

She continued to lead the way downhill through the trees. We weren't on a path but the going was easy enough. The boundary wall loomed up ahead.

"What was Jerry doing here?" I asked.

"He's often here when he's not in San Francisco or at the ranch," Elvira said, without looking round. "I guess Magnus sent him in case I headed this way."

It made sense: Magnus didn't realize that Elvira knew of Jerry's involvement; and Mike Izmidlian had no doubt been left to cover San Francisco, in case

Elvira had turned up there. Like all Magnus's plans, this one had been characterized by a certain ruthless simplicity. I guessed that Jerry had been told to snatch Elvira if she appeared, and leave her on ice until Magnus returned. Jerry had driven the Ford Mustang away in order to give the impression that Elvira had left Summerville Palms; by this time he would probably be looking for somewhere to dump the car in Santa Barbara. He would also want to call Magnus to report what had happened.

"Won't the security people notice that Jerry's driving the Ford Mustang?" I said.

This time, Elvira looked at me. "If he sits well back in the car, the cameras won't pick him up. And he'll use the secondary exit from the estate. Normally there's no one on duty there."

"How will he get back in?"

"The same way as we're leaving." She pointed through the trees. "There's a gate to a path that leads down to the beach."

The trees petered out. Up on the left, perhaps fifty metres away, was the corner of a brick building.

"They're garages," Elvira said. "That's the back of the house up there."

We rounded a bend. Another wrought-iron gate was set in the wall. There was an electronic keypad beside it.

We walked down to the gate and stopped. She punched in the exit code and held the gate open so I could go through first. As I passed by her, she put her hand on my shoulder.

I stopped. "What is it?"

She reached up and kissed my cheek. She let go of my shoulder and backed away.

"What was that for?"

"You saved my life back there."

She gave me a smile that dazzled, pushed past me and went through the gateway.

We spent most of the next twenty-four hours on the move. First we walked. Then we found a bus that gave us a ride into Santa Barbara. A cab took us out to the airport, where we snatched a sandwich while we waited for our flight to Los Angeles. When we landed, we travelled from one of the domestic terminals to the international terminal.

I used my credit card to pay for our tickets in case some of Magnus's hirelings were still on the watch for Elvira. I shut my eyes to the possibility that she might not get around to paying me back. At present, running into debt was the least of my worries.

It was all right, or at least bearable, while we were actually on the move. The worst part was the couple of hours we spent pacing up and down the departure lounge and biting our nails. We didn't talk much. We were both too busy waiting for something to go wrong.

At last our flight was called. Once we were on the plane, the load of worries became a little lighter. Even so, we didn't say much until we were above cloud level. It felt safer up there.

"How did you get on to Carson in the first place?" I asked.

"Magnus hired an English PI. Guy named Vane."
Elvira stared out of the window. "I saw one of the
reports he did for Magnus. It was faxed to Menlo Park,
and it came through to me by mistake. I just glanced
at it. Carson's name leapt out at me."

"It actually said that he was Gregory's son?"

She shook her head. "Just that he was the best
candidate so far. Didn't say for what – the report was
very discreet. If I hadn't seen my mother's letter, it
wouldn't have meant a thing."

"Vane gave the address?"

"Yes. And there was a mini-biography too. His
mother's name was Mary Lorna Carson – that sort of
stuff."

"Did you guess what Magnus was planning?"

"That's a dumb question. Of course I didn't. You
don't think that someone you know would kill people,
do you? Let alone someone you've known all your life.
Your uncle. Your mother's brother. The fact I never
liked him much has got nothing to do with it."

She glared at me. In a sense I deserved it, because I
had temporarily forgotten the relationship; a blood link
isn't something you can lightly put aside. On the other
hand, I wasn't going to stop asking questions just
because they might have unpalatable answers.

"But you went to England to look for him yourself.
Why?"

She yawned. "I figured I'd better take a look
myself. OK, I knew Magnus had to be up to
something. He always is." She stared out of the
window: in body language, she was making it clear that

300

she had had enough of this conversation. "And he wasn't meant to know that Carson even existed."

My sister Becky acted just the same way when she was trying to conceal something without actually telling a lie.

"And?" I said, refusing to let Elvira off the hook. "What else?"

"I guess I was curious." She swung round to face me. "If you really want to know, I felt I could use another relation. Does that seem strange to you for some reason?"

At that point, the stewardess arrived with a meal I needed but didn't want. We ate in silence. I had time to think about Elvira's other relations. Her parents had been killed. Her grandparents were dying. She was lonely, as anyone in her place might be. You don't expect the rich to have the same problems as ordinary people have.

Afterwards, Elvira announced that she was going to take a nap. She tilted her seat back and closed her eyes. I envied her ability to switch off. I was too wound up. My thoughts kept running back to what had happened at Summerville Palms. Once again, we had been lucky. No one stayed lucky for ever.

If Jerry had thrown Elvira into the boot of the Mustang and driven her off the estate, I wouldn't have been able to follow. If Jerry had been a little more ruthless with Elvira, there wouldn't have been anyone left to rescue.

But Jerry hadn't been more ruthless.

In a way, this had been Magnus's problem all along:

he hadn't been able to hire people who were as ruthless as he needed. Where possible, he delegated. But the main thing he hadn't been able to delegate was murder. As Jerry had shown at the ranch, and by implication at Summerville Palms, he was willing to be an accessory, but he would go no further. It had been the same story in England. People like Vane and Jason Ford would do most of the dirty work that Magnus wanted: but they wouldn't kill Carson for him. That was why Magnus himself had made the attempt at the hospital.

The stewardess asked if I wanted to watch a movie. I shook my head. No story on earth would be strong enough to distract me from what was going on in my mind. I glanced at Elvira. Her eyes were closed; she was breathing easily and quietly; and the corner of her mouth had turned up in what might have been a smile. I wondered what she was dreaming about. I wished I knew why she had kissed me. I wished most of all that the rich weren't different.

Thinking along those lines wouldn't get me very far. By now Magnus Lange was in England. He was there because he wanted to have another shot at killing Carson. He thought he was relatively safe because there was nothing to connect him with his intended victim.

Sooner or later, I knew I would have to tell Inspector Anthorn everything I knew. I had to accept the fact that Carson's life was just as valuable as Elvira's grandmother's. He had as much right to live. If I could persuade Elvira, well and good. If not, I would have to go to the police by myself.

A voice in the back of my mind whispered, *But they won't believe you...*

It made no difference whether the police believed me or not. I had to tell them what was happening. The results of the blood tests would give some support for my story: they would link Jason Ford in with the attack on the Sanctuary; and if all went well they would also connect Gregory Lange with Carson.

I just didn't know how Elvira would react. Her shoulder was touching mine, but we were doubly removed from each other – by nationality and by money. Apart from her, there was no one who could corroborate my story – though I knew that Phyllis and Jack Bream would do their best. Maybe, I thought wildly, maybe Mrs Fettercairn could help: maybe her mother told her about the wartime affair with Gregory Lange.

It would be so much easier if I had a fragment of hard evidence against Magnus Lange: something the police couldn't shrug away. I remembered the portrait of Gregory in my bag. In those days, Gregory looked as Magnus did now. I rummaged for the photograph, hoping that the sight of that strong, proud face would jog my memory. It must have been Magnus who had tried to kill Carson at the hospital. If only I could be so sure that I could swear it in a court of law.

I lifted the photograph out of the bag and looked at it. The more I learned about Gregory Lange the less I liked him. Like son, like father. His eyes stared into mine. He was smiling. It was strange to think that I had seen him in the flesh a few hours earlier. In the wheelchair he had looked like a wizened doll. I flipped the frame over on my lap, to get away from those eyes.

The cardboard backing was coming adrift. Pins holding it in place had rusted, and two of them had fallen out. A corner of the photograph had actually slipped out between the backing and the frame itself. I frowned and turned the frame face upwards again. The photograph of Gregory Lange was level with the mount. There must be a sheet of card behind it.

Automatically, I turned the frame over again and eased the backing away from the frame. My mind had drifted back to the doll in the wheelchair. All I wanted to do was to make the frame a little more secure. I lifted out the backing. Underneath, there was a white rectangle, slightly askew, resting on the mount containing the photograph of Gregory Lange. I lifted it out and turned it over.

I was looking at another photograph. It showed a woman wearing a fur stole and smoking a cigarette in a long black holder. In her way, the woman was very beautiful. She was also familiar. There were a few words scribbled in the bottom left-hand corner.

For Gregory, with my love, Julia.

I sat up so sharply that I jarred Elvira's arm. She stirred; her eyelids fluttered and then she went back to sleep.

According to Phyllis, Carson's sister, Mrs Fettercairn, had acted under the name of Julia Bliss.

304

TWENTY-FIVE

In Cambridge, the first person I recognized was my father.

He materialized from his study as I opened the front door of the Master's Lodge. I followed Elvira into the hall. My father hovered under a full-length portrait of an eighteenth-century Master. He was wearing another of his undertaker's suits, and his face looked tired and old.

"Ah," he said. "Adam. Good to see you."

This sort of enthusiasm was practically unheard of. Before I left home, he usually greeted me with a grunt when he bothered to greet me at all. I said hello and introduced him and Elvira to each other. He was polite to her as well – even charming; when he wanted to, he could produce a brand of old-fashioned courtesy that some people found very attractive.

Becky appeared on the stairs. She and Elvira exchanged cautious, assessing glances. Elvira smiled and said hello. She was looking a little dazed. I don't know what she had been expecting, but it hadn't been the Master's Lodge of Jerusalem College, Cambridge.

"I have to go out and see someone," I said to Becky. "I'll only be half an hour, if that."

"Is it OK if I stay and take a shower?" Elvira said, looking at Becky. "Adam said you wouldn't mind. We spent the night on a plane."

"Come upstairs and I'll find you a towel."

Becky and Elvira went away together. I backed towards the door.

"By the way," my father said to me. "Could you spare a moment later? I'd like a word."

"Sure. When I get back?"

It was only when I had let myself out of the house that I noticed that something was missing. Something inside me. Interviews in my father's study generally involved me hearing how, yet again, I'd failed to make the grade – his grade. Less than a year ago, the prospect of sparing a moment for my father would have worried me. Now it meant nothing at all except another minor commitment to be fitted in when I had time. Seeing my father again made me realize how much I'd changed.

I left the Polo outside the Master's Lodge and walked. It was good to get a little exercise after too many hours cooped up in cars and planes. When I got to the department, Simon was in the middle of a late supervision with two anxious-looking undergraduates, but he broke off when I poked my head round the door. He took a folder from a drawer and came into the corridor to talk to me.

"You look tired," he said accusingly.

I looked at the folder. "Are they the results?"

He took off his glasses and rubbed the mark on his nose. "Yes. I did you a summary on the first page – something for lay readers. I used the department's stationery."

I nodded, thinking of Inspector Anthorn. "The more impressive it looks, the better. What did you reckon?"

"The two samples come from different sources." He was watching my face. "But the sources almost certainly had the same parents. Is that what you wanted to hear?"

I smiled with relief. Now we had evidence that the bloodstained feathers from Well Farm had come from one of the hybrid chicks which were stolen on the night of the first attack. "How sure are you?"

"Something like seventy thousand to one. That's a conservative estimate. Will that do?"

I took an envelope from my pocket. Simon's eyes narrowed. Inside the envelope there was the blood sample Elvira had persuaded the nurse to take from Gregory Lange, telling her vaguely that the lawyers needed it for a paternity case; the nurse was well paid to obey orders without asking unnecessary questions.

"Could you do another comparison between genetic profiles?"

Simon's eyes shifted away from mine. I had used up most of the goodwill he had owed my mother.

"Listen, Adam. I know it's near the end of term, but this is not a good time for me. I've got to—"

"This one isn't a favour," I said. "This is a fee-paying job for an American client. You can name your price, within reason. And the money can go towards any aspect of the department you like."

Almost all university departments needed money, and I knew that Simon's was no exception. He cheered up.

"Of course, that puts a different complexion on it. Not that I wouldn't have done it for you in any case, but—"

"It's all right," I said. "Here's one sample." I gave him the envelope. "I'll send you the other as soon as I can. It'll be a bloodstained towel. Can you handle that?"

"No problem." His fingers ripped open the envelope. "What are you looking for?"

"A relationship. If it's there, it should be father–son."

Simon held the transparent container against the light. He pretended to be absorbed in tilting the sample to and fro. "Isn't this rather unorthodox? Unless, of course, it's a forensic investigation."

In theory, the last sentence wasn't a question. In practice, it was. Simon wasn't prepared to admit it directly, but he was bubbling with curiosity.

"Yes," I agreed, "you're right. It is rather unorthodox. Now – how soon can you do it?"

We spent a couple of minutes discussing the timescale he would need and the fee he was going to charge. As Simon answered my questions, he hopped from foot to foot, torn between a desire to know what all this was about and a need to get back to his students. The direct approach having failed, he tried a more oblique one.

"You'll want the results as soon as possible. I'll call you, shall I? Do you want to give me a phone number?"

I smiled. "I'm not sure exactly where I'll be. But don't worry, I'll phone you."

I said goodbye and left him to go back to his supervision. I walked slowly back to Jerusalem College. The streets seethed with students and tourists. It was still very warm, but since we'd landed at Heathrow earlier in the day the sky had clouded over. There was no wind, and the city seemed airless. There were dark, rain-filled clouds coming in from the south west.

I knew I should phone the Sanctuary again. I had phoned when we reached Heathrow. I found myself talking to the answering machine. Phyllis's voice had told me that there was no one available to take my call, and would I like to leave a message.

So I had said, "This is Adam. I'll be in touch soon. Look after Carson."

I walked past the long, eighteenth-century façade of Jerusalem College, turned right and let myself into the private entrance of the Master's Lodge. The door to my father's study was open. I closed the front door.

"Is that you, Adam?" he called.

He had been waiting for me. I went into his study. He was sitting behind the big leather-topped desk. The screen of his computer was blank. There were no papers in front of him. All the books on the desk were closed. It was unthinkable. My father was doing nothing.

"Are Elvira and Becky still upstairs?" I asked.

"No – they went to look at the college gardens. Have you a moment now?"

"Yes, of course."

He got up and came round the desk. The

expression on his face was unreadable. Our eyes were on a level now. I could remember when it had seemed impossible that I could ever be as tall as he was.

"Let's sit at the window."

The study had a long window overlooking the Master's Garden. A window seat ran the full width of the embrasure. I perched in one corner and my father in the other. He was trying to create a relaxed atmosphere, for his sake perhaps as much as for mine.

"I owe you an apology," he said.

"Why?"

"The cannabis."

There was a long silence. A convoy of ducks wandered into the garden from one of the college ponds; according to my mother, undergraduates had been known to make them drunk by feeding them bread dipped in brandy.

My father cleared his throat. "Becky told me all about it while you were abroad. I understand that she brought the wretched stuff into the house, not you." He waited for me to say something, but I didn't. "I leapt to the wrong conclusion, which was unforgivable of me."

I shook my head. "It was a natural mistake. I'm the older. It was much more likely that I'd brought it into the house."

"But you didn't deny it." He raised his voice as he said that. He was trying to defend himself. He was hurt. I had been hurt too.

I remembered the scene only too well. Becky had gone to a party, her first night out since our mother died, and a friend of a friend had given her a minute quantity of cannabis: they were just a pair of kids trying to show how wicked and adult they were.

Becky had been terrified, of course: she had only accepted it because she hadn't wanted to lose face. She had come home and asked me what she should do with it. She stood there in the sitting room in her party finery, looking like a scared seven-year-old.

I told her I'd flush it down the lavatory for her. Least said, soonest mended. Becky trailed off to bed. Then the telephone rang. I rushed to answer it. I had been in a hurry because I'd thought it might be a girl I fancied: now – not much more than six months later – I could hardly remember what she looked like – only that I was trying to get her to go out with me by simulating an intense interest in medieval memorial brasses. When I went out of the room, I left the little foil-wrapped package on the open pages of the book I was reading.

It wasn't the girl, of course. An old friend of my mother's was phoning to find out how we were: how we were coping. I talked to her for fifteen minutes. And in that time, my father came back from dining at High Table with the Home Secretary, a member of the college. He strolled into the sitting room. As luck would have it, the little parcel of silver foil had caught his eye. He had unwrapped it and found the cannabis.

When I came back, he was waiting for me. He turned into a combination of prosecuting lawyer, jury and judge. I hadn't bothered to defend myself for two reasons: if he was so ready to think badly of me, there was little point in my trying to change his mind; and I could only defend myself by telling the truth, which would have meant bringing Becky into it.

The ducks advanced purposefully across the lawn and formed a line under the window. They could see us. The Jerusalem ducks had learned over generations to think of human beings as food machines.

"Why?" my father said softly. "That's what I can't understand."

I shrugged. "If I'd told you the truth, you'd have been angry with Becky. It was better to say nothing."

His anger that night had washed over me like the freezing water in the underground river at Gold Valley Ranch. At the time, so soon after my mother's death, we had all been a little crazy. Emotions had been twice life-size and liable to behave like bolting horses. My father had told me icily how irresponsible I had been; he mentioned the danger of leading Becky astray; he touched on the possible political consequences for the Home Secretary, if the police had arrested me on the night he was dining in college; and he asked at least to show respect to others, even if I'd shown none to myself.

I had stood there in front of his desk, with my head bowed. When at last he asked me if I had anything to say, I shook my head.

This had seemed to anger him more. In the circumstances, he informed me, bearing in mind the fact that I was under considerable emotional strain, he had decided to deal with the matter himself, rather than report it to the police. I had a place at university for the following academic year. If I wanted financial support from him, I would have to agree to certain conditions. These included living at home, never staying out after midnight, and generally acting as if I were on probation – which of course I would have been.

"Well?" he'd said. "What do you say?"

"No." After what seemed like an age, I'd added, "No, thank you."

The colour had drained out of his face, leaving it a chalky white. We had had our quarrels before; but before there'd always been my mother to mediate between us.

I'd said, "I'm leaving in the morning. You won't mind if I keep in touch with Becky, will you?"

His eyes had widened with shock. "Where will you go? What do you intend to do for money? It would be stupid to throw away the chance of going away to university."

"That's my affair."

I wished him good night and went upstairs. The next morning I left the house. It wasn't as grand a gesture as it seemed. The previous summer I'd worked for Carson at the Sanctuary, and he promised me a job if ever I needed one. At the time, I had thought I was right to go. Now I wasn't so sure.

The ducks waddled away. My father stirred at the other end of the window seat.

"The other night, I took Becky out to dinner. She blurted it out then." He hesitated. "It goes without saying that you're welcome to come home again."

"I don't think that would be a good idea." I smiled at him, wanting to take the sting out of the remark. "I've got used to being independent. Do you understand? You can never go back, can you?"

"No." His face was bleak. He forced himself to smile. "But what about university? There's still time. I could have a word with—"

"No, I'd rather you didn't do that." I spoke more sharply than I'd intended. "I don't want to go to university at present. Maybe later. I'll see."

To someone like my father, whose whole life had revolved round universities since he was my age, this was the next best thing to heresy. But he nodded, as if it made perfect sense to him. "You must do as you think best," he said. "So what are your plans?"

It occurred to me that I wasn't the only one who had changed.

"I don't know if Becky told you, but I'm working at a bird of prey centre – the one I worked at last summer."

"The Sanctuary? I understand they've been having some trouble there."

I nodded. That was one way of putting it. Breaking and entering, theft, arson and attempted murder seemed very remote from this quiet, calm room. Then my father surprised me once again.

"You'll look after yourself?" he went on gruffly. "And I hope you'll let me know if there's anything I can do."

The ducks scuttled under the gate at the bottom of the garden.

"One day you must come and see the Sanctuary," I said. "I know it's not your field, but I think you'd find it interesting."

"I'd like that very much. How long can you stay here?"

I told him that Elvira and I would have to leave very soon. I found it very hard to think about the future because for the last few days I had been so completely involved in the present. My father looked at his watch and announced, with a faint air of surprise, that he was a quarter of an hour late for a meeting. I had never known my father be late for anything before.

His meeting was in college. I walked with him for part of the way. We went down the Master's Garden, out through the gate and into the college gardens beyond. I saw Elvira and Becky sitting on a bench beside one of the college ponds. A flotilla of ducks was cruising in front of them in the hope of light refreshment.

My father stopped and said, "If I don't see you again, good luck. And would you say goodbye to Elvira for me?"

We shook hands. Tall and dignified, he walked along the arcade that led to Front Court. I set off towards the pond. As I drew near the bench, the girls saw me and started to giggle.

"What's so funny?" No one likes to feel ridiculous.

"You look so stern," Becky said. "Just like Dad does sometimes."

Elvira moved up the bench so there was room for

me to sit down. "I've been getting all the dirt on you."

All the laughter fled from Becky's face. "Have you talked to Dad? I had to tell him."

"I talked to him. Everything's fine."

I wasn't sure that everything was fine, but I knew that it was better than it had been.

"Will you come back home?"

"As a visitor."

Becky stared at the ducks. "I suppose it had to happen some day."

I nodded.

Elvira said: "I didn't expect all this." As she spoke she waved her arm in a gesture that embraced the whole college.

"It goes with the job. We'd better get moving soon. But I need to make a phone call first."

We went back to the Lodge. Becky and Elvira disappeared into the kitchen to make sandwiches and a flask of coffee. I went into my father's study and closed the door. I dialled the number for the Sanctuary. The phone rang on and on. I was about to give up when suddenly the ringing stopped and I heard Phyllis's familiar squawk in my ear.

"Hello," I said.

"Adam! Where the hell are you?"

"In Cambridge."

"In England or Massachusetts?" she snapped. "That man from Rampro – Mike, is it? – he thinks you've gone missing."

"Good," I said. "Let's keep it that way."

"What do you mean?"

"I wouldn't want him to think I've turned up. So don't mention you've heard from me if he phones again." I overrode Phyllis's attempt to interrupt. "Listen, I'm in England. I'll be coming back this evening. I'll explain everything then. But how's Carson?"

A match rasped at the other end of the line. "You haven't heard?" Phyllis had a bout of coughing. "Of course you haven't. Carson came out of his coma yesterday. He's furious with you. He wants his keys back."

TWENTY-SIX

As we drove west, the sky darkened and the atmosphere became more humid. I pushed the Polo as hard as I could. I was hoping to reach the hospital before the end of visiting hours for the evening. But for the last six miles, we were at the tail end of a queue behind a convoy of caravans. We got to the hospital ten minutes too late.

"We can come see him tomorrow," Elvira said. "What's the rush?"

"I'd like to see how he's getting on for myself."

"He'll need lots of rest. The important thing is, he's safe. He's got a twenty-four hour guard on him. And if he has a relapse, hospital's the best place to be."

I knew she was right. But I had nerved myself up to seeing Carson tonight. There was so much to discuss. The adrenalin was pumping through my bloodstream. I wanted to do something – anything.

"I know – let's go to the police station."

"Why?"

"The sooner Anthorn gets Simon's report, the sooner they can get moving against Jason."

"Yes – but what's the hurry?"

"Jason's a part of your uncle's support system. The less effective that is, the less effective he'll be himself. We've got a chance to get him at a disadvantage. He's in a strange country now."

That was true as far as it went, but I had another, less rational reason for wanting to see Anthorn: to be precise, I wanted to see his face when he read that report and realized that I'd been right all along about the involvement of Jason Ford in the first attack on the Sanctuary and Carson. Besides, I had had enough of being out on a limb. I wanted to be on the same side as the police. It would make a nice change.

We drove to the police station. It seemed years since I had last been here – on the occasion when my memory had failed to produce a convincing Photofit portrait of Carson's attacker at the hospital. We parked in the yard at the back and went into reception.

The desk sergeant shook his head when I asked for Inspector Anthorn.

"He went off duty at seven. He'll be in around nine o'clock tomorrow. I can take a message or you can see someone else if you want."

I didn't want to see anyone else. I put the folder which Simon had given me on the desk.

"Could I leave that for Inspector Anthorn? It's urgent. I'd like to write a note to go with it."

The sergeant gave me a sheet of paper and an envelope. I wrote standing up at the counter. I was conscious of Elvira beside me – close enough to read what I was writing.

Dear Inspector Anthorn,
    The enclosed report compares blood taken from hybrid chicks at the Sanctuary with feathers found at Well Farm.

Jason Ford told me that these feathers belonged to one of his birds. I have an independent witness both to the discovery of the feathers and to the taking of the other sample. The genetic profiles show that the two samples derive from birds with the same parents. I look forward to hearing from you.

Yours sincerely,

Adam Davy.

Writing the note gave me a childish satisfaction. I gummed down the envelope and left it with the sergeant. Elvira and I went back to the car. Neither of us spoke. I started the engine and manœuvred the car out into the street. I took a turning which would lead to the ring road.

Elvira said softly, "That guy Anthorn has really got under your skin, hasn't he?"

I nodded but said nothing.

The last few miles passed quickly. As we drove through the village, I noticed that there were no lights in the windows of the Breams' veterinary surgery. But Jack's Land Rover was parked outside the pub a little further on. I was tempted to stop and talk to him. But he wouldn't be alone, and there would have to be too many explanations. We had more urgent things to do at the Sanctuary.

On the far side of the village we took the turning that led past the Ardross Hall Hotel. We began the long climb to the Sanctuary. We passed Quarry Hill, the lane that led to Well Farm. The road rose higher and higher. Our headlights picked out a line of railings on the right. Elvira stirred in the passenger seat.

"This is where we met," she said, echoing my own thoughts. "And it was about the same time too."

"Tonight it's not raining."

"Not yet."

The road levelled out. The little lay-by near the Sanctuary fence was empty. We drove past the lighted windows of the farmhouse and turned into the car park. The only cars were Mrs Fettercairn's Jaguar and Phyllis's MGB. I parked beside the Jaguar.

The adrenalin had stopped flowing. Instead a dull, unsatisfied ache filled my body. It was all over. Now the police would take charge. Now Carson was going to be all right. Now it could only be a matter of time before Magnus was rounded up. Soon Elvira would go back to the States and leave me to be Carson's deputy at the Sanctuary.

"Look – am I in the wrong place?" Elvira said suddenly. "They won't want me here. Maybe I should book myself into the hotel."

"There's four empty bedrooms here."

"That's not what I meant."

"It'll be easier if we're both there to explain things."

She looked at me in the half light and I looked back. "Is that your only reason?" she said.

"No, it isn't."

There was a long silence. I felt that anything could happen, but nothing did. Elvira opened her door and grabbed her bag.

"Let's go then."

The side door through the shop was locked at this

hour. There was no sign of the security men whom Mrs Fettercairn had hired. We went round to the front door that faced the road. I rang the bell. A few seconds later, Phyllis flung open the door. The lines in her forehead were deeper than before, and her skin was grey with tiredness. Leila ran outside and sniffed my hand.

"Adam—" Then Phyllis saw Elvira standing beside me, and her face closed up. "Elvira Bladon?"

"There's a lot to talk about," I said.

"You're telling me. For God's sake, what's happening?"

"I'll explain later. Is Mrs Fettercairn still up?"

"She's in the drawing room."

"And Kenneth?"

"He went to bed hours ago." Phyllis stood back and we filed into the hall. She rubbed her forehead as though trying to erase the lines. "It's been a difficult day."

"How come?"

Phyllis lowered her voice to a whisper. "The men from Custodemus left this morning. There was rather an altercation, I'm afraid." She glanced behind her in the direction of the drawing room, and lowered her voice still further. "I understood that Mrs Fettercairn was taking responsibility for paying them. But apparently there was some sort of a hold-up." She hesitated, glanced at Elvira and hissed, "The cheque bounced."

I shut the door gently behind me. "Phyllis, did Mrs Fettercairn make any movies in the States?"

She was about to lead the way down the hall. She turned and frowned. "What? Why on earth do you want to know?"

"That's something else I'll tell you later. It's all tied in."

Phyllis stared incredulously at me. Then she shrugged, as if deciding it would be simpler to humour me. "There was one — a sort of gothic mystery called *The Raven on the Water*. Come on, you'd better come and see her. She heard the doorbell."

I didn't move. "Are you sure about this film?"

"I looked her up the other night. I've got an encyclopædia of films and actors at home. Actually meeting her in the flesh made me want to check her out."

"Was the film a failure?"

"I imagine so. It was the last one she did — just before she retired and got married." Phyllis pulled a face. "A lot of British actors couldn't make it in Hollywood. And Mrs Fettercairn was never exactly a potential superstar. No charisma. Couldn't act very well, either."

Over the last few days, exposure to the reality of Mrs Fettercairn had clearly affected Phyllis's opinion of Julia Bliss as a star of stage and screen.

"I do wish you'd tell me what all this is about," she went on, eyeing Elvira. "Are you both intending to stay here tonight?"

"Yes," I said. "Elvira can have my room. I'll use a sleeping bag in one of the spare rooms."

"Phyllis!" Mrs Fettercairn's voice wasn't loud but it

had the carrying quality you need to get to the back of the stalls. "Who is it? What are you mumbling about?"

"You'd better go in," Phyllis murmured. "Let's get it over with. But I hope you can keep it short and sweet. I need my beauty sleep even if you don't."

I dumped our bags on a chair. I unfastened mine and took out the photograph of Gregory Lange. We walked down the hall. Elvira hung back. I glanced at her. She looked almost shy.

The sitting room was stiflingly hot. Despite the warmth of the night, the curtains were shut and a wood fire was crackling in the grate. Mrs Fettercairn sat in a large wing armchair close to the fire. She was wearing the long, burgundy-coloured dress she'd worn before. When she saw me, she held out a hand encrusted with enough rings for a diamond knuckleduster. The general impression was of Good Queen Bess greeting Sir Walter Raleigh on his return from what she hoped had been a lucrative trip to the New World.

I shook the hand, rather than kissed it. Mrs Fettercairn was looking not at me but to the right.

"And this is Elvira Bladon," I said.

The huge, watery eyes dilated, as though obeying a direction to portray astonishment for the benefit of a close-up shot. "This is a surprise," Mrs Fettercairn said. "How do you do?"

They shook hands warily. I said how pleased we were that Carson had come out of his coma. Mrs Fettercairn brushed this aside.

"You have a lot of explaining to do, Adam. I

suggest you start now."

The rest of us sat down as far as we could from the fire. The warmth of the room was almost unbearable. For a few seconds, I hesitated, knowing I had to choose my words with care.

"Elvira's grandfather is a man named Gregory Lange."

I watched Mrs Fettercairn's eyes. She wasn't a good enough actress to suppress the shock of recognition which the name gave her.

"He owns the computer company Rampro which offered us sponsorship. He's a very rich man. Unfortunately he's got Alzheimer's Disease, and he hasn't got long to live."

"He doesn't even know he's alive," Elvira said a low voice. "He doesn't know who he is any more."

There was a moment of awkward silence. Mrs Fettercairn broke it by sucking in her breath.

"While he was able to," I went on, "he made a will leaving the company to his children or to their children." I was watching Mrs Fettercairn. She had her features under control now. "This means there are two, or perhaps three, heirs. First, there's Magnus Lange, Gregory's son. He's the current CEO of Rampro. Then there's Elvira, whose mother was Gregory's daughter." I glanced round the room. "Finally, there may be an illegitimate child, a child that Gregory Lange fathered when he was stationed in England during the war. That child may be Carson."

"Twaddle!" Mrs Fettercairn snapped.

"Elvira has a letter which Gregory wrote to her

mother. It contains a detailed description of his affair with a woman called Mrs Lorna Carson. She worked in a jeweller's in Lewes, in Sussex. Her husband was in Italy with the British Army. He was killed. According to Gregory, Lorna Carson went to her parents in the north to have the baby. He also said there was an elder child, a girl."

Mrs Fettercairn slowly and gracefully bowed her head, neither accepting nor denying what I had said.

I had to press on: "Can you confirm that? Or does it at least fit with what you know of your parents?"

She nodded slowly.

"We think that Magnus Lange has been embezzling while he's been in charge of Rampro. When his father dies and they sort out the estate, anything like that is bound to come to light – unless Magnus is the only surviving heir."

Phyllis leant forward and grabbed a cigarette for reassurance. "You mean he's going round killing all the other heirs? That's ridiculous. It's like that film—"

"Ridiculous?" I said, more loudly than I'd intended. "Magnus may have killed Elvira's parents already. We know for a fact that he tried to kill me and very nearly succeeded. He also arranged to have Elvira kidnapped, and there's no reason to believe he intended to let her go. You may find it ridiculous. We find it frightening."

Phyllis sat there with the cigarette halfway to her mouth and the box of matches in her other hand. "I'm sorry – but unless you can prove it, that's what everyone will say. And why did he want to kill you? Are you saying that's why Rampro asked you over?"

326

"It was almost certainly Magnus who attacked Carson in hospital. He thinks I can identify him. That's why he wants me dead."

In the silence that followed, I got up. I showed Mrs Fettercairn the photograph in the silver frame.

"That was Gregory Lange, forty years ago," I said. "Apparently he was a dead ringer for what Magnus looks like now."

Her lips twitched. She made no comment.

I passed the portrait to Phyllis. She studied it for a few seconds.

"Not a face I know." She handed the photograph back to me.

"Carson may recognize him."

"I wouldn't bet on it." Phyllis hesitated. "But what about all the other people? That man Jason who did the raid on the incubator room. The men who attacked you in Turkey. The man with a beard in the white Metro. You're not trying to say that Magnus is a dab hand at disguise, are you?"

She stuffed the cigarette in her mouth and lit it. She stared triumphantly around the room. I sat down and grinned at her.

"Magnus has been pulling a lot of strings, calling in a lot of favours, past and future. Rampro is the Izmidlian family's biggest customer. They're happy to do the boss a good turn. We think they're already involved in the embezzling. The men who attacked me in Turkey thought I was Carson. The guy Mike you talked to on the phone is John Izmidlian's son. They're all a part of it."

"But murder?" Phyllis shook her head. "That's not just a favour."

"Magnus probably has to cope with that himself," I said. "Except in places like Turkey, where John Izmidlian has the right contacts. But Magnus was on the spot both here and in the States. Which is why it's rather disturbing to learn that he's back in England again."

"Then we must talk to the police," Phyllis said. "I'm surprised you haven't done so already."

"It's not as simple as that. Even if Carson says he recognizes that photograph, we haven't got the sort of proof that would stand up in a court of law. We don't know where Magnus is, or what name he's travelling under. We can't even prove he's been embezzling without getting access to Rampro's records. We'd need some sort of a court order for that. Elvira thinks the shock of it all could kill her grandmother and—"

"She's dying," Elvira interrupted. "I was wrong about that – we mustn't let her stop us."

I shook my head. The heat was making it harder to think straight. "We've been through all this. The police would laugh at us. And Magnus would get the lawyers busy. When you're as rich as he is, you can afford the best advice. You can buy people."

Mrs Fettercairn sat back in her chair. "We can't let this man go around murdering people in their beds."

"What we propose to do," I said, "is to try to prove that Carson is Gregory's son. Then we'll publicize the story of Gregory's will and the illegitimate child."

"My brother won't allow it," Mrs Fettercairn said.

328

"It's a slur on our poor mother's memory. It's—"

"Carson will go along with it," I interrupted. "He'd sell his soul for a chance to put that sort of money into the Sanctuary."

Elvira lifted her head. The firelight gleamed in her hair and turned it to gold. "Even if he isn't my grandfather's son," she said, "I guarantee the sponsorship. If necessary I'll use my own money."

Mrs Fettercairn folded her hands on her lap. Her mouth tightened until the lips were almost invisible.

"I'm sorry," I said gently. "I know this will be upsetting for you, but I don't see how else to play it. Up until now, Magnus has been kidding himself that no one except him knows that Carson could be Gregory's son. He doesn't know that Elvira's mother had that letter. He thinks I'm dead. He thinks Elvira is in a safe place and either dead or about to die. As far as he knows, he's only got Carson to deal with, and he believes that there's nothing to connect them. He thinks he's almost home and dry."

"It will take time," Phyllis pointed out.

"That's why we want to speed things up by putting the pressure on from other directions. We've got evidence that ties in Jason Ford with the first attack on the Sanctuary. We dropped it in at the police station on our way here. Anthorn can't ignore it. We can also make things awkward for a couple of Magnus's people in the States – including Mike Izmidlian. If we're lucky, someone will crack and implicate Magnus. But even if they don't, it's going to warn him off."

"How does Jason Ford come into this?" Phyllis

asked. "He doesn't need the money, does he?"

"I think he wanted to smash up the incubator room simply for revenge," I said. "And he nicked the hybrid chicks on impulse. What he didn't realize was that there was a witness."

"The beard in the Metro?" Phyllis said.

"I always thought that the Metro was the name of the underground railway in Paris," Mrs Fettercairn said.

"He must be working for Magnus. Maybe he and Magnus were planning to attack that night, but Jason got there first. I heard the Metro's engine. The starter motor's got a whine you can't miss. So the man with the beard called off his attack and recruited Jason instead. It must have been the man with the beard who got Jason to have a go at me. That was a diversion to get me and Phyllis out of the way while he searched Carson's study. And he started the fire to make it seem like the break-in was part of a local vendetta."

"But who is this guy?" Elvira asked.

"I wish we knew."

"I can tell you his name, if you want," Mrs Fettercairn announced. Our heads jerked towards her. "It's Vane – V – A – N – E."

She looked smugly at our bemused faces. Then she admired the rings on her left hand.

"Are you going to tell us how you know?" Phyllis asked, in a voice which suggested that if Mrs Fettercairn didn't, Phyllis would knock her over the head with the nearest blunt instrument.

"He came to see me in Edinburgh about six weeks

ago," Mrs Fettercairn said. "He showed me a card which said he was a private investigator. He claimed he was engaged in a genealogical enquiry on behalf of an American client." Her gaze swept round the room. "Naturally I sent him packing."

Elvira said, "Did he ask about Carson?"

Mrs Fettercairn nodded. "I told him I did not propose to discuss family affairs with a stranger."

"But when I told you about Elvira saying she might be related to Carson," I said, "you said that it was most unlikely because you didn't have any American connections at all. You were lying. You knew about Gregory Lange, didn't you?"

She waved a hand which sparkled in the firelight. "One can't be too careful. At the time, I hardly knew you." She stared down her nose at me, like Good Queen Bess on the verge of accusing a courtier of treason. "Indeed, I hardly know you now."

"OK, so Magnus hired Vane to trace Carson," Elvira said. "I bet it's Vane who deals with Jason Ford."

"So what do we do now?" Phyllis said.

"Try and keep Carson in hospital and under police guard for as long as possible," I said. "That's the main thing. And in the meantime, we get this out in the open and try to assemble a case against Magnus."

"I shall have to consider this very carefully," Mrs Fettercairn said grimly. "To be perfectly frank, you haven't convinced me."

Elvira fanned herself with her hand. She yawned. She covered it up with her hand, but a few seconds later, Mrs Fettercairn followed suit. Then it was Phyllis's turn. The evening slipped into another gear. We all realized how exhausted we were.

"Shall I show you where you can sleep?" Phyllis said to Elvira. "And would you like a sandwich or something? A drink?"

I was secretly relieved – for two reasons. First, by the way Phyllis spoke, it was obvious that she had decided to accept Elvira, at least on probation. Second, if Elvira and I could convince Phyllis that there was something in what we were saying, there was a good chance that we could convince other people.

"Come on," Phyllis said to the room in general. "Can't sit here yawning all night."

She and Elvira went upstairs to have a look at Carson's room. Leila pattered after them. Mrs Fettercairn didn't move. She asked me to pass her one of her black, gold-tipped cigarettes from the mantelpiece. I felt exhausted. I wanted to lie down in a cool room and sleep for ever. But the evening wasn't finished. The worst was yet to come. I moved towards the door.

"Where are you going?" Mrs Fettercairn asked.

"I want to shut the door."

I sat down again and turned the photograph face down on my lap. Mrs Fettercairn had always seemed old to me, but tonight I thought she looked even older. It was hard to imagine how she could ever have been Elvira's age.

"How will you try and prove that my brother is Gregory's son?" she said.

"Elvira got a blood sample from Gregory. We'll have it compared with Carson's. And perhaps with yours as well." I glanced across the room at her. She was sitting very still and upright in the big chair. "It's amazing how sophisticated these genetic profiles can be. They can extract an enormous amount of information from them."

She made no reply. I took the back from the frame and lifted out the photograph which she'd given Gregory. I stood up to hand it to Mrs Fettercairn. She balanced her cigarette on an ashtray and examined the face she had possessed near the other end of her life, nearly forty years before. A few seconds later, she asked me to pass her her handbag. She made a great performance of finding her glasses and putting them on. She went on studying the photograph.

For Gregory, with my love, Julia.

"Do you know anything about DNA testing?" I said.

She didn't look up. "Of course I don't."

"It's as if they put your genetic blueprint under a microscope. They isolate what makes you an individual. What you inherit from your parents. You can even show which bits come from which parents."

"Fascinating, I'm sure." Mrs Fettercairn rested the photograph on her lap. "My mother told me about Gregory Lange. Couldn't avoid it when she got pregnant..."

"And?"

"I went to Hollywood to make a film. It was in the fifties, before I married. I didn't know anyone out there. My mother suggested I write to Greg, send him a publicity shot: she thought perhaps he'd take me under his wing...for old times' sake, as it were."

I wondered why she had really sent that photograph: a genteel attempt at blackmail?

Mrs Fettercairn picked at the material of her dress. "But he didn't get in touch. In a way, I was glad." Her face was pleading with me even though her words weren't. "You can understand why I didn't want to publicize the business. Reflects badly on my mother, and not much fun for my brother either."

"Your brother?"

She stared at me. Her eyes dropped down to the photograph.

For Gregory, with my love, Julia.

"But Carson's not your brother, is he?" I said softly. "He's your son. That's why it was so important to cover everything up. Important for Gregory, and for you, and probably for your mother as well. Important even now."

Her stillness frightened me. She was holding her breath. But I had to go on. You can never go back.

"The day you came here, you told me you were ten or eleven in 1940. So in April 1944 you'd have been fourteen or fifteen. That was when you knew Gregory Lange, wasn't it? That was when he had sex with a minor."

"Nonsense. I refuse to listen to this...these slanders."

"Gregory lied in his letter to Elvira's mother – or perhaps he never knew the truth. Did your mother bring Carson up as her own son? I bet that even Carson doesn't know what really happened."

Mrs Fettercairn didn't answer. Her expression looked as though she had half a lemon in her mouth. A log fell into the grate and discharged a shower of sparks, but neither of us moved. Flames shot higher in the chimney.

I got up. I reached my hand over her head to the high back of the armchair. She flinched. I picked up a long grey hair which stood out on the red upholstery. I showed it to her.

"That's all they would need," I said. "They can get an adequate sample of your DNA from that."

Her eyes widened again. She wasn't acting. The pupils were black pools.

"But it's all right," I said gently. "There's no reason why anyone should know, is there? Not if we all put up a united front."

We stared at each other. For a second it was as if the years between us had vanished. We were hardly human: merely two wills locked in a duel. Then, slowly, she lowered her eyes and nodded.

The door burst open. It smashed into a stool, knocking it over. Phyllis rushed into the sitting room. Leila started to bark.

"Adam! There's someone outside!"

TWENTY-SEVEN

When I opened the side door, Leila slipped between our legs and ran silently into the darkness. Elvira and I followed.

An owl hooted in the valley below. Two of our own owls replied. A fourth owl answered from high in the hills. I wondered whether the chain of call and response would eventually reach Jason Ford's Great Horned Owl at Well Farm.

"Which way?" murmured Elvira.

I took her arm and guided her on to the grass verge that ran beside the path down the hawk walk. I had Carson's stick in my hand – more as a reassurance than as an effective weapon. Though the temperature had dropped, the atmosphere was still close, almost stifling.

At the bottom of the hawk walk we turned right on to a path which eventually brought us to the boundary wall dividing the Sanctuary from its car park. There was another entrance here – one which we occasionally used for coping with coach parties or disabled visitors.

My eyes adjusted to the darkness. To the west, the clouds blotted out the sky. To the east, a sprinkling of stars was visible near to the horizon. The net result was a deep, grey twilight which left plenty of room for the imagination to get to work.

Phyllis's bedroom overlooked the car park. She had gone upstairs and, without switching on the light, she had crossed to the window to draw her curtains. She had looked outside. She was sure that she had seen the flash of a torch beside the Polo, and glimpsed the silhouette of a human behind it.

Elvira and I reached the gate. I pushed the key into the lock and turned it gently. With the faintest of clicks, the lock shot back. I picked up Carson's stick and stood up. I glanced at Elvira. At Phyllis's suggestion, she was armed with a compact camera which had a built-in flash. She touched my arm to tell me she was ready.

I twisted the handle and pulled. The door wouldn't budge. I swore to myself. I had forgotten the bolts. The top bolt moved back easily and quietly, but the bolt at the bottom resisted my fingers. I forced myself to slow down, to ease it gently backwards. I put the pressure first on one direction and then on the other, trying to free the bolt by rotating it.

A lorry changed gear in the valley below. An owl hooted.

My concentration wavered. The bolt gave way and slid back. Metal snapped on metal with a crack like a whiplash. I stood up and twisted the handle.

I was too late. Even as the door moved, a starter motor whined. The car drove away, the sound of its engine rapidly diminishing. The engine backfired. I couldn't tell how far away from us the car was, or even the direction. But it was certainly further away than the lay-by at the other end of the Sanctuary.

"At least that's progress," Elvira said, no longer bothering to whisper. "We know it was Vane's car. So Magnus is still interested in the Sanctuary."

We turned and began to move back to the house.

"The question is," I said, "did Vane get the answer he wanted?"

"What do you mean?"

"He was sniffing round the Polo. He probably wanted to find out who was paying a late-night visit to the Sanctuary."

"Will he connect the car with you?"

"No reason why he should – everyone uses it here."

Inside the house, we told Phyllis and Mrs Fettercairn what had happened. None of us thought it was worth phoning the police; this was just one more item we could add to the account we would give Inspector Anthorn tomorrow.

Mrs Fettercairn armed herself with the sitting-room poker and announced her intention of going to bed.

"I think I'll do the rounds outside," I said. "Shine a torch along the fence."

"I'll come with you," Elvira said.

Leila came too, but only out of a sense of duty; she would much rather have settled down to sleep in the kitchen. We took a torch and walked slowly around the Sanctuary. Most of the birds were asleep. The humidity and the jet-lag made me feel fifty per cent heavier than usual.

"I wish it would rain," Elvira said as we were crossing the flying ground. "Feels like I've got an ice pick between my eyes."

We reached the yard where the barns were. I switched on the outside light.

"Do you mind if I get something?" I asked.

Elvira shook her head. I took Carson's keys from my pocket and unlocked the door of the barn on the left. We went inside. It looked better than when I'd last seen it. Most of the mess had been cleared away – the eggshells, their sticky contents, the broken glass, the shattered shelves, and the machinery that would never work again. The floors had been swabbed and swept. It was difficult to believe that in this clean, bare room Jason Ford had snuffed out so many tiny lives.

"What is this?" Elvira said, looking up at my face.

"It's where the captive breeding used to take place. This was the incubator room. Carson's pride and joy."

I bent down and opened one of the cupboards beneath the counter. Inside was a towel with a rusty stain on it. I took it out and folded it up into a square.

Elvira watched me. "Blood?"

"It's Carson's. He had this under his head after the first attack."

"Why do you want it? Surely you can get a sample through the hospital?"

"Getting a blood sample could take time – especially if someone feels like being awkward."

"Someone like Mrs Fettercairn?"

"She won't be a problem."

"Are you sure? It didn't sound that way to me back there."

"I talked to her while you were out of the room."

Elvira glanced at me. "Is there something I don't know?"

"Yes."

"Are you going to tell me about it?"

"I'd like to." I moved towards the door. "But it's not my secret."

Elvira followed me out of the room, turning off the light. When we were back in the yard, I turned to lock the door. Leila ran up. Elvira stroked the dog's head, and Leila nudged her nose against Elvira's leg. I switched off the outside light. The darkness closed around us.

"I don't know why the hell I should trust you," Elvira said. "But I do."

"Leila trusts you," I pointed out. "Who knows why? She's not usually like that with strangers."

There was a roll of thunder directly overhead. It drowned out Elvira's reply. The words sounded like, *But you're not a stranger now*. Leila whimpered.

I waited to see if Elvira was going to repeat what she had said. Her attention was concentrated on the dog. I slipped Carson's keys back in my pocket. I stretched out my hand towards her.

At that moment the rain began to fall – a dense curtain of heavy drops like a tropical storm. For an instant, sheet lightning filled the sky. I glimpsed Elvira's face half-turned to mine, and I couldn't read her expression.

She straightened up. She grabbed my hand. We ran through the storm towards the house.

I didn't sleep well. While I was dozing, I had dreams;

and they were the sort of dreams that make you see the advantages of getting up early. I felt as pumped up and ready to go as a flat tyre.

I got dressed and went downstairs. I heard movement above me. Elvira was behind me. Before I could speak, Kenneth's stooping figure filled the kitchen doorway.

"Ah." In the harsh, early-morning light, Kenneth's face looked greyer and more lined than usual. "It's – um – Adam." His nose twitched. "You're back?"

As he spoke, he caught sight of Elvira coming down the stairs. He squirmed, and darted back into the kitchen. We followed him. We found him cowering by the Aga and looking as if he were about to burst into tears.

"Kenneth," I said firmly. "This is Elvira. We think she's a relation of Carson's. She's come to help us."

Kenneth nodded. He was still bewildered, but he looked a little further from the brink of tears than he had been.

Leila settled the matter. She scrambled out of her basket beside the Aga and pattered across the tiled floor to sniff me and Elvira. Elvira stroked her head. I knew that Kenneth noticed – and I knew, too, that he was aware of how choosy Leila could be. A recommendation from an animal was the shortest route to Kenneth's approval. He had a point: only humans are liable to tell lies.

I made some coffee, and we sat round the table to drink it. The rain had eased off during the night, but the atmosphere wasn't much lighter than it had been before the storm. Mrs Fettercairn and Phyllis were still asleep.

I had expected Kenneth to be surprised to see me, but I'd forgotten what he was like: his world was the Sanctuary, and anything outside it had very little reality for him. He was glad to have me back because he wanted to tell me how the birds had been in my absence. He had requests, complaints and suggestions to make. For him, talking about the birds was a form of refuge: it meant he didn't have to worry about the risk of Elvira making conversation with him.

I watched her out of the corner of my eye while I answered Kenneth's questions. She was wearing jeans and one of my jerseys, which she'd found on the chair in my room. She caught me looking, half-smiled and turned away.

Kenneth wanted me to do the rounds of the Sanctuary with him, and Elvira asked if she could come as well. He could hardly refuse, though he would have liked to. The three of us stumbled outside with the dog at our heels. The sky was grey, with a band of darker clouds moving in from the south west. Only Leila seemed to have any energy.

The rounds took longer than usual, because Kenneth wanted to have an in-depth discussion about each bird. He pointed out a peregrine with a bad case of bumblefoot, and a Harris hawk with suspected lead poisoning. I said I would phone Jack Bream for him; Kenneth didn't like the telephone.

We helped him clean out the pens and feed and water the birds. Elvira's willingness to help with the dirty work earned his grudging respect. Once or twice he actually spoke to her. Finally, we reached the yard with the barns. We admired the hybrid chicks, siblings of the ones that Jason had stolen.

"We think we know who attacked Carson down here," I told Kenneth. "We've got some evidence to show the police."

"Murder," he muttered, meaning the destruction in the incubator room. He nodded at the pen containing the hybrid chicks. "And those?"

"The stolen hybrids? They're dead. I'm sorry."

Kenneth said no more, but I watched his big, capable hands clenching into fists. His eyes were dull, as though they were looking not at the outside world but at something unpleasant inside his head.

"Come on," I said. "Let's get moving. I want some breakfast."

It was just after eight by the time we finished. As we were walking back towards the house, the phone began to ring. Usually, if the phone rang before nine o'clock, it meant that someone had a problem. When we got into the house, I discovered that the someone in question was us.

Phyllis had taken the call in the dining room; the study was still out of action. She wasn't saying much besides saying "Yes", "No", and "Are you sure?"

Mrs Fettercairn was in the kitchen. She was dressed and sitting at the head of the table. Her face brightened when we came in.

"Good morning. I think I might have a poached egg today. And Phyllis bought some splendi

Columbian coffee yesterday."

Before we had time to reply, Phyllis herself came into the kitchen. She looked dazed. "That was Carson. He's decided to discharge himself."

"What do the doctors say?" I asked.

"I don't think he's asked them. Some people never learn."

Mrs Fettercairn picked up a teaspoon and rapped it on the table to attract our attention. "We shall need to hire nursing staff. Twenty-four hour attendance will be essential. One can't be too careful. And what about an ambulance? Perhaps we should hire one to bring him back from the hospital. I imagine a private ambulance would be far more comfortable than a National Health vehicle. Phyllis, would you be a dear and sort it out after breakfast?"

No one said anything.

"We must get his room ready too." Mrs Fettercairn stared round the room. "Perhaps we shall need to purchase some special equipment. No doubt the hospital will be able to advise us."

Phyllis was the first to find her voice. "All this would cost a great deal of money, Mrs Fettercairn."

"Don't worry. Tell them to direct the bills to my solicitor. He copes with that sort of thing for me."

"But that's what you said before – to the Custodemus men. Remember? Your solicitor phoned up and said he had no authority to make payments on your behalf. So you wrote a cheque and it bounced."

Mrs Fettercairn waved a hand with grubby nails. "A clerical error, my dear. Don't you find that mistakes are increasingly common since they introduced these wretched computers everywhere?"

"I'll pay," Elvira said. "Have them send the bills to me."

"How very sweet of you, dear," Mrs Fettercairn purred. "And not inappropriate if dear Adam is correct. That would make my brother your uncle, wouldn't it? Blood is thicker than water."

I went over to the sink and began to fill the kettle. "We'll need to talk to Anthorn about this. There's a security angle. Does Carson realize his life is still in danger?"

"I tried to tell him," Phyllis said, "but he wouldn't listen."

"Then you'd better hire someone," Mrs Fettercairn advised. "But not those Custodemus people. They weren't satisfactory at all. One of them was actually rude to me."

Kenneth, who had been standing listening by the larder door, sidled up to me in the silence that followed this last remark. "Carson's coming home?"

"It looks like it."

"Good. That's good."

"Do you know," Mrs Fettercairn said, "all this excitement has given me quite an appetite. I think I shall have two poached eggs."

In the end, Mrs Fettercairn had to make do with toast and marmalade. The rest of us were too busy to poach eggs. After breakfast, Phyllis spent half an hour on the phone sorting out a nurse, an ambulance and securi

She also talked to the ward sister responsible for Carson. The sister, who sounded like my old enemy with a perm like a guardsman's busby, said that if Carson wanted to commit suicide, it was none of her business. She added that there was at least a fifty-fifty chance that he would survive.

Most of the non-resident staff of the Sanctuary trickled in around nine o'clock; one phoned to say he was ill and two were on holiday. I sorted out their jobs – and discovered that there were too many jobs for too few people. Fortunately, we were not expecting any large parties. Even so, I had to ask Kenneth to take the till in the shop for the first two hours of the morning, a job he hated. A grumpy expression settled over his face.

"I – um – I was going to trim the hedge at the front."

"You can do that later."

"I can't. Got to repair the buzzards' aviary. Wire's loose."

"Then the hedge will have to wait. I'm sorry. We're shorthanded."

His lower lip stuck out like a sulky child's. "It needs doing now. Carson likes the front looking smart."

Elvira came into the office. "How about if I do the hedge?" she suggested.

Kenneth brightened. "Or – ah – the till?"

"No," I said. "We haven't time to show her everything. Elvira does the hedge – you do the till. OK?"

He nodded reluctantly, and slouched out of the

346

room.

Elvira waited until he was out of earshot. She said, "You know something? I envy you."

"Why?"

Her face was sad. "Because you've got something you have to do. Something you chose."

"What's all this?" I asked, trying to joke her out of it. "Poor little rich girl?"

She shrugged. "When you feel you're near to dying – like when Jerry left me in that basement? – well, being rich ain't what it's cracked up to be."

Suddenly the thought of all that money made me feel ill. "There are plenty of good causes around," I said. "Why don't you go and find one?"

"Why are you being so aggressive?"

I was being aggressive because the money was like an enormous wall between her and me, and I didn't know how to knock it down. But I had nothing to lose by trying to explain.

"Listen," I began, "the problem is—"

"Adam! Elvira!"

Mrs Fettercairn put her head round the door and announced that she had decided to go to the hospital; Phyllis could drive her in the Jaguar.

"It will be reassuring for the poor boy to see a familiar face," she said. "Besides, I must warn him about Elvira. One mustn't shirk one's responsibilities."

She glanced at me with eyes which were as hard as the diamonds in her rings. She was reminding me of the deal we worked out last night: her cooperation in return for my silence. This was the reason why she was so keen to be the first at the hospital. She wanted to make sure that Carson had her preferred version of his parentage.

Elvira and I went out to the car park with them and helped Phyllis get Mrs Fettercairn into the passenger seat of the Jaguar. Phyllis backed the Jaguar rapidly out of the car park and roared off down the hill. She drove the car as if it were her MGB, and it responded remarkably well.

"Now," Elvira said. "You were about to tell me something."

At that moment, the telephone began to ring. I swore.

"Tell me later, huh?" she said, and stalked off.

I went through the shop and back to the office. I grabbed the phone.

"Sanctuary," I snapped.

"Is that Adam Davy?"

"Yes." I recognized the voice. "Inspector Anthorn?"

"I've been looking through that material you left for me last night. And I've been on the phone to Cambridge, too."

I said nothing.

"You've got some useful connections there," he went on. "That's assuming that the samples are what they're claimed to be."

"You can check that with Jack Bream."

"Don't worry, I shall. Are you free this morning?"

"No," I said. "But I'll be at the Sanctuary all day."

"Then I'll see you in an hour or two."

"Before you go, there's something you may not know."

"You do surprise me," he said.

"Carson has decided to discharge himself."

"When?"

"He phoned us early this morning. He wants to get out as soon as he can."

"Being realistic, that probably means lunchtime at the earliest. This is against medical advice, I presume?"

I ignored that one. "Will you still keep a guard on him? There's all the more need for it now."

"We'll consider that in due course," Anthorn said. "First we need to talk to Mr Carson. The hospital wouldn't let us. There's a chance that he'll be able to describe the man who attacked him."

"The man's name is Magnus Lange," I said. "I can show you a photograph if you like. He's American, but he's in England, and he wants to have another try at killing Carson."

"These are very serious allegations. Are they as unsupported as some of the other allegations you've made in the past?"

The temperature between us dropped a few more degrees. "There's a witness you might like to talk to. She's up here at the Sanctuary. She's Magnus's niece. Will that be good enough for you?"

"I shall look forward to finding out. Goodbye."

Anthorn put the phone down without waiting to hear if I had anything else to say. I shrugged. Anthorn didn't like members of the public trying to do his job for him. I went out of the office and into the shop, hoping to find Elvira.

I was out of luck. Kenneth was at the till. He was surrounded by a large, German-speaking family. One was a pensioner, one was a student and one was a baby: things were getting complicated, so I moved in to help.

Most of my mind was still going over what Anthorn had said, and the rest was dealing with the Germans. That's my only excuse for delayed reactions. I heard but did not recognize the whine of a starter motor among all the other noises outside; I even glimpsed the white Metro driving swiftly out of the car park but it didn't register in my conscious mind.

Not at once – not until the last of the Germans had filed through the turnstile into the Sanctuary; not until the car backfired.

"Kenneth," I said urgently. "Was there someone else in here? Someone before that family?"

Kenneth recoiled. "Um – well, let me see..." The pause was agonizing, but trying to hurry him would only make it longer. "Yes, a – ah – a man. And two women and a toddler, a little girl."

"The man. What did he look like?

"I can't remember..."

"Did he go inside?"

Kenneth shook his head. His face was a mask of worry. He stared at the floor.

"A car drove out just now. A white Metro. Did you see the driver? Was it the same man?"

"I don't know, I didn't notice..." Kenneth looked up. "I think he had a beard. He said he'd forgotten something, he'd be back in a moment."

At first I couldn't believe that Vane would take the risk of coming here in broad daylight. Then I saw it from his viewpoint. He would have calculated that there was no risk at all. To the best of his knowledge, the only person who could recognize him was Mrs Fettercairn: but her Jaguar was no longer in the car park, and he might even have seen her going out. He wasn't to know that I'd seen his face before, and that the sound of Metro's engine had become his signature tune.

"Did he say anything?"

"He – er – wanted a ticket."

I tried to keep the impatience out of my face and my voice. "But did he try and make conversation?"

"He asked how Carson was..." Kenneth beamed – he was pleased on my behalf that he'd remembered. "So I told him Carson was coming home this morning."

At that moment, a pair of cyclists arrived at the till. I left Kenneth to deal with them. If Vane knew that Carson was coming out, it could only be a matter of time before Magnus knew as well. On the other hand, there wasn't a lot that Magnus could do about it in the short term. Carson was still safely tucked up with a police guard in hospital. But it was another item to pass on to Anthorn. I didn't want to phone him for another dose of muted sarcasm, but it would be wiser not to wait until he came to the Sanctuary later this morning.

Kenneth was by himself again. I went back to him.

"Did the man ask anything else? Did he mention me or Elvira?"

He shook his head. "He just went." He hesitated. "This man...is he one of them?"

"What do you mean?"

"One of the men who killed the chicks and hurt Carson?"

"Only after the event." I saw that Kenneth was looking confused. "The guy with the beard was around that night. He saw what Jason Ford did – but he didn't actually join in. But now I think they're working together."

"Jason Ford...he killed them?" Kenneth frowned with the effort of concentration. "Well Farm? Up – um – Quarry Hill?"

I nodded, my mind elsewhere. I wanted to find Elvira and discuss this with her. But first I had to phone Anthorn. Another family came in from the car park and Kenneth lumbered behind the till to serve them. I took the opportunity to slip away. Later I wished I hadn't been in such a hurry.

I went into the office and dialled Anthorn's number. The station switchboard put me through to CID, but Anthorn himself was no longer in the office. I left a message saying that an Englishman called Vane was working for Magnus Lange, and that Vane knew that Carson was coming out of hospital today. The guy at the other end made me feel I was making a fuss about nothing.

I went outside to look for Elvira. It didn't take long. I heard the snarl of the hedgetrimmer as soon as

I reached the car park. I walked on to the road and along to the front of the house. A dusty box hedge ran the length of the façade. The hedge was straggly and overgrown: Kenneth had been right – it badly needed a cut. Elvira had only done about half a metre on one side. The wheelbarrow beside her was almost empty and there were few cuttings on the ground. As I approached, she turned off the trimmer and put it down. Sweat glistened on her face.

"Vane's been here – in the shop. Did you see his car?"

"I've only just got out."

"Kenneth told him Carson's leaving hospital, but not about us."

She shrugged. "You told the cops?"

I nodded.

"Then there's not much more we can do." She picked up the trimmer.

"I didn't mean to upset you in there," I said.

"You didn't. Now I'd better get on – I've got work to do."

She fired up the trimmer, and the noise of its engine made further conversation impossible. I went back to the office, wondering why I had to upset Elvira every other time I opened my mouth. I was angry with both of us, but more with myself than with her.

There was enough paperwork to keep me busy for a week. Phyllis had had to let things slide while I was away. I tried to concentrate but I couldn't. I wanted to be doing something that needed physical activity, not sitting on a chair and trying not to think about

Elvira Bladon.

I remembered the towel that I had to send to Cambridge. I'd wrapped it up the previous evening before I went to bed, and addressed it to Simon at the department. The sooner he had a sample of Carson's blood, the sooner he could compare it with Gregory's.

I collected the parcel and the Polo's keys from my room. I told Kenneth where I was going. He nodded, but his eyes stared through me as though I were a sheet of glass.

"To the post office in the village..." he murmured. "OK."

I left him to it. I drove on to the road. Elvira was working away with her back towards me. For a second, I was tempted to put my foot down and drive past her. When you are hurt, you can be amazingly stupid.

So I compromised. I let the car slide to a halt beside her. She turned. I rolled down the driver's window, showed her the parcel and pointed down the hill in the general direction of the village. She nodded. She didn't turn off the trimmer, and I didn't try to say anything.

On the way down the hill, I tried to persuade myself I had behaved with dignity. The railings slipped by on my left. A little later, on the right, was the narrow opening to Quarry Hill, followed almost immediately by the gates of the Ardross Hall Hotel. The gates were closed and padlocked. There was a painted sign on them asking people to use the entrance at the west lodge on the main road.

I came to the T-junction and turned left into the

village. I parked outside the post-office-cum-general-shop. Fortunately, there were no other customers. The woman behind the counter recognized my face. She tried to pump me about the Sanctuary. Between them, the Sanctuary and the Ardross Hall Hotel were better than a soap opera for the people who lived in the village.

I was only in the shop for a few moments, but by the time I got outside the grey of the sky had darkened. It looked as if we were in for more rain. Down here on the valley floor, it was even clammier than it was in the hills.

I glanced up the road. The veterinary surgery was only a few metres away. I remembered the case of bumblefoot and the suspected lead poisoning which Kenneth had mentioned earlier in the morning. There was a chance that one of the Breams would be around, and if not I could leave a message with the receptionist. I could have phoned from the Sanctuary, of course, but this seemed a perfectly reasonable way of wasting a few more moments.

The Breams' battered Land Rover was parked among the cars at the front of the surgery. I was lucky: I met Jack coming out as I was going in. At the sight of me, his dark, mournful face split into a smile.

"When did you get back? How was San Francisco?"

We moved outside to get away from the ears of the receptionist and the other people in the waiting room. I gave him the abridged version, promising to fill him in properly when we had time. It was typical of Jack Bream that the first thing he said was, "Is there anything I can do?"

I shook my head. Then I remembered the bumblefoot and lead poisoning and mentioned those.

"Sure – I'll be up around lunchtime. What about those tests?"

"On the feathers? It was a positive match. Jason Ford's got some explaining to do."

"I saw him this morning – going up Newton Hill with Victrix. Remember – the Great Horned Owl? That bird did not look happy."

Newton Hill was the long, crescent-shaped ridge at the back of Well Farm. If Jason had gone up there with the owl, he might not come back until the evening.

"He's by himself at present," Jack went on. "Even that woman of his had enough of him. They had a stand-up fight in the pub the other night."

But I was hardly listening. A tractor towing a heavily laden trailer was slowly passing the Polo. A horn tooted behind the trailer. It went on tooting like a demented SOS signal. A car began to overtake the tractor and trailer while they were still in the middle of the road. It was Vane's white Metro.

Simultaneously, a second horn blared behind us. This one was deeper, more melodious – and louder.

Beside me, Jack swore. "They're going to crash."

Coming at speed from the opposite direction was Mrs Fettercairn's Jaguar. I glimpsed Phyllis crouching over the wheel in Grand Prix mode and Mrs Fettercairn sitting beside her.

The Polo, the tractor and the Metro filled the

width of the road. The horns blared and tooted again. The tractor driver braked. The Metro cut in front of the tractor and veered on to the left-hand side of the road. Its nearside wheels mounted the pavement. I saw Vane fighting for control of the steering wheel.

The Jaguar, its horn still ringing out, surged through the gap and was gone. The Metro straightened up. Vane revved the engine until it squealed and drove off in a cloud of burning rubber.

A few seconds later, an ambulance passed by. It was following the Jaguar.

TWENTY-EIGHT

I must have looked as dazed as the others. The man on the tractor rubbed the side of his nose. Jack and I stared after the ambulance. The tractor driver gave us a shrug that invited us to share his opinion of other people's stupidity. He let out the clutch and the tractor rumbled forward.

"Is Carson out already?" Jack said. "Someone's been cutting red tape."

"One of Carson's specialities. I'd better get back."

Jack returned to the surgery. I held up the traffic with a quick three-point turn. Vane's urgency had infected me. Why had he been driving so dangerously?

The urgency grew on me as I drove further up the hill. I dropped a gear and pushed the car harder and harder round the bends. Suppose Vane had been running away. What would really scare him? I kept coming back to the same answer: the risk of getting involved in murder.

The road levelled out. The ambulance was parked behind the Jaguar in front of the house. A uniformed attendant was opening the doors at the back. Mrs Fettercairn, attired in her fur coat, hovered nearby. She was talking to a nurse. She saw the Polo and beckoned me.

I pulled up behind the ambulance. The attendant

took out a wheelchair and unfolded it. I caught a glimpse of Carson before the nurse's broad back blocked my view. He had his arm round the shoulders of the second ambulance man. His grey hair stuck up in spikes. He looked like a geriatric punk.

Phyllis came out of the house followed by a woman with red hair, one of our student part-timers. I got out of the car, and the slam of the door made her look up. Her face was bewildered.

I noticed the hedge-trimmer lying on the ground near the gate. Half of it was in the roadway, as if Elvira had dropped it without caring where it landed. I'd left Elvira beside the hedge not much more than thirty minutes ago. And where was Kenneth? If he had still been in the shop, he should have seen the ambulance's arrival through the roadside window.

I called to Phyllis: "Have you seen Elvira?"

Phyllis came out to the road, licking her lips to moisten them; she looked as if she wanted to be sick. "We passed her as we were driving up the hill."

"Where was she going? Why?"

"She was driving Jason Ford's Lotus. There was a—"

Mrs Fettercairn was bearing down on us. "I nearly had a heart attack," she interrupted. "The man in the passenger seat looked exactly like Gregory Lange." Her voice rose higher and higher, and you could see the pallor underlying the layer of make-up. "The likeness was quite uncanny."

"But what happened? And where's Kenneth?"

The student edged closer to us. "He asked me to

359

take over in the shop. It was just after you went."

"Apparently he went off on his bike," Phyllis said.

The nurse detached herself from the group round the wheelchair and came across to me. "Mr Carson would like a word with you."

"In a moment." I turned back to Phyllis. "Jack Bream and I saw you and Vane in the village."

"The moron. I thought it was him. He nearly killed us."

"Vane was up here earlier this morning and Kenneth told him Carson was coming out of hospital."

Phyllis understood at once. "Vane tells Magnus, Magnus comes up here to do a reconnaissance. Then he gets the shock of his life when he sees Elvira trimming the hedge. And she sees him. So he makes her get into the car and drive him—"

"What on earth are you talking about?" the nurse asked. "My patient—"

"Do be quiet," Mrs Fettercairn snapped. "You silly woman."

Phyllis was frowning. "But you must have passed the Lotus on your way up the hill. You were only a moment behind us."

"But I didn't."

"Adam," Carson said.

The voice was so thin and strained I barely recognized it. I turned round. Carson was just behind me. One of the ambulance men had pushed him towards us in the wheelchair. He was wearing a dressing gown, pyjamas and slippers. Pain had scored vertical lines between his eyebrows. He had lost weight, which made his face look thinner. The cheekbones were more prominent, the eyes seemed larger. A ghostly family resemblance linked him to Magnus Lange on the one hand and Elvira on the other.

"Where's Kenneth?" he demanded in a whisper. "I'll need him to push me around."

"He's probably gone to Well Farm." I knew that with Carson there was no need to take refuge in half truths. "Jason Ford was the man who stole the hybrid chicks, smashed up the incubator room and hit you on the head. I think Kenneth's gone looking for revenge."

"We really should be getting you into bed, Mr Carson," said the nurse.

Anger gave him a shot of energy. He glared at the woman, and she shied away. "Adam," he whispered. "You've got to find him. He could do damage."

I thought of Kenneth's dull eyes looking inwards at something unpleasant, of his hands clenching into fists.

"I hoped there wouldn't be any need for this to come out," he went on wearily. "I've never known anyone with more of a knack for handling birds." He paused for breath. "Twenty-odd years ago Kenneth strangled a man who was torturing a kitten. He wasn't much more than a boy then. Had a history of mental illness. But they said he was fit to plead, which he wasn't, of course, and he ended up serving fifteen years in jail."

"I think Elvira's at Well Farm too."

"Who the hell's Elvira? By the way, I want my keys back."

I took the keys from my pocket and dropped them on his lap. His hand reached for them. I noticed that in hospital they had let his fingernails grow until they were long and horny, like talons.

The fingers closed round the keys. Carson's eyes stared into mine. He tried to say something else. His eyelids fluttered. The nurse elbowed me aside and started shouting orders.

I grabbed Phyllis's arm. "Ring the police. Get them to come to Well Farm."

She nodded, and I knew from her lack of surprise that we had reached the same conclusion. I hadn't passed the Lotus on my way up. The hotel gates were padlocked. The only turning Magnus and Elvira could have taken was Quarry Hill – the road that led to Well Farm.

I ran back to the car. The road was too narrow to turn. The motor howled as I reversed at speed to the lay-by and backed into it. I drove down the hill. Flecks of rain dotted the windscreen. My head felt as though it belonged to three people. One was so anxious he wanted to bite his fingers off. The second was calculating road speeds, engine revolutions and gear changes. The third was trying to sort out what had happened at the Sanctuary.

Magnus must have seen Elvira, and Elvira must have seen Magnus. The sight of her must have hit him like a totally unexpected punch in the gut. He probably believed that she was safely tucked up in the cellar of the Langes' guesthouse in Summerville Palms. Otherwise he wouldn't have dared come here. So

Magnus had been faced with the need to make a split-second decision about what to do. I guessed that he had had three options, though he wouldn't have had the time to make a considered choice between them.

I took a bend too fast and almost lost control of the car. Usually an incident like that would have shaken me. I hardly noticed it.

Magnus could have killed her, but if he had done that he wouldn't have been able to find out what she knew and what she'd told other people. Besides, leaving a corpse by the roadside tends to attract more publicity than simply removing someone from the scene.

He could have driven off. But in that case he must have known that she would raise the alarm. Not only that, the Lotus would connect him with Jason Ford and Well Farm.

So his only practical option had been number three: point the gun at her and order her to climb in. He must have had a gun because otherwise she wouldn't have obeyed. From his point of view the option wasn't perfect, but it offered him a much better chance of limiting the damage than the other two did.

I braked hard and changed down. The turning to Quarry Hill was approaching on the right, just before the gates of the hotel. It struck me that there might be another reason why Magnus wanted Elvira with him. He might have calculated that a hostage could come in useful.

The implications of that possibility distracted m
I took the corner too fast, and this time there w
price to pay. The driver's door scraped again

abandoned seed drill that was rusting quietly on the verge. There was a cracking sound. The next time I checked my wing mirror, it wasn't there.

The lane meandered uphill with the park wall of the hotel on the left. I drove higher and higher into the hills. The sharpness of the bends and the narrowness of the lane forced me to cut my speed.

The rain had grown heavier and by now the windscreen was streaming with water. I switched on the wipers, something I had been too preoccupied to do before. A pulse throbbed in my head: it felt like a fingertip tapping my temple. I reached the little crossroads and slowed. The turnings to the left and the right were no more than muddy farm tracks. The one on the left framed a distant view of the Ardross Hall Hotel. During the spring, tractor tyres had dug deep parallel grooves in the mud. The Lotus was too low-slung to cope with such an irregular surface. It must have gone straight on.

The lane seemed nothing more than an endless procession of ill-kempt hedges and unexpected bends. I began to think I must have made a mistake. Either I'd taken the wrong track or they'd somehow managed to camouflage the entrance to the farm.

Suddenly the white-painted five-bar gate appeared. It was ajar.

Like Magnus, I was in a hurry. I pushed the gear ever into first and charged the gate. There was a jolt. offside headlamp broke. The gate rocked back on inges. The car shot through the gap and roared up ive.

No one was in the yard. A dog was barking with monotonous savagery inside the picture-postcard house. The only vehicle in sight was the Toyota pick-up, which was standing in the barn with its bonnet up.

I scrambled out of the car, leaving the engine running and the door open. The Land Rover wasn't there, which presumably meant that Jason was still on Newton Hill with his Great Horned Owl. There was no sign of Kenneth or his bicycle, either. The two horses were grazing in the far corner of the paddock. The other barns were empty. So too were the three pens where Jason kept his birds. He seemed to be using only one at present, presumably for Victrix. It was filthy.

At a run, I followed the drive round the house. On this side there was a garden and an imposing front door with a porch. The windows looked west towards Newton Hill, which lay like an enormous green croissant about a mile away. In the centre of the hill was a bite-shaped scar just below the skyline. I guessed the scar was the quarry which had given the lane its name. A track led from the turning circle at the end of the drive in the direction of Newton Hill.

I peered in the nearest window of the house. A Doberman leapt up at the glass. I jumped back. The window vibrated in its frame but didn't break. Trying to ignore the dog, I rubbed the rain from the glass. curved my hands round my eyes to shield the light ; tried to see what lay beyond the reflections.

Directly in front of me was a wall cupboard doors hung open. There were keys in the lock the cupboard was a rack of guns. The sight of them sharpened my fear. Jason wouldn't have left the keys in the lock. Kenneth wouldn't have known where to find them in the first place, even if he could have got past the dog.

I ran on, glancing in each ground-floor window I passed and trying not to panic. I went right round the house, returned to the yard. I tried the back door. To my surprise, it opened.

There was a big kitchen with a stone-flagged floor. The table was stacked with dirty crockery and open tins. Flies and wasps filled the air with their buzzing. The smell of decaying food made my stomach churn. The dog's barks were muffled, which suggested that it was shut in another part of the house, on the other side of the door beside the big pine dresser.

I went inside, hoping to find a phone. I was out of luck. There was no phone – and the dog heard me moving about. Its barking grew even more frenzied, and it began to fling itself against the inner door. I went back outside.

Suddenly my mind registered what my eyes had already seen: there was a key in the lock on the outside of the back door. It was unlikely that Jason had left it there – he hadn't been in a hurry. The implication was that Magnus had needed to collect something. Possibly gun – but almost certainly he already had one. Or he needed to dump Elvira's body? The possibility my mouth go dry. But if he'd killed her, why he need to leave her in the house? Besides, you a hostage before she's served her purpose.

Magnus wasn't a fool. The most likely explanation was that either he was trying to delay pursuit or he'd needed something to secure his line of retreat. Money, perhaps, or documentation for a false identity. We should have realized before that Magnus might have bought himself a safety net.

Even as the possibilities were chasing one other through my mind, I was running back to the car. Magnus still had the Lotus. He had been to Well Farm, but I hadn't met him coming away from it. Therefore, he must have gone on – which left only one possibility: the track that led to Newton Hill.

I drove round to the front of the house and turned up the track. The rain had stopped, though judging by the sky there was more to come. I reached another gate. This, too, was hanging open, which supported my hunch that Magnus was heading for Newton Hill. Jason played too hard at being a countryman to go around leaving gates open.

The track zigzagged westwards between the fields. It was several feet lower than the surrounding ground. The hedges and trees marking the field boundaries arched across the track and turned it into a green tunnel. There was just enough width for the car. The track had once been a hollow way – one of the network of prehistoric roads which used to cover this part of the countryside.

The car forged on. Branches slapped t' windscreen. There were scrapes along the wings occasional bumps underneath. But if the Lotus make it, so could a VW Polo.

I slowed for a 90-degree bend. It was just as well. On the other side of the bend was the Lotus Elan. There was no warning. I tried to brake, but I was too late.

The Polo was travelling slowly, but still the impact threw me hard against the seat belt. The cars ground together. Metal crumpled. Glass broke. The Lotus shifted a little. My car stalled.

I got out. There was hardly room for a person to get by, let alone a car. I wriggled round the bonnet of the Lotus. It had caught on a low boulder of rock that projected from one of the sides of the track. I bent down to look through the windscreen. The car was empty.

The hollow way stretched upwards. The fifty-metre stretch ahead was empty. Then the track hit another bend. Magnus and Elvira couldn't be far ahead. I hoped that the police weren't far behind, but they'd have to come on foot the rest of the way. The two cars blocked the track like a pair of corks in the neck of a bottle.

I began to run uphill. The track grew steeper and rockier. Even someone with Kenneth's determination and physique must have found it hard to use a bicycle on it. I was aware of my tiredness, of the clamminess of the air, and even of a sneaky little voice deep inside me saying, "Wouldn't it be better to wait for the police? Leave this to the experts."

At first I went flat out, but in a moment I was gasping for air. I was making a lot of noise too. I forced myself to slow down. If I wasn't careful, they would hear me coming for miles off, and when I found them I would be too exhausted to do anything.

I passed a stile leading into a field. Kenneth's bicycle was propped up against it. There was still no sign of him. Shortly afterwards, the path cut through a shallow stream which ran from one side to the other. In the soft mud of the ford there were different sets of footprints between the deep parallel stripes of the Land Rover's tyre marks.

Round the next bend, I came to another gate. It was unlatched. On the far side, the track continued through a narrow belt of conifers. Pine needles lay thickly on the bare earth and muffled the sound of my footsteps. I totted up the times and the distances in my head. I had made good progress on foot – almost certainly better progress than Magnus had managed with Elvira. She might be only moments away from me. So were three violent men with conflicting priorities.

I came out of the trees. The quarry was immediately in front of me. The track continued uphill, separated from the quarry on its right by a rusting barbed-wire fence. The quarry was set in the side of the ridge. It was roughly circular, and the top diameter was about fifty metres. The bottom was lined with weeds, bushes and small trees. Someone had thrown an old refrigerator down the sheer, fifteen metre drop from the ridge above. On the left of the path was a pile of rocks and small stones, debris the quarry.

I took all this in but barely registered it.

swooped upwards. No one was in sight around the quarry or in the small strip of open ground above it. Beyond the top of the ridge was the grey dome of the sky. Something was moving.

A great bird hovered in silence just beyond the brow of the ridge. It was Victrix. I had never seen a Great Horned Owl in the air, but I recognized her at once. She was waiting for exactly the right moment to dive on her prey. I knew that immediately below her would be Jason, with the baited lure on its line and the bag of meat slung across his shoulders. Raptors aren't stupid – they stay close to where the easy pickings are.

Again from deep inside me came the sneaky little voice pointing out that the sensible thing to do would be to wait for the police. Or even to go back and guide them.

A man shouted. I barely recognized the voice as Kenneth's. The stream of abuse lasted for five seconds. It stopped as abruptly as it had started.

I bent down and scooped up two small rocks from the pile of spoil. They were made of dull pink sandstone. Neither was much larger than a tennis ball. I stared stupidly at them, wondering how they could help me cope with three maniacs, one of whom was armed.

I heard the clap of a shotgun blast – a double clap, ɛcause its echo was immediately behind, treading on ˙heels. The sound of it sent fear pulsing through my · the effect was as physical as an electric shock.

˙th a stone in each hand I advanced up the track. ˙ the top of the quarry. There were sheep droppings here but no sheep. High above me, Victrix wheeled to and fro.

Almost at once, the ground levelled out and then began to slope away. The track ran downwards towards the broad green smudge of Forestry Commission land, which stretched from the foot of the ridge to the horizon. No more than twenty metres away from me was a derelict stone enclosure, perhaps a sheep pen, with a small, roofless barn at one end. Jason's gleaming Land Rover was parked beside the enclosure.

I broke into a run. My feet made no sound on the springy turf beside the track. I reached the Land Rover and, using it as a shield, edged closer to the pen. There were voices inside. I heard Elvira saying something in a quiet voice. The relief rushed over me: she was still alive.

I crouched down and inched along the front of the Land Rover. The wall was broken by a wide opening which had once had a gate. I had a clear view of all four of them.

Magnus had his back to me. He was blocking the gap. The others were a few metres away near the back wall of the pen. They were standing apart from one another. Elvira was in the middle, and closer to Magnus than the others. There was no sign that the shotgun blast had hit any of them.

"Why don't you just go?" Elvira was saying Magnus.

He was wearing jeans and a red check shirt. not realized he was such a big man – tal!

Kenneth. An airline flight bag was slung across his body. He cradled an over-and-under shotgun in his right arm. On his head was a cap made of brown tweed, with a fur lining. It was like a deer-stalker -- with earflaps which could be buttoned across the top of the head – and it made him look ridiculous. I wondered if he was wearing it not just to keep his head dry but also as a disguise. Hats are like policemen's uniforms or even doctors' white coats: they, not the faces, are what people notice.

"I will, honey," he said. "All in good time."

Jason was pressed into the angle where two walls met. He had lost his good looks. Fear tends to strip its victims down to their essentials. The lure was dangling from his right hand. No wonder Victrix was going crazy up there.

Kenneth was closer to Elvira. He was staring at his hands. His face was working as though something under the skin was bursting to get out.

"I want you all flat on your faces," Magnus said. "Move!"

Jason began to get down on his knees but he stopped when Elvira spoke.

"But you've only got one barrel left," she said calmly. "There are three of us. Something doesn't add up."

"Cut that out, Elvira," Magnus yelled. "You do as I and you do it fast."

Jason dropped on to the ground. Magnus swung between Kenneth and Elvira.

"Magnus," Elvira said. "Have you thought this

through? You know something? We could help you."

Her voice was cool, clear and disdainful – just as it had been on the night we had met.

Cautiously I straightened up. Magnus was three or four metres away. Elvira saw me, though she gave no sign. I hefted the stones in my hands and mimed what I would do. It wasn't subtle, but there was no room for subtlety. I was going to fling my body as fast as I could across the few paces separating me from Magnus. I would bring down the stones, one in each hand, on his skull. He'd hear me coming, but I doubted that he would have time to react. If the gun went off, I just hoped it wouldn't hit anybody. The plan wasn't perfect, but I didn't have time to think of a better one.

Jason lifted his head from the wet ground. His face was smeared with mud. "For God's sake," he shrieked at me. "This guy's trying to kill us."

I charged. Before I even started, I knew it was too late. Jason had cost us the vital split second of surprise.

Magnus half-turned. He saw me. He leapt sideways, swinging the gun round not at me but at Elvira. I stopped. Kenneth gave a great howl of anger and lurched towards Magnus. He was trying to put himself in front of Elvira.

Magnus didn't pause. In a fluid, beautifully co-ordinated movement, he swerved, lifted the gun in both hands and swung the butt into the side Kenneth's head.

The blow connected with a thud. Ke— stopped. Amazement spread over his face. He His legs gave way. He toppled forward on to and knees. He stayed there, slowly swinging his head from side to side.

Magnus had already reached Elvira. He rammed the twin muzzles of the shotgun in her stomach. She tried to pull away. But there was nowhere for her to go. Her back was flat against the side wall of the pen.

"Get over there with Jason," Magnus ordered without turning round to look at me.

I compromised and moved halfway towards him. Magnus glanced at me. For an instant his face filled with terror. He thought I was a ghost.

"Who – who the hell are you?"

"Adam Davy."

"It's not possible."

"Because you thought you'd killed me? Like you killed your sister and her husband?"

The skin tightened over his face. He didn't deny the accusation. He took a second to digest the shock. Then his face relaxed. He looked almost relieved.

"It's all over now," I said. "Mike and Jerry are going to talk, and so is Vane. There's no reason why they should take the rap for you, is there? Carson's recovered. He'll testify that you're the man who tried to kill him. We know why, too, because we've done genetic fingerprinting. So do the police."

Magnus pushed the gun a little further into Elvira's mach. She winced and cried out.

"You guys listen to me," he said. "You there" – he his head at me – "drop those rocks." He waited eyed before he turned his head towards Jason. eys in the ignition?"

"Yes." Jason added, just to show he wanted to be helpful: "And the tank's almost full."

"All right," Magnus said. "Elvira's going to take me for a little ride. The rest of you are staying here."

"They'll find you in the end," Elvira said.

"They'll be looking for the wrong person," Magnus said. "You think I'm stupid or something? I set up a fallback identity months ago. Get behind the wheel."

He took a step backwards, to give her room to move. With her head high, she walked slowly towards the Land Rover. I saw what was going to happen with harsh, uncompromising clarity, and I couldn't see any way to prevent it.

Magnus knew that the way he'd come was blocked. So he'd make Elvira drive on down the track and into the vast forest below. For a while they would be safe under cover of the trees. Magnus might already have looked at a map. If not, there was almost certainly one in the Land Rover. They would cut through the forest, using Forestry Commission roads and tracks, to one of the main roads.

Where they would go from there was anyone's guess. The motorway was within a few minutes' drive. They could be at any one of three provincial airports within a couple of hours. They wouldn't use the Land Rover any longer than they'd have to. Magnus would ditch that, and perhaps Elvira with it, and steal or hire another vehicle.

Elvira opened the driver's door. Magnus s beside her. The gun was resting in the small back.

"I'll ride behind you," Magnus said.

Kenneth groaned. His eyes focused on Magnus. He struggled to his feet. He lumbered a couple of paces towards the opening of the pen. His arms flailed. His fists hit nothing but air. His face was working, and tears were flowing down his cheeks.

Magnus smiled. He lifted the gun. But there was no need for another blow. Kenneth fell before he came within range. This time he lay flat on the ground. He tried to pull himself up but failed. Magnus turned away.

"Get in," he said to Elvira. "We haven't got all day."

He glanced round at Jason and me. He looked almost happy. I suppose he felt in control. He'd forgotten one thing, however. It plummeted from a grey sky.

Victrix gave him no warning. An owl's wings are covered with thick feathers so it can move silently at night. She swooped down on his head. What attracted her was not the man but his hat. Jason's failure to give her meat had driven her into a frenzy. Her eight talons ripped through the cap, through Magnus's hair and into his scalp.

He screamed. I wouldn't have thought an adult man could have screamed at such a high pitch. He tried to lift the gun – it was as if he had some crazy idea he could shoot the bird. Perhaps he didn't even realize it was a bird astride his head.

Victrix sank her talons deeper. The more Magnus struggled, the more tightly she gripped him. Great Owls are savage birds, even compared with other raptors. They match aggression with aggression. Her massive wings mantled round his head. Magnus dropped the gun and tried to pull the bird away. Her beak slashed at his hands.

Blood was flowing – from his hands and from his head. Magnus's face was a mask of blood. The sight and taste of it enflamed Victrix still further. Magnus broke into a run, jerking his head from side to side in an effort to dislodge her. He ran up the path towards the quarry. The screams were the only sounds in the world.

Elvira bent down and scooped up the gun.

I ran after Magnus and tried to grab Victrix. I saw the bird's eyes, the mad orange irises like fires beyond control. The beak jabbed at my right hand. I reeled back. A triangle of blood grew on my hand and went on growing.

Magnus staggered on. He was still on the track, with the quarry on his left and the conifers in front of him. I broke into a run again. Victrix was pecking at his face with her beak. If Magnus could see anything at all, it must have been through a red haze.

"Come here," Kenneth shouted. "I'll get her off you."

Magnus turned, and so did I. Kenneth was on his feet, clinging to Elvira. They were standing by the fence round the quarry at its highest point. Kenneth was the only one of us who had any chance of coming the berserk owl from Magnus's head.

I approached Magnus cautiously, intending him by the arm and guide him. The dang

Victrix would transfer her attentions to me. Magnus staggered up the track towards me. His mind was blinded by the pain as his eyes were blinded by the blood.

"I'll help you," Kenneth said softly. "I want to help you."

Magnus forced himself in the direction of the gentle voice. First one step, then a second step. On the third step he reached the fence.

"Wait!" Elvira screamed. "You're too near the edge."

Magnus blundered into the fence. The top strands had gone, though the lower ones were sound. I shouted and tried to grab his arm. The wires caught his jeans at the ankle and the knee. My fingers closed on the rough cotton of his shirt. He pulled away with a jerk. His weight went against the strands of wire. The upper part of his body toppled over the fence.

He fell through the air, the momentum pushing him out so that by the bottom of the arc his body was parallel to the ground. His legs hit the wrecked refrigerator with a dull thump. His head hit solid rock. Victrix leapt into the air, a bundle of outraged feathers. Magnus's legs slithered silently from the refrigerator to the ground.

Blood tricked from his mouth. He didn't move. bird rose higher and higher in the sky. She glided vards and disappeared beyond the belt of pines.

lked back up the path. My legs trembled. It ed raining again, though I hadn't noticed much more heavily than before. Kenneth

378

was crouching on the ground. As I drew nearer, he screwed up his face and rubbed his forehead, as though trying to erase a memory. Elvira put an arm round his shoulders. Jason was not in sight.

Elvira sighed. We looked at each other. The rain trickled through our hair and ran down our cheeks. We had to try to do something for the man in the quarry. We had to fetch help.

She held her free hand up to me. I took it in mine, and our fingers locked together.

Lions Tracks

The Outsiders by S. E. Hinton
£2.99

This is the chillingly realistic story of the Socs and the Greasers, rival teenage gangs, whose hatred for each other leads to the mindless violence of gang warfare.

Rumble Fish by S. E. Hinton
£2.99

Rusty-James has a reputation for toughness: he runs his own gang, and attends school only when he has nothing better to do. But his blind ambition to be just like his glamourous older brother, the Motor-cycle Boy, leads to an explosive and tragic climax.

That was Then, This is Now
by S. E. Hinton
£2.99

Caught in the violent and frustrating atmosphere of an American city slum, Mark and Bryon, who had always been like brothers, now find they are drifting apart. And then one day Bryon discovers the awful truth about Mark...

Taming the Star Runner by S. E. Hinton
£2.75

Travis's life in the country with his uncle after t' bright lights of New York is pretty dull, but the ch is that or reform school. The only thing to liven it the girl with the horse called the Star Runner he's never thought much of girls.

Lions Tracks

After the First Death by Robert Cormier
£3.50

A busload of young children is hijacked by terrorists whose motive is to render useless one of the major secret service units. The general heading the unit is forced to employ his sixteen-year-old son Ben as a go-between, exposing him to appalling danger.

Eight Plus One by Robert Cormier
£3.50

These nine stories probe the feelings and reactions of people in life's most trying situations: a first love, leaving for college, a boy's discovery that his father is all too human. The stories are warm, touching and intensely personal.

Fade by Robert Cormier
£3.99

Paul inherits a strange gift: the power to become invisible. At first he thinks this is a thrilling trick, but when he finds out more, he gets scared. Is the fade a gift or a curse?

Tex by S. E. Hinton
£2.99

ife is fine for Tex until he comes home one day to his horse has been sold to pay the mounting bills. then on things get uglier – his father seems erned about the trouble Tex is in at school, and her is determined to force matters to a head. he truths revealed are devastating.

Lions Tracks

Children of the Dust by Louise Lawrence
£3.50

"There's only one thing worse than dying in a nuclear war, and that's surviving," said Sarah. *Children of the Dust* is a chilling warning about nuclear war and a moving tribute to the human spirit.

Talking in Whispers by James Watson
£3.50

Sixteen-year-old Andres Larreta becomes a wanted man, a prime target of the security forces, an outsider. Yet he finds friends, Isa and Beto, people who will help him. For, as Isa says, "After a while you come to hate talking in whispers..."

The Passionflower by Margaret Hadley
£3.50

Pash has always been the one to run the home. Her mam's just not the organised type, too taken up with feller-of-the-month, probably, though Pash isn't any too keen on the latest one. Too young for Mam, all muscles and gold chains, and jeez! talk about conceited! Still, Pash didn't expect him to do over the flat while she was out at work and leave Mam lying in a pool of blood ...

Order Form

To order direct from the publishers, just make a list of the titles you want and fill in the form below:

Name ....

Address ....

....

....

Send to: Dept 6, HarperCollins Publishers Ltd, Westerhill Road, Bishopbriggs, Glasgow G64 2QT.

Please enclose a cheque or postal order to the value of the cover price, plus:

UK & BFPO: Add £1.00 for the first book, and 25p per copy for each addition book ordered.

Overseas and Eire: Add £2.95 service charge. Books will be sent by surface mail but quotes for airmail despatch will be given on request.

A 24-hour telephone ordering service is avail-able to Visa and Access card holders: 041-772 2281